THE NINETY AND NINE

WILLIAM BRINKLEY

THE NINETY
AND NINE

1966

DOUBLEDAY & COMPANY, INC., GARDEN CITY, NEW YORK

All of the characters in this book
are fictitious, and any resemblance
to actual persons, living or dead,
is purely coincidental.

Library of Congress Catalog Card Number 66-13194
Copyright © 1966 by William Clark Brinkley
All Rights Reserved
Printed in the United States of America
First Edition

To
Roger Joel Waybright
gallant in War
wise in Peace

CONTENTS

The destinies of two great empires . . . seemed to be tied up by some god-damned things called LSTs.

WINSTON CHURCHILL

THE NINETY AND NINE

Prologue

It is dawn off Anzio and the destroyers are underway, furling huge billows of white across the anchorage to screen it from enemy aircraft and submarines as always at each dusk and each dawn. In a while the smokepots set on the destroyers' fantails are shut off and still a little later the white shield begins to lift, revealing a small harbor crowded with ships and among them, moving toward the land, a strange vessel of a type not before seen in the long history of war. She makes her way steadily to the beach, unhindered by a shell which kicks up a geyser of water a distance off her starboard quarter, and soon puts her bow directly up on it. The bow opens, a ramp comes down, and troops begin to move off and then vehicles of war. After a while the ship backs off the beach, swings awkwardly around, churns out of the harbor, and stands out to sea, headed south to pick up more troops and cargo and come up again on the same errand.

The ship's usefulness lies in her ability to put part of herself up on land and take herself off again. But to give her this very talent she has been strangely contrived. She is 328 feet long but has a draft of only 13 feet and has no keel, meaning that in any kind of sea she rolls like no other ship ever devised by man, and she has a blunt bow which likes to club the sea instead of riding through it. These various specifications make her about as ungainly a vessel as you would ever see in a harbor or at sea, and also one of the slowest and least maneuverable. With the hull newly scraped of barnacles, the shrapnel holes smoothly patched, the hull painted, a favoring wind, and her engines straining, she can do 11½ knots. Usually she cruises at 8. Naturally this also makes her an excellent target equally for enemy subs below and enemy planes above the sea, not to mention enemy artillery on the land and even tanks, which have been known to rake her point-blank from stem to stern. One of her other chief characteristics is her generous amount of freeboard: More of her is out of the water than in, so that she is blown by the wind almost as much as she is moved by the current of the water and in this respect is more like a sailing vessel than any ship in the Navy Register. The ship is called the LST, for Landing Ship, Tank. This particular ship is the *LST 1826*, complement nine officers and ninety men.

The landing craft are the forgotten ships of this war and in a way the outcast Navy, the glamour having been staked out by the more classic vessels such as the destroyers, the submarines, the aircraft carriers, and the PT boats; this, even though there could not possibly be the type of war that there is without them and a fair case could be made for the proposition that of all ships they are the most indispensable part of the Navy in the war. The men of the landing craft are a decided breed, made so partly by this not particularly resented knowledge that they are the underprivileged branch of the Navy, and with it the more or less stoic acceptance of getting the short end of the stick in general, despite the fact that it is their fate to fulfill one of the toughest of sea duties and to endure some of the dirtiest and most dangerous work of the war while receiving so little of the credit; put-upon and low-caste within the naval hierarchy, and yet beautifully independent and resourceful; and yes, even proud.

The *LST 1826* is even a happy ship. To read the stories of the war one would think no such ship ever existed. It is difficult to say just what makes her so. There is an old Navy saying that "a taut ship is a happy ship." But there is nothing taut about the 1826. The captain doesn't care what kind of clothes the men wear, for instance, and there are some pretty weird combinations aboard. During one period Capri sandals, which some of the men discovered on a liberty boat trip to that island, are the most popular footwear aboard; and after a visit to Mers-el-Kebir the famous Arab "baggy pants" are worn for a while by a number of the crew until they discover that they are as impracticable for working aboard ship as is a full skirt for a lady ascending a ship's ladder. And while the ship is by no means without discipline, there is an irreducible minimum of spit and polish. To some the 1826 is known as the children's ship because of a rather remarkable closeness that has grown up between the crew of the LST and the children of the little towns clustered around Pozzuoli Bay, which is home port for the ship while it is making its runs to Anzio. The children are forever hanging about wherever the LST puts in. The crew gives candy and food and clothes to them but the relationship is not just one of calculation on the children's part. It is something a good deal more, and the children seem to sense a fondness on the part of the sailors, and they return it eagerly. The sailors play games with them on the mole. Carpenter's Mate Second Class George Wiley has made some stilts for them to stride around on and a seaman second named Red Carlyle often plays his guitar while they gather around him. They have developed a great liking for the guitar music, without understanding the words which Carlyle sometimes sings. When the ship leaves for Anzio the children are there to see it off and the day after next they will be waiting to welcome the ship home. They are always relieved that she is home safe once more from Anzio. Even the children know that ships do not always return from Anzio. Even they have a peculiar consciousness of the mines and the submarines that lie in between and of the German guns and aircraft once the ship gets there.

To say that it is a happy ship is not to say that any of its company of nine officers and ninety men loves the war. To a man they hate the war, they *loathe* the war. But beginning with the captain, there has developed a technical competence, a marked ingenuity for making do with what they have or somehow laying hands on what they haven't, and a norm of treating each other with a certain allowance. Within this broad framework, each of the ninety and nine has evolved his own, quite personal and individualistic pattern. So it is that they can be singleminded about the war, and still, taking the circumstances in which they find themselves not of their own free will, of having been taken from their homes, their families, their women, and their ordinary daily freedoms, meet the conditions—in some cases, as will be seen, head-on—and not only make the best of them but, now and then, even reach some fairly memorable plateaus.

At the time our story opens the LST 1826 has been through three invasions, at Sicily, Salerno, and Anzio, and has performed and fought creditably at each. As visible witness to the life she has led she carries her scars in the form of shrapnel dents too numerous to count and—though there is nothing visible to testify to this part of her experience—a number of men have died on her decks. Now she is engaged in carrying supplies and troops to the forces of the Allies pinned down on the beachhead, which is thirty-seven miles from Rome. Since Anzio (the birthplace of Caligula and of Nero, though few aboard the vessels know this or would consider the fact of much importance at the moment if they did) is cut off from the main Allied lines, the beachhead is supplied entirely by sea, and in large part by the landing craft, which make the overnight run from Pozzuoli (where Saint Paul landed as a prisoner also trying to get to Rome, to see Caesar, though few aboard the vessels know this either), thus skirting the Germans, who are holding up our land arm at the monastery at Cassino in between. It is a considerable undertaking to keep enough men and materiel on the beachhead to prevent the Allies from being shoved off it into the sea, besides which the LSTs are as always in extremely short supply, which is why they have to keep going all the time. The LST 1826, along with the others, has been making the run for two months now and no one can predict with any confidence how much longer she will continue to do so, for the Germans are dug in on all available high ground and are fighting very hard; there is not a square foot of harbor or beachhead but what is accessible to their artillery the day and the night long.

I

THE NURSES GOING TO ANZIO

The LST 1826 had carried many things. She had carried C-rations, ammunition, jeeps, tanks, barbed wire, Aqua Velva lotion, toothbrushes, penicillin, atabrine, cement, and almost anything else you could think of. In addition she had carried American, British, Polish, Gurkha, Sikh, Rhodesian, Canadian, Australian, New Zealand, French, and Moroccan Goum troops, also Italian and German prisoners of war, also horses and mules. But none of these items or creatures, not even the mules, evoked quite the stir aboard ship of the news of still a new species of cargo the ship received word one morning it would be taking on that night. The captain announced the nature of the cargo to the assembled officers over coffee in the wardroom.

"Myself I intend to spend this war fat, dumb, and happy," the captain began. "That means you officers will have to be bright-eyed and bushy-tailed. I'm actually too old for this job." It was the way the captain invariably started his talks and everybody relaxed.

"Gentlemen, we shall be making yet another run to the beachhead tonight," he said heartily. "I imagine after the last two days in Naples most of us can use the rest I'm told a voyage at sea unfailingly affords."

The captain was given, on these occasions, to speaking in phrases of mock formality. The officers laughed appreciatively at this little jest, and the captain continued.

"The LST 1826 is well-known throughout these waters and possibly even in its numerous ports for the self-control and willpower of its entire ship's company. Naturally in all such matters it falls somehow on the officers to set a proper example for the enlisted men. If on some extremely rare occasion all of us have not in every detail completely lived up to what might be called an ideal of perfection in these matters, it is imperative that no such lapse attend our imminent mission." The captain's voice took on a firmer note. "My hope—I might say my instructions to you, and to one and all—is that you will continue to display the previously mentioned self-control and willpower throughout the hours of our forthcoming beachhead run."

This was quite cryptic and the captain continued.

"Gentlemen," he said, "this vessel—if one can properly call a flat hunk of steel a vessel—has carried numerous items to our fighting forces at Anzio. Indeed, gentlemen, I fancied that we had carried every item conceivable to the needs of land troops. Gentlemen, I was wrong. I have just returned from Navy headquarters where I learned that we shall tonight transport an article novel even to our broad cargo experience. Gentlemen! Tonight the *LST* 1826 will carry to the beachhead a consignment of fifty-four—I repeat that figure—fifty-four Army . . ." The captain paused and his eyes looked down at the green billiard cloth of the table and then up at the officers, and in a voice very quiet he let the rounded, almost caressed word drop . . . "nurses."

There was a moment of profound silence. Then Ensign Eliot Horner, the communications officer, who was less than two years out of Dartmouth College, said very quietly:

"Nurses, Captain?"

"Nurses," the captain said more briskly. "American nurses, going up to staff a field hospital. Now gentlemen."

The captain sipped at his coffee. "Gentlemen, I wish above all one thing." He looked penetratingly around the circle of officers. "That thing is that we shall make the brief voyage aboard our ship of these good, brave women as pleasant as is possible, given the circumstances."

"You can count on me, Captain," Ensign Horner said.

"We shall, of course," the captain continued smoothly, ignoring this comment, "break out our very finest rations. As a matter-of-fact, after receiving the cargo orders, I dropped by the base commissary and was able, employing various lies and exaggerations, to talk those misanthropists into a supply of steaks for all hands tonight including passengers. Aside from all that we shall require, it hardly needs saying, special security arrangements." The captain turned crisply to the officer at his immediate left. "Barclay, that of course, if it is not inconvenient, will be your pigeon."

"Yes, sir," Lieutenant (jg) Matthew Barclay said. "I'll see to the security, Captain."

"Well, gentlemen, that about wraps it up. I don't need to say that of course we shall all quit ourselves like gentlemen. We all know what the penalty for striking a fellow officer is. You can well imagine what it is for *touching* one."

Lieutenant (jg) Richard Abernethy, the engineering officer, laughed rather uproariously at this.

"Gentlemen! Pass the word to all hands and see that this vessel looks as worthy as we can make it to its imminent cargo."

"Flowers, Captain?" Abernethy said.

"I only wish we had some," the captain said somberly. "I really do."

"Fifty-four nurses," Ensign Horner said in some awe. "That's over half a nurse apiece."

It must have been one of the most satisfying missions of the war, the delivery of those nurses to Anzio. From their arrival on the mole to their departure through the massive jaws of the tank deck at the beachhead, a wonderfully gentle, almost tender air held between the nurses and the men of the 1826. After the wardroom meeting the word spread like a prairie fire through the ship. Men who had liberty suddenly discovered they could more profitably spend the day aboard, and all hands turned to, to make things as convenient and comfortable as an LST could be. As first lieutenant, Lieutenant (jg) Barclay was in immediate charge of most of these arrangements. His duties included bedding down the nurses, so to speak, so that he was to have unusual opportunity to know them. The nature of the passengers being what it was meant that certain passageways had to be sealed off but it was clear that no one of the crew was going to mind the extra steps that this would entail in going from one part of the ship to another. Barclay saw to the painting of large signs for which he had composed the legend, NURSES COUNTRY—DO NOT ENTER, and the posting of them on appropriate doors. Boatswain's Mate First Class Andrew Nelson even took it upon himself to go ashore and find some red and yellow sprigs of flowers, independently of the captain's casual wish, and tuck them brightly around the NURSES COUNTRY signs as a kind of frame. The decks were scrubbed, the entire ship made as clean as possible, and then the men turned their attention to their personal toilets. As the hour for the arrival of the passengers approached, they shaved and took showers and dug out their dress blues to wear instead of the dungarees and T-shirts which for so long had been their only shipboard attire. Radioman Third Class Nathaniel Middleton, who had acquired a pair of barber clippers, had his busiest day since the commissioning of the ship. Some of the crew were hardly recognizable when they appeared topside. Thus scrubbed, coiffured, and uniformed, all hands were standing by to lend whatever assistance might be required when the first weapons carriers bearing the nurses pulled up on the mole at promptly 1600 hours.

They were a lovely sight. For one thing they were the cleanest-looking things the men had seen in all their time out. One and all, they looked unbelievably trim and neat and they bore to the ship a magic potion commingled of womanly softness and nursely briskness. As they walked up the bow ramp, each was escorted by one of the crew, swinging swiftly down out of a long line which had formed like something at the Radio City Music Hall, carrying her barracks bag aboard. The captain stood at the top of the ramp wishing each passenger as heartfelt a "Welcome aboard, Miss!" as had ever been tendered to anyone boarding that ship. A faint aroma of perfume made its way along the decks, strangely overcoming even the essence of diesel oil which was eternally the prevailing scent aboard the LST. In the men there was not the faintest suggestion of rapaciousness. Quite the opposite, their entire mien was one of respect, even awe, before the presence on the ship of something almost forgotten.

The voyage up could not have been more pleasant. The nurses were wearing field clothes, but this did nothing to decrease the marvelous freight of femininity they brought aboard. If anything it increased it. To see the delicate, entrancing bulges from their coveralls, to see a little harvest of curls emerging from a woolen field cap, to feel from these fragile packages, as ship's company viewed them, strange and wondrous scents . . . well, the clothes, we say, did nothing to decrease the awareness of the femininity now aboard. The nurses, for their part, were eager to learn about the ship, and the men willingly explained the difference between a bitt and a winch. One nurse asked ship's Cook Second Class Gerald Mason, "Is the water soft—I want to wash my hair," and Mason, who wished her to be happy, stuttered out, "It certainly is, Miss. I'd say we have about the softest water in the Mediterranean aboard this ship," neglecting to mention the fact that the shower water at that time *was* the Mediterranean. After a longer-than-usual chow everyone went out on deck.

The nurses were laughing and having a good time. They liked the sailors. Besides being one of those glassy, motionless seas, rarer in the Mediterranean than is generally believed, there was a full moon. With the nurses standing silhouetted by the life lines talking with members of the crew and watching the moon pour down upon the sea, their hair blowing back in the soft wind created only by the passage of the ship through water, an occasional sound of girlish laughter erupting around the decks, and above all that distant odor of perfume, the voyage had aspects of a Mediterranean cruise. Except that Navy men never like a full moon, which so spotlights their ship in a sub's periscope or a bomber's sight. But no one, of course, was so crude as to disturb the nurses' enjoyment of the voyage by mentioning this fact. On the fantail Seaman Second Class Peter Carlyle, who was only a boy, seventeen, and who ten months ago had never seen the sea or even been out of Iowa, broke out his guitar and a group of nurses and sailors soon collected around him to listen to him play and often to join in song. They sang many things, such as "Midnight Special" and "John Henry" and occasionally a hymn which Carlyle played, such as "Lead On, O King Eternal" and "The

Old Time Religion." But especially "Shenandoah," which Carlyle
kept returning to because it was his favorite song, so that the
blended voices of the nurses and the sailors telling of a wide
American river drifted out over the Tyrrhenian . . .

> O Shenandoah, I long to see you,
> Away, you rolling river,
> Shenandoah, I can't get near you,
> Away, away, I'm bound away,
> 'Cross the wide Missouri . . .

There was little sleep that night, no action but much talk.
Nothing much happened, only a feeling that was to last for
several weeks before the war made the crew forget most of it.
Lieutenant (jg) Barclay had been checking around the ship and
he finally found himself, not quite knowing how, standing by the
starboard life line midships talking quietly with one of the nurses.
Now and then they could see artillery fire on the Fifth Army
front spring across the night sky. It was a little eerie since you
could see but not hear it, the shelling coming in great flashes,
broad and flat, quick and gone, like voiceless summer lightning.
They would watch it for a while in unconstrained silence before
talking some more. She seemed sincerely curious about the ship,
not just encouraging a man to talk, and he told her about the
things they had carried. She seemed most interested in the mules.

"I didn't know there were mules fighting the war," she said.

"Oh, yes. The mules are right in there," Barclay said. "They use
them to pull howitzers up those mountains over there and to carry
up supplies."

"But weren't they a problem aboard here? They're animals of
their own mind, aren't they?"

"Yes, but I think just for that reason they are realistic and
face facts," Barclay said soberly. "I think they knew they were in
there for a trip and so had better make the best of it and not
waste their energies just yet. I do know that those mules were
very well-behaved passengers generally. We put an eight-inch
layer of sand on the tank deck, stretched lines and put them into
little corrals. Ship looked like a ranch. Wagons, saddles, horse-

shoes, spurs, feed above on the main deck here where we're standing; tank deck full of mules below. When we got going they
began to bray a little but that was all. They didn't get seasick.
Of course the soldiers took good care of them. They fed them
water out of their helmets."

He looked at the flashing artillery fire for a moment across the
sea. They would be almost opposite Cassino now.

"Tell me more about the mules," she said.

"Well, everything went well until the ship beached—this was
at Salerno. There were pontoons in front of the ramp and the
mules started across. They began slipping into the slits in the
pontoons, getting their legs stuck. Two soldiers would get on
either side of a mule, place a board under its mid-section and start
lifting. Another soldier would lift the mule's tail at the same
time. One mule didn't like the tail-lifting part and kicked the
soldier assigned to that end of the detail flat on the pontoons.
He picked himself right up and went to work on another mule.
'Nothing at all,' the soldier said. 'I've been kicked by mules before.' It almost seemed the mules didn't want to *leave* our ship.
Anyhow, finally we laid boards over the slits and with the soldiers
pushing them from behind, instead of lifting their tails, the mules
went right off. As soon as they got off they began rolling in the
sand on the beach. Then they started over the dunes to a green
pasture."

Soon they could see, far up ahead off the starboard bow, a
kind of light different from the artillery flashing. This was the light
of red flak and flares, and he knew there was another raid going
on at Anzio. He started talking about something before she should
ask about it. Then the strains of the guitar and the singing were
drifting up faintly to them from aft and she sang softly a verse
of it . . .

> Shenandoah, I love your daughter,
> Away, you rolling river,
> For her I've crossed the stormy water,
> Away, away, I'm bound away,
> 'Cross the wide Missouri . . .

He could see her quite well under the moon. She had walnut-colored hair cut short and occasionally she would raise her hand to brush it back from the wind. There was grace even in the simple movement. She was a slender girl, almost fragile looking. He was very aware of the smell of perfume from her. She was going to Anzio. It seemed strange to him that they would be leaving her there and that he would be going back. After a while Barclay escorted her down a ladder to a door bearing one of his own signs, NURSES COUNTRY—DO NOT ENTER.

"I'll see you in the morning," he said. "And I hope you're comfortable."

"Oh, I will be. Thank you."

"You won't get seasick?"

"No, I don't get seasick. I'm like the mules."

"Good night, Miss. I mean Lieutenant."

"Good night—Lieutenant."

The crew had a difficult time getting to sleep that night. In crew's quarters, a seaman second leaned over and spoke to a seaman first in the bunk below him.

"There's nothing really like an American girl, is there?" he said. "Didn't they look clean, though? And didn't they *smell* so good. I had to restrain myself to keep from going around just smelling them. But just imagine. Women like that going up to fight the war."

And at about the same time, in the nurses quarters, one of them leaned out a little and spoke to another in the bunk above her.

"Most of them are so young, aren't they?" she said. "Just imagine. Boys like that fighting the war."

Next morning when the ship came into the mole, and the bow doors came open, and the ramp swung down, Lieutenant (jg) Barclay stood there seeing the nurses ashore. One of them was whistling "Shenandoah" when she disappeared up the dusty road. Then the nurse he had talked with came by and he said the same thing to her he had to the others.

"Well, goodbye, Miss. It was certainly nice having you aboard."

"I'm glad you feel that way," she said. "Since I'm staying aboard."

"Oh. Is that so?"

"Yes. You see, I'm assigned to go back with wounded."

"Well, we'll be glad to have you aboard again. I'll see you later, Miss. I mean Lieutenant."

She seemed already to be smiling inside at him.

"Roger, Lieutenant," she said. "I'll be right back."

He watched her walk across the beach to the first of a long line of ambulances which had begun to pull up in front of the LST.

The LSTs always arrived shortly after dawn and as soon as there was a vacant spot in the busy little harbor they would scoot in and unload. Someone searching for an interesting statistic had come up with the one that at one time during the operation the harbor at Anzio was the fourth busiest in the world. Barclay hadn't had time to check that one out, let alone inclination, but it was very busy in there all right. They tried not to stay in the harbor any longer than was necessary. It had not taken much brightness for the Germans to learn the schedules of the ships and beginning with their arrival off the harbor in early morning from the south the Messerschmitts came in low over the land and dropped their bombs and got away fast, and the shelling could always be counted upon, especially from a 280-mm railroad gun up the coast in the hills. They dropped a lot in the harbor, just lobbing those enormous shells down, and now and then one fell on a ship. There was nothing in the world the ships could do about the guns. They couldn't see them or where they came from. All you could hear was a rushing sound and then very presently see a splash or a geyser of water, which gave you the very academic information of the approximate size of the shell. For this reason the art of getting in and out quickly was fined down as much as possible. Cargo, for example, was never taken up "loose" to be hauled off by the slow process of men carrying it. It was taken up in trucks, the loaded trucks driven off over the bow ramp, and other waiting empty trucks driven on for the return voyage to Naples, where these trucks would then be loaded up for another trip. Wounded in litters took a little more time to load but even they were always readied and waiting close by the point where the LST beached. Then the LST got out as fast as possible so as not to make the job of the railroad gun any easier by sitting too long in one spot. Not to mention the smaller German field guns, which were very good, and more accurate than the railroad gun.

That morning, as soon as the nurses were off, the wounded were brought on. Barclay stood at the bow ramp directing the U. S. Army bearers. The worst-wounded, as long as space lasted, were put in troops quarters in the bunks just vacated by the nurses and the lesser-wounded on stretchers in the tank deck, where the passage here in the bottom of the ship would be rough if the sea came up. Considering their number, the job of loading them did not take long. A couple of shells dropping nearby, and creating considerable fountains of water, inspired everyone to get the job done. The nurse stood by Barclay during the loading. Most of the wounded were silent but one kept saying something when he was brought aboard. His tag showed he was full of pieces of a land mine he had stepped on. The soldier-bearers stopped with him a moment, and Barclay could make out what the man was saying. "There's something under my leg." The nurse raised up the blanket and seeing the leg was gone pretended to take out something where the leg should have been. The man quieted down. "Troops quarters," the nurse said quietly, and the man was carried on. It had held up the parade only a couple of moments and they kept coming on; some to go on back to the States; some to return, repaired, to the beachhead; and some to die. Soon the LST raised her bow ramp, closed her bow doors, backed off, swung around and headed out. The shelling seemed to be increasing and one big one jarred the tank deck. Barclay could see some of the wounded sit up sharply in their litters, their glassy eyes dilating, in some cases in fear, in others in outrage that they should still be after them after all they had already taken. Barclay went topside just as the ship was out of it and standing out to sea.

He spent that evening checking around the ship. There were

several nurses aboard and he didn't run into her, which was not surprising since they all had their hands full. The dimly lit tank deck was one great mass of litters, with the nurses moving down the narrow aisles between the wounded, and stopping to give infusions of blood plasma, change a soaked dressing, and do whatever they could to rescue from death or ease the last part of the road to it. Lighting cigarettes and placing them carefully in the mouths of those who wanted them and had mouths left to smoke them; or if a man had his mouth left but no hands to hold the cigarette, kneeling beside him and carrying it back and forth while he took heavy drags on it. Barclay did not like to think what would happen if the ship should take a mine or a torpedo now. Not one soul would get out of that tank deck, he knew that.

The sea came up rough after a while and the sensitive LST took on a considerable roll. Barclay was surprised how little the men whimpered or groaned, even when one hard sea hit them and lifted several of the litters off the steel deck before setting them down again sharply. Those that retched seemed almost ashamed of it and did it as quietly and almost secretively as possible, leaning their heads close to the deck. There was no smell of perfume now, only of iodoform, various other medical smells, mansweat, blood and vomit, and the nurses moving down the aisles would slip a little now and then. Barclay turned in shortly after midnight to get a little sleep before the 4-to-8 watch which he had.

Taking the conn at 0350 hours he noticed the one line in the log: "Three of wounded passengers died between 0030 and 0330 hours. Sea six feet, rising." Both he and the officer he relieved he knew were thinking the same thing: The rough sea may have killed them. Neither said it. The sea was now spreading tossing whitecaps everywhere and foam licked high along the ship and under the black and starless sky it was as if they were traveling over a white sea. He could see the bow rising and falling and feel the ship straining beneath him and creaking like a porch swing. It was cold in the conning tower and the chin got quickly stiff in the chilling wind which raked across it. The ship ploughed through the churning sea with her strange movement. The black night and the rough sea were a partial protection against subs but thinking of the wounded soldiers he kept hoping for the sea to settle and it did begin to die down the nearer they got to Pozzuoli. Then he could see the humpy outline of Italy rising beyond the sea-mists and they came in on long gentle swells into perfectly smooth waters. The captain came up to take the ship in and for Barclay to do the offloading. Already up ahead Barclay could make out through his binoculars the red-crossed olive ambulances lined up on the mole. He watched them a moment then went down to the tank deck. There was not the incentive of the shelling for anyone to rush this time and it took awhile. The last ambulance was loaded and he had just turned off the ramp and was starting topside to get breakfast when he saw her leaving. She looked pale and very exhausted and he knew she had had no sleep at all that night spent with the wounded in the tank deck. She seemed such a bit of a girl for that kind of work.

"Hello, Lieutenant," he said. "I thought maybe you were stowing aboard."

She smiled. "I wouldn't mind."

"Anytime."

"Thank you. Well, I've got to go now."

"Where do you go—ashore, I mean."

"The 300th General. Up on the hill."

He thought of asking if he could see her. But then thought no. At least not now. But he did ask one thing.

"I don't know your name."

"It's Sarah Clark."

"Thank you," and he told her his.

She smiled a little. "Goodbye. I enjoyed our talk about the mules."

Suddenly above them the church bells in the town began to ring. They both looked up toward the sound. They seemed to be ringing for them, welcoming the ship and the wounded of the war home. Then he remembered that they rang every day. They stood listening to the sound a moment. Then she turned and walked toward the last ambulance.

He watched her, and just before she climbed into the back of it, she turned and waved, just barely raising her hand in that movement that seemed to him to have such grace in it. Then the door closed and the ambulance was driving away. He walked back through the ship. The scent of perfume was all gone now, obliterated by that of the wounded, the dying and the dead. The first had lasted but a short time, it occurred to him, but they would be a while getting that second smell out of the tank deck. He went on up and ate breakfast. Already he felt more lonely than he had in a long time. He went to his room and got into his bunk for a little sleep before getting up to help get the ship ready again for another run to Anzio.

2

LORD NELSON AND THE SPELEOLOGISTS

The cave was discovered by Boatswain's Mate First Class Andrew
Nelson, known inevitably aboard the *LST 1826* as Lord Nelson.
Boatswain's Mate Nelson was a professional Navy man and proud
of it. He had spent very little of his eighteen years in the Navy
ashore. In fact, he didn't really approve of the shore. He supposed it was a necessary evil in order to keep the ships out at
sea, but himself wanted as little of it as possible and couldn't
see how anyone who got in the Navy in the first place could
possibly feel otherwise.

"If a man wants to be on the shore," he said, always pro-
nouncing the word with a certain disdain, "why there're plenty
of outfits for him. The Red Cross. The Army. Even the Marines.
But a Navy man. A man shouldn't be in the Navy if he wants
to be on the shore." He sometimes spat after using the word.

Lord Nelson was just about the one kind of man whom if
the Navy didn't have, it might as well fold up its anchors tomorrow and go out of business. He was an unexcelled seaman and
deck man. After all it was his craft, and he took great pride in
it. His word in any matter of shipboard skill was infallible. If
Bo's'n's Mate Nelson reported to the officer of the deck that
something was lashed down and ready for sea, you could be
certain it was so. You needn't check it. In fact any watch officer
on the *LST 1826* would have been a little scared to do so after
such a report. His measured, Klaxon-like voice, able to carry half
the length of the ship if necessary, could sing out quickly enough
if a man was caulking off. At the same time he was fairly

gentle with new seamen and ensigns while they learned their jobs. He always gave them a certain time—not too much, but some time, anyhow—to learn things. He was a good man to be with on liberty. From his years of prowling around ports all over the world, he had an instinct for knowing the best places to go, and if any trouble broke out he was very handy with his fists. He was not a big man, being short and broad, but he had muscles like rocks. He was the last man to go around clobbering people just for the sake of exercise, looking upon the shore only as a place where one could have a few pleasures not available aboard ship. But he was also the last to back away from a fight that was thrust at him. Once in a bar at Oran he had laid out three Army men, with that many uppercuts to the chin that went off like depth charges. The Army men had made the mistake of voicing mincing remarks about "that little pajama suit" he was wearing. He hated to have to do it, but it happened to be a uniform he was highly proud of. He was an old Navy man.

"Now, men," he said, helping the Army people stagger to their feet still wondering what kind of piledriver had hit them, "let's try to have a little inter-service respect, shall we? After all, we're in this together. Now what would you men like to drink?"

The cave discovery came about as a result of some more inter-service cooperation. On the rare days when it was warm enough the men of the *LST* 1826 used to borrow a Duck from a small Army detachment stationed in Pozzuoli. The Duck was one of the more versatile vehicles developed during World War II, being able to navigate on both land and water, and used principally to unload cargo ships anchored out in a harbor, from where it would then chug through the water, crawl up on land, drive down a road dripping water as it went, and go directly with its cargo to an Army dump. It saved a lot of extra handling of cargo and was a very useful vehicle. The crew of the 1826 discovered an additional use for it. It could be driven out through the flotsam and debris that make any harbor unfit for swimming, to a place where the water was clean, and at that point parked for swimming purposes. It even made a good place to dive off of. The men appreciated the Army's setting this model by lending them the Duck and tried to reciprocate. The sergeant who really controlled the Duck was very fond of cigars and never got enough of them through regular Army channels. The crew of the 1826 kept him well supplied with cigars consigned to the ship—no one aboard smoked them so they had to be got rid of somehow, preferably in a useful manner—and got to use the Duck occasionally. It was a fine arrangement for everybody as well as being a good example of inter-service cooperation.

Lord Nelson came along on a swimming party one day not to enjoy its primary purpose—he didn't like being *in* the water—but because he got fascinated by the idea of a conveyance which could operate on both land and sea and wanted to observe it work. Coxswain Jerry Boland drove his load of a dozen or so men on out through the harbor, turned down the coast a way, and finally parked the Duck in a patch of good clean water deep enough for diving. The men took off their clothes and were soon diving off the Duck, splashing and yelling and swimming around in the water, in general having a refreshing time. Nelson busied himself with inspecting the Duck, shaking his head a few times, and finally deciding that while it was a nice toy it would really never get very far. It was no real threat to the Navy's supremacy of the seas. This accomplished he stood at the Duck's side looking idly over at the stretch of coastline. It was wooded and very peaceful looking over there, and seemed entirely uninhabited. His experienced eye inspected the shore and traveled down it until it came to a long rocky promontory jutting out to sea. His eye continued down this formation and was about to turn back when it held a moment near the end. The water there appeared to be making a curious kind of movement. Against most of the rocky arm the water washed quietly and fell back, in gentle, natural waves. But near the very end the water appeared just to flow on. There was no soft brush of white froth, no indication of the water falling back, as on the other part of the promontory. It appeared very strange and he wished he had a pair of binoculars. Since he didn't he waited until the men had had their fill of swimming and had climbed back into the Duck

then suggested to Coxswain Boland that they re
by way of that promontory. It was in the opposi
Coxswain Boland would never have thought to qu
that Boatswain's Mate Nelson told him. He stal
ward the end of the promontory.

"Slow this goddamn monstrosity down a little," Nelson gently
instructed the coxswain as they neared the end of it.

Coxswain Boland did so. They were now no more than fifty
feet from the promontory's end and edging up on it. At about
that moment Nelson said quietly, "Well, I'll be damned. Look
at that, men."

The men looked and saw an opening in the rock. Nelson
told Coxswain Boland to ease the vehicle to a stop and the Duck
lay rocking gently in the water while from its forward part Nelson
inspected the opening very carefully. Then he walked back and
spoke crisply to Boland.

"Cox'n," he said, "I think it'll just clear if you take this
contraption in very slow and easy and if you men all stay down
in the welldeck there. Let's see."

The coxswain moved the Duck forward very slowly, the men
kept low, and as they came to the mouth the coxswain and
Nelson crouched themselves. It seemed to just fit, both ways. It
was just wide enough for the Duck to get through and just
high enough. The vehicle rocked through it in the dark, then
the men stood up. They beheld an awesome sight.

It was a huge sea cave. The roof went vaulting up like a
cathedral's. Leaning over the side of the Duck the men looked
down into the most translucent water. It was like a Pacific
lagoon. It was full of shimmering colors and it looked about
twenty feet deep. The men looked in awe and silence, too overcome to speak. They saw that the water came up against an
enormous platform-like ledge. Nelson instructed the coxswain to
bring the Duck up against the ledge and the men stepped out
upon it. They stood there in absolute wonder. The ledge must
have been fifty feet in each direction and the rock was smooth
as silk. Then some of them saw that the ledge led off somewhere
and, excited with the explorer's fever of discovery, they hurried

_o see where. They found something else equally charming. The ledge opened into a kind of hallway and from this hallway a half dozen smaller caves gave off—smaller, but still each large as a medium-sized bedroom, of lower ceiling than the main room. If anyone had ever been in the cave—it seemed impossible that no one had—it had certainly been a very long time ago. There was no sign of man's presence whatever. The men came back out and pulling off what clothes they had got back on started jumping off the ledge and into the pool with ecstatic yells, their sounds coming back to them in eerie, wavering echoes from the walls and ceiling of the great rock chamber. They had never seen such water. The better swimmers dived clear to the bottom where they found a bed of white sand soft as a woman's face powder. From the top a man could see them as clearly as if he were looking through purest air.

They were in there for an hour and the men had not begun to get their fill of it. They would have stayed on had not Coxswain Boland mentioned something.

"Listen, men, I hate to break this up, but if we ever want to use this Duck again we better get it back to the Sarge."

That brought everybody out of the water and into the Duck. Boland drove it very carefully out of the cave, everyone keeping his head down again. Outside Nelson had the coxswain drive the Duck briefly along both sides of the promontory while he inspected carefully. The end of the promontory led back along a high ridge of rock which was extremely jagged and covered with thick, forbidding-looking, maquis-like growth. Nelson saw what he wanted to see, which was that the cave was approachable only by water. An experienced mountain goat would have had trouble reaching the end of that promontory by land. Then as they were driving back he said something to the men dressing in the well-deck while still talking excitedly of their discovery.

"Men, for the time being," he said thoughtfully, "I think it might be just as well if we didn't say anything about this little discovery to anyone. Especially anyone like the Army. I think we might find some kind of use for it and it would be a shame to spoil anything as virgin looking as that cave is by making it too public a place. Anyhow that is a sea cave which means that it belongs rightfully under Navy jurisdiction."

Everyone agreed it would be best not to talk about it, especially to the Army. Even a good thing, such as inter-service cooperation, can be carried too far.

For a short period following the liberation there had been a house in the little town but it had not lasted long. The town was much too small for anything of that kind to operate without those guardians of naval and military morals, the shore patrol and the military police, knowing about it. It was closed down quickly and a rigid eye kept on it. The men in the arm brassards were determined that nothing of the sort should come by land. It must never have occurred to them that it would come by sea, so that the sea approaches to such enterprise were left wholly unguarded.

The Duck's welldeck was designed to carry a good load of inanimate cargo. It was easily deep enough to shield the new, quite animate cargo it now began to carry. "We'll just have a little party," Lord Nelson had put it. "A little outing in the fresh air." The Duck would pick a few of them up at a prearranged place, the girls would be told to sit down in the welldeck, and the Duck would drive right through the main street of the town with nothing showing but sailors' heads. It would drive on down the street until it reached the water, drive into the water, and then proceed leisurely through the harbor and turn down the coast. Only when the Duck was well downshore and its passengers not discernible to the naked eye—Lord Nelson may have underestimated them, but after all he had had eighteen years of dealing with the shore patrol and military police and he did not believe them resourceful, or at least suspicious, enough to follow the Duck with binoculars—were the girls encouraged to stand up and get a whiff of sea air. It was a pretty drive in the sea down the coast and the girls enjoyed it. When the Duck reached the cave everybody, girls and sailors, sat down again in order to clear the entrance and the Duck glided softly in and parked. Once inside they were completely cut off from the world. The girls took as much delight in the cave as did the sailors, frolicking around it, once they were put ashore, like schoolgirls.

The men would sometimes get hold of a case of beer and chill it in the cave's pool, which was quite cold, by lowering it on a heavy line they had brought along for the purpose—Nelson knew every knot in the Navy. It was a very peaceful, content scene, the sailors and the signorine sitting around drinking their Pabst Blue Ribbon and conversing genially, as in a salon. The signorine developed quite a taste for the beer. Once one of the men, Mason, having had a couple of beers, suggested in his euphoria that they all go swimming in the cave lagoon. But the girls, having no bathing suits, were much too modest for that and appeared, in fact, quite shocked by the suggestion. After that no one suggested such an improper thing again and as a matter-of-fact Nelson chewed Mason out thoroughly for suggesting it at all.

"Do you want to scare them away, jughead?" Nelson said.

"I'm sorry, Boats," Mason said contritely. "It won't happen again."

"See that it doesn't. I don't know what you're used to but these are decent girls, Mason. Get that through your head."

"Yes, sir."

"And don't call me 'sir'!" Lord Nelson roared, as if he had been given the ultimate insult. "I ain't no officer!"

The Duck was, after all, intended to carry cargo and the men saw no reason not to use it for this purpose to make the cave even more comfortable than it naturally was. The rocks, for all their smoothness, did get a little hard at times. So they began bringing things to it. They brought some blankets from the ship— those superb, foamy cream blankets that say U. S. Navy in big blue letters on them. They even got some mattresses and, from the Army and by way of some more boxes of cigars for the cigar-chain-smoking sergeant, some cots. They had traded for some of these before to use in sleeping topside on warm, fair nights on the Anzio run, so that the Army saw nothing strange in the Navy wanting cots. The girls even contributed to the cave's décor, some throw pillows of various colors, which brightened things up a good deal. Gradually the cave became quite nicely furnished and a most comfortable place, very restful.

The entire crew of the *LST 1826* soon knew about the cave. The Navy has an institution which it calls the "happy hour," a term for a recreational period such as movies, baseball, volleyball, or whatever other means of diversion may be available in the circumstances of the particular ship. None of these was available in the case of the *LST 1826* but the crew felt it had found an adequate substitute. Excursions to the cave soon became the favorite form of "happy hour" among the men of the 1826. The cave's feature of having a half dozen distinct sub-caves leading off it like rooms also greatly increased its utility, enabling several men to have their happy hour simultaneously. The officers had also heard about the cave. They thought it an ingenious arrangement and in fact felt a definite pride in the crew for having figured out this method of solving a pressing problem. After a while Duck outings became so popular that they had to be rationed among the crew so that everybody who enjoyed this form of recreation could share and share alike. It became necessary to sign up two weeks in advance to be sure of space. Every day the ship was in port a Duck outing was laid on. On certain cool days when the men still went out, some of them so decidedly cold that a jungle-cloth jacket and a Navy wool watch cap did not provide an excess of warmth, the Army sergeant seemed a little surpised that anyone would want to swim in such weather.

"Well, we got some of those fanatics aboard," Lord Nelson explained one such cold day. "You know, some of those kind of freaks that would break ice to swim."

"Yeh, I heard of that kind," the sergeant said knowingly, flapping his hands to keep warm. "Never did understand anyone like that."

"Yeh, we got a few of those fanatics, Sarge. Now be sure and let us know if you ever run low on cigars. We've got to take care of the Army."

"Thank you very much, Boatswain's Mate," which was what the sergeant called Nelson. "I'll tell you frankly, I was never too sure about the Navy before. I was sure wrong and I don't mind saying it. You Navy men are all right," the sergeant said in a glow of good feeling.

"I appreciate you saying that, Sergeant, and I'm glad you feel that way. I guess all you got to do is get to know us," Nelson said piously.

The idyll of the cave had become an established part of the life of the crew of the *LST 1826* when Rear Admiral Haynes Doddridge, Commander Amphibious Forces Mediterranean, made an inspection visit to the Naples area. It was unfortunate that Admiral Doddridge happened to have the hobby he did. The admiral's hobby was speleology.

The cave had been in operation about a month when the admiral came over from his Algiers headquarters to have a look at how his Navy was doing in the Naples area. As part of his inspection trip the admiral came out to Pozzuoli one day, making the short trip by water from Naples in his glittering barge. He took a rather casual look around two or three ships in port, the last one the *LST 1826*. Then, being a thoughtful man, he asked if anyone wanted a lift into Naples. Ensign Eliot Horner was about to go into the city on shore leave and decided it would be pleasant to travel in style in an admiral's barge rather than on the rickety, crowded interurban that made the trip by land. He had never been in an admiral's barge. For that matter he had never been this close physically to an admiral before for any time and he felt the trip might be educational. He piled in and the barge went scooting off over a fine smooth sea down the coast toward the city in the distance. They had hardly cleared the harbor when the admiral instructed the coxswain to proceed slowly and rather close inshore. It was a very pretty and sunny day and the admiral felt he would like to enjoy the ride and be on the water as long as possible. To his everlasting regret, he seldom got away from his desk-bound job in Algiers, and it gave him a warm pleasure to be on the sea again, even if only in coastal waters and only in his barge. He said something of the sort now to Ensign Horner.

"Doesn't this air smell great, son? And the feel of this sea water under you, even in this little scooter."

"Yes, sir," Ensign Horner said dutifully, without sharing the emotion. He felt nothing but sea water under him most of the time and what he looked forward to feeling under him right now was the land of Naples, with a good recreational plan he had in mind.

"Sometimes I wish I could take every desk in the world and take it out to sea and drown it," the admiral said, a little forlornly. "But I guess there have to be desks to keep you boys on the ships at sea."

"Yes, sir," Ensign Horner said. "I know what you mean. We need those desks all right."

Somehow this didn't come out quite right. It even had a certain condescension in it. The admiral frowned a moment— this pup sounded almost as if he were judging *him*, who had had one cruiser and one aircraft carrier shot out from under him so far in this war, for being on the shore. Surely he was mistaken and he sat back gazing lovingly at the sea and at the pretty shoreline and again chatting occasionally with Horner. The ensign was suprised at the admiral's friendliness and easy talk and felt a distinct sense of warmth toward him. A very democratic man!

"How do you like LST duty?" the admiral inquired conversationally as they glided along.

"Well, it's the only Navy duty I've ever had, sir," Ensign Horner said carefully. "So I have no real basis of comparison. I like it I guess, sir."

"They do a good job," the admiral said.

"Thank you, sir," Ensign Horner said, as if accepting the compliment on behalf of the entire landing craft Navy. The admiral looked rather closely at him then back to sea.

"That's a very pretty formation over there, isn't it?" he said.

"What formation is that, sir?"

"That promontory. Coxswain," he spoke up to the spotlessly uniformed man at the helm of the barge. "Bring us a little closer to that point of land there."

"Aye aye, sir," the coxswain said smartly and immediately the barge came to port a good ten degrees. It handled beautifully, Horner thought idly. It was certainly a beautiful boat to the eye, too, as well as the seat, with comfortable white leather transoms and braided white tassels on the blue boat cloth. Its brass fittings gleamed in the sun and bow to stern it was an immaculate boat. Ensign Horner became aware that the admiral was looking rather earnestly at something.

"Coxswain, just let me have those glasses a moment, will you."

With one hand the coxswain deftly took the binoculars from around his neck and Horner got up quickly to serve as messenger. As he handed the binoculars to the admiral he noticed that their power was 7×50. The admiral, without moving his eyes from whatever he was looking at, took the glasses from the ensign and brought them up to position. Only then did Ensign Horner, who had been concentrating on saying the right things to the admiral and when he wasn't doing that thinking of what he would do on his shore leave in Naples, look up casually and notice the object of the admiral's study. He was looking very intently through those glasses, as though at a possible periscope from his bridge, at the end of the promontory.

"Son-of-a-gun. You know what I think, son? I think that's a cave in there," he said in rather reverent tones. "A sea cave. Coxswain! Bring her down to slow speed and approach the end of that promontory."

Horner was almost electrified out of his idle thoughts. Presently he observed, with intense alarm, that they were bearing directly on a course for the promontory's end, far off though it still was. Before he knew it, he heard a burst of words from his own mouth.

"Admiral!" he yelled so suddenly and so loudly that the admiral's head jerked around at him. His face was that of a man who was not accustomed to being shouted at from such close range, or at any range by an ensign. "Sorry, sir," Horner said more quietly. "But there are shoals in there, sir, I'm told. We've all been cautioned to give a wide berth to that promontory—on LCVPs, I mean—so as not to get our bottoms scraped. Sir."

It was a rather clumsy speech, but then Ensign Horner had had to improvise. He had not had time to compose a more proper one and he felt in any case he had got the central point across. The admiral, however, remained entirely cool under this navigational warning.

"Thanks for letting us know, son," he said. "That was a very proper thing to do. Coxswain! Send one of the men to the bow with a lead line."

"Aye aye, sir. McDermott!" the coxswain sang out. "On the bow with a lead line!"

The man McDermott was there in an instant. A very efficient crew! Horner thought in some terror. But then he imagined a crew of four commanded directly by a rear admiral would be. Then before he knew it the man was sending back fathom soundings.

"By the deep four!" he sang out.

The admiral turned to Horner. The ensign was astonished to see on his face now the look of eager anticipation one might expect on a boy setting out on a treasure hunt. "Do you know what I have for a hobby?"

"No, sir, I don't, sir."

"Speleology!" the admiral exploded the word as if it were the name of some esoteric rite in paradise.

"What's that, sir?"

"You mean you don't know what speleology is?" the admiral said in dumbfoundment. "Where did you go to school, son?"

"Dartmouth, sir. That's in Hanover, New Hampshire."

"So I've heard." The admiral looked at Horner as though dubious, or so Horner thought, that he had actually attended the school. Horner concentrated on remembering back. He remembered the graduation ceremony quite clearly. It was only two years ago. It seemed ten.

"You mean you never learned what speleology is?" the admiral was saying incredulously.

"Well, it's a pretty small school, sir. Just liberal arts mostly you know. Daniel Webster said about it, 'It is a small school, but there are those who love it.'"

The admiral gave Horner a curious look. "Did he? At any event, speleology is something of a branch of geology."

"That explains it, sir," Ensign Horner said. For some reason it made him happy to have any kind of explanation for what the admiral seemed to regard as rank stupidity. "I flunked geology."

"By the mark three!" McDermott sang out from the bow.

"Speleology," the admiral said, "is the science of cave exploration."

"That's very interesting to know, sir," Ensign Horner said. "I wouldn't have thought a regular Navy man would have much opportunity to practice cave-exploring."

"I got into it when I was stationed in Washington," the admiral explained. In the glow of discussing his hobby he now began speaking to Horner almost as if the ensign were his equal. "I did it to save my sanity from being stationed in that snake pit. It was very therapeutic—and very convenient, just across the Potomac. Did you happen to know that the state of Virginia is almost entirely hollow underneath?"

"No, sir, I didn't," Ensign Horner said. "That's very interesting."

"And a half, two!" McDermott sang out.

"The caves of Virginia!" the admiral said with enthusiasm. "I used to go out every weekend. I fell absolutely in love with exploring caves. Maybe one of those psychiatrists they have so many of around these days would say it was a repressed urge to be in submarines. And maybe he would be right," the admiral said with a touch of sadness, as if talking to himself. "I got turned down on the physical." Then he pulled himself back from this. "There's nothing quite like speleology. It saved my sanity from being stationed in Washington," he said again. "We used to tag bats."

"In Washington, sir?"

The admiral laughed appreciatively. "Well, no, I wouldn't undertake to tag *those* bats. We tagged bats in the caves. We put these little tags around their feet."

"What was the purpose of that, sir?" Horner, who was not entirely without intellectual curiosity, found himself suddenly fascinated by the idea of the admiral putting tags around bats' feet.

"Why, scientific, of course," the admiral said. "It was to find out how long a bat lived in those caves."

"How long did you find out they lived, sir?" Horner asked. He was becoming quite engrossed in the subject.

"Never did find out," the admiral said with real regret. "I got transferred. Thank the good Lord. The only thing I've ever missed about that duty was the speleology part. There's nothing to touch exploring caves. Even today I never pass up any chance I get."

This brought them both, Horner especially, looking up and dead ahead. They were getting quite close. The ensign felt a certain return of nervousness, even though, since his first outburst over the shoals, he had begun to reason more calmly that the admiral's only intention was to hover off and take a look at the cave's mouth. It was really all he could do. Horner had heard how closely the low-slung Duck fitted and was almost certain the admiral's barge, with its higher overhead, would never make it. Still, he would be just as happy when they were out of that vicinity.

"By the mark two!"

"I don't think there are any bats in the caves over here," Ensign Horner said.

"Oh?" the admiral said. "You've been in the caves of Italy?"

"No, sir," Horner admitted. "It's just a feeling I have. Somehow I don't feel there would be bats in Italy."

"Never give that kind of opinion except on the basis of first-hand observation, son," the admiral said in mild reproof. "Anyhow the bats are only incidental. It's the general idea of exploring caves that is the essential thing. Probably some atavistic urge."

"Doubtless comes from the primitive in some way, sir," Horner said, to make it clear he understood what the word meant.

They were getting so close that to Horner's inner agitation the leadsman had put aside the lead line and was poking as best he could with a boat hook.

"Ten foot!" he sang out.

The admiral and the ensign looked and now they were no more than fifty feet from the cave. The admiral ordered the coxswain to stop the boat. As it lay rocking a little in the water he looked toward the mouth of the cave, entranced.

"How I'd like to see what's in there! Of course it may be almost nothing. That's the excitement of it, of course. You never know until you get inside whether it's going to be a gopher hole or St. Patrick's Cathedral."

"This one looks more like a gopher hole to me," Horner said. "I doubt if we'd find St. Patrick's in there, sir."

"Probably not," the admiral said. "Most of them are gopher holes. But you never know. If I had a pair of bathing trunks here I'd be tempted to have a look. I might almost be tempted without the bathing trunks."

The idea momentarily brought a fresh alarm to Ensign Horner. He had never considered that the admiral would do such an undignified thing. Then he told himself the admiral could not be serious.

The admiral gave a regretful sigh. "All right, Coxswain. Take her out."

The coxswain had just put the boat on slow stern when a sound like nothing Horner had ever heard for penetration, a sound of the most piercing laughter, shattered the still afternoon. It rose above the quiet coughing of the engine and brought the admiral up out of his seat and looking with instant alertness at the source of the sound. He was looking directly into the mouth of the cave.

Now the air was invaded by another burst of laughter. This one was entirely different from the first, being decidedly more shrill. The first round of laughter had appeared to emanate from a man. The second clearly from some sort of female.

"Must be some Italians in there, sir," Horner said promptly.

A barrage of words, carried on more waves of laughter, erupted from the cave. The words were not identifiable as to meaning but the nationality of them was. They were unmistakably English, that is to say, American.

"*What the hell goes on here?*" the admiral said loudly.

"Coxswain! Take us back in as close as possible! Edge up on it! Proceed with care now! McDermott! Look alive with that lead line!"

The rapid-fire burst of orders seemed to come from a different man than the one who had been discussing the science of speleology so amiably with an ensign. Horner could well imagine the admiral on the quarterdeck. Already the boat was starting back in. The admiral was looking fixedly at the mouth of the cave and appeared to be pondering rapidly which of perhaps two or three courses he would take. The only thing not in doubt was that he would take some course. Horner searched frantically for some course of his own.

"No, I don't think we should try to take the barge in," the admiral was saying aloud but as if conferring with himself. "I don't think we'd clear overhead. Not to mention we don't know what's in there and might run aground. Stop here, Coxswain."

Instantly the admiral started taking off his clothes. Horner looked with incredulity as he shed them with bewildering speed. Maybe a quarter century of general alarms had taught him how to dress and undress quickly, the thought pushed through the great agitation in Horner's mind. Then without knowing he was doing so the ensign suddenly became aware that he was starting to remove his own clothes, probably because he could think of nothing else to do. The admiral was far faster. Horner was still working on his shoelaces when the admiral stood poised in his shorts on the gunwale. Horner just had time to glimpse a barrel of a chest with a light covering of black and white hair, the flat midriff of a man who kept in perfect condition, and a set of muscular shoulders. Then this figure had given a magnificent leap off the barge, entered the water like a torpedo, was surfacing, and moving swiftly toward the cave's mouth. By the time the ensign had got down to his shorts and executed a far clumsier disappearance over the side—a belly-buster in fact—and come up and commenced his own rather rug-beating stroke, the admiral was a good thirty feet ahead of him and he was disappearing into the cave. Horner fought and flailed his way inside. A colorful scene greeted him.

Strung out across the great ledge were a dozen men from the *LST 1826* and an approximately equal number of signorine. The signorine and the sailors were paired off in an easy comfortable arrangement, laughing and chatting gaily, and they all appeared to be drinking beer. The signorine looked lovely if somewhat professional to Horner's view and the men looked happy. The entire impression was one of relaxed merrymaking. Then Ensign Horner saw the admiral ascend from the lagoon, like some mythological god of the sea.

Calling himself a coward, the ensign nevertheless tread water, unable to merge into the developing scene. But he had a beautiful fish's-eye view of it. Signorine and sailors both looked up in mild surprise at the apparition. Horner noticed as a detail that some of the signorine were looking with a coy, almost professional interest at this new arrival. The admiral was a very handsome man in his way. Then, raising his head a little more out of the water, the ensign could make out that Boatswain's Mate Nelson had stood up in a position of spokesman for the group, and was looking in a curious and kindly fashion at the dripping figure before him whom he obviously took for a wayward swimmer of Italian extraction.

"What can we do for you, Pops?"

The boatswain's mate, obviously deducing from his silence that the man didn't know a word of English, spoke to one of the signorine. "Will you translate for me, Angelica? Ask him what the Navy can do for him."

Ensign Horner, wanting to go down in the water, preferably to the bottom and stay there, but finding himself helplessly raising his ears even more out of it, heard the even, steely voice which was that of the admiral, not of the speleologist.

"Translation will hardly be necessary." The admiral looked at Nelson then at the young woman who had stood up to provide her translation services. She was a package. "Young man." He turned back to Nelson. "Let me introduce myself. I am Rear Admiral Haynes Doddridge, Commander Amphibious Forces Mediterranean."

"Ten-shun!" Nelson's boatswain's voice crashed through the

cave. A shattering echo came back from the rock ceiling and walls. Then to the astonishment of the signorine all the Navy men came to a position they had never seen them in. They leapt to their feet and along with Nelson stood at rigid attention before the man in shorts. Somehow even this attire did not rob him of his dignity. The admiral looked evenly at the boatswain's mate and along the line of men.

"I want a straight answer. Who is the man responsible for finding this cave?"

"I am, sir!" Nelson spoke up immediately. "Nobody here is to blame except myself, sir. It's entirely my responsibility, sir."

"I see." The admiral looked appraisingly at the boatswain's mate. "And who are you, young man?"

"Lord Nelson, sir!" It was the only time anyone could ever remember when Nelson had lost his bearing. "Beg your pardon, sir. Andrew Nelson, boatswain's mate first, *LST 1826*, sir!"

The admiral looked across at Horner in the water.

"The 1826, is it? Come on out and join your shipmates, Mr. Horner." Then the admiral looked up in awe at the great vaulting roof. "It's not a gopher hole. It's St. Patrick's."

The admiral turned back to the boatswain's mate. Abruptly he put out his hand.

"Lord Nelson," he said very courteously, "I want to congratulate you on discovering one of the most esthetically perfect caves I have ever seen. I hope only you will forgive this intrusion on your privacy. It is in a way unforgivable, except for one thing. Would you mind showing me briefly around the cave before you and the lovely signorine here return to your conversation—I can only admire your choosing such a magnificent place in which to conduct it—and before I go on my way. You see, I, like all of you, am a speleologist."

Nothing as good as the cave was going to last. There were always too many people around whose job it was to put an end to anything as good and as healthful as that arrangement was. The end for the amateur speleologists came, not because of Admiral Doddridge's visit, but because, about a month after it, the men took the Duck out in a rather rough sea, and several of the signorine becoming seasick, decided reluctantly when about halfway out to return to shore for the day. The Duck, which had very little freeboard, was almost swamped itself before it finally chugged up on shore and, as seasick people always do, the signorine started disembarking immediately to get their feet on solid land. The commotion attracted a curious crowd, mostly civilians, but attracted also, unfortunately, a couple of shore patrol men cruising around the waterfront. In any event the cave gave a good many happy hours, while it lasted, to the men of the *LST* *1826*.

3

DEATH AND BIRTH

The main road led around the small harbor and into it fed other roads like dusty tributaries. The jeep turned up one of them. Up ahead was an intersection with a church beside it, its bell-tower half decapitated. An MP was standing in the middle of the intersection directing the traffic that was hurrying off the LSTs and down the road. He waved the last of a line by and for a moment the intersection was empty, save for the MP standing there in a swirl of dust. The jeep was bouncing toward the intersection and the MP had turned to look at it and was just bringing up his arm to wave it on through when the shell landed. A much larger cloud of dust flew up and the MP disappeared in it. The jeep kept coming then stopped and Barclay and the driver got out of it and walked through the dust toward the intersection. They entered it like entering a cloud and felt their way through it until they found him. The top of the MP's head was blown away just on a line with his eyebrows and already the dust was settling into the wound. The soldier leaned over him.

"Anyhow he never knew," he said.

They carried him out of the dust and off the road and laid him in the shade of a tree. They saw another jeep coming down the road. It had two MPs in it. One of them got out of the jeep to take over the traffic-directing job in the intersection and the other drove on away to get someone to come after the body under the tree. Barclay and the driver went on back to their jeep and continued along the road. Very soon they pulled into a large clearing where the weapons carriers were already loaded. Barclay got out and went over and talked with the Army captain in charge. It was very dusty in there and the captain's face under his helmet was solid with it with his eyes showing through. You could have drawn your initials on his face. Barclay and the captain talked for a moment and then the captain climbed up on top of one of the trucks and holding a megaphone addressed the people in the trucks in a shout.

"This Navy officer," he said in Italian, "has come to take you down to his ship. The ship will be taking you away from Anzio back to Naples, away from the war. Everything is very safe there now. The war is over in Naples. The war is only here, and at Cassino, which is why you cannot go overland but must go by sea. The Germans are between us here and Naples but the ship will go around Cassino. This Navy officer speaks your language, just as I do, and you will be cared for on the ship and it will get you to Naples. Do whatever this Navy officer tells you to do and you will be all right."

There was a stirring in the trucks and a little jabbering. "Are there German submarines in the water between here and Naples we have heard so?" a voice came from somewhere in the trucks.

"That is right, there are," the captain shouted back. "But then there are German shells here, and German bombs, as you know."

"*Mangiare sopra questa nave?*" a high thin rather whining voice came from another truck.

"Yes, you'll get to eat on the ship," the captain shouted back through his megaphone. "Now I think we should all be a lot safer by making an end to the questions and for you to be on your way instead of being congregated here so invitingly for some of those shells and bombs just described."

This put a prompt end to all questions. Barclay got into the jeep and the driver led out, the long string of brimming weapons carriers following. Looking back Barclay could see a great whirlpool of dust, obscuring all but the truck immediately behind him. They came to the intersection and the new MP waved them through. Then pretty soon the procession of vehicles turned into the road that ran around the harbor. They followed it until they came to the LST and Barclay got out, went back to the first truck, and told the occupants to follow him onto the LST. He detailed some men from the first truck to go back and tell the occupants of the other trucks to do the same. Soon he was leading them up the bow ramp. When he got to the ramp and looked back he could see just what a long line of them there was.

He stood on the bow ramp directing them onto the ship by the elbow. Closer up he could see how, without exception, their flesh had a scooped-out look, of long hunger, and the skin stretched tight over the bones of their faces. Moving them on, he continued to speak their language, never stopping talking, and smiling now and then, and in general he hoped being reassuring. Shells fell sporadically in the water around the ships and they looked in fear at the splashes. Some of them looked in almost equal fear at the ship, as if it were a strange ship which could open its bow like a mouth so that you could walk right on and as if it possibly might be going to get them all aboard, snap its mouth shut, and take them out to sea and drown them. These various trepidations made some come aboard with a certain reluctance, and for these Barclay's hand on the elbow had to be crisply convincing to induce them on at all. Most of them, however, looked more dazed than frightened and came stolidly aboard, amenable to any hand that would guide them. Nearly all of them clutched or carried by a stick over their shoulder some kind of tattered bundle or basket which would contain all that the war had left them. As they entered the tank deck they passed from Barclay into the hands of members of the crew who led them to their home for a day in troops quarters. As soon as the last one was on Barclay told the bridge so from the phone by the bow ramp and almost at once the ramp started up, the bow doors folded shut and the ship backed off.

They were out of the harbor without incident and Barclay kept going through the ship handling various minor problems that arose with these passengers and trying to answer their questions. They had quite a few of them and the ship was well down the coast before Barclay got up to chow. Afterward he went up on the bridge wing and stood there awhile watching them down on the main deck. It was a bright, clear and warm day and a smooth sea, fortunately, and they appeared to be relaxing a little. They sat around on the hatch covers and stood by the life lines watching the wake of the ship. They were every age except one age, he suddenly was aware, now that he began to separate them as individual persons. There were old men and old women and there were boys and girls and there were young women. But there were no young men at all. He went down and circulated among them some more. They seemed a good deal more relaxed now. They had been fed for one thing, but mainly it was that they were leaving the war behind them and were fairly confident now that the ship was not going to cast them to the bottom. They had some forebodings about the situation in Naples, where a good many of them had relatives and where some of them had even lived themselves before going north ahead of the war until they got pinned in a corner at Anzio with the Germans on one side of them and the arriving Allies on the other, or, filtering through the war-filled lines from the hills above Anzio, had emerged upon the beachhead and presented themselves to the Allies for disposition. Barclay had to keep reassuring them that though Naples had suffered damage the city was still there and operating.

"They even have the San Carlo going," he said, thinking that they would identify the fact of opera performances with a fairly stable situation. "They have opera every afternoon at 2:30. Myself I saw Aïda there only a week ago."

"It is a pretty good opera," said an old man. "Personally I prefer Puccini."

"Perhaps that would be the fault of your taste," said another old man. "Everyone knows Verdi is the superior artist."

"I will take Puccini," the first old man said stubbornly.

"Did you not hear the lieutenant say he likes Verdi?" the second old man said. "Are you trying to insult this brave American lieutenant who is taking us back in his ship to make it possible in the first place to see opera again, not to mention saving our lives which must seem to him a thankless task judging from the reaction of some of us."

"Do you think the lieutenant is so ignorant as to consider me ungrateful because I admire Puccini? You misjudge the Americans. The Americans have no wish to be dictators to order everyone they must prefer Verdi to Puccini." The first old man turned to Barclay. "Lieutenant, you do not think me ungrateful because I admire Puccini, do you?"

"Not at all," Barclay said. He felt things were really all right now. "In Naples they were showing both of them—Puccini and Verdi—and both of you gentlemen will have an opportunity to see them both once more and thus have a fresh basis of comparison."

"I doubt if anything could change my mind about Puccini," said the first man.

"Lieutenant," an old woman in the large crowd that had collected around Barclay spoke up, "if these two goats will stop bleating about their opera for a moment I would like to ask what part of Italy your ancestors are from."

"Rome obviously," the second old man spoke up at once.

"Nonsense," said the first old man. "He is of course a Florentine," and Barclay at least knew the home city of each of the two old men. "He has that grace and assurance which are the stamp solely of the man of Florence."

"I'm afraid they didn't come from Italy at all," Barclay got in. "They came, I am afraid, at one time from Scotland."

"The Scots are very much like the Italians," said the old man from Florence.

"Almost an identical people," the old man from Rome at last agreed to something his compatriot had said.

"But how do you speak such immaculate Italian?" the woman asked.

"I went to school in Italy for a little."

"Where, Lieutenant?" the woman asked.

"It was only a year," Barclay said. "At the University of Florence . . ."

"Didn't I tell you so!" the old man from Florence said triumphantly. "Don't I know a Florentine when I see one?"

"Lieutenant," the old man from Rome said, "did you ever visit Rome?"

"Many times," Barclay said. "I . . ."

"I knew it," the old man from Rome said. "I tell you, when a man has spent such a long time in Rome as has the lieutenant here, I can tell it, that mark of the true dignity possessed alone by the Roman."

"I only spent . . ."

"You have a beautiful Roman accent," the old man from Rome said, "which is to say, no accent at all."

"Mr. Barclay," a very obviously American voice said at his side. "The captain requests your presence in the conning tower, if that is convenient."

It was Seaman Second Class Peter Carlyle, who had never been to either Florence or Rome. "It is convenient," Barclay said. "My presence will be right there." The two men grinned at each other.

"Excuse me," Barclay said to the Italians. "The captain wants me. I have enjoyed our talk and we will be doing some more of it." He looked at the two old men. "Actually I like both Puccini and Verdi."

Everybody laughed and they bowed as Barclay went away.

"A most educated and mannerly young man," he heard one of the old men say behind him, the Florentine, he thought. "Didn't I tell you that all Americans were not uncultured ignoramuses?"

"Who said they were?" the other old man flared up. "Was it not you who said the Americans would put us on a ship and . . ."

By that time he was out of earshot. He went on up to the conning tower. A very short old man wearing nothing but long underwear, a shabby coat and a straw boater, of all things, above it, was standing there gesturing vividly and saying something which appeared to be of the most vital importance to the captain, who could not understand a word of it and himself had begun to gesture rather frantically so that the ludicrous-looking old Italian and the American two-stripe lieutenant stood there making windmill hand-motions to each other and getting nowhere.

"Barclay!" the captain turned on him as soon as he came up. "What in God's name is he saying? And I wonder where in the hell he got that boater."

Barclay talked to the old man a moment, about the first not the second part of the captain's question. Barclay's eyebrows flicked up and he took a breath.

"Captain," he said. "He's saying there's a woman below who is going to give birth to a baby."

"What's that?" the captain blurted out. He seemed equally astounded and outraged by the news. "What's that? What's that?"

Barclay repeated the intelligence he had gathered from the Italian.

"Ask him why in the hell they didn't keep her ashore where she could get proper medical care?"

Barclay spoke quietly again with the man. The Italian's gestures now became less vigorous and more subtle. He began to speak elaborately as if explaining a very complicated and technical problem for the benefit of these naval people. Barclay turned to the captain.

"He says she had no idea then that it would be so soon. He says that his experience is that a sea voyage brings on birth sooner. Undoubtedly, he says, it is due to the motion of a ship . . ."

" 'His experience'!" the captain blurted in absolute outrage at the phrase. He looked at the man in underwear and straw boater and then at Barclay. " 'His experience!' What does he know about sea voyages?"

"Shall I ask him, Captain?"

"Never mind, never mind!" the captain said.

"Captain, I . . ."

"A baby!" the captain exploded. "They can't have a baby on this ship. This is a man o' war."

He turned to Barclay. "How soon?"

Barclay talked to the Italian. "He says in his experience it could happen almost any time."

"He has lots of experience, doesn't he?" the captain said, gazing coolly at the absurd-looking little Italian. He turned to Barclay and spoke crisply. "Go have a look."

Barclay, accompanied by the old man, went below and was back in five minutes verifying the report.

The captain looked out to sea a moment. "Son-of-a-bitch!" he said, turning to the Italian. He was not calling the old man a name, but simply airing his outraged perplexity. Then he was silent for a moment, staring at the water moving past.

"Thank God for this sea anyhow," he said almost to himself. The sea was an unbroken sheen, not a whitecap anywhere. They were silent for a bit and Barclay knew what the captain was thinking: that an LST carried no doctor except during an invasion and shortly thereafter. It had been two months since he left.

"Well," the captain said, turning back again, this time toward Barclay. He gave a deep sigh. "I guess it's up to Latimer. He's the senior medical authority present aboard, I believe."

"Yes, I guess he is, Captain."

The captain sighed again. "Pharmacist's Mate Second Class Latimer," he pronounced the ship's available medical skill.

"He's a pretty good pharmacist's mate, Captain," Barclay said.

"Who said he wasn't?" the captain said irritably. "And I'm a pretty good ship's captain and you're a pretty good first lieutenant. What we're talking about here is delivering babies." Then, as if in fear of weakening what small structure of hope they had, he said crisply to Barclay: "Don't communicate any lack of confidence in him to him, you understand?"

"I certainly won't do that, Captain. We couldn't afford to. He's all we've got."

Abruptly, coming to decision, the captain issued a rapid series of orders.

"Barclay, I want you to take personal charge of this entire matter starting right now. You will accompany this gentleman—and for God's sake get him some pants somewhere will you—to the woman. You will see to it that she is given every care and comfort available. Take her to the wardroom. You will assign Latimer to attend her. Ask Latimer if he can handle it and report his answer to me. On second thought don't ask him. *Tell* him. Tell him he has to handle it. May God help him. Latimer, with whatever knowledge of these affairs he may have or be able to invent, and you with your Italian lingo, are to stay with the woman until she—delivers. Carlyle here will remain with you at all times as messenger. And you will call upon whatever other help you may require. You got all that?"

"Yes, sir," Barclay said quietly. "We'll . . ."

"In addition! You are to make frequent reports to me personally on the woman's condition. You are to advise me if we are going too fast, causing too much movement of the ship—which seems to bring these things on," he said, glancing coolly at the Italian, "for her comfort and welfare. Especially as the time approaches. Is all this clear, Barclay?"

"Perfectly clear, Captain," Barclay said. He was very fond of the captain.

"And Barclay."

"Yes, sir?"

"Wait a moment."

The captain turned and dictated a message to the watch recorder. Barclay heard it but read it again when the captain handed it to him. The message read:

ORIGINATOR: LST 1826

ACTION: COMPHIBMED

URGENT

HAVE ITALIAN WOMAN ABOARD SCHEDULED TO GIVE BIRTH
VERY LIKELY BEFORE THIS VESSEL REACHES POZZUOLI.
NO REPEAT NO DOCTOR ABOARD. REQUEST SAME BE DISPATCHED
IMMEDIATELY VIA PETER TARE BOAT TO THIS VESSEL FOR
TEMPORARY EMERGENCY DUTY. MY POSITION IS 15 MILES
BEARING 160 FROM CAPE CIRCEO. IF REQUEST IS
GRANTED WILL KEEP PT INFORMED MY POSITION AT
ALL TIMES

"Well, what do you think?" the captain said.

"It means breaking radio silence."

"I'm quite aware," the captain said drily, "that you can't send a message without breaking radio silence. Anything else?"

Barclay sighed deeply. "PTs are pretty scarce around here, Captain. We'll be lucky to get a PT. And if what our experienced emissary here says is true, it's going to happen anyhow long before any PT gets here."

"Women are always mistaken about the exact time," the captain said authoritatively. "And invariably their mistake is on the side of prematurity. I have seven children and my wife thought everyone of them was coming before it did in fact come. The doctor *might* get here in time. Any further comments?"

"Just that I'm glad you're sending it, sir."

"Very well. But before I do so I want you and Latimer to have a look at her. Do that, then report immediately to me. I'll hold back the message until you do."

The captain turned rather abruptly, looking at the sea again. He turned back to Barclay.

"All right, Barclay. Carry on and both of you assume all the way Latimer's going to have to do it. By the way. Do you know how old he is?"

"I believe he's nineteen."

"My God. Carry on."

"Yes, sir. *Adèsso* . . ." Barclay started talking to the Italian. With the little Italian almost trotting at his heels to keep up, and Carlyle bracketing him from behind—both Americans were a foot taller—the long-legged Barclay swung swiftly down the ladder and made his way forward to troops quarters. There the Italian guided him through an excited and chattering crowd of other Italians, with an importance in no wise diminished by his attire telling everyone to stand aside.

She was lying in a bunk with just her head sticking out above the cream blanket that said *U. S. Navy* on it and her long black hair framing her face on the pillow. Barclay had been startled at how young the face was. She looked hardly more than a child herself. The face looked very pale right now and very afraid. Barclay sensed—it was hard to tell now, or even deal with the thought—that she must be very beautiful. He could tell one thing, that under the blanket she was clutching at her belly.

"The husband," Barclay said aside to the Italian. "Is her husband aboard?"

The man shrugged his shoulders and cocked his head. "No one, Lieutenant," he said importantly, "knows where the husband is. Or who."

Barclay could see other Italians hovering around in the gloom, some squatted on their haunches, watching. He told Carlyle to get Latimer wherever he was, and have him bring a stretcher and to get four men for bearers. "Big men," he specified. Carlyle hurried off and Barclay knelt by the bunk and began to talk to the woman.

"Be patient a few moments, signora," he said to her. "We have a man who knows about medicine. He is coming now. All will be well," he said, a confidence he didn't feel at all. She seemed very fragile for the undertaking, thin and underfed.

Momentarily he placed his hand on her forehead, his large hand enclosing it entirely, and feeling the sweat of pain and fear there. He kept talking to her, and the talking, or perhaps merely the fact that there was at least someone with authority who knew her language and to whom therefore she could communicate her urgency, seemed slightly to soothe her.

"I am afraid," she said in a small voice. "And I am beginning to hurt. What are you, signore?"

"I am a lieutenant aboard here."

"You won't leave me, Lieutenant?"

"I will not leave you, signora. I'll stay right with you all of the time."

"This medical man," she said. "He is a doctor?"

Barclay looked at her, and knew somehow he would never fool her. "No," he said. "But he is a man who helps doctors in their work."

"I understand, Lieutenant," she said, and it was then he knew she had courage. She would need it.

"How old are you, signora?"

"Seventeen."

"Seventeen, signora?"

"I am seventeen, Lieutenant. I am old enough."

He saw Latimer, Carlyle, and some men for bearers led by Boatswain's Mate Nelson coming down the passageway. Carlyle must have had the good sense to have told Latimer what it was and what he was going to have to do because the pharmacist's mate's face masked whatever alarm he felt, which Barclay imagined must be plenty.

"Let's get her up to the wardroom," Barclay said.

Latimer's voice shook only slightly. "Carlyle! Go get the Navy medical book from sick bay and bring it to the wardroom."

"Nelson, let's get her onto the stretcher," Barclay said.

"All right, you men," Nelson said, in that voice of crisp, rather menacing authority he had. "I want you men to take it very easy with the signora. You understand? I said *easy*."

Moving her with great care the sailor-bearers got her onto the stretcher. She groaned out even so. They took her very slowly along the passageway to the foot of the ladder, where Carlyle, already back from his errand, was standing. They hesitated a moment, looking up the steep ladder, and Barclay decided it would be better not to try to get her up it on the stretcher. He turned to Carlyle, whose feats of strength on the ship were legendary.

"Can you carry her up, Red?" he said.

"No problem at all, Mr. Barclay."

"All right then. Let's go."

Very gently, but with no more trouble than if she had been a baby herself, Carlyle picked her up off the stretcher and took her in his arms up the ladder and along the passageway into the wardroom and placed her on a dining table, which he had previously cleared and spread with blankets and pillows. Latimer took the big Navy medical book over to the Silex stand, more than anything else to steady his nerves and give himself a chance to think. He flipped through the book but of course could find nothing to help in this situation, which the Navy seemed to have overlooked. Barclay came over and stood by him.

"Good God, Mr. Barclay," Latimer whispered. "I don't know the first thing about delivering babies. They never taught us that in Navy pharmacists school. The subject never even came up!"

"Well you'll just have to learn," Barclay said firmly. "By practice."

"A *baby!*" the pharmacist's mate exclaimed. He seemed appalled by the very word, as if the enormity of what was expected of him was just coming over him. "Well, all I've heard is that you're supposed to have hot water. So I guess we better start getting lots of that in here."

Then, and Barclay could almost see it happen, a change came upon Pharmacist's Mate Second Class Hugh Latimer. Drawing himself up, he spoke distinctly and his voice didn't shake a bit.

"Carlyle!" The seaman messenger, who had been standing over to the side looking very contemplative and a little awed, snapped his head up. "Get a couple of men and start fetching plenty of hot water from the galley! On the double!"

Carlyle, almost leaping out of the wardroom, took off on the hot-water mission.

Barclay took one more look at the girl where her head moved from side to side on the pillow and at her ghostly face, and he listened for a moment more to the low, unceasing, animal moans that came from her. Then abruptly he stepped over to the phone and called the conning tower.

"Captain, I think you should get that despatch off immediately. She's in for a rough time of it."

Within an hour the captain phoned down to Barclay and read him this answer:

ORIGINATOR: COMPHIBMED

ACTION: LST 1826

URGENT

COMMANDER WILKINS JONES, UNITED STATES NAVAL
MEDICAL CORPS RESERVE, ENROUTE YOUR VESSEL IN
PETER TARE ONE ONE ONE NINE. SEAS OF FOUR
FEET AND INCREASING REPORTED BETWEEN PT BASE
AND YOUR VESSEL THEREFORE UNABLE GIVE ANY ETA
BUT MINIMUM IS SIX HOURS. UNDERTAKE DIRECT
CONTACT WITH ONE ONE ONE NINE ON FREQUENCY
THREE SIX. GOOD LUCK TO YOU AND MOTHER.

Then he sent it down. Barclay showed it to Latimer.

"It's certainly nothing we can count on, is it, Mr. Barclay?"

"No, it isn't," Barclay said. "It depends on the girl—and the sea."

Now, as the ship ploughed south toward Naples, a long vigil began in the wardroom. The captain came in frequently to get a progress report. He seemed to take the matter as a personal challenge to his ship and his seamanship. Once when the sea came up just enough to make it felt in the wardroom he phoned Barclay from the conning tower.

"Can you feel it down there?"

"A little. Only a little, Captain."

"I think we'll rev down a couple of knots. Wouldn't that make it easier on her?"

"It might, Captain. It certainly wouldn't hurt."

"Very well, we'll rev down. Let's hope for the PT."

"Yes, we'll hope, Captain."

The captain waited a moment. Then he said: "She appears to be a very lovely girl, doesn't she?"

"Yes, I think she must be very lovely, Captain."

And the ship was slowed.

But more than anything Barclay marveled at Latimer. He was tireless and he was thorough. He did the medical things—the pulse and temperature readings—with a quiet coolness; and the things of comfort—such as the cold cloths—with an apparently instinctive gentleness. And above all he made his whole air radiate assurance, some of which communicated itself to the girl. He had plenty of fears about what would happen, as Barclay discovered when they went off briefly from time to time to talk. But the girl never saw them in him.

The girl's pain continued erratically and Barclay never got beyond the range of her call. Most of the time he just sat by her, talking when she wanted to or when she had a need to communicate with Latimer, but otherwise just being there. He found out that she had a cousin in Pozzuoli with whom she intended to live. He explained carefully that they would take her to the American hospital and care for her until she was able to leave. And something made him decide to make sure to get the address in Pozzuoli. At one point in the talking Barclay discovered that she liked music and he told Carlyle to break out his guitar. The tall seaman second sat on the wardroom transom with his legs crossed playing quietly and sometimes softly singing. The music, dealing with such faraway places and strange-sounding names as the Chisholm Trail, Gilgarry Mountain, and the Erie Canal, must have seemed rather esoteric to her but it appeared to soothe her, a smile of something like comfort coming over her face as she listened. Once Barclay happened to look at Carlyle's face while he was playing. The sailor was watching the girl, with a strange look that seemed to combine wonder, hope, and fear. By suppertime nothing had happened and the officers took their meal below with the crew.

Very late the captain called Barclay from the conning tower.

"Not good news," he said at once. "We're getting off and on contact with the PT and the story is this, she's running into heavy seas. I guess it doesn't take much for a boat like that."

"What's the earliest she estimates here?" Barclay said.

"Four hours at the very earliest. Probably more. Will she be that long?"

"I doubt it. I've never seen this before but I doubt it, Captain."

Barclay could hear the captain's sigh. "Well, we're doing everything and we'll do everything."

The word of the struggle taking place in the wardroom had by now spread through the ship and the crew waited, completely caught up in it. Virtually nothing was being done now around the ship, except the necessary watches, and except that the carpenter's mate constructed a crib and brought it up and installed it in a corner of the wardroom. The wardroom had settled also into a waiting silence, broken only by Barclay's quiet talking, almost a litany now, with the woman, and Carlyle's equally quiet playing of his guitar. Occasionally the woman would go off into a kind of mumbling delirium and once she reached at Barclay and pulled him down to her as though she had something of great urgency to impart to him.

"Lieutenant, if the baby comes and stays and I don't, will you see about the baby?"

"Yes, signora. We'll see about the baby. But you'll be all right. You'll be there to see about the baby yourself."

"But you promise if I'm not here? Don't worry that I talk this way, Lieutenant. It's only that I am very realistic. You promise about the baby if I'm not here?"

"I promise. I promise about the baby."

"I believe you. My mind is better now." But her head moved restively, feverishly, on the pillow.

They kept getting reports from the PT—three hours away, two and a half, two and finally only one hour. But now she had reported extreme seas and she was going very slowly for a PT. Then, it happened very suddenly, the ship ran into what must have been the same sea and in the wardroom they could feel the LST begin to take on deep rolls. A fresh terror came over the girl's face. Barclay put four large-sized men of the crew in position, one on either side of the wardroom table and one on each end, their bodies pressed against the table to keep her from rolling off. Latimer was leaning over the woman and Barclay could see the deep concern in his face.

"Mr. Barclay," the pharmacist's mate said. "I think if we can get the ship slowed down, we should do it. She's not too good."

Barclay stepped over to the phone and called the captain in the conning tower. The captain ordered the ship slowed to almost a creeping pace; the decision was made without hesitation, no one mentioning the added invitation this action extended to any German submarines that might be around. In the wardroom the men at the woman's sides braced themselves to the roughening sea, and never moved. Barclay could hear the mixture of rain and sea begin to spatter against the dogged wardroom ports. Turning, he could hear the woman cry out and at almost the same instant hear Latimer say: "Here we go." And the pharmacist's mate, a Catholic, crossed himself, and bent to a work he had never known. Barclay stepped quickly to the woman's side.

"I am hurting, Lieutenant," she was saying. Her face on the

pillow seemed whiter than the pillow itself, and it was contorted
in savage pain. "I am hurting very much."

"What's she saying, Mr. Barclay?" Latimer asked.

"That she's hurting—very much. How is it, Latimer?"

"I don't know, Mr. Barclay." His voice was grave but it was
steady. "If she can just hold on . . . tell her if she can just
hold on."

"What is he saying, Lieutenant?" she asked.

"That it will not be long now, signora. It will be soon."

She looked very beseeching, her wide eyes not leaving his now.
"Don't leave me, Lieutenant!"

"No, I am right here," he said. "I'm not going anywhere."

One hand came out from under the blanket and held at his,
her fingernails biting into his palm and then the small fingers
stretching out between his large ones, interlacing, and holding
on hard, very hard, straining hard against his.

"Only a little bit more now, signora," he said. Her face had
an unearthly whiteness and he felt great fear. He felt no confidence at all. At that moment he hoped only that they would
save one of the two out of it. "It will be over very soon now,
signora," he said.

"Am I hurting your hand?"

"Hurt it some more, signora."

And she squeezed tighter, holding terribly to his hand as if
to life itself.

They would remember later that it happened almost at the
precise moment at which the sea itself quieted, as if in its own
expectancy. For they had sensed that the rolling had stopped
and Barclay had just looked up and become aware, with a kind
of wonder, that no water was splashing against the ports, and
felt, simultaneously, her hand in his, biting hard enough that
small drops of blood ran down. At that moment he heard a tiny
cry break through the wardroom of the 1826.

It was just first light, Barclay could see through the wardroom
ports, which someone had undogged. Latimer wrapped the baby
in a pillowcase, and laid it in the blanket-lined and pillowed

crib the carpenter's mate had fashioned. Barclay leaned over the mother to tell her. She was white as death now, but the ordeal had passed over her, and spared her.

Barclay phoned the captain in the conning tower. Presently the captain could be heard on the p.a. system addressing all hands, most of whom had stayed up through the night in vigil.

"This is the captain speaking. Now hear this. The LST 1826," and his voice rose in pride, "has just had a baby." He said it almost as if the ship itself were the father—as, in a way, it perhaps was. "The baby is a boy. Mother and child are doing fine. The delivery was made by Pharmacist's Mate Second Class Hugh Latimer. Correction. He has just been recommended for Pharmacist's Mate First Class Hugh Latimer. Unfortunately the Navy doesn't permit commanding officers to confer M.D. degrees."

Almost immediately the captain was striding into the wardroom and congratulating Latimer, the mother, and, so it seemed as he stood over the crib grinning widely and shaking his head, the baby itself, each on a brilliant performance.

"Well, I'm fat, dumb, and happy," he said. He stuck his finger down and the baby's red tiny hands struggled around it. "And isn't he bright-eyed and bushy-tailed?"

The wardroom phone buzzed and Carlyle took it.

"Captain, the O.O.D. says there's a PT broad on the port bow, two miles and closing.

"Well, well," the captain said. "Tell the O.O.D. to put the jacob's ladder over the side, Carlyle, and prepare to take a passenger aboard."

The PT came alongside and lay there bobbing a good deal, so that it would require some agility to get across and the passage would have to be timed cannily for the split-moment when the boat and the bottom rung of the ladder were about level. Along the gunwale of the PT crouched a middle-aged naval officer with the stripes of a full commander and the insignia of a doctor. He didn't look terribly happy as he stood there on the bouncing PT looking warily at the ladder. Nelson threw a line over and one of the PT men secured the black bag to it and Nelson heaved it in. Finally, the commander ventured his own transfer and managed to get a precarious hold on the ladder. The PT immediately shot off, leaving the three-striper plastered against the side of the LST and hanging wild-eyed just over the sea lapping against his legs. He managed to mount a few rungs until Nelson, leaning far over, grabbed him by both shoulders and helpfully yanked him aboard. Lord Nelson's first words, meant harmlessly enough, did nothing to enhance his equanimity.

"Well, you're not needed, fortunately, sir," Lord Nelson said. "It's all over and everything's fine. But we're glad to have you aboard all the same, sir."

"You're more than kind," the commander said. "Would you care to lead me immediately to the scene?"

"Oh, yes, sir," Lord Nelson said happily. "You're going to get a big kick when you see that baby."

"I can hardly wait," the commander said.

"Yes, sir," Lord Nelson said. "Just follow me, sir."

The commander followed Nelson into the wardroom. Without bothering with introductions he took an immediate professional look at the baby, then the mother.

"Well, that is quite a nice-looking baby," he said of the first. "And she seems to be all right," he said of the second. "Who did this?"

Barclay introduced Latimer. The commander glared at him. "Have you ever done this before?"

"No, sir, this is the first time. The opportunity never arose before."

"No, I suppose not. Well, young man, all I can say is, you probably ought to be a doctor."

"Thank you, sir," Latimer said. "I intend to. If the war ever gets over."

"They tell me they plan to get it over with some day. If you keep that ambition, check in with me. I know something about medical schools, I might say. Must have been a very difficult case," he said, almost as one colleague to another. "That narrow pelvis, you know."

"Yes, it's a pretty narrow pelvis, sir," Latimer, who had been too busy even to think about pelvises, said thoughtfully.

The captain was particularly gracious with the commander.

"Sir," he said, "we appreciate your trip just the same."

"It was damn rough," the commander said. "Have you ever been in a PT boat doing 40 knots in a rough sea?"

"No, sir. I haven't had that privilege."

"I thought I was going to have a baby myself. Very conducive to seasickness. Matter-of-fact, if I'm not needed here—and seeing everything is in such good hands—I wouldn't mind lying down for a few minutes."

"Latimer," the captain said at once. "Will you take the commander to my cabin and give him anything he needs."

The commander was led out and after Latimer had administered aspirin he came right back. The crew kept coming in to get a look at the baby. A strange kind of joy leapt through the ship. Ship's company furthermore looked upon the fact of having a baby born aboard as a kind of omen of good fortune for a ship to have; a sign; that nothing really bad ever could happen to a ship where such a thing had taken place. And they all took great pride.

The captain signaled ahead a message to the base. It read: PLEASE HAVE AMBULANCE STANDING BY. HAVE THREE-HOUR-OLD BABY ABOARD.

The ambulance was waiting on the mole when the ship came in. Down in the tank deck the Italians all stood politely aside, their tattered bundles over their shoulders, for the mother to be carried off first and most of the crew were lined up, too, to get a last glimpse of the baby. The mother was brought down the deck, borne on her stretcher by the same four towering sailors who had stood by her at the wardroom table. She was accompanied by Barclay and by Latimer carrying the child bundled in a Navy blanket, and by Carlyle carrying the crib. And leading the entire procession, with a bearing that suggested he was in some way responsible for the whole successful enterprise, was the short old man who had originally brought the situation to the captain's attention. He still wore his straw boater though below it, covering his long underwear, he now also wore a pair of Navy dungarees Lord Nelson had dug up for him, and as he led the procession along he kept repeating to his fellow Italians, with an air of importance and a brushing movement of the hands, something which translated "Attention! Make way for the signora and the baby!" As the procession moved toward the bow ramp suddenly a mighty cheer went up from the refugees.

"Viva the American Navy!" they shouted.

At the bow ramp Bo's'n's Mate Nelson handed Barclay a quite good-sized bag of white drill cloth with a drawstring.

"The crew took up a collection, Mr. Barclay," Lord Nelson said. "For the baby."

Barclay tucked it, unnoticed by her, under the mother's pillow. Then, just before the bearers put her into the ambulance, the mother motioned to Barclay and he leaned down close to her.

"Lieutenant," she said. "Will you tell me your first name, Lieutenant?"

"It is Matthew," Barclay said.

"And the name of the medical man?"

"His is Hugh," Barclay said.

"Lieutenant," she said, "the baby will be christened Ugo Matteo."

The ambulance drove off, many of the crew and the Italians standing there watching it until it had disappeared. Barclay saw to the loading of the Italians in the waiting weapons carriers, wondering where they would all go, and if he might ever see any of them again in the city. Most of all he wondered where that new mother would go. Then, in a reflex, his hand felt his shirt pocket. He remembered that he had her address there.

He went on back to the ship. Walking up the ramp it occurred to him that he had seen one die and one born that day, which he figured made it even. It had been a pretty good day, for the war.

Next day the crew painted on the conning tower of the LST a baby in a crib, as some ships paint there representations of enemy ships they have sunk and planes they have brought down.

4

A TRIP INTO NAPLES

If the *LST 1826* had the beachhead on one end of it, there was some recompense in having Naples on the other of the Anzio run. Week after week the ritual was the same: Up to Anzio overnight, back the morning after next, maybe one full day in Naples, then repeat the whole thing.

It was always good to get back from Anzio. There must not have been any city anywhere like Naples in those days when soldiers and sailors of so many nations and even tribes were there from all over the earth, some back from Anzio or Cassino for a few days before returning, or in for a few hours from the sea, others waiting to be taken for the first time to one of those two high-priced battlegrounds. In a couple blocks on Via Roma you would encounter Americans, British, French, New Zealanders, Rhodesians, Dutch, Poles, Greeks, South Africans, Goums from Morocco, tiny brown Gurkhas and towering turbaned Sikhs—both from India and both as good fighting men as lived and died—and even Brazilians in their over-green uniforms. They all explored the city with the voracity of men who were not sure they would ever explore any city anywhere again. They swarmed up and back Via Roma, its narrow air filled with the smells of lust and wine and almonds, looking, watchful, hunting for something that would divert or excite them for a little while. Their search, for whatever it was, was eagerly assisted by many Italian civilians of all ages who sidled up urging on them their anodynes for war—vino of doubtful ingredients, rosaries for those who might feel the need for this added armor in their coming collision

with the German enemy, and above all women, peddled often
by their own kin, by some small boy whispering, "*Mia sorella* . . ."
Sometimes the same vendor conveniently sold all three.

It was always good to get back from Anzio. It was even better
if it were your turn to have shore leave into Naples. If added to
all this you had a date with a nurse it was about as good as it
could get, during the war.

Mid-morning Barclay went over to the field phone at the little
Navy shack on the mole at Pozzuoli to check with her on what
time she could get away. It took a very long time to get her.

"What time was that?" he said when he did. The connection
was never very good over that phone and he was practically
shouting at her. Even so it seemed a remarkable thing to be
talking over a phone with a woman.

"That will be twenty hundred hours," she shouted back and
he heard her light laugh as from a great distance.

"I'll be there," he said. "I may even get there at nineteen
fifty hours."

At that moment Barclay had no transportation, which was
always a problem for anyone coming in off a ship. But he was
pretty sure where he could get some. Other than that, he would
like to spend some time with Shanley if he was around. There
was no better man to spend time with than Shanley, when he
was around.

Lieutenant (jg) Allen Shanley was out to enjoy the war. He
had a tremendous appetite for enjoyment and he found Italy
an unending source of it. He couldn't have been happier than
to be where he was, doing all the things he was doing. He
was a big man in every way. Physically he was a good deal like
an Alaskan bear. He must have been a good 230 pounds and six
feet five inches, big-boned and solid but not fat, and he moved
his body along with a kind of rumbling lurch. He had a lot of
very black hair and this added to the impression. But the bigness
in size was the smallest part of it. It was Shanley's constant
finding of so much to enjoy around him in the war that was

the important thing. His job helped a lot. Shanley had about the most dangerous job you could have during the war. He was a bomb-disposal officer.

One of the most appealing things about Shanley's job was that it afforded him such a lot of time to fool around. There were only so many bombs to be defused and Shanley would go weeks sometimes literally doing nothing whatsoever of a professional nature. This left him free to devote immense amounts of time to other interests. There were the signorine. There was the good cognac if you knew where to get it. There was what was known as "liberating" enemy possessions, which he enjoyed very much and practiced assiduously.

Shanley's job put him in an exceptionally good position for this last form of enjoyment, since bomb-disposal officers were among the first men into a captured city and after doing his defusings he could browse at his ease, before the main body of liberating troops moved in, the choicer villas and headquarters buildings vacated by the departing Germans. Sometimes, after casing the basement of a villa and rendering harmless any bombs he found there, Shanley would proceed immediately to the up-stairs floors and there look around for anything that might deserve liberating. Even then he kept his knowledge of explosives and ingenious ways of implanting them very much in mind. The Germans were very good at this kind of thing and once Shanley found a 250-pound charge arranged in such a way as to go off when the glass door to a case of rare books was opened. He admired the Germans for thus trying to extract a penalty for greed. He was also happy to outsmart them by spotting the device first, dealing with it, those enormous hands of his moving over the bomb's mechanism with the delicacy of a master watch-maker, and then opening the door. Shanley had liberated a great many things and packed them off dutifully to his mother in Chevy Chase, Maryland, a dear lady who, assuming they were purchased with solid coin, was grateful to have a son so thoughtful as to select and ship so many interesting gifts, and right in the middle of a war, including fencing foils, an occasional painting, a brace of ornate sixteenth-century dueling pistols in a velvet-lined case, and very often gifts appropriate for a pretty woman, such as a matching set of malachite and silver earrings and bracelet, and once a twenty-seven-piece tortoise-shell dressing set. Shanley had done a little bit of liberating in Africa, where he and Barclay used to see each other when Barclay's ship put into port, but he found the materials around Oran, Algiers, and Bizerte not too enthralling, though he did come up with a rather fine bronze cup from Leptis Magna. It was only in Italy that his liberation had reached full flower, and he was certainly looking forward to the invasion of France.

It was clear that Shanley had not gone into bomb-disposing because of any of its fringe benefits. He could hardly have foreseen these golden opportunities when he volunteered for the work. In fact Barclay could never understand what it was that prompted a man to volunteer to be a bomb-disposal officer. The attractions of other types of hazardous duty he could appreciate readily. The mystery of being in a submarine, for instance—he had tried to get into them himself. But to spend the war disconnecting strange bombs in wayward cities—it seemed a lonesome job at best, and not really set to glory. He could never understand it, until he and Shanley talked about it once, and then he understood only in part.

"The real attraction of it," Shanley said, "is that it's the one job in this bloody war I know anything about where no one can tell you what to do. I mean no one, mate." Shanley had picked up a habit of using British expressions. "You take submarines— it's a group activity. Fighter planes—even they fly in formation, and there's something called a squadron leader. PT boats— there's still a captain of the boat, and men giving orders and other men taking orders. But when I'm down in a pit or a drydock it's just me and the bomb trying to work it out. No one standing over me telling me what to do. I was never a bit good at taking orders. This way I'm my own man."

"It's a good thing everyone isn't that selfish," Barclay said, swallowing some of his drink, "or we'd have no one out there doing the important work of manning the ships."

"And there's one more thing," Shanley said.

"What's that, Allen?"

"The suspense of it." He laughed, that loud, deep laugh of enjoyment he had which sounded like a large bear amused by something. Sometimes Barclay felt there was a kind of madness in Shanley, and maybe there had to be. "When you're working you're never entirely sure of what will happen next. Yes, sir, boy, the suspense of it."

He refilled their cognac glasses. "No, sir, I wouldn't trade jobs with anybody. There's nothing like being a bomb-disposal officer. It's the only job in war for an independent man."

It was not always you saw a man so satisfied in his work in the war, and it must have been this that made Shanley about the easiest man to be with that Barclay had come across during it. He was a very good man to have for a friend, and the first thing Barclay got in a new port he always made it a point to check if Shanley was there.

There was one other interesting thing about Shanley. It had come out in a conversation he and Barclay had once had, in Oran or Bizerte, Barclay couldn't remember which. The thing happened very quickly, but Barclay always felt afterward that it contained the real reason Shanley was in the job he was in, even though they had been pretty tight that night and even though Shanley never took anything seriously, least of all himself.

"Do you believe in this war, Shanley?" he had asked.

The question was half facetious of course, if not nine-tenths so, as any such question would be, and Barclay was surprised when Shanley, for once, appeared to give an entirely serious answer.

"I don't believe in any war," he said. "Do you believe in *this* war?"

Barclay hesitated. "Yes, I do. Yes. I believe in it."

"Well, I don't. I most certainly don't."

"You don't? Then why did you ever become a b.d. officer?"

"So I wouldn't have to kill anyone. You see, mate, I'm opposed to killing, for any reason."

"You could always be a conscientious objector."

"Hell, I don't object to anything, conscientiously or unconscientiously. Besides it'd be too dull. Waiter," Shanley said, quickly getting away from the subject, "that'll be two more cognacs."

You always had a good time with Shanley. After talking with the nurse Barclay called him from the field phone.

Shanley came all the way out and picked him up. The jeep said BOMB DISPOSAL on the front in tremendous block letters, just under the windshield. Shanley got out and came toward him like a tank. He grinned widely, and assaulted Barclay with both of his pawlike hands, shaking his hand with one and with the other squeezing his shoulder so hard it hurt to the bone.

"My God," Barclay said when he was loosed, "I didn't know you had a personal jeep."

"Oh, yes indeed," Shanley said, and laughed hugely. "You never know when they'll need me, as I pointed out to the commandant, and in a critical situation like that we certainly wouldn't want for me to go through all the red tape of getting a jeep from the car pool, now would we, mate?"

"No, I'd prefer you had a permanent one," Barclay said. "You can certainly tell whose it is."

"Yes, I thought it was a nice idea of mine to paint that little identification on there. I've found it will get you through anywhere—absolutely anywhere. There are no off-limits streets for that jeep. No questions are asked if you're in that jeep. Well, let's go, boy. Let's not waste our valuable time in this dump," he said, looking around at the little town of Pozzuoli. "Let's get out of the sticks and into the big wicked city."

They were coming into it when Shanley asked, "What would you say, laddie, to accompanying me on my cultural rounds?"

"Your what?"

Shanley laughed richly. "You know, I find myself with a little spare time on my hands. I've always wanted to learn fencing."

"Fencing?"

"I was very fortunate to come across Signor Candela, my fencing master," Shanley rolled on. "The signore was an Olympic champion three times—in the sabre. I go for thirty minutes a day. Tuition is a carton of cigarettes a week. That got me started and I decided there was no reason to stop there. I met the Contessa D'Oriani."

"Who?"

"My language tutor. She's the real article. You know, one of those noble Italian families down on their luck on account of *la guerra*. She's a born teacher. I go to the Contessa an hour a day," Shanley continued in the tones of a dedicated scholar. "That comes to six cans of C-ration a week and one of peaches. The Contessa loves C-rations. Then there's Signor Serafini."

"My God, who's he?" Barclay said.

"My tutor in the Italian civilization. A former professor at the University of Naples. The Contessa put me onto him."

"What does he cost?" Barclay said promptly.

"Only a five-gallon can of gasoline a week. He sells it, I imagine. Naturally I've never been so coarse as to ask him about a delicate matter like that. But he certainly knows his history of the Italian civilization. Right now we're going through the rise of Florence."

"The Navy is staking you to a first-rate education, I can see," Barclay said.

"Aren't they though?" Shanley said eagerly. "If the war just holds out I ought to be a very learned man—one of the more knowledgeable Americans anywhere in the Italian field."

"Well, let's just hope it does," Barclay said.

"What?"

"Let's just hope the war holds out."

Shanley burst out laughing. "Barclay, it's good to see you. You know how it is, boy."

Actually it had been a very pleasant day. Barclay had sat in on the lesson in Italian civilization with Signor Serafini. Then they had tooled over to the Contessa's villa—it was actually a villa, if a small one, and Barclay would not have been surprised if she was a real Contessa. He had sat in on that lesson and he could testify that Shanley was doing quite well in the language. Then Barclay had sat by while Shanley and Signor Candela leapt around and slashed away at each other with sabres in the hallway of the Candela home—the hallway was so small and the pupil so large that it was as if someone had shut a bear in a baby crib and it had decided to get out, and with Shanley threshing and slamming off the walls you felt the whole house might go at any moment. All three of his tutors seemed to look upon the big burly naval officer with a kind of fond awe, and to enjoy him as much as he did them, laughing a good deal with him.

On their way back from the lessons to Shanley's room they stopped by the naval base so that Shanley could pick up his mail. The bomb-disposal officer jumped out and went into the head-quarters building while Barclay waited for him in the jeep. A building next door had a sign on it, ENLISTED MEN'S MESS HALL, and Barclay noticed idly that it was chow time. The men were just finishing supper and were walking by some large garbage cans in a slow line and scraping the leftovers from their mess trays into them. It was not for a moment that Barclay saw, beyond the cans, another line. It had the appearance of having been formed and waiting there for some time. He couldn't see how long it was for after about fifty people the line disappeared around the corner of the mess hall. But the ones he saw presented a curious sight. There were women in it of all ages, a number of middle-aged or older men and no young ones, and a number of young children. Now Barclay noticed that all of them, of what-ever age, had something in common. Each was carrying some kind of small container—various kinds of old cooking pots and even tin cans. The tableau of the two lines, one of the Navy men walking silently by scraping their mess trays into the large cans, and the other line beyond them, standing there looking at the Navy men and patiently waiting, fixed itself into Barclay's vision but for a moment he did not understand the purpose of the second line. Then the last of the line of Navy men had passed by and a large man wearing a cook's apron and carrying a long-handled tin ladle of the kind used to dip out soup emerged from the building and took up a position by the can nearest the second line. A certain almost trembling restlessness now began to move through this line. Then as if on signal the line began to move forward. As each person in it came abreast of the garbage can, he held out his container—cooking pot or tin can. The Navy man in the apron brought his ladle down into the garbage can, scooped out a cupful of the garbage, and deposited it in the container. He ladled out without looking either into the big can or at the face of the waiting person in the line, as if to be certain of his impartiality with the contents of the garbage can—not, that is, to try to pick out special pieces for the person currently waiting, not to be influenced by his face, age, or whatever. Regardless of the size of the container he held out, each person got one cup. Immediately the person was out of the line, Barclay could see him pick down into the container, obviously to see how lucky or unlucky he had been, whether he had dragged up mostly a liquid mixture of vegetables and bread pieces or had been fortunate enough to land a piece of meat. Having made this examination the person—whether child, woman, or old man— alike attacked the contents of his container with his fingers and began feeding it rapidly into his mouth. Barclay felt the scene burn into his memory and he knew that it would be with him until the day he died. Shanley came out of the headquarters building flipping through a handful of mail and whistling "Love Is the Sweetest Thing."

"Do they always do that?" Barclay asked as the jeep started up.

"What's that, Matteo?" Shanley said.

"That line. Those people lined up for their cups of garbage."

"Every night," Shanley said. "Breakfast and lunch are scraped into the big cans too but it's set up so that the line is only once a day, after supper. Some of them start lining up in the morning."

They drove back to Shanley's room for a bath.

"Well, how do you like it?" Shanley said when he had thrown back the door. He stood there beaming. Barclay, in his astonishment, could only gape. It was a corner room in a villa the base had taken over for a BOQ. The villa, which was almost a palazzo, must have been just about the nicest Bachelor Officers Quarters anywhere in the Navy.

It was a huge room with statuary in the four corners and from the high ceiling myriad cherubs in their customary nakedness looking happily down, possibly on the bed, which was of fitting size to the room. The military articles here and there mixed uneasily with the Italian palazzo furnishings. A foot locker set alongside an elegant chaise longue. A sea bag nestled against a maritime Aphrodite in one corner. A canvas musette bag hung from a corner of the mammoth marble fireplace. There was a grand piano. The room overlooked a garden through tall Moorish-arched windows. It was some room.

"Of course, the basic materials were already here," Shanley said modestly. "I just added a few furnishings and decorative effects I found in neighboring villas. That chaise longue. I particularly admire that. Did you ever see one more beautiful? It's Louis Quinze and I liberated it very near here. I want to ship it home to my mother eventually—she'd love it. Likewise the Turkish rug and that almost unique bedspread. The bed—did you ever see a bigger one—was already here fortunately. I call it the Cherub Room."

"Very touching," Barclay said.

"Now, now," Shanley said. "We mustn't be cynical, my boy."

A bathroom with a sunken mosaic bath large enough to accommodate a water buffalo came with the room and they took turns bathing. They dressed and sat and had a drink. Shanley insisted on letting Barclay have the jeep and for him to go on alone for the nurse, but Barclay insisted more on his coming along.

"All right then, I'll go with you," Shanley finally said. "I tell you what we'll do, old man. We'll go over to the club and have a couple of drinks—you really ought to see the club anyhow—and I'll soften her up a bit for you. Then you can come back here for *tutta la notte*."

"For God's sake," Barclay said in real alarm. "This isn't anything like that! This isn't a starved signorina who has to earn her living on her back. This is a nurse, Shanley. An American nurse, and she and I are just having a date, do you understand that? *Tutta la notte*, my God!"

"Don't you worry a bit about putting me out," Shanley said. "I've got plenty of other places to stay. I'll just soften her up for you and then fade out."

"Shanley," Barclay said patiently, "I tell you it isn't *remotely* like that. And for God's sake, don't talk about softening her up!"

"Now don't you worry about a thing," Shanley said. "I'm glad to do it."

Barclay sighed. It was impossible to explain anything like this to Shanley. He looked hopelessly up at the ceiling and his eye caught the naked cherubs, who seemed to be smiling, or possibly leering, down at him. He and Shanley finished their drinks, got the jeep and drove on up the hill to pick her up. Shanley had fished out a bottle of cognac for Barclay—three-star Hennessy cognac—from a big armoire in his room which looked like a combination ship's store and wine mess jammed with tins of food, packages of soap and toothpaste, cartons of cigarettes, and a good many bottles of cognac and Scotch whiskey, wrapped it in a towel, and laid it between the front seats of the jeep.

"You know, I've never gone with a nurse over here," Shanley, as they drove along, said in the benevolent, meditative mood he was feeling from the day's educational labors. "The signorine keep me so occupied. And now, of course, my various studies in the Italian field on top of that. Are you sure you're not making a mistake, Matteo, neglecting all the rich Italian material here— and I could introduce you to plenty, *amico mio*—for something after all you can always get back home? Why come three thousand miles to a country that has had beautiful women since the Ptolemies to date someone from Boise, Idaho?"

"The Ptolemies? Shanley, you've been boning too hard on that five-gallon-can-of-gasoline course in the Italian civilization. Anyhow I don't think she's from Boise."

"Well, it sounds pretty provincial to me, this running around with an American nurse. Provincial—even bourgeois."

But when they were standing in the big lobby waiting for the nurse to come down and she was coming toward them, but was still a distance away, Shanley had whistled softly and spoken in an undertone to Barclay.

"Brother. That's no ordinary nurse. That's quite a package, Matteo."

"Not too bad—for someone so provincial and bourgeois."

Then the nurse was there. "It's exactly twenty hundred hours," she said, and smiled at Barclay.

It was quite a place. It was certainly the most lavish place Barclay had been in since leaving the States, or possibly even before that.

"Look at all those women," Shanley said happily. "Aren't they a fine-looking group of women, though! Barclay, don't you find it an interesting thought—sociologically, if nothing else—that you can have any lady in this room for a carton of cigarettes. Not including you, of course, Nurse."

"No, I come a little higher," the nurse said.

"How high do you come, Nurse?" Shanley said.

"More than you can pay, Lieutenant."

Shanley laughed. "I'm a pretty substantial man."

"Do you suppose you could get us some more of these substantial drinks, Lieutenant?" Barclay said.

"*Camerière!*" Shanley called. A waiter dressed in black, tapered trousers and a slashed white jacket came stepping briskly over.

They were in the Navy base officers club. It was in a former villa—everything was in a villa, it seemed—and it looked all glass and red velvet to Barclay. There were rich heavy draperies and rich heavy rugs and an enormous chandelier which sparkled brilliantly under the high ceiling upon a gleaming dance floor. There were a lot of officers in there having drinks, both at the tables and at the long bar, and a lot of women at both. The bar glowed as dazzlingly as the chandelier, with highly polished glasses and rows of bottles on the mirrored shelves. The women were nicely dressed, some of them rather flashily so, and they filled the air with an almost intoxicating promise of erotic experience to be had, of the flesh of woman rich in availability. The women tended to be pretty young, and one didn't need to be told that almost none had been professionals before the war. The sounds of laughter rose in the room, from both the officers and the women. It was a glittering, rich, and satisfying place to be.

"*Camerière,*" Shanley said, "we'll just have one more round of these if you please. That'll be two more Scotches for the lieutenant here and myself, and one Dubonnet for the officer-lady here."

"I think I'm all right," the nurse said.

"You're better than all right," Shanley said. "You heard the order, *Camerière*."

She was certainly looking much different, better now, Barclay was thinking, than when he had last seen her after all night in the tank deck with the wounded from Anzio. In a way it was his first real look at her. She had the very white complexion of an English girl and had brown eyes to go with her walnut-colored hair. The eyes were as brown as autumn leaves and against the very white skin made an effect one would quickly notice. She seemed to be fascinated by the women all around, though she tried clearly not to stare.

"Nurse, I want to plant a comforting thought with you in case you ever need comforting. Though Barclay here is in only infrequently, you might bear in mind that I am in residence in the city practically all the time."

"But you have all these signorine, Lieutenant."

"True. But I would have to feel that any American girl would have first call on my services."

"That's very patriotic of you, Lieutenant. I haven't felt any especial urgency just lately to be comforted. But I'll remember it in case of extreme need."

"I hope you do that, Nurse. After all Barclay here is away most of the time."

"We have to have the seagoing men, you know," Barclay said. "Everybody can't be a dry-land sailor if we're ever to win this war."

"He's very interested in winning the war," Shanley said.

"I don't think I want either of you to comfort me," the nurse said.

"Have you ever heard a more selfish statement than that, Barclay? A very selfish young lady for a nurse. *Camerière!*"

"I'm going to drown in Dubonnet," the nurse said.

"Would you like to switch to martinis?" Shanley said helpfully.

"Heavens no."

"Well, Nurse," Shanley said after the waiter had brought the order, "how long have you been with us?"

"'With us,' Lieutenant?"

"In *la guerra*. The war. Serving your country like this."

"Well, let me see. About two and a half years. About a year of that over here."

"Two and a half years! That's a good record, Nurse. A good record! And before that?"

"Well, if you really want to know, I was in music school, in New York."

"Music school! Why would anyone leave a music school? I suppose you wanted to do your bit, like the rest of us?"

"Well, I don't think it was so grand as all that, Lieutenant, though it's nice of you to think so. I suppose I wanted to be in on it. I never wanted to miss the excitement."

"Excitement, Nurse?"

"I've always wanted to be where things were going on."

"Well, you've come to the right place, Nurse. I find personally this war excites me more every day. *Camerière!* We must have some more of these exciting drinks."

"I believe I will switch to Scotch," the nurse said.

"Very sound decision. It's very easy from here on in, *Camerière*," Shanley said to the waiter. "Three Scotches."

Barclay wished Shanley wouldn't try to "place" her. He knew exactly what he was doing and that he was only trying to help Barclay—to "soften her up," as he said. Only he didn't want anybody to soften her up. What he liked about her was his conviction that she couldn't be softened up. Then it struck him that this, right now, was the first thought of a personal, judging nature he had had of her.

"Nurse," Shanley was continuing, "it's quite a time since I talked with an American of your particular sex. So let us meditate on those fellow women over there, if you please. The signorine, at the bar and at the tables. You have the *ufficiale* offering the carton of cigarettes, and you have the signorina taking it. Which is degraded, if that's the word, more, Nurse? The girl who accepts the carton—or the bar of soap, piece of chocolate, or tin of C-ration—or the man who gives it? That's tonight's philosophic, metaphysical riddle before we move on to more serious matters."

The nurse smiled a little. "That isn't a very difficult riddle, is it, Lieutenant? The girl does it in order to eat. One has to eat. I'd say the man is the one who makes any degrading possible—even necessary."

"Necessary? Isn't that rather moralizing, Nurse?"

"I'd say moralizing is when you give an opinion without being asked. Wouldn't you, Lieutenant?"

"You know, she's a pretty clever girl, Barclay, this one."

"I told you all that, Shanley. I remember very clearly—it was while we were driving up to the hospital, I believe—telling you that she was not merely clever but very close to brilliant."

"What a pair of liars you two are," the nurse said.

"Nurse, I want to say right here that you've passed the course; you have the applying mind; you have awareness. So that we are left with this, that the war degrades the conquerors considerably more than it does the conquered. The conquerors, otherwise known as the liberators." Shanley slapped his hand on the table as if enjoying some huge private source of joy. "Glance around us at the liberators! But let us pass on to more serious matters. Where do you live, Nurse?"

"Why, I live in the hospital. And you, Lieutenant?"

"I live in a villa. A very pretty villa. I live in a pretty room in a pretty villa. Isn't that so, Matteo?"

"It's a very pretty room, all right," Barclay said. "It has cherubs on the ceiling."

"It sounds very poetic," the nurse said.

"It's the most poetic place I've seen lately," Barclay said.

"Do you play the piano?"

"Oh, yes, I play the piano," she said.

"The cherub room has a grand piano. I wish you'd bear that in mind."

"That I will bear in mind."

"I hope you do. I'm a very cultural man myself. That puts me in mind of just this one last thought. Actually both the signorine *and* the *ufficiali* are merely following what should be the daily password for us all these days, all of us warriors and nonwarriors alike, namely: Anybody should get anything he can while he can. Isn't that so, Nurse?"

Shanley stood up. "Nurse, it's a great privilege to have known you. I want to leave you now with absolutely my final thought. Don't get tied up with anyone on a ship. They're here today and gone tomorrow. What you want, Nurse, is to place your chips on the man ashore. That's my final thought, Nurse. Never get tied up with anyone on a ship like Barclay here."

"Thanks a lot," Barclay said.

"Nothing personal, old boy. I'm just thinking of the young lady."

"Is he always this thoughtful?" the nurse said to Barclay.

"Yes, you'll have to go a long way to find anyone more thoughtful than Shanley here. I've always found him most thoughtful."

Suddenly Shanley reached down and pressed something into Barclay's hand and was gone. Barclay opened his hand, holding his palm flat and up. It was a key ring, with two keys. Barclay knew one of them was for the jeep, and he had a pretty good idea what the other fitted.

Outside a boy of about ten came up to them and asked Barclay if he wanted a woman.

"My sister," he said. "My sister will give you a very good time."

"I'm sure of it," Barclay said. "But I've got a woman here and I'm not sure she'd wait."

"Do you want a room?" The boy kept walking by them on their way to the jeep. "I have a very nice room for you and the signorina, Lieutenant."

"No, I don't believe we want a room. Thank you all the same."

"You're making a mistake, Lieutenant. She's a very beautiful signorina, this one you have here."

"Yes, I know that."

"You shouldn't miss the chance with a signorina like this one, Lieutenant," the boy said. He was real salesman. "It might never come your way again, Lieutenant. It can happen to you, Lieutenant. Or to the beautiful signorina."

Barclay, startled unaccountably, looked down at the boy as if at some kind of genie. Then he reached into his pocket and got out some lire for him.

"Any time you want a room, Lieutenant," the boy said. "I have very nice rooms."

They got into the jeep that said BOMB DISPOSAL on the front of it.

"What was that all about?"

"He wanted to sell something. What time do you have to be back at the hospital?" Barclay said as they were driving away.

"Well. I'm on duty at eight o'clock."

"That would be eight hundred hours?"

She laughed. "Yes, that would be eight hundred hours."

He felt very shy with her but he said: "How much sleep do you have to have?"

"It depends. I can always make it on two hours, if I have to."

"I don't get a jeep often. I thought we might drive down the coast toward Amalfi. Coming back we could see the city by early light."

She waited a moment. "All right, let's do that," she said then. "I'd like that."

There was very little traffic in the city and once they got out of it almost none whatever. They were quickly in the mountains and under the moon and they could see the sea far down below them.

"That's quite a club," she said. "I've never seen them before, close up."

"Seen what?"

"Well—girls who make their living that way, have to. And I liked Shanley." He could hear her laugh quietly.

"Yes, Shanley's all right. I always try to be with Shanley over here."

"How did you get to know him?"

"We were in midshipmen's school together in New York, and

we went around the city a lot together. I think he's become about my best friend. He's quite a man."

"That's not a very good job he has, is it?"

"I wouldn't want it."

They were taking the curves easily and he had a sense of her hair, which was nurse-length, held out behind her in the wind the jeep made. He felt very comfortable with her, although he had forgotten how to talk to a woman. And it felt good to be driving this jeep. There was no evidence of the war anywhere around them, no sight, sound, or smell of it. Then the road was dipping toward the sea.

The little beach in the cove was entirely empty and they got out and walked along it in the moonlight. Enfolding rock promontories went out to sea on either side. It was very quiet, the sea. He found a poncho in the jeep and spread it out on the beach and they set on it and looked at the sea.

"Are you glad you're over here?" he asked.

"I think it's better than it would be at home. I wouldn't have liked waiting at home, waiting for the war to end, I mean."

"Yes. I can understand that."

"No matter what anyone says I think it's better to be in it than entirely outside it. You. Are you glad you're over here?"

He laughed a little. "Well, there isn't much choice with a man, is there?" He waited a moment. "But I like the sea. What choice there is, I like being on the sea. I've always liked the sea—more, I guess, than anything. So I have that, in a way, even now."

"Yes." Now she waited a moment. "Are you still making the trips to Anzio?"

"Yes, we're still making them."

"What did you take up the last time?"

"British. They'd been in the desert."

"No more mules?"

"No more mules—and no more nurses. Maybe you could arrange for some more nurses for us. Everyone really liked having the nurses aboard. It's been our favorite cargo."

"How often are you and your ship in here?"

"The ship once every two or three days. Myself, about once a week into town."

They were silent a moment then she asked: "How long do you think the beachhead will go on?"

"I wish I knew. They keep saying we're going to break out of it and at the same time break through at Cassino, then everybody will meet in Rome. But then they've been saying that quite awhile.

"As long as Anzio is there you keep coming in here?"

"Yes," he said, and suddenly he saw the implication of it. "That's about it."

"Then they take your ship away somewhere else? After the beachhead is over, I mean."

"Yes, they'll certainly do that."

Nothing about it was a good thought, either way, and he pushed it away.

He could tell from the sky that first light would not be far away and he wanted to see the sea and the city in the sunrise from the hills and thought she would like to see it that way too. They started driving back, climbing rapidly in the little mountains that clung down upon the sea. First light was just coming on when they came onto the city and they stopped on the road high up and watched the dawn begin to push the darkness back from the sea and the city. No one seemed about except themselves. Far over to one side they could see the red cone of Vesuvius, which had been erupting, and to the other down below them the city spread out. There was no bay so beautiful, clasped in its hills, and from here the scars of the war were all hidden. It was a good way to see it. It was a very beautiful sight, and Barclay liked that neither said it was. Then, coming down the hill, they were back where they could see the evidences of the war; some sheared-off buildings; some heaps of rubble; and above all, the gray ships in the harbor. It was these that seemed natural and familiar, and the other was the unfamiliar and strange-seeming.

They drove by a church where some hunched old ladies wearing black shawls were going in.

"Can we stop a moment?" she said.

"Sure."

They went in and she brushed her fingers in the little font of water and dipped her knee quickly and crossed herself. He thought again, as he had several times now, of the grace that was in everything she did. Then they went to a pew and while she knelt for a few moments there Barclay sat on the bench by her and looked at the church. It was a rather garish small church on the outskirts of Naples, a church built for the poor, one felt, with murals and wood statuary of yellows and blues that were too bright. There were a dozen or so people in there, all women, all old-looking. After a while some of them went up to the altar and knelt for the wine and wafer. Barclay wondered if they had trouble getting flour for the wafers nowadays, and if even they were smaller. She stood up and they went outside and got in the jeep.

"Thank you for stopping," she said.

"I was glad to."

He drove up the hill to the hospital and stopped and looked at his watch.

"You just have your two hours sleep, almost," he said. "This has been a very good time for me. I haven't had a time like this over here."

"I haven't. What does the ship do next?"

"Tonight we go to Anzio. And back day after tomorrow morning but there's no shore leave for me then. Then we go up the next day again probably . . ." He was telling off the days on his fingers now . . . "Four nights from now I should have shore leave. May I see you?"

"I'd like it. Will you call me when you get in?"

"I'll call, never fear."

He walked her into the hospital and then came back and drove slowly away in the jeep and back down toward the harbor. He imagined Shanley would get her. But then he wasn't altogether sure. He felt very fatalistic about it, as he did about everything these days having learned to, and would see the next time he was in port. He believed the nurse might already be falling in love with Shanley. But you never could tell. He would call her. He would certainly call her.

Meantime it had been a good day, today. He wished he didn't have to go back to the ship. The ship was always there, and they would always be going again to Anzio. That was the one reality, and Naples was only a pleasant dream, something that didn't really exist, and so was she. Shanley would probably get her, if anyone did. But he wasn't sure that anybody would. Then he found himself hoping not.

5

THE RED-HAIRED SAILOR

It really began when Carlyle scooped her off that stretcher in troops quarters, as easily as he might have a child, carried her up the ladder, and placed her gently on the wardroom table. Something happened to him from that act. Even so it took quite a bit of courage for him to ask Barclay. If it had been any other officer, he probably could never have done it. Barclay was Carlyle's favorite officer aboard. He had a kind of sixth sense about the ship—it seemed sometimes to the men that he had memorized the ship, a considerable feat in view of how complicated an LST and her workings could on occasion be. It appeared that nothing ever upset him. If a man didn't do something right, Barclay never chewed him out, but carefully, and above all, privately, went over with him how it should be done. After that the man would make a big effort to see that it was done right, whatever it was. And finally, Carlyle had seen Barclay brave in battle, when at Palermo with the harbor under severe air attack, a piece of shrapnel had all but taken off the leg of a gunner's mate named Colwell who was standing directly next to the officer in the forward 40-millimeter gun tub and Barclay had immediately picked the man up and carried him under heavy fire down the wharf to an aid station. Barclay seemed to Carlyle all that a naval officer should be, and he was also as easy a person to talk with as he had known, in or out of the Navy. Still it took him awhile to decide to ask him this.

He went to his stateroom the night they were headed back to Anzio carrying a load of vehicles and drivers and he knew

Barclay was off watch. Barclay was sitting up in his bunk writing a letter and at the knock on the bulkhead he said "Come in" and Carlyle parted and stepped through the curtains.

"There's something I'd like to talk to you about, Mr. Barclay."

Barclay put his letter aside and sat up on the edge of the bunk. "Have the chair."

Carlyle settled his big frame gracefully into the only chair in the room, sitting up very straight as he always did. There was no constraint of any kind between the two men. Still it was a pretty difficult question, somehow, to ask *anybody*. Carlyle thought he would talk a little about the recent event as the easiest way of leading into it.

"That was quite a job Latimer did, wasn't it, Mr. Barclay? On the baby, I mean."

"Yes, it was that," Barclay said. "Latimer must be the only pharmacist's mate in the Navy now qualified to deliver babies."

Carlyle grinned. "I wonder how they're making out. The mother and the baby I mean," the seaman said and swallowed. Here it was. "You wouldn't know where she is, would you, Mr. Barclay? I thought I'd like to go over and see them when we get back in."

The officer looked at the sailor a moment. "Why, I think that's a fine idea," he said.

"You really do, Mr. Barclay?" Carlyle said, brightening. "You know where she is?"

"Why, as a matter of fact I did get her address from her. Would you like it?"

"I'd appreciate it very much, Mr. Barclay."

Barclay reached over to the desk and found a scrap of paper. The ship took a deep roll right then. The sea had been coming up all the way up. Barclay grasped the desk for a moment and Carlyle braced his feet on the deck as the chair slid a little.

"Here it is. Her name is Coco Comparo. The address here says Via Giuseppe Mazzini 36, Pozzuoli. It shouldn't be hard to find in Pozzuoli."

"Coco Comparo," Carlyle said thoughtfully. "That's a very pretty name."

And that was all there was to it. It had been a lot easier than he had expected. As he walked aft in the passageway another sea hit the ship and, as she rolled hard, held him for a moment against one bulkhead, then, as the ship completed the roll, against the other. Then he straightened up and went on along the passageway.

Like many other Americans, Seaman Second Class Peter Carlyle had had his education interrupted by the war. In his case the interruption came in the tenth grade. Up until the time he enlisted in the Navy, he had never even seen salt water, and in fact had never been out of the state of Iowa, where he was born and grew up on a farm, except for a trip he made with his father once to take a truckload of hogs to sell in Omaha.

Though he had never set eyes on a ship before, Carlyle took to the sea and to shipboard life as though he had been born in a hammock. From the first he liked the sea and he liked being aboard ship. Consequently, since he was also bright, he was very good at it. Whether it involved handling of lines, taking depth soundings, or hoisting an LCVP into its davits, he mastered it quickly and soon it was as if he had been doing these things all his life instead of milking cows, slopping hogs, and ploughing earth. There was no faster loader than himself at his battle station on the forward forty. He had the best pair of eyes on the ship and everybody aboard, from the captain on down, felt a little easier when the ship was going through mined or submarine-fraught waters if Carlyle was one of the lookouts on watch. His shipmates, with pardonable hyperbole, liked to say that he could spot a fly on the conning tower of an E-boat ten miles away.

He was a very good-looking young man. He had a body that might have stepped off of one of those pedestals that support characters in mythology and come to life on the deck of an LST. The sailor's uniform, the trousers tight at waist and seat and bell-bottomed, the blouse open-necked and middy-draped, is calculated to make a man of any age at all, especially if he has a bit of fat on him, look faintly ridiculous. But it was made for a man like Carlyle. He stood six feet and one inch, all of it lean, with a flat belly and narrow hips. His strength had become a byword among the crew and if something really heavy needed lifting someone always said, "Get Carlyle." He had eyes as blue as the sea his ship sailed and fair skin which had yet to feel a razor. He was seventeen. He was very blessed physically. But what really gave distinction to these various physical endowments was his hair. It was really remarkable hair. There was a lot of it but its distinction was no matter of abundance. This was supplied by its color. It was about as red as hair could ever be. It seemed to glow like some kind of fire on top of him, and the crew liked to say that if the ship ever sunk, the main thing would be to save Carlyle, and they wouldn't need to worry about Very flares to attract rescue vessels. Carlyle's head would do it.

Only once in anyone's memory had Carlyle been known to use his strength for any personal reasons. A sailor new to the ship and some other men had been working one day in port on the anchor windlass when the new man unwisely began to address Carlyle as "Pretty Boy" in tones obviously not intended to convey flattery in the appellation. For quite a while Carlyle paid no attention to the needling. Then abruptly, with no warning whatever, he walked quietly over to the man, picked him up, lifted him over his head, walked over to the side and dropped him in the water. With not a word. It was a successful maneuver. The man never so addressed Carlyle again.

Men on ships, living in their tight world, inescapably judge one another more critically than in perhaps any other society on earth. There no quality of character or habit, whether good, bad, or in between, can long remain hidden, and no artifice will enable it to do so. In addition to his good looks and his strength, Carlyle did not drink, or smoke, or swear, or even patronize those places in Mediterranean ports so conveniently signalized by OFF LIMITS signs. Had he been vain about his looks or strength, or proud about his abstentions, Carlyle could easily have become an object of severe dislike aboard. But his only consciousness of his strength appeared to be that it was an asset now and then around the ship. As for his looks, he seemed actually unaware of them. As for the other things, it was just that he found a satisfied life in working aboard ship and, when he was on liberty, visiting the places in port that any very proper tourist might have visited in peacetime. Red had promised his mother to read a few verses out of the Bible every day and he faithfully kept the promise. During the Anzio run he was going through the Psalms and sitting on the edge of his bunk he read a chapter each night before turning in. No one thought it strange. There is nothing worse about a ship than the crowdedness of its living quarters and nothing better than its leaving a man alone with his private world. The one makes the other necessary. It is as if the men knew that, thrown so closely together as they are, unless this were done a man would soon have nothing left of himself. A ship is ordinarily a highly tolerant place of any kind of peculiarity—even nondrinking and nonwenching—provided it not impinge on the peculiarity of another and that the man who practices it does not do so with any air of superiority. Nothing told more about Carlyle than, being what he was, he was thoroughly well-liked by his shipmates. Also he played the guitar, and this helped the crew pass a lot of empty hours at sea. Sometimes Red Carlyle would sing as he played. He had a good voice and it was a pleasure to hear him and one felt the varying emotions of his songs. He would sing . . .

> I been doing some hard traveling
> I thought you knowed,
> I been doing some hard traveling
> Way down the road . . .

And the men would be taken back, lonely and far away, to the homes they had known in America. Or sometimes it would be a lively gospel hymn such as "Bringing in the Sheaves" or the loneliness of another hymn such as "In the Sweet Bye and Bye," "The Old Rugged Cross," or "O God, Our Help in Ages Past."

It was the guitar which had brought Carlyle's one intersection with the Italian populace, which was with the children. When the ship was in Pozzuoli he would sit by the hour on the mole or bow ramp and play it, while a score or so children gathered around him and listened in the only form of recreation some of them had. They seemed as intrigued by his red hair as by his guitar playing. It was something that most of them had never even seen and being so novel it was as fascinating to them as if someone had had *green* hair. He seemed to have a way with the bambini. They would clap loudly after he played and sometimes pile all over him. It was starting with Carlyle that the ship became such a favorite of the children at Pozzuoli so that often when it came in from Anzio they would be waiting there on the mole for it, and in particular waiting for the sailor with the red hair to come down and play the guitar for them.

He put on his dress blues and walked over into Pozzuoli. He had the address on the slip of paper and he asked directions in the town. It was a small town and no trouble finding the place. It was an old stone house in a solid row of them and an old lady was sitting in front. She seemed a little deaf and he had to practically shout the name.

"*Sigaretta?*" she said.

Carlyle didn't have any but he usually carried some candy for bambini purposes and he gave this to her. She opened the Life Savers and popped one in her mouth. This stimulated her to point indifferently up the stairway and to indicate through gestures that the place he sought was in the front of the house. Carlyle climbed the stairway, walked to a door by the front and knocked. But not before a baby's cry from inside confirmed that this was probably the place. In a moment the door was opened and she was standing there. She looked startled to see him but immediately recognized him, held back the door, and said some Italian words which must have meant "come in."

It was the barest room Carlyle had ever seen. The total furniture consisted of a narrow bed, one straight-backed chair, a small table with two drawers, a chest of drawers, and a crib. Nothing else. The girl herself was no more adorned than the room. She wore a black dress, wooden shoes, no stockings, and no make-up. She looked very young, and if one had not known otherwise one would have thought she was the baby-sitter instead of the mother of the contents of that crib.

Carlyle knew no Italian except a handful of words he had picked up from the bambini. She knew no English whatever. He had brought with him one of those language-and-vocabulary books issued to the military forces and this first day this booklet, supplemented with gestures, was their sole instrument of communication. It reminded him of one of those me-Tarzan-you-Jane conversations in the Tarzan movies that came through the little town in Iowa near which he lived. It was very slow going. He gathered that she had been treated well at the American hospital. And that when she returned to this building her cousin and her belongings were gone—where, she had been unable to discover—so she had moved into this room. She picked up the baby from the crib and held it for him to see. It was wonderfully tiny and its hand went out immediately to his red hair, causing the baby's mother to laugh. The baby was put back. Presently they had used about all the gestures and looked up all the words they could think of, in sum, had exhausted the limited range of communication of two people who cannot speak each other's language. Perhaps it was the sudden awareness of this limitation that gave him the idea, or perhaps, standing there, he was overcome with embarrassment from the fact that he could think of no reason for coming to see her again. And since he wished to, without even thinking about it he leafed through the language book and was able to come up with the message that he wanted someone to teach him to speak Italian, that he would pay, and would she undertake this work? She hesitated a moment, then indicated that she would. And he arranged also, using the booklet, to come there each time he had liberty.

Now he had been coming to that room for a month. The lessons were very long, four hours or more. Between times Carlyle studied incessantly on the ship when he was off watch, using some books he had got Barclay to pick up for him in Naples. Even on watch, when it was with Barclay, he talked the language with him some, for practice. With two teachers in effect, with the long lessons, and with his unceasing studies otherwise, it was about as crash a course in a language as one could put oneself through. And since Italian is one of the easiest languages to learn anyhow, and since Carlyle was intelligent, and since, above all, he had a great incentive to learn it, at the end of four weeks it was hardly surprising that he was handling himself pretty well in the language. The more he learned of it, the more he could communicate with this girl . . . the more enjoyable the visits to the room on the Via Mazzini became.

The first thing he ever bought her was a chair. He had early looked up in his dictionary the Italian for "I want to buy a chair" and said the words to a man in a store in Pozzuoli which sold cheap souvenirs to the sailors. The proprietor, instead of directing him to another place, immediately got up out of the chair he was sitting in and sold him that. Carlyle carried it down the street and up the stairs to her room. After that they could both sit at the table to work on his Italian.

It was toward the end of a lesson one day. They were doing some exercises in which she would ask questions in the language and he would give formalized answers.

"How many men are there on your ship?"

"There are ninety men on my ship."

"And how many officers?"

"There are nine officers."

"Do you ever get seasick?"

"I got seasick crossing the Atlantic Ocean. So did everybody else," he felt he had to add. "I have not been seasick since."

"Do you like being on the ship?"

"Yes, I like being on the ship."

"Do you prefer being here?"

She would sometimes insert, with no change of expression, unexpected questions like this. They always laughed when it happened.

"Yes, I prefer being here."

"What will you do after the war?"

"After the war I will probably be a . . ." he had to pause and look the word up, "a farmer."

She corrected his pronunciation of the word and continued.

"Do you like my baby?"

He smiled. It could be a game as well as an exercise.

"Yes, I like your baby." And indeed he did. Often in that room the sailor would pick the baby up and hold it and say something, all of which seemed to please it enormously. He looked over at the baby now and repeated, "Yes, I like your baby very much."

"So do I. Do you know how I remembered you? It was from your playing of the guitar."

He decided he would ask a question. "Do you remember that I carried you to the room up above?" he put it.

She looked very surprised. "No, I didn't know that. That I don't remember at all. That was very good of you."

"Shall we continue with the lesson?"

She waited a moment then said: "What do you pay me in for your lessons?"

"I pay you in lire for my lessons."

"Why do you not pay me in things instead?"

"I do not pay you in things instead because . . ." he had started, not immediately realizing it was not just a lesson question. He looked across at her and continued . . . "because I do not know what you mean by things."

"I mean things from the ship," she said. "Food, for instance. Why spend your money? You could save your money."

That was the way it happened. He began to bring her packages of food from the ship. Small things, such as cans of C-ration, boxes of K-ration—things like these were always lying around the ship. He also insisted on continuing to pay her lire for the lessons.

"The others are just presents," he said.

During the lessons she had to stop sometimes to feed the baby, which informed them of the time by a series of little yelps and a flapping of hands and feet. They never mentioned it but since she nursed the baby, he would go downstairs and walk around the town for a while, always using the excuse that he wanted a break from the lesson. One day he was caught in a rain. When he came in wet she apologized.

"There's nothing to apologize for," he said.

"If I had an apartment," she said offhandedly, "you could go in the next room when the baby gets hungry."

The talk embarrassed him a little. "Well, I don't mind going out," he said. "But I think a little better place would be good for you. Not that this place isn't very nice," he added quickly, for politeness sake. "But well . . . another place."

"A better place? I cannot pay for a better place."

He thought they were on another subject when a few moments later she said, almost absently: "Perhaps if you could bring me other things. Things like cigarettes."

"But you don't smoke," he said.

She smiled. "I won't smoke them."

She waited, then said quietly: "Do you realize what I could buy with one carton of your American cigarettes? *One* carton of cigarettes."

Carlyle said nothing and they got on with the lesson. Actually he didn't think about it again until he was returning to the ship and then it just crossed his mind briefly. He'd have to think about that one.

6

JOSEPHUS DANIELS VS. SAINT PAUL

Not a man or officer aboard the *LST 1826* would have traded off Lieutenant Jacob Adler as a ship's captain. It was not that Captain Adler was in any sense soft in his job—a quality which, in Navy captains, never makes for popularity anyway. Any man who ever put to sea would prefer, if the choice came to that, a tyrannical and competent captain to a "democratic," incompetent one. Better to lie in your bunk knowing that a devil who knows his job is on the bridge than a saint who doesn't, affability being small comfort if a ship runs aground or if men die because she is fought ineptly in battle. The thing about Captain Adler was that he knew his job very well, giving the men such sense of assurance as is available in war, but that he was also aware that his crew were certified members of the human race. He could be very tough indeed if anything that concerned the functioning of the ship—its navigation, its gunnery, its deck work, the fitness of its engine rooms—was conducted in a slipshod manner, and everyone aboard knew it and acted accordingly. But he was also wholly approachable, and seemed to think almost—not quite—as much as did the crew themselves in terms of what would make their life as bearable as possible given the circumstances.

Captain Adler ran his ship on the basis of a discovery he had made after being in the Navy awhile, that most of the regulations dealing with Navy conduct and performance were there for a reason and actually made sense. But he was the first to cast aside, and in fact literally forget the existence of, any which he felt not suitable to the particular needs of his particular ship and his particular ship's company. Uniforms were an example of his attitude in both respects. He insisted on whatever dress was ordained by local naval authorities when the crew went ashore on liberty parties. He felt he had enough to do without having to deal with complaints from base commanders or any undue number of arrests by the shore patrol. On board, however—everything there coming under *his* jurisdiction, for even the captain of an LST is its absolute monarch—the men were free to wear whatever they pleased. Most wore the standard dungarees and T-shirt most of the time but most also had dyed the standard white hat a medium-blue since this was more easily kept clean. And odd articles of apparel sometimes blossomed reflecting the ports the ship had visited and the desire of the men for a little variety in their lives. The captain let the men alone on such matters. Captain Jacob Adler, in sum, took an even strain on life, and particularly on Navy life. He had early decided that the war, however long it went on, would be too short to try to squeeze nine officers and ninety men, virtually all of them straight out of civilian life with a little training in between in boot camp or midshipmen's school, into the mold that was perhaps fitting for someone who had spent four years at the Academy on the Severn. And he felt all this particularly about the landing craft, which was a bastard Navy to start with.

Captain Adler had a kind of combination of his own, a peculiar technique of fierceness and deadpan-ness, for moving around a regulation when he had decided to do so. It was a ritual the crew knew well by now—and knew exactly how far they could go, and went no further. Once when Latimer, the pharmacist's mate, who the captain knew for a fact was holding a secret sick bay to treat v.d. cases, these being something that would get a man on report—the captain overlooked the practice out of sheer realism, namely that no amount of being put on report for v.d. contraction would ever deter a man off a ship who wanted a woman from fulfilling this want if he could—came to him with a request to hold *another* sick bay, this one on the mole for the children when the ship was in port, the captain looked outraged and had the matter decided in less than a minute.

"Don't you realize you'd be using naval supplies, Latimer! My God, man. That's highly irregular, don't you know that—and in time of war too."

"Yes, sir," Latimer said sheepishly. "But one thing we're never short on, Captain, is supplies."

"Hardly the point, Latimer. It's some kind of highly punishable offense to hand off Navy materiel to non-Navy personnel. Are you interested in seeing us both in Portsmouth?"

"No, sir," Latimer said. "I certainly wouldn't want that to happen, sir."

"Permission denied!" Captain Adler said loudly. "Under no circumstances are you to hold this bambini's sick bay more than once a day. Is that understood?"

"Thoroughly," Latimer said, "sir."

Jake Adler had come from not merely one, but two of New York's oldest, highest, and wealthiest Jewish families, so wealthy that at the time of his parents' marriage many people had said churlishly that it was scandalous that such a rich boy should marry such a rich girl instead of spreading it around. The money thus joined was immense and had left the union's only son free to devote his life largely to his two chief loves, which were sailing and having children. From his sailing he knew the sea well, and a good many of its enormity of hidden surprises of which no man ever knows all, and he had added to this knowledge what the Navy had to teach him about LSTs. From his wife he had obtained the children at the pace of one a year for the first seven years of their marriage. Jake Adler kept a photograph of the seven children on the desk in his cabin. They were exact stair-steps starting at six and ending at twelve, their ages on the day he started his LST across the Atlantic Ocean. The measure of the war to him was the aging of those children. The captain wrote long letters to his family, and got long, fat, happy letters back, often with pictures enclosed. Comparing these fresh photographs with the one on his desk always gave him a sense of incredulity. He could never get over how fast it was happening while he was away and the worst thing the war did to him was that there would be, how many years? during which those seven

children would go through a great deal of growing up without his
being there to see it and take part in it. It was the one personal
thing that really tore at him, and once he almost asked his wife
not to send any more pictures. He refrained, knowing the request would sound bizarre to her, and also because it would be
greater misery not to see their growth even through the terrible vicariousness of a camera. As it was, he went through periods of almost savage loneliness for them. Although noticing
their change so strongly in the photographs, he was not even aware
that some white hairs had begun to appear in his black.

It was due a great deal to Captain Adler that the LST 1826
was a bountiful ship to the children who were always hanging
around her at Pozzuoli. Nothing fashioned by the war was so
bone-chilling, to him, as the degradation in which it enveloped
the children he saw in Italy. Often when the sailor Carlyle sat
on the bow ramp or the mole playing his guitar for them, if anyone had looked he would have seen Captain Jake Adler at the
back of the crowd looking on, and there was one terrible moment
once when, after doing so, he went back to his cabin, shut the
door and sat on his bunk weeping, both for them and for his
own—and for himself, the truth was. It was only in that moment
that he realized a full hatred of the war. The incident shocked
him. Nothing like it had ever happened to him and he made certain it never happened again.

He kept on the desk, by the photograph of his children, a piece
of metal about the size of a lemon. It was jagged and very solid.
It must have weighed three pounds. It had come out of a twenty-
one-year-old boy named Harrison, for whom Ensign Horner was
the replacement. The hunk of shrapnel had jumped up out of the
water at Salerno and into Harrison, who was standing on the
bow ramp helping direct traffic off the ship. Harrison was lying
on the wardroom table when they took it out of him and he was
dead by then. The captain kept it on his desk to remind him
that, within the limitations of seeing that his ship performed well,
his job was to bring as many of the nine and ninety as was possible through the war and home to America.

Captain Adler was a prowler of the ship. Not to spy. He did it because he liked it and because he slept very little any more, and because, too, he liked to expose his presence to the men—to be available for problems that might come up. Actually the men liked to see him coming.

The ship was halfway back from Anzio and the captain was sitting in his cabin attempting to sew up a torn pocket on his shirt when a delegation of the men came to him with an odd new request.

The United States Navy is the only navy in the entire world in which no alcoholic beverages are permitted aboard ship. It was not always so. The situation came about during the tenure of Josephus Daniels as Secretary of the Navy in World War I. It has probably served to make the memory of Secretary Daniels a little less hallowed aboard U.S. naval vessels sailing the various seas than it might otherwise be. The reason for the edict in the first place, or at least it is so commonly held aboard these vessels, was the belief that the Navy would fight more effectively without such beverages than with them. Apparently there was some fear that sailors and officers might be staggering drunkenly to their guns in the midst of battle, and thus their marksmanship be affected, or that captains of ships or watch officers would load up on the stuff and run their vessels aground. It seems a curious fear in view of the fact that all other navies of the world have their daily alcoholic portion for the men and sundry alcoholic drinks available for officers, and that many of these have quite acceptable records as navies. The Royal Navy, for example, where if the British sailor were not given his legally assigned tot of rum at 1100 hours sharp or if engaged in battle as soon thereafter as is practicable a mutiny rivaling that of 1797 would undoubtedly erupt as though on signal throughout the fleet, has quite a good record of naval performance and even valor extending over the years and there is no record of one of His Majesty's ships ever having failed to perform properly due to shipboard intoxication. Indeed, the U. S. Navy itself had a thoroughly good record before Josephus' ban, as good as it has had since. Nevertheless the thing somehow got through, and ever since has been one of the burdens the U. S. Navy has to carry. The only thing that can be said for it is that it perhaps has abetted inter-Navy relations on the ship level by increasing the number of social calls paid by personnel of American ships when they are in harbor with such ships as those of the Royal Navy.

Not all the men of the LST 1826 knew the history of the ban but all, with not one exception, knew the ban existed. Most probably believed it had always been so, like the fact that a ship floats. Some of the more thoughtful members of the crew had been devoting a good deal of that thought to the matter for some time now, and looking, not very actively or hopefully, for a solution. When Radioman Third Class Nathaniel Middleton came down with an acute case of stomach poisoning the morning after visiting several of the local bars, to a point where in fact his life was moderately uncertain for a time, some of them decided to make the most of Middleton's misfortune.

The men chose the personnel of a committee of four with great care. On it they put Pharmacist's Mate First Class Hugh Latimer, Cook Second Class Gerald Mason, Motor Machinist's Mate Second Class Joel Chatham, who in private life had been a bartender and barowner in a small New England town, and Seaman First Class Edgar Allan Poe Porterfield, who was a ship's helmsman and the ship's unofficial chaplain, having been studying for the ministry when the war came on. It was this delegation which went to see the captain and interrupted his sewing-on of his shirt pocket. The captain received them in his cabin and invited them to sit down. Mason, Chatham, and Porterfield sat on the edge of the captain's bunk and Latimer sat on the edge of a chair. Latimer had been chosen as chief spokesman of the delegation, the medical approach having been adjudged the principal, though by no means the only, armament.

"Captain," the pharmacist's mate led off, "we wanted to speak to you about the trouble some of the men have been having with their stomachs."

"Their stomachs?" the captain said. "What trouble is that?"

"Well, sir, there's been an unusual amount of stomach trouble lately. Middleton is the latest and the worst, that's all. A lot of the men have been having either stomach or intestinal trouble," Latimer said professionally.

"Is that so?" the captain said. "Well, that's very interesting and a little disturbing. I'm sure we'll have to do something about it. What's the problem? Something wrong with the food, Mason?"

"No, sir, it ain't the food, I'll guarantee you that, sir," the cook said earnestly. "We serve about as good chow on this ship as you'll find in the landing craft, sir. Not as good as them big cruisers, of course, but then in the landing craft we don't get the supplies a cruiser does."

"Yes, I'm aware we get the short end of the stick compared with the cruisers, Mason," the captain said, a little briskly.

"I just wanted to set your mind at ease that it ain't the food, sir," Mason said.

"All right, it's at ease. Or was before you men came to visit me. Now what is it?" the captain said. There was a trace of impatience in his voice.

"Well, sir," Latimer said. "It's what the men have been drinking ashore. No doubt about it. Chatham here can bear me out on that. Chatham was a bartender, you know, sir, and he knows about drinking." Latimer looked promptingly at his expert.

"It's true, Captain," Chatham said soberly. "That's pretty bad stuff they drink in some of those bars, sir. I'd hate to tell you what they put into some of that stuff they sell over on the beach, Captain."

"Yes, sir," Latimer confirmed this. "I was talking with one of the base pharmacist's mates—I made a special trip in just to confer with him about this problem—and he said their medical department had analyzed chemically some of that vino and, sir, they found things the mere mention of which should turn a man's stomach."

The captain looked thoughtfully and even admiringly at the pharmacist's mate for this speech. They certainly had prepared their case well, he thought, and wondered idly how long they had spent on it—not to mention what the case was.

"That's interesting research, Latimer," he said. "Very interesting. It's commendable of you to go to all that trouble."

"Well, I tell you for a fact, sir," the pharmacist's mate continued fervently, "I hate to see them come into sick bay, all doubled up and moaning. They're very pitiful cases, sir."

The captain meditated a moment on this gruesome picture. "Yes, I imagine so."

"I don't think there's anything worse than vino poisoning," Latimer said.

"Myself, I'd rather have the syph," Mason said, and Latimer gave him a quick look which suggested that he had made his contribution, the negative one on the food, and had best be quiet about medical matters.

"There's just one thing, Latimer," the captain said. "No one *requires* them to drink it, do they? I mean it isn't like an atabrine pill."

"No, sir, but you know how it is, sir. They're going to drink *something*. And some of them are going to drink a lot. You know how all this is, Captain."

"All right," the captain said, a little wearily. "I know how it is. They're going to drink. What do you want me to do about it? Get a chemist to accompany liberty parties?"

"No, sir, we've thought of something simpler than that." Latimer took a deep breath and said it. "We figured if the men could get a little wine on the ship, why, then they wouldn't drink so *much* ashore. Chatham here knows about wines and he could make sure we got *wholesome* wine direct from one of those vineyard places. We thought we could keep it in one of the five-gallon cans," Latimer added, as if the storage of the proposed wine was one of the central problems in having it.

The captain looked carefully around the circle of the four men. "Are you men seriously suggesting we serve *wine* aboard this ship?"

"Not exactly *serve* it, sir," Chatham said. "Our idea is that if we had this five-gallon can and kept it full of *good* wine . . . well, sir, it would be a lot better for the men."

"We figured also," Latimer hurried on, "that a man could have a glass of wine only when he came off watch. Not before. Chatham here could keep the key—we'd rig up a lock for the five-gallon can—and could be in charge of dispensing it. Like he used to do in peacetime," and Latimer laughed, somewhat feebly. The captain did not join him.

"I see. A very interesting plan," the captain said slowly. "Very carefully thought out." He paused then said evenly: "Did you men ever happen to hear of someone by the name of Josephus Daniels?"

Only Porterfield, who was the best-read of the four, had. "Wasn't he Secretary of the Navy once, sir?"

"That is correct," the captain said. "Do you men know what Secretary Daniels has to do with this conversation?"

No one, not even Porterfield, knew that Josephus Daniels was at the root of their problem. The captain explained.

"It was Josephus Daniels who laid down the regulation that there would be no drinking aboard vessels of the United States Fleet."

"Why the son-of-a-bitch!" It shot out of Mason's mouth before he knew it and startled everybody. "I'm sorry, Captain," the cook apologized, reddening. "I forgot myself."

"I understand your feelings, Mason. However, none of us can forget the memory of Secretary Daniels. His memory will be long preserved."

The men sat glumly for a moment in the face of this specific information of Josephus Daniels' role in naval history. Then Chatham had an idea.

"Did Josephus Daniels include vino in that ban, sir?"

"Vino? Why," the captain said, "I suppose so." He appeared to think a moment then added: "But I'm not absolutely sure. I don't carry a copy of the Josephus Daniels Edict around with me so I don't know *absolutely* whether it applies only to things like Scotch, bourbon, and gin, or if it embraces vino from around Naples, too."

The captain stood up, walked to the port and looked out it a moment. What a pretty sea today, he thought. He turned to the former bartender.

"What would you say the alcoholic content of that wine was, Chatham? I have an idea—this is just from memory—that the

Edict may have specified all alcoholic beverages of three point two percent or more," the captain added before Chatham could answer.

"Well, sir," Chatham said. "I don't know for sure—I could find out—but I'd say the wine here is about three percent."

The captain waited a moment, looking thoughtful. "I tell you what I'll do," he said then. "I'll send off for a copy of the Edict. Then we can know for sure whether it applies to three-percent vino."

The men looked very glum.

"It'll sure take a long time to get a copy of that from Washington, won't it, sir?" Latimer said. "I mean the red tape and all."

"That is true," the captain said. "By the time I put it through the necessary channels—ComRonPhib, ComDivPhib, ComPhib-Med, ComNavMed and so on—it would probably take three or four months, I'd say. At a minimum."

"By that time," Latimer said, "we might have a lot more cases of vino poisoning, sir."

The captain reflected. "That could even affect our combat efficiency. Couldn't it?"

"If it keeps up, I wouldn't be a bit surprised, sir," Latimer said earnestly. "There's nothing knocks a man out like vino poisoning."

The captain reflected a few moments more. Suddenly he turned to Porterfield, who had said not a word but was obviously there for some purpose.

"How do you feel about all this, Porterfield?"

"Well, sir, it was Saint Paul," Porterfield answered, looking somewhat reverently at the overhead, "who said: 'Use a little wine for thy stomach's sake.' I Timothy 5:23."

The captain looked thoughtfully at the helmsman. "You mean Saint Paul should overrule Secretary Daniels?"

"Well, sir, with all due respect to the former Secretary, he is, I believe, a somewhat higher authority," Porterfield intoned piously.

The captain looked out at the sea again then turned back. "I tell you what I'll do. Since we don't know the exact language of the Daniels Edict, I'll do this. I'll send off for it. Until such time as I receive it and find out for certain if we're following the regulation to the letter you can go ahead with the five-gallon-can plan. For the sake of our combat efficiency," he added.

"Thank you, sir," each of the men said, and got out of there as quickly as discreetly possible. The captain took another look at the torn pocket, decided it wasn't worth it, simply ripped the pocket off and sat down and began reading *An Occurrence at Owl Creek Bridge* by Ambrose Bierce, a non-Navy man.

The men chipped in and when the ship was in port Chatham took the five-gallon can out to an excellent vineyard he had found in the countryside and had it filled. Aboard, the former bartender measured out a portion of wine daily to the men, following the British system. No one could ever see that the efficiency of the crew was in any way impaired. As regards Josephus' Edict, the captain somehow forgot, in the busyness of the war, to send off for a copy of it. It was very easy, with so many important matters concerned with the ship's operation to deal with, for an administrative detail like that to escape his attention. And so the men of the *LST* 1826 had wine. Good wine, not the stuff that was sometimes served under that name in the bars of Naples. There was always good morale on the *LST* 1826 and this seemed if anything to improve it, perhaps in line with what Saint Paul had in mind.

7

TWO ROOMS

In the barren room on the Via Mazzini they were toward the end of a long lesson when it happened. It happened like an explosion, with no warning. The lesson that day dealt with items of dress and articles of food and she had been saying the Italian words for them and having him say them back to her, correcting his pronunciation. Biscuit, cheese, beef, flour . . . shirt, shoes, hat, dress. Then all at once she was sobbing into her hands.

"I am so ashamed," she said. "I do not have enough even to buy underclothes."

The statement, coming so abruptly like that, startled Carlyle.

"One pair of shoes," she said. "One dress. Can you imagine what this means to a girl, what it *does* to her? You on your ships, with your clothes and food and your warmth! I don't even have a coat to wear when it gets cold. Oh, it is terrible, terrible, the war is so terrible."

Her body was shaking violently with her crying. It was something entirely outside Carlyle's experience.

"Do you know," she said, "that when I know your ship is coming in I have to stay in this room all day because I have washed my dress, to have it clean for you, and cannot go out?"

He remembered he had never seen her in anything but that same black dress but he had never thought anything of it.

"Do you know what it is to be hungry, really *hungry*? And all the time?"

"No," Carlyle said quietly. He had grown up on a farm and there were certainly always great amounts of food around. "No, I've never been hungry."

Then, from exhaustion if nothing else, her crying quieted
a little.

"I am sorry," she said. "But I get very desperate." Now a certain determination came into her voice. "There is nothing to do,
except that there is one thing. Others do it. I will do what the
others are doing."

"What do you mean?"

"Unless I get things," she said, "I will have to do what so many
others are doing. If other girls can do it I can do it. I will have to
become a . . ."

Before she could say the word and before he even knew what
he was doing, his hand shot up over her mouth. It was several
moments before, slowly, he let his hand drop.

"Don't say it," he said. "That is one Italian word I don't want
to learn. Don't ever say that word about yourself."

He was astonished to realize he was shaking. He waited until
he could speak quietly.

"You are not to worry any more," he said then. "And you are
never to think again of what you have been thinking. And I will
take care of everything. Do you understand me?"

She looked up at him this time. In her youngness she seemed
as helpless as a child. And she said: "I will believe in you."

But that night in his bunk on the ship was a sleepless one
for him, as he fought with his choice. It was, in fact, the first
great moral choice of his life, of the seventeen years of his life.

Next day Seaman Second Class Peter Carlyle was seen leaving
the ship carrying a musette bag. As he walked up the street into
the town he consoled himself with this thought: The Navy has
lots and lots of things over here. They wouldn't miss it. They
certainly wouldn't miss it.

And then he thought something else: Did not the Navy have a
certain moral obligation to help a child born on a Navy ship,
and its mother?

In the cherub room Lieutenant (jg) Matthew Barclay, USNR,
reclined on the Louis Quinze chaise longue listening to Second
Lieutenant Sarah Clark of the Army Nurses Corps play the grand

piano. Through the French doors came the purple of bougain-
villea and the scent of honeysuckle. Shanley had gone up the
coast to look at a bomb, so they had no jeep today. But they had
his room, to which he had left Barclay the key.

Pivoting on the piano stool, she glanced around it, at the
Aphrodite and the Mercury, at the towering fireplace and mammoth bed, at the general marble enormity of the room, at the
vaulting ceilings where flew the riotous profusion of cherubs. Then
she looked across at him and laughed a little. She had a very nice
laugh, not loud, not deliberate.

"I've never seen such a fantastic room. It's wonderful to find
a piano. Especially one like this. It's well tuned, too. I haven't
played in over a year now."

He thought how very easy it was to be with her. She was intelligent and she was comfortable. And she played very well.
Also this was one hell of a comfortable place to be with her,
piano playing or not.

"I miss the music, the playing, more than anything else," she
said. "I guess everyone misses one thing most, though."

She sighed, but a happy sigh, and got up and walked around
the room, looking. She came to the enormous armoire. "May I
look in here?"

"I'm sure Shanley wouldn't mind where you looked."

She opened it. "Why it's dresses!" she said in astonishment.
"I never saw so many dresses."

Barclay got up and stood by her. The armoire was full of dresses
—thirty or forty of them, he would guess. Beneath were stacks of
cartons of cigarettes, bottles of whiskey, even ten-in-one rations.
These held Barclay's eye but she paid no attention to them. She
could see only the dresses.

"I also miss these." She took one out. "How lovely!"

She held it against her. It appeared not far from her size.

"I wonder whose they were."

"Probably the owner's wife. More likely her daughter's."

"She had good taste," she said. She let her hand flick along the
rack.

"You look almost covetous."

"I am."

"Try one on," he said impulsively.

"All right. That's just what I'd like. You pick it out."

She took it, black and silk, and went into the mosaic bathroom and in a moment came out. She was smiling, happy as a girl in an attic. Turning mockingly, laughing, she modeled it for him.

"I wanted to see how you looked in a dress," he said. "I mean not in an Army dress. You look—lovely."

She looked exceedingly feminine—but she did that even in the Army dress, which still didn't hide it. She had looked as feminine when he first met her, in her field clothes on the deck of the LST. Still the dress—well, it did something.

"May I try on another one?" she said shyly.

They must have spent well over an hour at it, and she must have tried on ten of them. He was enchanted by her complete enjoyment of it. She was so alive, so capable of extracting joy from life and sharing it with others; the way she made the simple thing of trying on the dresses into a thing of such pleasure, for both of them.

"Which do you like best? I think I'll just keep one on for a while."

He had her hold one or two out in front of her again. "The blue one, I think."

She went back in and changed back into it and came out. "Shall I play for you some more?"

The sunlight from through the tall windows with their Moorish arches fell across her and its light caught in her hair. She seemed to him very beautiful. Lovely and wrapped in grace as she sat lightly there playing. Then after a while they walked out into the garden and she took his arm and they strolled. The garden had been well kept up, for the war, and had long pebbled paths bordered by hedges.

"In this dress I can forget everything about the war," she said. "Forget that you have to go back to your ship. Forget that I have to go back to the hospital. I want to thank you for bringing me here. A day to forget in, that is what one wants, isn't it?"

It was precisely what one wanted. And with her, for a few hours every week, he could forget it all. She gave him about the most valuable thing there was in the war, and the hardest to get, which was forgetfulness of it for a little time.

As night came on she changed back into her uniform and they had dinner in the officers mess in the villa. The meal was elegantly served by Italian waiters in white jackets and it was quite a meal, starting with bits of native lobster in stem glasses. Then there was a light veal with lemon and there were delicate whipped potatoes and hearts of artichoke. There was a dessert of chocolate mousse. There was Bel Paese cheese and there was fruit—pears and grapes. They could have white or red wine. The cutlery and plateware were excellent; the linens beautiful and immaculate.

While eating she told him a little about her family. "My father teaches Greek. Greek and everything about Greece, that is his love, sometimes I think he's actually living back then." She laughed. "That's exactly, no other reason, why I got sent to Baltimore, to the Bryn Mawr School for Girls, because Edith Hamilton had been headmistress there once and Father always said she knew more about Greek and Greece than any woman in America or probably any man. And she wasn't even there then. He does one thing extremely well—the Greek—and nothing else, except that he's always been very good to us. I have a brother."

"In the war?"

"Just starting. In the Marines. Boot camp at a place called Parris Island."

He asked about her music. "The music school was not to make a concert pianist out of me. I never had the aspiration for that— or the ability, I'm sure. But I wanted to learn the piano as well as I could, for my pleasure—for I loved it."

Afterward they went back to Shanley's room and she played and they talked some more. They were sitting there when Shanley got back. He looked dusty and a little beat in for him.

"Well, I want a fat drink," he said, and routed out a cognac bottle and poured drinks out for them. They had a nightcap with him while he was having three.

"I had to work for a change," he said. But he didn't talk about it. "What's been going on here in my absence? I'm sure I was greatly missed."

"I played your piano and I tried on your dresses," she said. She was still happy with it.

"My dresses?" Shanley said quizzically.

"In the armoire," she said.

"Oh, those dresses. Well, I wish I had been here to see it." He sighed. "Matthew, I talked with some fellows up the line today. They really think the big push, as we used to call it in World War I, is about here. Anzio *and* Cassino, breaking out of both at the same time then meeting up and going to Rome."

"They've been saying that a long time," Barclay said.

"They said it a little different this time." Shanley shrugged. "Well, we shall see what we shall see."

He swallowed some of his brandy. "This goddamn war. That goddamn hill. Those goddamn Germans. Soldiers, they *are* soldiers. Even those fourteenth-century stones are on their side."

It had surely become the most famous monastery in the world, sitting upon a hill holding up an entire front, and for so long; first the Allies being unwilling to shell or bomb the monastery, because of its fourteenth-century religious antiquity; then having done so after much soul-searching, ironically improving the enemy position there by adding the rubble of the monastery itself to the fortifications which the Germans had previously built around it; and now the Allies dug in below and on the slopes of the hill of the Benedictines, taking daily ever more death and frustration, the latter Shanley having felt that day.

It was time for her to go. She was on duty at midnight.

"Help yourself to a dress to take home," Shanley said. "As many as you want."

"Thank you but they wouldn't let me wear them."

"Well, come down anytime and try them on."

"I may do that. Thank you for the use of your room today. And the piano. It's a nice room."

"It is a nice room, isn't it?" Shanley said, suddenly beaming.

He was still working on the cognac bottle when they left. Barclay borrowed Shanley's jeep to take her back. Up on the hill they sat in the jeep awhile. They had fifteen minutes before midnight and they always used all of it until the last minute she had to be in.

"Matthew," she said, "I like our days together."

"I like them. I'm glad you were here."

"When are you coming in again? I know. Start counting on your fingers."

He laughed a little, for he had already begun to do so. And he told her the time.

"I'll be here," she said. "I'll be here waiting for you."

"Be sure you wait," he said.

"I'll wait," she said. "Be sure that I'll wait."

He walked her slowly into the hospital lobby.

"Let's have them, Matthew," she said. And then she added rather somberly, almost urgently, "Let's have the days while we can."

She turned quietly and started up the stairs. He turned back across the lobby. He stopped to let a man in a wheelchair, and the stumps of both legs sticking straight out, cross in front of him then walked on. It didn't take you long to get back to the war.

8

THE STOWAWAY

The odd thing was that it hadn't happened before. The big bow doors of the ship were kept open most of the time at Pozzuoli to permit the crew to go back and forth, and though there was a sort of watch maintained there it was kept so loosely that an elephant could probably have walked aboard without anyone's knowing it. The ship was two hours out of Pozzuoli and steaming north toward the beachhead. Dark had just come on and in the wardroom, supper was over and the captain and three or four of the officers were lingering around the table having a comfortable second cup of coffee. The captain, in a genial mood, was telling a story about something that had happened over on the beach and, pausing in it as he reached toward the story's climax, was just raising his cup to his lips when he heard someone rather gruffly clearing his throat over to one side. Looking that way, he saw standing just inside the doorway the chunky, broad form of Bo's'n's Mate Nelson.

"Yes, Nelson?" the captain said pleasantly.

"Captain," Lord Nelson said, "I just found this."

The boatswain's mate stepped aside to reveal an astonishing sight. Standing there was a small boy, barefooted. He was very thin and was wearing a ragged, dirty shirt, and ragged, dirty pants. His hair looked as if it had not been cut in several months, and he looked at least as dirty himself as his clothes. He looked as if he had not eaten much for a very long time.

"God in heaven," the captain said, setting down his cup in a clatter. "What's that? Who is he? Where did he come from? Where did you find him?"

The questions sounded like the twenties in action. Lord Nelson hurried out an answer to the last question, at least, as if in some kind of defense against the barrage.

"I found him in the bo's'n's locker, Captain," he said.

"The bo's'n's locker! How in the hell did he get in the bo's'n's locker?"

"I wouldn't know, sir," Nelson said. "I don't speak Eye-talian."

The captain turned sharply to Barclay, who with the other officers was looking on with keen interest.

"Barclay, ask him how he got here! Ask him how he got in the bo's'n's locker! Ask him how he ever got aboard in the first place!"

The boy was trembling slightly in the wash of all this noise and Barclay spoke quietly to him.

"What's your name, lad?"

"Rebi," the boy said.

"Rebi what?"

The boy shrugged. "Just Rebi."

"What's all this?" the captain broke in. "What's he saying, Barclay?"

"He says his name is Rebi, Captain. He doesn't know the rest of his name."

"His name! What difference does it make what his name is!" the captain exclaimed. "Never mind about his name! What I want to know is how he got aboard this ship."

"Rebi," Barclay said quietly, leaning forward toward the boy. "How did you get on the ship?"

The boy kept his eyes rigidly on Barclay, in whose corner he at least discerned less frightening sounds, and off the captain. But he said nothing. He simply stood there shaking a little.

"No one's going to hurt you, Rebi," Barclay said. "Just tell me how you got on the ship."

The boy took a deep breath. He talked awhile to Barclay while the captain waited rather impatiently. At last he stopped and Barclay related the essentials to the captain.

"He says he just walked up the 'mouth' of the ship—he means the bow ramp obviously—and walked into a little room there—

that would be the bo's'n's locker—and stayed there until he felt the ship move out. He says it was very rough down there."

"That's too bad," the captain said crisply. It would have been rough, Barclay thought. Near the very bow of the ship and virtually on the bottom, the bo's'n's locker would be about the roughest place aboard, and they had had something of a sea coming out.

"Ask him who helped him," the captain said.

Barclay did. "He says no one, Captain. He says it was his own idea."

"I don't believe it. How could he get aboard unless someone helped him?"

"Well, it's a pretty big bow ramp," Barclay said. "And we don't keep much of a watch there, Captain."

The captain turned and looked at Barclay for several moments. "Are you trying to describe the physical aspects of an LST to me, Barclay, as well as depict the condition of our bow watch?"

"No, sir, Captain," Barclay said. "I certainly wouldn't do that. I know you know the size of the ship and I certainly wouldn't undertake to characterize the condition of our bow watch to you, sir."

"Please don't," the captain said briskly. "Now we'll just see who helped the boy aboard—and why. And may God help who did it. Barclay, I want to see if there's anyone aboard who knows the boy."

"I think if anyone would, it would be Carlyle."

Barclay was sorry the moment he said it.

"You mean," the captain said slowly, "that Carlyle had something to do with this?"

"No, I don't mean that at all, Captain," Barclay said emphatically. "It's just that Carlyle knows so many of the children at Pozzuoli, from playing his guitar for them. I only thought Red might know the boy."

"Nelson," the captain said. "Go get Carlyle."

Presently Carlyle was stepping into the wardroom. The boy was to the side and for a moment the sailor did not see him.

"You sent for me, sir?" he said, looking at the captain.

Then he followed the captain's eyes. "Rebi!" he burst out.

"Rosso!" The boy broke into a wide grin, walked up quickly to the sailor, and stayed closely at his side.

"A friend of yours, I see," the captain said drily.

"Yes, sir. He's one of the children at Pozzuoli. His name is Rebi."

"Never mind his name!" the captain said. "Did you have anything to do with this?"

"With what, sir?"

"With the lad's being aboard here, what else!"

Carlyle swallowed. "No, sir," he said.

The captain sighed. "I believe you," he said immediately. "You wouldn't know how to lie if you tried to." To Carlyle it didn't sound like much of a compliment the way the captain said it. "Barclay, there's one more thing. We appear to know *how* he did it. I propose to believe the lad—half because I think he's telling the truth and half because I have no intention of questioning every man aboard this ship. Now ask the lad *why* he did it."

Barclay did so and the boy replied.

"He says . . ." Barclay turned to the captain. "He says he had watched the ship go out many times. He says he wanted to see what it was like where the ship went all the time."

"Oh he did, did he?"

The captain's voice was still stern, and he looked straight at the boy. But a little something seemed to have happened in him. There was a silence for a moment and then the captain spoke.

"Ask him how old he is."

Barclay did. "He says twelve, Captain."

"Twelve? He doesn't look nine."

"They all look younger over here, Captain."

"Yes, I guess so," the captain said, looking at the small creature. "I've got a boy about that age," he said absently. He waited a moment. "Well, I guess the first thing we'd better do is feed him, isn't it?"

"I think that would be a fine idea, Captain."

"Carlyle!"

"Yes, sir!"

"Carlyle, take the lad below and feed him."

"Yes, sir," Carlyle said promptly. He took the boy's hand. *"Mangiare,"* he said.

The boy looked up at the sailor eagerly. *"Mangiare?"*

"Mangiare," Carlyle said, and started to lead the boy away by the hand.

"And oh, Carlyle?"

"Yes, sir?"

"After you've fed him," the captain said, looking the boy up and down critically, "you might wash him."

"Yes, sir. We'll feed him and then we'll wash him, Captain."

In crew's quarters the boy was first stuffed with food while several of the crew sat around. He looked as if he probably would never stop eating until Carlyle promised he could resume this occupation a little later.

"I think he needs a bath," Carlyle said.

"And a haircut," Nelson said.

They put him in a shower and then something occurred to Nelson. He looked down at the little pile of clothes on the deck. It was hard to tell whether they were distinguished more by their raggedness or by their dirt.

"We can't put him back into these when he gets out of that shower," Nelson said.

"No, Boats. The shower wouldn't have been much good if we did that."

The boatswain's mate looked hard at Carlyle. "That's what I mean, what did you think?" Then he said: "Let's go see Rutledge." They put a Navy-issue towel around the boy and started down the passageway.

The LST had no formal "tailor," such as were carried in large ships, but Machinist's Mate Third Class Timothy Rutledge doubled in this job when absolutely necessary. He was convinced of the necessity in this case and he dug up a pair of dungarees and shirt and went to work. He got the smallest pair he could find but even these were of course much too large. However, with shears, needle, and thread, Rutledge, after several fittings on him, was able to do enough to the garments that they would not fall

off the boy. They put him in them and then Radioman Third
Class Middleton gave him a haircut. "Never cut so much hair off
anyone in my life," Middleton observed. Fed, washed, hair cut,
and in his new clothes the boy looked considerably better.

"*Mangiare?*" he said.

They fed him again. As the ship approached the area where
an increasing number of submarines and JU-88-sewed mines had
been reported lately, Lord Nelson decided he should be prepared
in case of general quarters. He got a battle helmet which he
stuffed with taped-in cloth. Even so the helmet almost swallowed
up the boy's head. It would have to do. Then they put him in a
kapok life jacket and kept him in it the rest of the way up. As
they came opposite the Fifth Army front Carlyle took the boy topside so that he could see, far off, the light of the shelling. He took
him into one of the 20-mm gun tubs and boosted him up on the
ammo box and they watched it across the sea. The shelling was
particularly active tonight and it engaged the boy in a fascination
that left no room for fright. The boy was full of curiosity about
the war, as if "the war," and all that went with it, were the only
world he had ever known, or was likely to know for some indefinite time. They were silent for a while, and watched the shelling.

"Will your parents worry about you?" Carlyle said.

"No parents," the boy said tersely, in a way that made Carlyle
sorry he had asked. It was so certain that they had been killed
in the war that the sailor did not ask that.

"Whoever you live with then," Carlyle said. "Will they miss
you out here?"

"No one misses me." The boy said it without self-pity or appeal
for sympathy, just as a fact, and even possibly to put the sailor's
mind at ease.

"Where do you live, Rebi?"

"In the sulphur caves at Pozzuoli."

"The sulphur caves?" Carlyle said in astonishment. He had
been in these caves. You had to crawl into them and could stand
up only briefly because of the hot sulphur fumes near the roof.
They were set in hills embracing a volcanic field abounding in

fissures from which rose sulphurous vapors and in small live craters bubbling lava. It looked like a setting in hell.

"It is not a bad place," the boy said, as if defending his dwelling-place against a slight. "It keeps me warm in there. Whenever I get cold all I have to do is stand up for a minute. Then I am warm and lie back down and go to sleep quickly before I get cold again." Then, obviously to get away from the subject of where he lived, he said, "Look, there is more shelling."

It was late when they went below to crew's quarters. Carlyle put the boy in an empty bunk near his, where, still bundled up in his kapok jacket, he fell immediately asleep.

Next morning, Carlyle took him topside and far forward, into the very bow, so that he would have a good view of everything. From the moment the beachhead came in sight through the morning mists, the boy was almost hypnotized by the sight of Anzio.

"Is this where you come all the time?" he asked.

"Yes, this is where we come, Rebi."

The boy looked eagerly at the large number of ships through which they were beginning slowly to pass. As the ship beached he went below and stood near Carlyle at his station on the bow ramp, watching the loaded trucks go off, and a long line of empty trucks come on. The sailor was glad he expressed no desire to go ashore. He seemed very content with the ship, as if it fulfilled all the drives for curiosity anyone might have in his most excited dreams. The ship was loaded with empties, backed off and headed out and Carlyle took the boy topside. The only shells that fell were some distance off and the boy, standing near the bow with the sailor watched their splashes. He seemed determined not to miss anything.

"Germans?" he said.

"Yes," Carlyle said. "Germans."

"How long do the Americans stay here? How long do you keep coming here?"

"Forever, I expect. For a long time, I think," the sailor added.

They were just emerging from the harbor and Carlyle was looking idly out to sea, where it was very quiet, when he heard the boy speak.

"Rosso. Something just went into that cloud."

Carlyle looked up toward a huge billowing cumulus that stood up ahead of the ship. He could see only the cloud high in the blue sky around it.

"What was it?" he said easily.

"I think it was a plane," the boy said.

Carlyle kept his eyes on the cloud and in a moment he could see a tiny speck come out of it. He vaulted up the ladder to the gun tub and spoke to the bow lookout.

"Boland," he said. "Let me have those glasses a moment, will you?"

Carlyle took the glasses and looked through them. He looked only a moment. He brought the glasses down sharply and grabbed the phone speaker on Boland's chest.

"Conning tower," he said. "There's a plane up ahead. Just coming out of that big cloud. I think maybe it's an FW-190."

It was only a moment before the general alarm, a series of pulsating gongs, broke over the ship. Carlyle jumped back down the ladder. The boy was looking up curiously toward the source of the sound on the bridge.

"What's that?" he asked.

Carlyle quickly made sure the boy's kapok jacket was tied securely and stuffed his helmet down on his head. "Whatever you do, make sure that helmet stays on."

Looking up, he could see the cloud and framed against it, like a small bird, the shape of the plane starting down. He pushed the boy under the gun tub. "It'll be noisy in there. Keep your helmet on—and don't come out until I say so."

He hurried back up the ladder to his battle station as loader on the bow 40-mm. Nelson, the pointer—a job not ordinarily rating a boatswain's mate first, but on LSTs people were put where they were best, whatever their rating, and Nelson was both good at and liked to fire the forty—and Porterfield, the trainer, were already in their gun seats, and both already turning their wheels, Nelson to elevate the gun and Porterfield to swing the mount to put the gun on the aircraft. Carlyle could see the plane sliding down the sky, seeming to gather speed and getting larger every moment. And now it came on. The bow forty was the first to open fire, and then he could hear the shriller twenties joining in. The plane was diving on them at an angle of about sixty degrees and Nelson and Porterfield lined up on the tracers. The plane came on in a rush and Carlyle and Mason, the other loader, sweated up the four-shell clips into the loader to keep the gun provided with its rapid fire. Then he was conscious of a large shape and then of the plane passing with an immense noise directly over the ship and low enough they could feel its engine's roar pass through them. It was unhurt. Almost simultaneously he saw a large geyser of water shoot up about seventy yards off the starboard bow. The ship vibrated and some water splashed over her. But she also was unhurt.

"He'll be back," Nelson said.

It must have been five minutes but it seemed much less. Carlyle had time for a quick look under the gun tub. The boy was lying on his belly and looking out. He looked all right though he was holding his fingers to his ears under the helmet. The noise under the tub must be fearsome, it passed through Carlyle's mind.

"Is it gone? Can I come out now?"

"It's gone, but it'll be back. Stay right there, you hear me?"

"I'll stay, Rosso. Don't worry about me."

Carlyle stood up and kept his eyes on the high sky. He could see the plane, and he knew it would be one more time. They always made their two runs.

"Here she comes," he heard Nelson say quietly.

Nelson let the German get in range. The plane had started its run earlier, and flatter, this time, and Nelson had depressed the forty and Porterfield swung the mount around dead ahead. Now the plane came roaring, raging in. The guns were all going now, shaking the ship. Nelson was firing very rapidly and still the plane came on. Carlyle was aware of it beyond the bow and he was caught up now in that most final of all knowledges, that the plane wanted the ship, and the ship the plane, and with it somehow a certainty that one or the other would presently have its desire fulfilled. The shells erupted from the Bofors with great noise. Carlyle could see the tracers racing out and the plane coming in on them at a fearful speed. He thought it was closer, but he knew later that it was a hundred yards beyond the bow, close enough at that, when he saw the plane swerve. The plane came on, veering to port now, and passed, not over the ship, but immediately to port, and very close, no more than a matter of yards away. He could make out the iron cross markings and a figure in the cockpit and Nelson had just said, "By God, I think one of us got him," when the plane, trying to turn upward, at that moment Carlyle could see smoke coming from her, the plane climb sharply, almost vertically, and angling so that he could see her underbelly, and then suddenly he could see no plane but only a great burst of flame, and, in a moment, pieces of objects falling down into the water, an explosion on the water, and very quickly the flame and all objects were gone to the sea, and only tendrils of smoke remained, seeming themselves almost like soft streaks of cloud against the sky and over the quiet sea.

He turned to see the boy standing up looking out at where the plane had exploded.

"How long have you been standing there?" Carlyle said sharply.

"Just at the last," the boy said. He shook his head a little to clear it from the noise. He didn't seem very apologetic. He seemed quite happy, almost transported. "I just wanted to see the last."

"I'm glad the last was out there," Carlyle said, "instead of in here."

It was the first full plane the ship had ever brought down, though she had been credited with half a plane twice, at Sicily and at Salerno, the other half of the credit going to the guns of other ships. Two half planes were painted on the conning tower. It would be nice to paint a full plane there for a change. Then Carlyle heard the mount captain say something to him.

"Carlyle! The captain wants you in the conning tower."

He went on up there, taking the boy with him. The captain, who was looking at the sky, turned as they came up.

"Carlyle, I just want to commend you for spotting that FW. You have good eyes, as I have always said."

"Not as good as the boy's, Captain," Carlyle said. "He spotted him first."

"He did?" said the captain in amazement. He stood looking down at the boy. "Well how about that." He sighed deeply. "Tell him well done, Carlyle. Tell him that's the best thing anyone can say to you in the Navy."

The crew put together a citation which they had Barclay translate for them and after a yeoman had typed a copy, presented it to the boy. It read:

> For conspicuously assisting the LST 1826 to bring down an FW-190 off Anzio beachhead, by sighting the plane the first of anyone on the ship.
>
> This citation will entitle bearer to eat on the LST 1826 anytime the ship is in port.

The boy was especially pleased with the second paragraph of the citation. When the ship got back to Pozzuoli, he had many things to tell his friends there about exactly what the ship did when it left the harbor each time. He perhaps colored it up a bit. He certainly had the ship going through fire and hell all the way up and back. He also said they ate all the time aboard. Thereafter he was the undisputed authority, among the children around the mole, of everything concerning the ship, where it went and exactly what it did. So much so as to start quite a universal desire among them to duplicate his experience.

The captain easily anticipated this development. And while even grateful, as matters had turned out, for Rebi's having stowed aboard, he was not anxious that his example be made a practice. Thereafter the bow doors were closed one hour before the ship shoved off and a detail of men assigned to search the ship, paying particular attention to out-of-the-way compartments—such as the bo's'n's locker. The captain assigned Carlyle, since he knew the children best of anyone aboard, to be in charge of the detail.

After that, just before sailing, a singular ceremony took place in the conning tower of the LST 1826. There a tall, red-haired seamen stepped up to the captain, saluted, and said, "Captain! There are no children aboard this vessel!"

Only then would the captain order, "Cast off!"

9

WINE AND K-RATIONS

They stopped in the hills and got a bottle of red wine. The sun lay across the campagna and the blue sky was interrupted only by a few thin strips of cirrus cloud out to seaward. The coast was one small beach after another, each U-shaped with rock arms pointing out to sea. Their beach was no different from another but they knew it by the particular way the road dipped down there and by an abandoned shed on one end which must once have housed fishing boats. He drove the jeep up to the edge of the sand and they got out and went walking along the beach. Out to sea he could see a ship aimed north. It was a destroyer, one of the new one-pipers.

They came back and he got the poncho out of the jeep and spread it on the beach near the water's edge. He got three K-rations and the wine and they settled on the poncho. He pulled the cork from the wine.

"Let's taste this first," he said and handed it to her. They had no cups so they swallowed from the bottle. The proprietor had said it was fresh Vesuvius wine. It was fresh all right but it had a good, bitter taste. He made a hole in the sand to rest the wine in.

"Would you prefer a breakfast, dinner, or supper K-ration?" he asked.

"What's the difference?"

"The breakfast has a tin of dehydrated eggs scrambled with some kind of meat. The dinner has a tin of cheese. The supper has a tin of some kind of vegetables mixed with some kind of meat."

"The cheese sounds more dependable," she said. "I'll take the dinner one please."

He opened that and the supper ration, and opened the tins and tore the cellophane off the hard brown biscuits. They ate, chunking off the contents of the tins with the biscuits and drinking the wine. She gave him some of her cheese.

"It's spooky here," she said. "I like it. Nobody anywhere. I feel the ghosts of the fishermen."

"This was certainly a fishing beach."

"Will you promise me something?" she said in a moment.

"Probably."

"Promise me that when Rome is taken you'll borrow Shanley's jeep and take me there for a day. I want to see Rome. I've always wanted to see Rome."

"I'll be glad to promise that. I don't know what year it'll be though."

"It won't be that long."

"Maybe not."

"I sometimes think it may, too," she said, "when I see them coming in at the hospital. There are so many, many of them coming in from Anzio and Cassino, both. To get so close to Rome and not to get there, those men."

He waited a moment. "I'd like to show you Rome. I'd like to take you to see the Forum and Hadrian's tomb and the Bernini fountain and the Palatine Hill and the Janiculum and have an audience with the Pope."

"Aren't the names exciting? I want so much to see them. You promise to arrange it?"

"I'll arrange the rest of it and you arrange the audience with the Pope."

"All right. After the war I shall tell my grandchildren of a Navy lieutenant who took me to Rome."

"Your grandchildren, if they've studied their geography, will ask, 'What was a Navy lieutenant doing in Rome?'"

"I shall tell them you sailed me in your ship up the Tiber. Doesn't it empty into the sea?"

"Yes, but I don't think it'll take much of a draft. But maybe the grandchildren . . . I would like to show you Rome," he said seriously.

"Then you will. You really promise it?"

"I promise to take you to Rome," he said, meaning it, if there was ever any possibility in the world of it at the time, if every effort could do it for one day, which was all he would ever get away from the ship, and that only with great luck.

They finished the K-rations and the wine and lay back on the poncho and looked at the sky. The wine had made them sleepy. They turned over and soon, lying with their backs to each other, were asleep.

He woke up and felt something had done it. It was getting dark. He listened and could hear nothing. Then he heard her crying a little in her sleep. Then he felt some drops of rain. He slipped off the poncho and doubled his part of it over her. He waited and soon the crying stopped.

He sat and watched the first stars come out above the hills but they were not out long. A good cloud cover soon hid them. It was very dark on the beach. He sat and thought how just being there with her, or talking with her, did it. How the presence of her took away the loneliness of the ship and the war. The loneliness was the worst thing by far the war did to you. But she took it away. It was a great gift she gave him.

He felt a few more drops of the rain. And then her crying again. Then she awoke and sat up with the poncho draped around her.

"Was I crying?" she said.

"A little. It was probably the raindrops."

"I've always cried in my sleep. It doesn't mean anything." Then, coming more out of her sleep and just becoming aware of it, she said quietly and as if to herself, "You covered me up with the poncho."

Then the rain came on suddenly and they got up and hurried into the jeep. He made her keep the poncho around her. They sat while it poured against the top and the windshield, coming mostly straight down and not on a slant, so that not too much got inside the jeep. When it slackened a little he started the jeep and they headed back over the wet mountain road.

He got her to the hospital a quarter hour before she was to go on duty. They sat in the jeep and could hear the rain, still falling a little, against the canvas top.

"That was a nice picnic," she said.

"Yes, it was. Even the K-rations tasted good."

She waited a moment then, without turning, said: "I want to tell you. I think I'm leaving here in about a month."

He looked across at her. "In a month?"

"About that. They're making up a new unit to go to Anzio and I'm on it."

"You're going to Anzio in a month?"

"If it's still going on there. Maybe you'll be taking me up in your ship."

"Maybe we will," he said.

He waited a moment. "May I see you again?"

"Yes," she said. "You may. You certainly may."

Then he was counting on his fingers again the time when his ship would be back in, and he told her. He walked her into the hospital and came back and drove back down to the ship. The loneliness was with him again the moment he drove away. It was worse than before he ever knew her.

Four more weeks, about a half dozen more times to see her, a half dozen more dates, he thought. And that would be it. And if they broke out of the beachhead before then, the ship would be going somewhere else anyhow. Either way they had him.

10

A NEW MEMBER OF THE FAMILY

It was the very next day after his trip to the beachhead that Carlyle brought Rebi over to see Coco. He did it as the most natural thing in the world, as if he wanted one friend of his to meet another. After a while the sailor mentioned, as if it were some interesting detail in a person's life, that Rebi had no place to live and as of the moment slept in the sulphur caves.

"I was thinking," Carlyle said. "Thinking of myself. I would feel safer about you out on the ship if I knew Rebi were around looking after you. He would be a protection."

Coco looked at Carlyle in surprise. "Him?" she said. She looked down at the very thin boy. "A lot of protection he would be."

"He would be some protection," Carlyle said. "He could do things like mind the baby when you go out. If he stayed here he could help you with the baby."

The girl was so stupefied, as it came over her that Carlyle actually meant that the boy would *live* here, that it took her a moment to take in the various problems entailed in this suggestion.

"Help me with the baby? Most likely he'll just eat. Little boys eat a lot."

"I won't eat much," Rebi said.

"I would see to it about the food," Carlyle said.

"Where can he sleep?" Coco addressed Carlyle, ignoring the boy. "There's only one bed."

"I can sleep on the floor," Rebi, who stayed to the side entering the conversation only when he saw a proper opening, said. He said it as if the floor were a bed in a palace. And after all it was an improvement over the dirt mattress of the cave.

"This room is not big enough for three people," Coco offered another objection. "Even if one of them sleeps on the floor."

"Maybe we could get you a place with another room," Carlyle said.

"We are going to get a lot, aren't we?"

"He could help you with the baby," Carlyle returned to that.

"I'll take good care of the bambino," the boy said. "I'm very good with bambini."

"Oh, I suppose you've had lots of experience?" Coco said.

"Oh, yes," the boy said. "I've known many bambini."

The boy walked over and peered into the crib. The baby's arms went up and Rebi picked the baby up. He held it with astonishing expertness.

"I guess he can stay," Coco said, and smiled a little. Then she turned briskly to the boy.

"You'll have to mind me," she said. It sounded comical to Carlyle. She was little more than a child herself, and it was like an older child saying this to one handicapped only by being slightly younger.

"Oh, I will, signora. I'll always mind you. In addition to helping with the baby. You don't have to worry about me, signora."

What had seemed a luxury before now became a necessity: Carlyle got them an apartment in the same building as the room. If anything it looked more bare since the furniture—a chest of drawers, a table, two chairs, a bed, and a crib—had now to be distributed over two rooms. With the larger space, and another occupant to be fed, Carlyle started bringing a bigger musette bag.

I I

THE NINETY AND NINE

It was warm and windless and a velvet sea when the ship left Pozzuoli, water melding into horizon to form one vast unbroken reach of dusty blue. The sea held thus for hours. Lieutenant (jg) Barclay had the dog watch, two hours only, from 1800 to 2000. But he would have a full watch again that night, from 0400 to 0800. He hadn't seen a better sea than when he came on watch for the short one. He got the course and speed and the rest of it from Ensign Horner, whom he was relieving, and soon was settled in with his watch boatswain, Nelson; his signalman, Abbot; Carlyle, his phone man; his recorder, Mason, who though a cook by rating had recently been eased out of that job on performance and had become a watch stander; and, just below in the wheelhouse, Porterfield, his helmsman, along with a quartermaster and an engine-room telegraph man. It was a remarkable sea, so lake-like that even an LST almost sailed itself. Now, later in the watch, Barclay looked down over the Number 2 hatch forward and saw that some of the men had come topside to sleep, it was that good a night. Warm, and paths of stars overhead to look at. He looked at his watch, checked the time with the wheelhouse down through the voice tube and ordered a course change.

"Right rudder to course two six five."

"Right rudder to course two six five," Porterfield echoed up through the voice tube. He could feel the ship come to starboard a little, then presently Porterfield's voice again. "Course is two six five, sir."

"Very well."

He and the five men had stood so many watches together that they knew everything, he supposed, that six men could ever know about each other, in a war.

"Do you realize this is our thirtieth trip to Anzio, Mr. Barclay?" Mason said.

"No," Barclay said thoughtfully. It was a solemn fact. "I hadn't realized that. I'd lost count."

"I keep track in a little book I've got," Mason explained. "Thirty trips." He gave a sigh as a sort of tribute to this number. "I wonder whatever happened to that saying, 'Rome by Thanksgiving, Berlin by Christmas.'"

"They didn't say which Christmas, brightness," Nelson said.

Barclay stood scanning the sea through his binoculars, and occasionally looking upward. Nothing showed but a flat sea below a star-ridden sky. Stirred perhaps by Mason's remark, he thought of what the men planned to do after the war. From innumerable watches with them, he knew exactly and in some detail. Abbot was going to be a schoolteacher; Mason longed to settle down in California and didn't care what he did, so long as he did it in California; Porterfield would become a minister; Carlyle would go back to farming; only Lord Nelson would keep on with what he was doing, on ships. Himself: Well, he had various plans, various dreams of a method of life satisfying and even exciting, and nothing like the end of the war so beckoned out of the loneliness; nothing so beckoned as the time when the control of your own destiny would be out of the hands of others and back in your own.

"I wish I had some fresh milk to drink," Mason said. "I'd rather have some fresh milk than anything else in the world. I could drink off the first quart without lowering the bottle."

This started a catalogue of articles of food they didn't have that they missed most.

"Fresh vegetables," Carlyle said. "I'd settle for any kind of fresh vegetables."

"I think I'd like a Maine lobster," Barclay said with some deliberation. "Or maybe stone crabs. Stone crabs if I had to choose, I believe."

"Ice cream," Abbot and Lord Nelson said at about the same time.

Fresh milk, fresh vegetables, stone crabs, ice cream, the merits of each were set forth by its advocate. No one knew quite why but somehow the more they talked about it, the more ice cream shaped up as the most desirable of all the items.

"I guess I would trade off fresh vegetables for good ice cream if it came to that," Carlyle admitted.

And finally they decided nothing in the world would be better to have than American ice cream.

"Say, they got ice cream on cruisers, don't they, Lord Nelson?" Mason said.

"They got everything on cruisers," Lord Nelson, who had served on almost every type of naval vessel, said authoritatively. "Yes, they got lots of ice cream. Matter-of-fact, they got a soda fountain on cruisers. You can order a malted milk, sodas, sundaes with chocolate or marshmallow sauce—all kinds of ice cream things."

"I wish you hadn't mentioned that, Lord Nelson," Mason said. "Think of a cruiser having malted milks and ice cream sodas!"

"Ah yes," Nelson said soberly. "A regular soda fountain they got." They all visualized the shining soda fountain.

By the time they were through examining the subject they were all perfectly ravenous for ice cream, even if previously they hadn't thought about it for months. But this very longing took their minds from other things, mostly from loneliness. It was time for another course change and he spoke into the voice tube.

"Left rudder to course two five five."

"Left rudder to course two five five," Porterfield said, then: "Course is two five five, sir."

"Very well."

Barclay kept looking through the night with his binoculars. Nothing anywhere. Nothing in sight and no sound except the familiar, easy creaking of the ship and the soft and rhythmical stroke of the sea against her. He had his love for the sea anyhow, he thought, a deep and abiding love. Even on an LST he still

had it. Abruptly he was thinking of this living thing called a ship
that had become his home, been so for so long now, and would
be for how much longer no one could know. Her history flashed
like a hurrying kaleidoscope through his mind: how she was put
together as a ship in a place called Jeffersonville, Indiana; how she
was then floated down the Ohio and Mississippi rivers to New
Orleans, where she was commissioned and her crew took her over
and started her across. The Navy had designated her "Landing
Ship, Tank" but it had not taken long for the crew to change this
to "Large Slow Target." He remembered the long crossing of
the mid-Atlantic which no ship built like an LST had any business
crossing, whose waters seemed almost to eat the ship up and
where every soul aboard had been desperately seasick time and
time again, and the passage through Gibraltar into the Mediterranean where she had been since and no one could tell, either,
if she would go once again through those Straits, going home.
He thought of the men who had died on her, and of the efforts
which would go on as long as the war itself went on to increase
the number, and he thought of all the troops she had carried
of whom so many were also now surely dead, on some mountain
slope, along some dusty road. He thought of Sicily, where a bomb
had landed on the fantail killing five of the crew and four Army
men; of Salerno, where in the landings she had immediately lost
an officer to that hunk of shrapnel now on the captain's desk
and where she had broached and had been on that beach thirty-
six hours, unable to get off by herself, the steel cable leading from
her powerful fantail winch to her giant stern anchor which had
been dropped routinely several hundred feet back for this very
purpose of retracting her from the beach having been severed
and they were on that beach at Salerno thirty-six hours before a
tug got her off and that was a bad time and they had lost eight
men to the 88s; of Anzio, where he had just learned she was now
making her thirtieth run. He thought of all the shrapnel dents in
her, of how battered she was, and he thought how it, meaning
the invasions and the war and the runs, seemed to go on forever.
Then for just a moment, in thinking of his watch crew, the
thought occurred rather solemnly to him that the only thing that

came out of war was a certain comradeship, and then came one
further thought of how ironic this was, to get that out of something that was such an exercise in idiocy, so foul, useless, evil; but
there was nothing else, absolutely nothing else. It was a type of
thought that he didn't allow himself and this one had got in for
only about ten seconds before he shut the thought off, as being
pretty useless itself. Nelson was off checking around the ship, Mason had gone below for coffee, Abbot had stepped down to the
radio shack and for a couple of minutes only he and Carlyle
were standing there.

"How's the mother, Red?" he asked when they had talked a
little bit.

"My mother?" Carlyle said in surprise.

"No, *our* mother. The one from the ship."

"Oh, Coco." He could almost feel Carlyle's grin in the dark.
"Fine, just fine. So's the baby. I've been seeing a lot of them."

"I can tell by your Italian. I've never seen anyone learn a language faster."

"Well, she's a good teacher," Carlyle said. "Very bright girl
also. I like her better every time I see her."

Nelson and Mason had both just returned when suddenly
a light, bright and startling, showed about 900 yards off the starboard bow and dead on the water. Everyone had seen it at about
the same time. The bow lookout, who reported it on the phone,
and the conning tower. Immediately it was under scrutiny by the
entire watch. Barclay stepped over to the speaker tube leading
from the conning tower to the captain's cabin. The captain left
standing orders to be called if anything strange, in particular any
strange light, was sighted. He was in the conning tower in seconds.

"I thought I'd better call you, Captain. I can't make it out,"
Barclay said.

"I'm glad you did." The captain studied it for a few moments.
"I can't either."

"Could be a fish," Mason said.

"Fish don't carry tail lights," Nelson said.

Then, as abruptly as it had appeared the mysterious light

had vanished. The captain stayed a little while talking quietly.

"What a pretty night!" he said, looking up at the stars. "Well, good night, Matthew. Good night, men."

"Good night, Captain."

Then he was gone. And presently so was the watch. The five men and Barclay turned a very pretty, quiet sea over to the oncoming watch and went below to get some sleep. They knew they would be seeing each other again at 0400.

"I can't get that ice cream out of my mind," Mason said as they started below. "Man, I'd love some ice cream."

They went below wondering a little what the strange light had been, but thinking mainly of how good some ice cream would taste.

Barclay knew there was something different the moment he was awakened by the watch messenger. When he stood up and started pulling on his khaki pants he had one leg in when he was slammed back into his bunk and planted there in a sitting position. He did the rest of his dressing from this position. He could hear the wind screaming from the sea and when he stood up he lurched to the doorway and then along the passageway as the deep roll of the ship took him first to one side and then the other down to the deserted wardroom. He managed to get a cup of coffee from the Silex over to the table, some of the coffee scalding against his hand as he poured it. He had just got some sugar into it when the sugar bowl decided to leave the table and hurl itself against the bulkhead, splintering dully. He held onto the saucer while he got some coffee into him and then took cup, saucer and spoon to the wardroom pantry and put them in the sink, to save some of the ship's plateware. Then he picked up the pieces of the sugar bowl and put them in the wastebasket there. Lieutenant (jg) Richard Abernethy came in from the engine room and started the same process of coffee-getting. "This is the kind of night that makes me most content—not that I'm not just wild about it anyhow, especially on a monstrosity like this—to be in the black gang instead of up on that deck," Abernethy said. "It's pretty snug down there, if you understand what I mean." "Oh, I understand all right," Barclay said. Abernethy shook his head. "Imagine a civilized human being having to spend four hours in that conning tower on a night like this. Only a sadist could have designed something like that," he said thoughtfully. Barclay grinned. "There's a great deal in what you say, Richard." "There often is," Abernethy said. "Be sure not to catch cold from becoming overheated down there—we need men like you," Barclay said, as Abernethy laughed hugely.

He negotiated the route back along the passageway and up the ladder to the wheelhouse by sliding and pushing alternately along one bulkhead then the other. Once arrived there his eyes confirmed what his ears and the ship's movement had already told him, that they were in one of those violent storms the Tyrrhenian Sea could lay on so suddenly. He went on up to the open conning tower. He had to shout to make himself heard to Lieutenant (jg) Scot Fairchild, whom he was relieving. Fairchild was glad to hand over the watch. The captain had been up several times, he said, and they had at last decided to secure bow and stern lookouts lest they be taken overboard by the sea.

"The son-of-a-bitch of a submarine skipper who could see up through this deserves to sink us," Fairchild said, and he was gone.

Barclay took a look forward. The storm was laid out in a savage pattern. The sea was foaming white everywhere and great slashes of cold rain tore in frenzied sound across the decks, stinging and near-blinding him, the wet wind slapping directly into his face. The forward part of the ship was entirely hidden, range of vision being scarcely beyond Number 2 hatch just forward of the superstructure. It seemed impossible that only a few hours earlier, in this same sea, men were sleeping there. The sea had the ship in a seizure, of both a hard pitch and roll. The roll wanted to throw you sideways. The pitch wanted to lift you off your feet. Each time the blunt bow of the ship slammed rhythmically into that sea you could feel the pitch through the soles of your shoes. As for the roll it was constant and far over so that a man had to brace hard to keep from going with it against the shielding, and sometimes to hold to the shielding itself to keep his feet.

Perched on a six by eight foot nest high above the ship, open entirely to the sky and with only a chest-high shielding for its sides, the conning tower gave almost no defense to men against the elements which attacked them viciously in such a storm. Yet stood there the watch had to be. There would be no talking on this watch, only the fierce dissonance of the sea, and the wind and the rain. The ship's habitual creaking had given way to something like a long, straining groan as she took the sea first hard on one side then, rolling back, on the other, and the groaning produced by the roll was embellished by the hard, slamming sound produced by the pitch. LSTs had had their seams opened in storms, and even, one heard, had broken in two, but this one was not enough to do that. Or so they thought, and hoped. Not that the sea was not trying hard enough, and at each pitch Barclay could see a great cascade of sea break just abaft the bow, and then rush in a torrent down the main deck. Then immediately on the roll the sea poured over the decks from the side and it was like two rivers in floodtide intersecting amidships. They were taking on a great deal of sea. He hoped the armored trucks and weapons carriers secured on deck would hold. One breaking away and sending its tons of metal hurtling down the deck could do a considerable bit of damage to the ship, not to mention to the cargo itself, especially if it ten-penned the others, but catching a momentary look at the shapes of them between the blasts of rain and sea, Barclay could see that they were riding grimly at their moorings.

The main thing now was to hold the ship on any course at all, responsive as she was to both wind and sea. He checked down into the wheelhouse. Porterfield had been strapped to the helm and Barclay could see his tall form which made the kapok jacket seem like a boy's on him hunched over it and those great bony hands of his gripping the wheel. Barclay was very glad to have him for helmsman. Getting through such a sea was a tense thing for anyone on watch, merely to be present on such a watch and knowing that you had the responsibility for the ship, but it was hardest on Porterfield. Barclay stepped out into the weather again, using his shoulder to get the blackout door open against the wind, and fought his way up the ladder and back into the conning tower. He was almost immediately nailed against its side. To keep his footing, he took a step forward and wedged himself between the gyro repeater and the forward shielding of the conning tower. The position gave him what vision was to be had through the elements and it would be difficult for them to dislodge him from there. He was enveloped in total blackness, with only the wild sound of wind and water, both from sky and sea, raging at will across the deck. It was very cold and the water slammed against them. They were opposite the Fifth Army front and Barclay wondered if the storm was there tonight, too, and if so, imagining that it might even be welcome by those ashore, by keeping activity down, and maybe, he thought, the storm had brought a rest for the soldiers so that this night because of it men would not die. There was no way to tell, since with no visibility the shelling could not have been seen, even if there had been any.

It was just in the first reaches of dawn that they came out of it, as if they had traveled through some tumultuous tunnel of water and wind where on either side all is quiet. For suddenly it was gone, when the watch was almost gone itself. The wind collapsed, the whitecaps fell away, and abruptly out of its hiding place, they could see the bow of their ship. In the light Barclay looked down upon a deck cargo very wet and with some tarpaulin lashings torn away, but cargo and ship had come through the storm. The first thing they could feel stop was the pitching of the ship. And then the rolling had greatly diminished, the clouds gave way, and up ahead they could see the shape of Anzio sitting on a peaceful shore overlooking still water. Coming in they could see something curious downshore—some men seemed to be standing in the water. Just standing there. The air was still quite cold and the water would be more so. Then the ship was beaching and it was over. They promptly got a message from the shore that the return load would not be coming on until 1600 or thereabouts that afternoon and were ordered to anchor out. Their watch, where the assaulting elements had stretched the mind and nerves but kept this very effect lidded down, being over, the exhaustion and tension from it flooded in on them. It was Barclay who made the suggestion before the ship could get off.

"Let's walk down the beach and see what those soldiers are doing," he said. "It's pretty cold for men to be walking around in the water—even with their clothes on."

So he and his watch, Porterfield, Mason, Abbot, Carlyle, and Lord Nelson took a stroll. As they walked they began to feel some of the tension drop away. Porterfield was the first to recognize what it was, perhaps out of his professional training. They were still some distance away and all the others could make out was the odd sight of some clothed men going into the water, then coming out of it dripping, then others going in and also coming out.

"Why, it's a baptismal service," Porterfield said quietly.

As they came up they could see about fifty soldiers, some just out of the water, some in it, and some dry ones sitting on their helmets watching, awaiting their turn. They were from an infantry division, Porterfield found out, and there were two chaplains there. One was a Baptist chaplain and he was standing chest-deep in the water. As soon as he had finished baptizing one man another would go in. Some of the soldiers took off their shoes, and some took off their shirts, and some didn't take off anything, walking into the water fully clothed in their fatigues or o.d.'s. The chaplain held each man, murmured "In the Name of the Father, and of the Son, and of the Holy Ghost," lowered the man backward until he disappeared completely for a moment under the surface, then lifted him back up in the symbol of the resurrection. The water must have been very cold and a chilling breeze had begun to fan across the scene. Out of the water the soldier-convert changed his clothes. Some of the men had exercised their option for the Methodist church and for these another chaplain standing on dry land dipped his fingers into a helmet containing water and sprinkled the drops over the soldier's head.

"I think I'll join the Methodists," Mason whispered, shivering a little. "I was thinking of joining the Baptists until I saw this."

The men from the ship watched respectfully. Occasionally a shell would kick up a spurt of water near the baptismal service. It was ignored. When all the men had been either immersed or sprinkled they stood in a group on the beachhead and bowed their heads while one of the chaplains offered up a prayer. Then they stood around and sang a hymn. Thanks to Porterfield, all the men from the ship knew it and they joined in. The hymn was "The Ninety and Nine" and the strains of it drifted thinly out over the beachhead.

> There were ninety and nine that safely lay
> In the shelter of the fold,
> But one was out on the hills away,
> Far off from the gates of gold—
> Away on the mountains wild and bare,
> Away from the tender Shepherd's care,
> Away from the tender Shepherd's care . . .

When it was over the men from the ship walked back down the beachhead. They had not gone very far when they saw an LCT taking on wounded to ferry out to a hospital ship they could see anchored out, white and waiting in the distance.

"Why don't we go along, Mr. Barclay?" Lord Nelson said. "A hospital ship is sometimes a very interesting place. There ain't nothing that's loaded like a hospital ship."

The litter wounded were being placed in a neat row on one side of the LCT's welldeck over which hung a tarpaulin with a large red cross painted on it, and the LCT's guns were covered. The walking wounded stood silently on the other side of the deck with their backs to Anzio and looking toward the hospital ship in the anchorage. Barclay and his watch got on and the LCT, as soon as its deck was entirely covered with litters and the standing, backed off, swung around, and headed out. The litter wounded lay very still, not even their heads turning, but looking up at the tarpaulin. Army nurses in field gear moved along the row tucking blankets in under shoulders. The face of one man showed nothing but lips, the rest a heavy white bandage over burns or wounds, and one nurse knelt by him all the way out holding a cloth which she kept soaking from a canteen to those lips while he chewed water from the cloth. Amid the wounded soldiers lay an incongruous passenger. She looked about five years old under the blanket and very tiny on the litter made for a grown, wounded man. Her face above the blanket was pale and quiet. An LCT sailor kept bringing her candy and K-ration fruit bars and she smiled and actually laughed. One of her arms, they were told, had been taken off by a shell at Anzio. A woman obviously her mother squatted beside her, her face blank of anything. Halfway out the small LCT ran into a rough harbor sea and Barclay could hear the mother begin to murmur anxiously in Italian, "What's the matter, what's the matter?" An American soldier lying on a litter directly by the girl's reached over and held the girl's one hand. Then he began telling the mother in her own language that everything would be all right. The mother cried a little then was silent. The little girl never cried at all.

The hospital ship looked very big and white and clean as they got near. A space in her side opened up and a horizontal gangway was laid across and the LCT came up and moored to it. While the wounded were being slowly shuttled over into the ship Barclay and his watch crew went aboard to take a look around. They found their way along passageways and topside. It was an incredibly clean place and made them feel very dirty and unshaven. Everyone was in blues with gold braid shining on sleeves and caps. The caps had white covers and Barclay in his spotted, worn khakis had forgotten the Navy wore such a smart-looking uniform, not having even seen it in so long. Lord Nelson had soon found a fellow boatswain's mate—boatswain's mates, wherever, form one of the closest of clans—and from him discovered that the ship was just out from the States and that this was her first run from Naples to Anzio to take back wounded.

"We left New York ten days ago," the hospital ship boatswain's mate said, and the LST men looked at him as if unable to comprehend the overpowering fact.

"Ten days ago in New York!" Mason said. "How about that."

"Yes," the boatswain's mate said pleasantly. "And that's where we're going right back to, soon as we pick up a load of wounded in Naples. We'll be back in New York in, oh, I'd say two weeks—at the outside, that is."

"Back in New York in two weeks!" Mason said in even more awe.

Barclay and the others walked down the deck, where they could see various officers, male and female, standing by the rail looking earnestly at the beachhead, but Nelson stayed behind to converse some more with his fellow boatswain's mate. Barclay happened to glance over a little later and they seemed to be engaged in a serious discussion about something. After a while Nelson detached himself and came over to Barclay.

"Mr. Barclay, can I have a word with you?"

Nelson had an air of both urgency and secrecy and Barclay stepped aside with him.

"Mr. Barclay," Nelson said. "Did you notice the man I was talking to?"

"The boatswain's mate? Yes, I noticed."

"Name's Rollins. Regular Navy man. He and I were on the *Vincennes* together, in the old days."

"Well, that's nice," Barclay said. "I'm glad you ran across an old shipmate."

"Yes, that was quite a ship, the *Vincennes*," Nelson said gravely. "I always liked Rollins." He waited a moment then said: "He asked me if we could give them some tours of the beachhead."

"Tours of the beachhead?" Barclay said in astonishment.

"Of the harbor, that is," Lord Nelson said.

"Why in the hell do they want to tour the harbor?"

"Well, you know how it is. New people fresh over from the States. Do you realize, sir, that these people were all sitting in a bar at the Waldorf-Astoria Hotel ten days ago?" Lord Nelson said in what seemed to Barclay a rather generalized metaphor. "They're curious, you know."

"No, I didn't."

"Yes, sir, they're real curious to see that beachhead close up," Lord Nelson said. "Rollins knows we've got LCVPs, of course."

"Listen, Nelson, the captain isn't going to let you use the VPs to give any hospital ship people tours of the harbor. You know that. Besides, what if they got hit."

"It's their asses, Mr. Barclay," Lord Nelson said, gazing solemnly down a row of nurses down the deck leaning protrudingly over the rail and looking intently over at the scenery of war. It—that is, the row—made a panorama far more interesting to Barclay and Nelson than the beachhead.

"Well, you can forget it," Barclay said. "We couldn't do anything like conducting LCVP-tours of the beaches. It's out of the question."

"That's exactly what I told Rollins, Mr. Barclay!" Lord Nelson abruptly burst out in fervent agreement. He seemed now almost outraged that Rollins would even make such a suggestion. "I told him it was out of the question, just like you said. I told him I knew you and the captain wouldn't dream of it. We could get in a lot of trouble doing a thing like that, I made that very clear to him. I told him there would have to be a very large consideration before you and the captain would even *think* about it."

"A consideration? What do you mean, a consideration?" Barclay said suspiciously.

Lord Nelson came a little closer, looked around him to see if there were any eavesdroppers, as if he were about to reveal the operation plan for some fresh D-day assault, and spoke in conspiratorial tones.

"Mr. Barclay, I found out something. You'd never guess. This ship is practically an ice cream factory."

"Oh it is?"

"Yes sir, that it is. Practically an ice cream factory! They can turn out any amount of it they want. By the gallon. Any amount."

"That's very interesting," Barclay said drily.

"That's exactly what I felt," Lord Nelson said. "That it was very, very interesting. Well, sir, I told Rollins that we might just be able to give them one or two tours if there was a consideration of, say, two gallons per tour. He tried to settle for one gallon—can you imagine that?—and I told him it was out of the question. It had to be two gallons or the tours were absolutely off."

Barclay, who had not known that the tours were ever even on, looked closely at Nelson. "What did he say?" he asked tentatively.

"'Done!' is what he said, Mr. Barclay. They really want to make those tours—all these nurses and civilians in officers clothes you see around you here. Beg your pardon, sir."

"You mean they'll *pay* us to take nurses on a boat trip around the harbor?" Barclay said.

"Well, we couldn't do something like that for free, Mr. Barclay," Lord Nelson said, shocked at the idea.

Barclay looked carefully into the boatswain's mate's eyes. "Nelson, tell me just one thing. Did Rollins actually suggest these tours or did somebody else maybe?"

"Oh, no sir," Lord Nelson said. "I would hardly do that. Let's put it this way. Let's say it came out about the same time, from Rollins and me. Of course I might have been just a *second* before him. But the truth is, Mr. Barclay, it was one of those what you might call *simultaneous* inspirations for everybody's good."

"I see," Barclay said. He looked over the side. The LCT was about to shove off. "Let's get the hell on that LCT and go see the captain."

"Come on, you clunkheads!" Lord Nelson immediately bawled out, his voice booming like a Klaxon horn down the deck. The heads of a covey of nurses and commanders snapped around startled, but Nelson was only addressing the visitors from the *LST 1826* in the friendly tones they recognized. They bounded below and were aboard the LCT seconds before it cast off.

They were going back when Lord Nelson mentioned some more of his conversation with his former *Vincennes* shipmate.

"There was just one other thing Rollins told me, Mr. Barclay. He said if we had any souvenirs, well, they'd be mighty interested in souvenirs of the beachhead."

"How much?" Barclay said at once.

"Well, we didn't get down to complete particulars. Naturally I'd want to clear something like that with you first. But anything of a German character," Lord Nelson said carefully. "Helmets, anything like that—well, sir, let me put it this way. I think it's a seller's market on that hospital ship. That's my judgment."

"Very refreshing," Barclay said. "Except that we don't have any German helmets—or things like that."

"No, but they do ashore. Rollins also said they would be interested in American helmets that had been in action."

Barclay looked carefully at the boatswain's mate. "They certainly seem interested in helmet-collecting."

"It's a good war souvenir," Nelson said in the tones of a connoisseur. "Nice and solid. Suggests the real thing. Mr. Barclay, I tell you, that hospital ship is a gold mine. They're just loaded with things we could use—lighters, fountain pens, I don't know what all. Not to mention all that ice cream. I don't think we should let them get away without transacting a little business. We might never have a chance like this again, Mr. Barclay."

The LCT, whose course to the beach went near the place where the 1826 was anchored, dropped them at the ship. Barclay went in to see the captain and explained the offer.

"The men have really got ice cream on the brain now, Captain," he said.

The captain gave Barclay about the same careful appraising look Barclay had given Nelson when the boatswain's mate first told him of the proposal.

"I hadn't exactly planned on our conducting Circle Boat tours of the harbor," he said. He thought a moment then looked at Barclay again. "Two gallons of ice cream—that's for each trip?"

"Two gallons for each trip," Barclay said. "That's the deal. Lord Nelson worked it out."

"Ice cream. I wouldn't mind some myself." Suddenly the captain's eyes narrowed. "Very well. Take one of the boats and put Nelson in charge. And do this. Put a signalman aboard with semaphore flags."

"A signalman, Captain?"

"If we're going to do it, we might as well do it right. Tell Nelson to keep in touch with the ship by semaphoring and we'll let him know when we're shoving off. He can keep those tours going until then. If we're going to have ice cream, we might as well have enough."

Barclay came back out and passed the captain's approval on to

Nelson. Just before the boatswain's mate turned aft to get the LCVP lowered away he paused thoughtfully.

"Would it be all right if we collected a few souvenirs for additional trading material, Mr. Barclay?"

Barclay decided he would grant that one on his own responsibility. "I suppose if we're going into business we might as well diversify."

"How's that, Mr. Barclay?"

"It's okay for the souvenirs," Barclay said.

Immediately the boatswain's mate moved aft, paused in a group of men, and for perhaps ten minutes stood giving various earnest instructions, and putting Gunner's Mate First Class James Plimpton in charge of the souvenir party as being most suitable to the job. Then he hastily assembled an LCVP crew of Boland for coxswain and Chatham for motor machinist's mate along with Porterfield, Abbot, and Mason to lend help to passengers assumed to be unaccustomed to getting in and out of small boats.

"Hadn't we ought to get cleaned up a little, Lord Nelson?" Mason asked. "For them nurses, I mean."

"No time, jughead," Lord Nelson said. "It'd cost ice cream. Besides they'll like it better this way. They see plenty of people in clean uniforms every day. What they want is local color."

"We got plenty of that," Mason said, looking over the crew in dirty dungarees, grease-spotted T-shirts, battered boondock shoes cut down at the tops, sailor's hats dyed with blue paint, and faces still unshaven from their watch.

The LCVP was lowered, the men got in, and Boland made over to the gleaming hospital ship. Soon the tours were underway. The nurses were immaculate in their crisp new uniforms but then so were the medical officers in theirs. The chief difference was in their shape, the nurses appearing exceedingly trim, while many of the medical officers were shielded with an amount of flabby corpulence unusual in a naval officer. The latter appeared all to be commanders and lieutenant commanders and the newness of their gold braid was almost blinding and the contrast to their escorting crew startling. The LST men helped both nurses and commanders very carefully into the boat. As the VP passed various ships enroute to the beach the ship's companies of many vessels hastened to the side to stare down at this astonishing cargo.

The reason for those uniforms looking as if they were just out of a box yesterday and their wearers commissioned hardly before, soon became plain in the talk overheard by Lord Nelson and the others. This was exactly the case of it. The hospital ship was staffed, it turned out, by a unit of doctors, nurses, and technicians lifted intact from a large civilian hospital and kept together. It was a system used a good deal by both the Army and the Navy during the war, the point being that such a team contained all the varieties of medical skills and its members were accustomed to working with each other practicing them. All you needed to do was take them out of their business suits and the like, drape them in naval clothes, and you had a first-class working medical unit ready to go. It was a sage system. But it did not mean that the unit's members, though wearing uniforms and gold braid, in some cases of decidedly high rank, knew the most elementary naval things. They were brilliant doctors and good nurses and they were as complete civilians as farmers in Idaho. Having discovered all this, more or less, Lord Nelson felt he had a good deal explained to him. He felt better. Nelson always liked to know what he was dealing with in any situation. These were just a bunch of civilians, really, and if he treated them more or less accordingly he would be all right. He found himself liking them. The doctors and nurses had obviously known each other a long time and they laughed and chattered like old friends on an outing.

"Isn't this exciting though, honey?"

Lord Nelson was snapped out of his reverie, but the little nurse with the blonde curls and the figure of an indented torpedo was only addressing a fellow nurse in her natural southern idiom.

"Sailor," he heard one of the full-bodied commanders address him, "we want to get just as close to the war as possible. So don't you be afraid of taking us in close. We want to see what it's like."

"I'll do my best, sir," Lord Nelson said.

"We want to see everything, sailor," the commander said.

"I'll certainly try to show you officers the whole works," Lord Nelson said.

Each trip Nelson had Boland take the LCVP in close and then turn upbeach. About the only things visible were shell-fractured trees, beach, and occasionally some soldiers who gawked back at them, but the passengers seemed very thrilled by it. Once when they saw a burned-out tank they were almost ecstatic. Nelson, since it was a per-trip arrangement, tried not to make any one trip too long, but he did try to give fair value by perching himself on the engine cover and offering a running commentary on Anzio to his enthralled listeners.

"At first there were quite a few mines in the harbor," his voice sang out, so clearly that it sometimes attracted the attention of soldiers on shore, who looked up curiously. "The Navy got them out—this is done with something called minesweepers. Now this very same boat you ladies and officers are riding in landed troops on the very beach you're looking at." The nurses and medical officers looked with keen interest around the historic craft. "We do that by going on the beach and putting the ramp down. The ramp is that part right up there in front of you ladies. The little rungs you see on it are for a lookout." Immediately some of the nurses, their attention called to the rungs, approached the ramp and climbed up a way to get a better view of things. "Now beyond those trees somewhere are the German positions. They have the advantage of having the higher ground. This is truly an advantage, the beach being at sea level . . ."

Meantime back on the LST the souvenir detail under Plimpton was keeping itself very busy. The word of the treasure-house of a ship anchored out there in the harbor, fresh from the States and ready for a fresh trip back there, spread quickly. Middleton, Wiley, Rutledge, and even Lieutenants (jg) Abernethy and Fairchild, as the day went on, and finally virtually the entire ship's company were caught up in the project and turned to with a will. One heavily laden working party under Abernethy's command was dispatched ashore to seek out souvenirs from the Army, to whom they traded off various ship items such as candy bars, cigarettes, and Aqua Velva lotion in exchange for German helmets,

German field knives, and assorted other former Teutonic possessions. Some of the German and American helmets Abernethy's
party brought back were defective in that they were insufficiently
damaged, which would have lowered their trading value seriously,
but Gunner's Mate Plimpton restored it by treating them with a
.45, so that soon all of them had appropriate holes and jagged
edges until the supply of .45 ammunition began to run low and
the crew had to use a sledge hammer to apply the needful dents.
The crew spent a very full day, both collecting and manufacturing
and improving souvenirs, and the ship rang with the sounds of
pistol-fire and metal crashing against metal. It was extremely hard
work, working as they were against time, especially getting the
steel helmets in proper condition, these having been designed to
withstand a good deal of assault of any kind whether by friend
or foe.

On the LCVP the men were enjoying their work. Everybody,
in fact, was having a fine time. These doctors were damn nice
guys, Lord Nelson decided. They may have looked a little pudgy
and lumpy in their uniforms, which they wore about like business
suits, the coats often unbuttoned, but he had always heard that
doctors never took care of themselves, they were too busy taking
care of other people. They shoved their braided caps back on
their heads if they felt like it and most of them smoked like
fiends, though often they had to have one of the crew light the
cigarette for them in the slight breeze the boat made by its
movement. An air of warm comradeship soon prevailed in the
small, 36-foot confines of the LCVP. The doctors chatted in a
very democratic way with the crew—they didn't act a bit like
officers—and the nurses, if anything, were even more democratic
and interested, judging by the frankly admiring looks cast by
them upon the boat's crew, who looked almost spectacularly male
and muscled alongside the pale and bloated doctors.

"You men certainly appear in excellent condition," the nurse
with the blonde curls, who incredibly seemed to be making every
trip, said to Lord Nelson.

"Well, we get lots of outdoor exercise, ma'am," Lord Nelson
said.

"I'll just bet you do. What do you do, honey?"

Boatswain's Mate Nelson could hardly believe she was addressing him but obviously she was.

"What do I do?" he stammered. "Why, I don't know how to describe it, ma'am. I do things around the deck."

"It sounds terribly interesting."

"Oh, it's interesting all right," Lord Nelson said. Christ, he thought, what a build. He knew he was blushing terribly from its obviousness. The nurse, however, seemed entirely unaware of all those sweet little bulges, or at least of the intensity of their impact.

"Hey, sweetie. I can't get this cigarette lighted. Will you do it for me?"

"Be glad to." The nurse handed the cigarette across. He could see the delicate trace of lipstick on it. Even Lord Nelson, who could ordinarily light a cigarette in a Force-Seven gale, required two matches to get this one on fire in his cupped hands. He passed it back to her.

"Why, honey, your hands are shaking."

"I've had this bad cold and chills," Lord Nelson said, laying on a racking cough. "Being outdoors so much I guess."

"Well, you take care of it, you hear now?"

Each time the LCVP headed back with its satisfied passengers to the hospital ship, Abbot stood up on the engine cover and using a pair of flags semaphored the ship to see if they had time for one more tour of the beachhead. The passengers were even fascinated by this display of seamanship and Abbot laid it on with a flourish, flapping the flags smartly. Late afternoon Nelson brought the boat by the LST and took on quite a large cargo of assorted objects. Dusk was not far off when the LCVP reluctantly made its sixth and last harbor tour. They had time to make that one only because Captain Adler signaled the boat that the ship would pick it up on the way out. Heading upbeach in the slowly ending day, Lord Nelson, while giving his beachhead commentary which he knew so well by now, got to thinking a great deal about the imminent ice cream. He was further relaxed by talking with the little blonde nurse who had almost attached herself to him. By now he realized that the words "Hey honey" and "Hey sweetie" were merely her method of addressing any and everyone, as someone else might say "Hey Mac" or "Hey jughead." Nevertheless, the words sounded astonishingly soothing on his ear when he heard himself so addressed.

"Why it's so peaceful here you could almost take a swim, honey."

This observation was hardly out of her very pretty mouth when a moderate geyser of water erupted in the sea about 1500 feet away. Lord Nelson, somewhat startled out of his beatific contemplations, realized suddenly that they must have come quite a distance upshore and be pretty near German positions.

"What do you imagine that was, honey?"

"What was that, sailor?" one of the officers asked Nelson in some alarm. His three commander's gold stripes flashed in the sun.

"I beg your pardon, sir?" Nelson said.

"That splash. Isn't that the kind of splash a shell makes?"

"Possibly, sir," Nelson said.

"Possibly? What else could it be?"

"It's hard to say, sir," Lord Nelson said studiously. "Anyhow it's nothing to worry about, I'm sure, sir. I think it's one of ours."

The officer pondered this answer for a moment and the more he thought about it the less satisfied he was with the explanation. In fact, he presently became quite irritated.

"What the hell difference does it make whose it is?" he said. "If one of them falls on us, I don't imagine it'll be of great importance whether it's American or German, will it?"

"You've got a point there, sir," Nelson said. "We just wanted to get you officers as close to the war as possible, like you wanted."

"We appreciate that, of course, but let's not overdo it, shall we? Don't forget, sailor, we have women aboard this craft."

"Oh, no sir, I couldn't forget that, sir," Lord Nelson said, looking carefully at a group of them by the gunwale studying the beachhead, as well as that part of the sea where the water had been disturbed.

At this moment another splash kicked up slightly closer, perhaps a thousand feet off.

"Boland!" Lord Nelson's voice sang out, but still in the tone of a casual command. "End of the tour. Take us back to the hospital ship. Now out there," Lord Nelson began addressing the passengers, focusing their attention seaward as the boat turned sharply, "you see one of our newer destroyers, the *Hilary P. Jones*. The *Hilary P.*, a two-piper, has a fine record of bombardment, being fitted out with five-inch guns . . ."

He thought how it was just as well that the little incident occurred on the last trip. Conceivably it could have discouraged subsequent tours. He was just reflecting on this fortunate circumstance when it happened.

Lord Nelson did not see her at first. He was contemplating with esthetic satisfaction the beautiful lines of the *Hilary P. Jones* and thinking with a certain nostalgia of the years he had done destroyer duty when his peripheral vision was caught by a figure on the bow ramp. Even seen peripherally it was a girlish figure beyond question and as something of a warning nature came upon him and he turned his eyes full forward he could identify her even in this arresting position as the little blonde for whom he had been lighting cigarettes. She was climbing up on the narrow, ladder-like rungs of the ramp to get a better view, presumably of the seascape in general and the *Hilary P. Jones* in particular. She went quite high up. Poised there on the bow ramp, she offered quite a view of her own, seeming for a quick moment like a ship's figurehead of older days and ships, a very delectable looking figurehead. About that moment the boat's passengers were electrified by a tremendous roar of five-inch gunfire erupting from the *Hilary P.*, which was apparently taking under fire whatever it was that was lobbing those shells out into the water. The LCVP by this time was close enough to the destroyer to feel the blast from her guns and even close enough to hear someone aboard her suddenly shouting with what seemed great anger through a megaphone: "LCVP! LCVP! Get the hell out

of here! At once! Repeat. At once!" The boat had apparently
wandered very nearly into the destroyer's line of fire. "That's
pretty discourteous to shout like that," Lord Nelson observed to
a speechless commander standing alongside him. "Probably some
new ensign. Boland! Bring her to port ten degrees." Turning, the
boat hit a hard groundswell of a sea wave, Lord Nelson knew
only that the figure which had been serving as the VP's figurehead was no longer doing so, and simultaneously he heard one
of the crew—Mason, he believed—sing out the terrifying words.

"Woman overboard!"

Coxswain Boland acted instantly, without waiting for any orders. He was a very good coxswain, Boland. He backed the boat
down, his reflexes telling him that the one immediate thing was
not to overrun this attractive object. They wouldn't have anyway,
as it turned out, but nonetheless it was a good and proper reflex.
The object had pitched overboard, it was seen immediately, not
directly over the bow but slightly to starboard of it, where they
could see her blonde head bobbing in the sea. Almost instanta-
neously, also without waiting for orders, three men—Mason,
Porterfield, and Abbot—were atop the gunwale and diving into the
water. Two commanders and one lieutenant commander had
started to climb up to jump in before Mason and Abbot shoved
them selflessly if rather roughly back, Lord Nelson hearing Mason
call out, "We'll get her, sir! We know these waters better!" It
had all happened in a flash. Boland turned and started circling
the figures in the water. From the boat the horrified onlookers
could see the three men racing toward the curly head. And presently as they reached her it almost seemed that the poor girl
would drown, not from the sea itself, but from what appeared
to be a process of the three men fighting over who should save
her. Doubtless it was only their eagerness to avoid catastrophe,
but Lord Nelson was certain he heard at least two voices sing out
rather angrily, "I've got her!"

The biggest of the men was Porterfield and due probably to
his strength he managed to take possession of the rescue-ee.
Presently he was towing her in. Many hands reached over the
gunwale as Porterfield, pushing up out of the water, hoisted the

dripping creature aloft and almost catapulted her into the boat and directly into the arms of Lord Nelson, where she clung for several moments, pasted against him. Then she had freed herself. Abruptly a trill of a laugh came from her.

"What a silly thing to do," she said.

She was neither abashed nor frightened. She might have returned from an impulsive swim with her clothes on. Lord Nelson didn't know what consistency nurses' uniforms were made of dry but wet they appeared to be made of clinging, very nearly transparent cellophane. He tried to look away in his embarrassment but that was obviously impossible with his duties in command of the boat requiring him to look dead ahead and indeed through her. He would just have to suffer the embarrassment. And the thing now was to get her immediately back to the hospital ship before she caught pneumonia or something. Nelson ordered Boland to put on speed and the coxswain had just revved up when they heard some shouts from the water. In focusing their attention on the rescued, they had almost forgotten the rescuers. Porterfield, Mason, and Abbot were pulled in and the boat got underway for the hospital ship with maximum rpm's. Returning, none of the doctors or nurses, including in particular the potential victim, was in the least alarmed by the experience. The blonde nurse's own reaction had changed the whole mood of the incident. From one of aghastness it became one which suggested this was the greatest of larks. Indeed by the time they reached the hospital ship they were laughing hilariously, almost hysterically about the whole thing. Unfortunately one of the larger doctors had given the nurse his coat. It came almost to her knees.

Back at the hospital ship the wet nurse went aboard first, amid a chatter of excitement from her shipmates and after kissing Porterfield thoroughly to show her appreciation. Then the others, with many thanks to the crew and a considerable amount of odd laughter, were handed off. And so the last tour was deposited safely back aboard. The payment of twelve gallons of rich, good, American ice cream was taken into the LCVP. Then the LCVP crew passed over a full dozen scarred, battered, jagged, and bullet-ridden helmets, both German and American, three German flags, two German field knives, four German canteens, a boxful of various German rank insignia, assorted items of German uniforms, and other German memorabilia. These were very eagerly received and in gratitude there passed back from the mercy ship to the LCVP, in addition to the ice cream, a number of cigarette lighters, fountain pens, several decks of fresh playing cards, two pairs of barber's clippers, four wrist watches, two electrical razors, some doctor or nurse's personal phonograph and a supply of records, and similar items, all of which had one thing in common, that they were very hard to come by in the Mediterranean. It was a good deal for everyone concerned, increasing the sum of human happiness for the soldiers, who got a large quantity of candy bars, cigarettes, Aqua Velva and a number of other usable articles; for the LST crew, which got the above haul in addition to all that ice cream; and even for the hospital ship personnel themselves, who besides the beachhead harbor tours got assorted real and doctored souvenirs of the war—and not a soul could ever then or in future years tell one from the other.

The LCVP was just finishing the happy task, taking on the last portions of its payment, when an extremely smart-looking craft slid in just aft of them and moored to the gangway. An older man stepped briskly out and Lord Nelson, who was directing the taking on of the cargo, idly noticed the two stars on his collar tabs. He was a little disturbed, on general principles, to see a rear admiral in the vicinity, and guessed that he had come out for some kind of inspection of the hospital ship. He decided, also just on general principles, that it would be on the side of prudence for them to get out of there as quickly as possible. He turned to tell Abbot and Mason to step lively. It may have been Nelson's voice that caught the admiral's attention. Nelson did have a distinctive voice. In any event the admiral turned and looked with a kind of idle curiosity at the proceedings. Mason and Abbot were just handing up the last of the souvenirs—two remarkably spent German helmets—and taking on the last of the barter, the phonograph and records. The admiral stood no more than fifteen feet away on the gangway, and appeared for a moment to focus through the light which was beginning to fail.

Something about Nelson must have interested him for he took a couple of steps nearer the boatswain's mate. At that moment something about the admiral intensely interested Nelson.

"Hurry up with that cargo, you men there!" he spoke up convincingly to Abbot and Mason.

"Young man, haven't I seen you somewhere before?" he heard a voice.

Lord Nelson looked up. He saluted. "Me, sir? Well, sir, I've served in a lot of ships, Admiral."

"Regular Navy, eh?" the admiral said approvingly. "How long, son?"

"Eighteen years, sir," Lord Nelson said.

"Eighteen years!" the admiral exclaimed in further approbation. Then a kind of light seemed to come to him. "You weren't just by any chance on the Vincennes, were you?"

"That's it, Admiral!" Lord Nelson brightened, in gratitude for meeting still another shipmate of his cruiser days. "The old Vincennes, sir!"

"A good ship, the Vincennes," the admiral said nostalgically.

"None better, sir."

"Well, I wish we had time for a chat about those Vincennes days," the admiral said. "But I'm due aboard here and I see you're about to shove off. Good luck, son!"

For the first time in his long Navy career, Lord Nelson was saluted first by an admiral, even though it was just a loose touch of the hat before he turned to go. Nelson saluted smartly back and turned urgently to Boland.

"Cast off, Cox'n!"

Lord Nelson saw the admiral pause halfway across the gangway and turn thoughtfully.

"You know, I think I've seen you somewhere else, though. I believe . . ."

By that time, however, the LCVP was already moving away. And it was soon some little distance off, enough to claim in any event to be out of earshot, when Nelson heard a voice come rather urgently over the water.

"Say there, I remember—I think. Nelson! That's it. Lord Nelson! Come back here a moment!"

They couldn't hear the admiral though, they figured. Lord Nelson had not the courage to look around, until they were still further off. As they made through the dusk with their precious cargo, they could see the nurses standing along the rail of the hospital ship waving down to them, including the rescued one who was wearing a white bathrobe below her blonde curls. She was a vision, she and the ship, big and clean and white and full of mercy there in the harbor, with the blue dusk coming on behind her in the Tyrrhenian sky. He worried about it for a little while on the way out to the LST, then forgot it. He had never been a worrier. He was glad, however, that his recognition vision was still acute, sufficient anyhow to detect fully clothed an admiral he had seen only in underpants. That recognition had just given him enough opportunity to speed things up and get the boat away. Then the LCVP was rendezvousing with the LST as the ship was leaving the harbor and was hoisted aboard, snug in its davits. The twelve gallons were handed down very carefully, then the other objects.

That night the twelve gallons were enough for every member of the ninety and nine to have two, large, stomach-filling dishes of ice cream. It tasted wonderful after the long abstinence and everyone agreed there was nothing to eat anyone would have chosen over American ice cream. Everyone agreed, too, that it was a nice way to end their thirtieth trip to the beachhead. Mason and Abbot went around calling "Hey honey" and "Hey sweetie" to Lord Nelson then laughing outlandishly. Someone suggested Porterfield should be put in for a life-saving medal and the helmsman said any good work contained its own reward, which brought forth an inordinate amount of ribald laughter. It was a very happy ship going back and in addition a smooth, summery sea again. Several sailors sat on Number 2 hatch contentedly listening to Carlyle play some guitar pieces, among them the hymn "The Ninety and Nine."

12

AN EVENING AND AN HOUR

That night Sarah was not off duty until midnight and had no liberty even then so that Barclay was to see her at that time, and only for one hour, in the hospital, to sit and talk with her. He had called Shanley and arranged to use his jeep. Shanley suggested he spend the evening until his hour's date with him.

"I have a remarkable treat in store for you, old man," he said. "Tonight you are going to meet positively the most beautiful, desirable thing in the entire Mediterranean theater."

"Haven't I heard that statement before?" Barclay said.

"Well, I have met a few over here—but nothing like this." Shanley did actually sound somewhat in awe. "This is the one we've all been waiting for. Everything that went before was just to pass the time."

Barclay arrived at the officers club about nine and looked around for Shanley's table. The place was so jammed with officers and their women drinking and dancing that for a while he couldn't find him. Then he saw Shanley waving to him across the vast room like a signalman semaphoring and he edged his way over, weaving in and out the tables. The girl was sitting sideways to Barclay's approach and not until he came up did he get a look at her. Shanley talked about girls so much that after a while most of it had ceased to register with Barclay. But when he saw this one, it registered very distinctly. She had a face classic in its Italian structure, smooth and light olive; a thinness that was very attractive, seeming, at least, from a natural build rather than from hunger. But most of all there was about her some quality, uncertain but visible as any feature, that seemed to embrace, as in a frame, something close to a purity of physical beauty; uncertain but seeming to Barclay to be close as he could define it to a kind of innocence, yet strong; innocence, or perhaps naturalness; a lack of hardness that made her seem entirely out of place with the rest of the women in that room. She did not seem a thing that could ever conceivably be bought and sold. She appeared very young. As Shanley introduced them she looked up at him and smiled. Then he realized that he had seen her before. He had last seen her being put into an ambulance, with her baby, from the LST. And he knew, too, that she had recognized him at the same moment.

"Buona sera, signorina."

"Buona sera, Tenente."

Later he had danced with her in that gay, crowded room. Everything about it seemed strange. The opulence of it was overpowering to him tonight, the bar with its teeming wealth of liquor, the rich velvet of the draperies, the softness of the chairs, the sparkling of the chandelier, the smoothness of the orchestra, the sensuous luxuriousness of the women whose availability for pleasure so shouted itself. All of it jarred against him tonight and then he knew why—it jarred against the sweetness he felt in her, the natural dignity she emanated. It didn't seem possible that she could be there. He kept remembering her on the wardroom table, where she had seemed to him, for some reason he never went into, and possibly, he thought, in a moment of excessive, wishful, or even irrational idealization, almost the very embodiment of purity.

"Lieutenant," she said. "May I tell you what you are thinking. You are thinking ill things of me, aren't you? You're thinking that I should not be here."

"Why shouldn't you?"

"Because of Red. I think you know about us. He talks about you."

"He talks about you to me, too."

"What does he say, Lieutenant?"

"Well, he says you're a very bright young lady, he likes very much being with you, and so on, and so on . . . That's my full report," he said lightly. "Yourself. Are you in love with him?"

"Probably not now," she said thoughtfully. "But perhaps it will be. He is a very good man."

"That he is. I am glad you know it."

"Oh I do. But it is not just that."

"It isn't? Oh, I see. You mean he's in love with you?"

"He has not said so." He felt she was very truthful. "But I imagine he is, or certainly will be."

She said this in such a way, so matter-of-factly as to take away any suggestion of vanity, but also as if no one she offered the opportunity of falling in love with her could possibly help doing so—an assumption which he believed might be entirely well founded, that he had to laugh.

"Yes, I guess he probably will," he said. "If all that love is going to be there, signorina, how can you do this?"

"How do you mean, Lieutenant?"

"I mean be here."

"They are two different things. I have to have some kind of life, Lieutenant. I would die in that room where I am. Here I can at least live a little. And Lieutenant Shanley is very nice."

"Yes. Shanley is an old friend of mine."

"And that is wonderful food they have at the villa where Lieutenant Shanley lives. Nowhere in Italy outside the military can one get food like that."

"Yes, I've eaten there."

"Do you know what I had for dinner last night, Lieutenant? One small can of cold C-ration. Nothing else."

"Yes, I know."

"Do you? And do you know what I had for dinner tonight? Macaroni, fish, steak, peas, potatoes, cake, fruit, cheese, and all the bread and butter I could eat."

He smiled. "You don't look as if all that would go into you."

"You should have seen me tonight and you would see how it went into me. However, I put it in me with manners."

He smiled again. "I'm sure of it."

"Do you know how long it is since I have had food like that, Lieutenant? Or even a decent meal?"

"I understand, signorina. Be clear that I understand. I don't find anything simple, believe me."

"Except that one needs to eat. That is simple. It is nice to be full of food just once in a while, Lieutenant. And one needs a little life of some kind," she said, looking around her.

"Some life," he said.

"Do you judge me, Lieutenant?"

"No," he said. "Things being as they are around here, Americans aren't in a very good position to judge."

"Are you going to tell Carlyle?" she asked.

He waited a moment. "I don't know," he said then.

She smiled up at him, her face free of all contriving, innocent, just liking him.

"Do as you think best, Lieutenant," she said. She smiled a little, as if whatever would happen would happen. And she held to him a little more tightly. He admired her absence of fear, and her refusal to worry, or to beg. No one could help liking her. She was as natural as a child.

As they turned in their dancing, he looked down at her again. There seemed to him something else familiar that he couldn't place. Then he remembered. Her dress. It was the dress Sarah had tried on that day in Shanley's room, the one he had liked best.

The musette bag had made quite a difference in Coco's life and, for a while, in her spirits. It came whenever Carlyle came and it transported items which gave her a great deal of satisfaction. Depending on their availibility at the ship's store Carlyle could buy limited amounts of cigarettes, soap, candy bars, chewing gum, toothpaste, and the like and he brought her all of these, along with such items as the K-rations and C-rations. It was a momentous occasion for her when he was able to get, from the ship's galley, a can of peaches. She ate them while he was there and she hardly needed to tell him how wonderful they tasted to her. Even to the baby, to whom she spooned out the syrup from the peaches, that was a very special occasion. These various items were no great trouble for Carlyle to bring and he felt fully rewarded by her happiness in getting them. It gave him a pleasure of a kind he had never known. Between one visit and another the items she didn't use disappeared. They never discussed what happened to them. Carlyle knew, of course, that she was disposing of them in some manner, and that they were responsible for a somewhat better life for her. For a dress for herself; a dress for the baby; for the food of which there was now more in the apartment. Even a few items from the ship went a long way. What it added up to was that the musette bag was supporting the girl and her child.

Yet life was still desperately hard for Coco. The things Carlyle brought and the money enabled her and her baby to live, but just that; the lesson money paid for one or at the most two bottles of milk on the black market, and while a bar of soap brought a hundred lire or one American dollar, this in turn purchased but one small loaf of bread. And she enjoyed the time with Carlyle very much. But there were the long days when his ship was gone. And her life had nothing resembling gaiety in it. It never had one full meal even. It had nothing but survival.

Without being at all aware that he was doing so, it was the boy Rebi who had introduced Coco to a much larger world.

One day when Shanley came down to pick up Barclay, Rebi, who often hung about the docks, approached the jeep. He grinned widely and spoke to Barclay. The boy had a very engaging way about him and Barclay smiled back and talked with him for a little. Rebi then asked if he could ride into the city with them. It was certainly all right with Shanley and the boy, with some kind of sack he was carrying, hopped into the back seat. On the way in Shanley heard the story of Rebi's stowing away aboard the ship and was delighted by it. It was the story which undoubtedly prompted Shanley to invite Rebi to stop by his room with them. The boy looked at the room in great wonder and before he left to go about whatever errand had brought him into Naples, Shanley gave him a couple of K-rations.

Rebi had, in fact, gone into the city to dispose of some of the items Carlyle had brought to Coco. She had been employing the boy for this purpose and Rebi was very proficient at it. He brought her back good sums for the cans of food, the bars of soap, the packages of cigarettes she entrusted to him. It was a good arrangement for both of them. It enabled three people to eat: Coco, Rebi, and Coco's child. The boy had been more useful than even Carlyle had visualized when he brought him to stay with her.

Thereafter, when he went to the city on his mission, Rebi sometimes dropped by Shanley's villa on the chance the officer was again going down to the ship and if so, to hitch a ride with him. Usually the officer was out, but one day the boy came up to the villa just as Shanley was coming out of it, on his way to pick up Barclay. The boy climbed in the jeep and they drove to Pozzuoli. If it had not been for the fact that the boy talked in such a winning way, and made excellent company actually, Shanley would probably have dropped him on some corner near his destination. But they were conversing enjoyably and he continued, dropping him by the very place he said he was going to.

Perhaps if he had been five minutes earlier, or five later, it would never have happened. In the first instance he would have seen Carlyle enter the house. In the second Coco would have been gone on the errand she was waiting to do as soon as Carlyle got there to stay with the baby. As it was she was just leaving the house when the jeep drove up, to go down the street to a place where she would trade the bar of soap which Carlyle had just brought her for a half litre of milk for the baby. She had the soap clutched in her hand now as she came down the stairs and out of the house and saw Rebi climbing out of the jeep. Shanley looked once at this girl, and made no move to drive on even when Rebi was out of the jeep. For a moment he looked from her face to the bar of American soap in her hand. Then, realizing she was embarrassed to be carrying the soap, he looked back quickly at her. Rebi, as if sensing everything and, with an intelligent boy's perception, everything that might be from this meeting, made no move to introduce the two of them, but, ducking his head, started around Coco and toward the stairs.

"Rebi," Shanley called. "Here, I've got something for you."

Shanley reached in the dash compartment, where he always kept something, and got out a K-ration. The boy walked back slowly to the jeep and took it almost reluctantly.

"Rebi," the officer said. "You haven't introduced me to the signorina."

The boy did so, hurriedly, then walked around the girl and started up the stairs.

That was all it took. If there was one thing on this earth certain insofar as Lieutenant (jg) Shanley was concerned, it was that he would never let a girl like that get away without arranging to see her. As for the girl herself, no one could have been more ready for a little gaiety in her life. And there was no place more gay in Naples than the officers club. In a way it was the only such place.

Rebi, feeling somehow guilty without entirely knowing why, never mentioned anything to his friend Carlyle. Nor did he go again to Shanley's villa to hitch a ride to Pozzuoli. The only thing new in his life was that Coco now needed him to baby-sit when Carlyle's ship was away. Anyway it was a nice baby.

It was a different life now. It even included differences that neither Rebi, nor any of the others involved in it, knew about. For some time now, as he went about his marketing of the things Carlyle brought and Coco passed on to him, Rebi had been followed by two men. They had, among other places, followed him to the villa that day and saw him get in a jeep marked BOMB DISPOSAL. These men who followed him were members of the American CID, which initials stood for Criminal Investigation Division.

For a few moments, driving away from the club, Barclay could not get out of his mind the image of her on the wardroom table, then this juxtaposed against the fresh memory of her in that club. For one moment he even thought of going back and telling Shanley to stop it, that the girl belonged to Carlyle. Then he thought, the hell with it. Nobody belonged to anybody, especially now. And he had never been fond of rearranging people's lives for them. He drove on up the hill.

Sarah had told him that if he wanted to come at eleven he could be with her some in her rounds and then when she was off at midnight they could sit and talk an hour. She could not leave the hospital that night and he would have to be out by 1 A.M. When he got there and she came into the lobby he thought how many different clothes now he had seen her in—the field clothes that first time on the ship; the nurse's "leave" uniform when they went out; the dresses she had tried on with such enjoyment that time in Shanley's room; and now the white working uniform and the white cap. She looked good in anything to him, and, he had an idea, to anybody.

"I'm glad you came up here even though I couldn't go out," she said.

"Well, I tore myself away from the officers club. It wasn't so hard."

"I'm glad it wasn't," she said.

They went in and she introduced him to the doctor and they went through a couple of wards, where the doctor and she checked down the long rows of the wounded. Most had some part or another missing, a Pfc. with a leg left on the slopes of Cassino, a second lieutenant blind from a shell burst, a destroyer ensign nearly one entire bandage from burns when his ship sank off Anzio. Barclay looked at the ensign's tag on the foot of the bed in case he knew him but he didn't. He was glad when it was over and they came back into the lobby.

"Let's sit in the jeep," she said. "That's probably the most private place around here."

They walked out of the hospital and down the steps. The big letters BOMB DISPOSAL jumped out through the night. She laughed as they came up to it.

"I don't know why it always seems so funny for us to be getting in a jeep that says 'Bomb Disposal.'"

"This is about the most un-private jeep on the Italian peninsula," he said. "I always feel a fraud in it. Everyone I pass thinks I'm the bomb-disposal officer."

They got in. "Matthew," she said in a moment, "you've never told me about yourself—your people I mean and where you were before the war."

"Well, I'll say this. I think my father might have liked your father. They could have held a conversation in Greek. But I'll bet yours couldn't in Hebrew."

She smiled. "No, he couldn't. Could yours?"

"Fluently. He's a minister and he studied Hebrew and Greek so he could read the Old and New Testaments in their original languages. And he really could. When I was a boy I went with him once when he was to speak in a synagogue. He startled everybody by giving his talk in Hebrew."

She laughed. "I believe I would like your father."

"I think so. Somebody said that intense religious conviction drives the person who has it to either the greatest good or the greatest evil; that the best things in history have been done in the name of religion, and the worst things. I think it may be true from what I've seen. Dad is one of the first kind."

"You never thought of being a minister?"

He laughed quietly. "No. I never did. Did you ever think of being a nurse after the war?"

"No." Then she added: "But I am glad I'm doing it now. For the duration."

"For the duration," he repeated. It was a phrase. Forever, he sometimes felt, would have been a better one.

"Continue, please. Where were you before the war?"

"Well. I was at a little college in Wisconsin. Lawrence College at Appleton. Except for one year in there, at the University of Florence. A freak which Dad worked out passing through Italy on a trip his church gave him to the Holy Land. Then I had one year of law school, at Yale. Then I was a ninety-day wonder for the Navy."

"Are you going back to law school?"

"Yes. But I've never been sure I wanted to *be* a lawyer. But I felt I'd like to study it."

"To do what then?"

"I don't know. I never quite figured it out. I felt I was getting pretty close to figuring it out before the war came along. Then I stopped thinking about it."

"Where had you got to in the figuring?"

He laughed shortly. "I'm not sure. I used to think I wanted to write. My father had a lot of books around, not just religious books. He had more non-religious books as a matter-of-fact. I read quite a bit."

"What did you read?"

"Oh, I read a lot. Mostly the standard things. Dickens, Thackeray, Conrad, James, Twain. I liked Conrad very much. Maybe I started loving the sea with him. And I liked St. Augustine, you'll be glad to know."

She laughed. "Will I? I've never read him."

"Well you should. And I read everything I could find about the English kings. I always liked reading about the English kings."

"You don't sound like a lawyer."

"Well, the law as practice isn't the big thing with me."

"What is?"

"I don't know. Mainly I want to look around some. I'd like to travel around the world for a couple years if I could and then I think I'll know. I've always felt I would never know until I got that traveling in. All I know right now is that I want to get the law degree, to travel—and to live a lot. Don't we all."

They were talking very quietly. "You sound as if you would do it. You're one of those who will do it."

"Am I?" He laughed a little. "Yes, I believe I am, as a matter-of-fact."

"You don't talk much about yourself, that's why."

"Don't I?" He laughed again. "It's the only thing I've talked about since we got in the jeep."

"But you never do unless asked. I have a theory that people who don't talk about themselves are the ones who do the things they intend inside them to do. One talks or one does things he thinks about."

"It may be true. I'd never thought of it that way but it may be true. I've always believed it was true about writers: You either talk about writing, or you write. But I haven't even thought about these things for a long time now."

"Matthew, I think I'm falling in love with you."

They were both looking straight ahead through the windshield. He remembered seeing through the doors of the hospital the shape of a man with one leg in an enormous cast thrusting himself slowly across the lobby on crutches.

"Don't say that," he said. "You shouldn't say that. This is no time to fall in love."

"I know," she said. "It's no time to fall in love. You have no idea how much I've been trying not to. Just wait a minute then take me inside, will you? My time is up, Matthew."

They waited quietly. He knew she was trying not to cry. He did not look. "Let's go now," she said then.

They went inside and they stood a moment in the bright lobby. She smiled at him. Then he laughed a little.

"It's no time," he said. "But I think I am too. We'll try to stop it, won't we? Good night."

He walked back out to the jeep. There was a row of jeeps parked there and it was one time he was glad his was marked so distinctively. He wasn't sure he would have found it otherwise. He did not want to be in love, in the war. He did not even believe in it.

13

DISCIPLINE

The ship actually feared mines more than torpedoes. Sometimes a torpedo would pass under an LST's shallow draft but a mine passed under nothing. The Germans had been sewing a lot of mines from the air recently. On some of their trips up to the beachhead they could even see the JU-88s far out to port doing it. The mines were one of the subjects that came up, in a rather peculiar way, during the conversation that day with the Germans.

The crew liked carrying German prisoners. They had done it a couple of times and it was always good for a nice long breeze session to help pass the time. It was interesting to get a look at some of the men who were holding up the war at Anzio. The Germans were equally interested in their captors. That day, as the ship pushed south, the Germans lounged around in the twilight on the main deck, the crew talking with them, something made possible by the fact that two or three of the Germans spoke English. No kind of guard whatsoever was kept over the Germans. What could they do and where could they go? If they wanted to jump over the side they were welcome to do so. None had. The conversation between the members of ship's company and the prisoners was amiable enough, if a little baiting here and there. They discussed why the Germans got into the war and why the United States got into the war. They discussed Cassino and they discussed Anzio. They discussed a variety of topics.

"It's obvious we are winning," a German sergeant said. "Look at Anzio. Look at Cassino."

"I hear we're bombing Berlin pretty heavily," Seaman First

Class Edward Polk, a Tennessee mountain boy who was quite a good arguer, observed in reply to this.

"There has been no bombing of Berlin," the German sergeant said. "That is propaganda they give you to keep your spirits up."

"Well, maybe so," Polk said. "We sure need something to keep our spirits up."

Several of the American sailors laughed quietly. Presently Polk continued. "What I don't understand is, why you should bomb one of our hospital ships. One of them was bombed up off Anzio. Why would you want to do a thing like that?"

"Oh no," the German said. "That couldn't be. We would never bomb a hospital ship. However, the Americans have bombed hospitals in Berlin."

"I thought you said Berlin hadn't been bombed," Polk said promptly.

The German blushed slightly. "Only a very little," he said.

"You mean only the hospitals?" Polk said.

Then Machinist's Mate Third Class Timothy Rutledge asked: "Who do you think will win the war?"

"The Germans will win the war," a German corporal said.

"Do you really believe that?" Rutledge said.

"Of course I believe it. How long have you been at Anzio and Cassino? You are stopped. The Germans will win. We will win the war if it takes fifty years," the corporal said.

"I agree with that estimate as to the length of the war," an American sailor in the back of his side popped up. The Americans laughed, the German translated the American's remark and then the Germans joined in with laughter too.

"What will happen when you leave Anzio?" Ensign Eliot Horner asked.

"We will never leave Anzio," the German corporal said. "We have now decided to hold all our positions. You will notice that this ship even now is opposite German-held soil," and he nodded over to the mainland.

"You want to swim over there?" Gunner's Mate First Class James Plimpton asked.

"I'm not much of a swimmer," the German corporal said, and

the Americans laughed again and the Germans, too, when the remarks were translated.

"You will never get out of Anzio or through Cassino," the German sergeant said.

They would never let the Americans forget how we had come to a standstill at Anzio and Cassino.

From time to time some of the American sailors drifted off, to stand watches or do other work they had to do. As Ensign Horner was leaving he noticed a German officer standing apart over by the life line, his back to the sea, looking with lofty disapproval on the conversation. He was a young, blond, handsome officer and Horner stopped to talk with him a moment, in the event he spoke English. Horner had seen him briefly before, when the German was eating alone in the wardroom before the ship's officers had their own evening meal, but no talk had passed between them, only a nod. Horner was a very friendly young ensign, and he now discovered that the German spoke excellent English. He was a Luftwaffe officer, as Horner could tell by the wings on his gray uniform. He said he had flown a JU-88 and was shot down only yesterday over Anzio harbor, and been picked up by an American PC.

"Before that," he said, "I had been flying up and down over here." He pointed over the bow to the sea. "I have been dropping mines for your ships."

"Is that so?" Horner said with interest. "Well, we know you boys have been dropping quite a few. We've even seen you doing it."

"That is true, we have been dropping many of them—especially just lately. Your ship will probably be encountering some of the mines in the nights to come."

"Is that so?" Horner said. "Well, we'll have to keep a good lookout for them."

"We're doing very excellent camouflage work on our mines these days," the German officer said. "You'll have great difficulty spotting them."

"Is that so?" Horner said.

"I myself," the German said, "dropped a good many down

there." He again pointed down the coast. "It would be very interesting, wouldn't it, if you should encounter one of those mines."

Horner laughed quietly. It did strike him, too, as ironic. "Yes, that would be interesting. It would be especially interesting if we encountered one of your mines with you aboard, Lieutenant."

The German, for the first time, smiled a little. "Yes, that would be possible. I was just standing here thinking of that possibility, Lieutenant," which is what he called Horner. "We will see if that is what happens. We know your schedules quite well and your habits and we try to drop them so that you will encounter them by night, when you cannot see them so well."

"Well, we shall encounter what we shall encounter, Lieutenant," Horner said sententiously.

The German officer glanced over to where Lieutenant (jg) Abernethy and a couple of enlisted men were lounging against the superstructure, chatting and obviously passing the time of day.

"That is very bad, Lieutenant," he said disdainfully.

"What's that, Lieutenant?"

"That is very bad for your officers to be fraternizing with the men like that. It breaks down discipline."

Ensign Horner looked at the group thoughtfully. "You know, I hadn't thought of that," he said. "But I think you have a point there. Yes, that kind of fraternization between enlisted men and officers is very bad."

"Any kind is," the German said.

"Very bad," Ensign Horner repeated. "I'll go speak to the captain about it right away."

"Discipline is very important," the German said, "in the military."

"Yes, you've got to have discipline," Horner said affably.

"One of the American faults," the German said, "is that you don't have a proper amount of discipline."

"Yes, we have many faults," Horner said agreeably. "I don't see how we're still in there."

"There's nothing more important in war than discipline," the German said.

"I suppose not," Horner said. "Except possibly winning, which we seem to be doing. Well, it was nice talking with you, Lieutenant."

Ensign Horner walked pleasantly away. Ensign Horner was an entirely pleasant young man, and still almost boyish. The Navy had plucked him out of his Dartmouth graduating class almost before he could get his gown and mortar board off, interrupting, temporarily, the plan that had been ordained from his birth to go from there to Harvard Law School then into his father's law firm in New York. At twenty, he was the youngest officer aboard. He was certainly glad he had been assigned to the Mediterranean instead of the Pacific, he was thinking as he walked away. It must be terribly dull out there in the Pacific, no cities even to get into, only those god-forsaken islands, and no Luftwaffe officer passenger to spend a pleasant quarter of an hour having a chat with.

It was late at night and some of the officers off watch sat around talking, mostly about the German prisoners. By a little after midnight all but the captain, Horner, and Barclay had drifted off and these three idled around the wardroom table having a final cup of coffee. Barclay had just come off the 2000–2400 watch and he mentioned that the sea was uncommonly smooth tonight. Horner talked a little about the German officer and the conversation about mines. Then, since Barclay hadn't heard it, he told him about the German's concern for discipline and they all laughed quietly. Horner said good night and, leaving the captain and Barclay to finish their coffee, left the wardroom and started along the passageway to his room. He chuckled a moment, remembering something else in that breeze session with the crew and the Germans. Then he yawned heavily. It had been a long day and he was very sleepy. He had never slept anywhere so beautifully as he did aboard ship. He could drink ten cups of coffee and still be asleep in a moment after he hit the sack. He put his hand to his mouth to stifle the yawn and at that instant felt something very hard jab into his back and heard a voice say in excellent English: "Kindly put your hands above your head, Lieutenant, and clasp them."

Ensign Horner did so and the voice continued quietly. "Lieutenant," it said. "This is an American .45 caliber pistol I have in your back. It has a shell in the chamber. You will do exactly as I say or it will go off. Now turn around and walk back to where you just came from."

Horner turned, still feeling the pistol pressing persuasively into his back, seeming almost to probe a little, as the German turned with him. He hesitated briefly.

"Now march, Lieutenant, and when you get inside that room, stop."

In the wardroom, the captain and Barclay, hearing a sound at the door, looked up to see Ensign Horner standing there with his hands held together above his head. For a moment they could see only Horner and at first thought it must be some kind of elaborate joke of which Horner was a part. Then they saw part of a gray uniform standing behind him. Then whoever was in this uniform had nudged Horner slightly forward and stood just inside. They then saw a German Luftwaffe officer standing there holding an American .45 caliber pistol, directed at the back of Horner's head.

"Stand up please, gentlemen," the German said quietly.

The captain and Barclay came slowly to their feet and the German satisfied himself they were unarmed.

"You may sit down, gentlemen," he said. "You are the captain?"

"I am."

"Now, Captain," the German said, "I will speak frankly. There are eight bullets in this gun, as we all know. If anything is attempted other than what I shall presently instruct, this will happen: The first bullet will go into this officer here," and he indicated Horner. "The next two bullets will go into you and the other officer there. I will then proceed out that door and put bullets into the first five Americans I encounter. I think I can do that before they get me. I have in my pocket another clip with seven additional bullets but I do not think we can count on my being allowed time to reload. But I think we can conservatively count on eight Americans being dead within five minutes from now if these instructions are not carried out both exactly and promptly. If they are fulfilled no one shall be harmed. It remains only to say that I am very serious, Captain, and that I am an excellent shot. I hope you will accept my word for those two facts. Now here is what you are to do."

The German then talked quietly, rapidly, and without interruption for perhaps just over one minute, giving the most explicit instructions. He was entirely fluent.

"Now, Captain," he concluded, "you will please go to that phone and call the bridge with my instructions."

The captain waited a moment, looking carefully into the German's eyes as though trying to satisfy himself about something. He must have done so because he stepped over to the phone and picked it up.

"Conning tower? This is the captain speaking. Let me speak with the officer of the deck."

There was a momentary wait then the captain was speaking again.

"Fairchild, this is the captain." His voice was even and calm. "Now listen carefully to what I have to say. Barclay, Horner, and I are here in the wardroom. A German officer who is our guest aboard has somehow got himself a .45 and he has it on the three of us down here. Now I want you to do exactly as I say. Have someone count off thirty-five of the German prisoners in troops quarters. Then lower the starboard boat to the rail and load the prisoners. Do this as quickly as possible and when you have done it call me. And you are on no account to make any attempt to rush the wardroom or to do anything other than what I have just told you. Is all this clear?"

The captain put the phone back and resumed his seat at the table.

"Now, Captain," the German said, "there is just one other thing. To accompany us on our voyage I shall need one of your men to handle the boat, and in addition an officer to give us, let us say, his protection. For various reasons we will not bother to assemble your entire complement of officers for you to make a selection from. That selection is to be made between the two officers present here."

"I see," the captain said. "It's a very thoroughly thought out plan, isn't it, Lieutenant?"

"I trust so, Captain. I had a good deal of free time to think today, as the lieutenant can testify." The German nodded slightly toward Horner.

"He's the one who talked about the mines, Captain," Horner explained dismally. "About the ones he's been dropping for us."

"Lieutenant," the captain said. "Before you proceed further with this, I think I should tell you something. I'm a very practical man. Your boat will get into the water all right. I shall not interfere with that, since I accept your assurance that such interference would cost at least three lives, very possibly eight. So that risking the two is a better choice. But let me say this, Lieutenant. I think you may have seen a few guns about this vessel today— you seem to be rather observant. You must have seen that we come rather well-equipped with 20- and 40-millimeters not to mention 50-caliber machine guns. It is my duty to tell you, Lieutenant, that we might open up anyway once you're in the water."

The German smiled a little. "I don't think you will, Captain. I may be mistaken in my judgment but it is my belief that you will let thirty-six Germans go rather than kill two Americans. You will never give that order, Captain."

"I frankly don't know, Lieutenant," the captain said, and Barclay suddenly realized that he really didn't, that this was not entirely bluff. "I won't know until I am confronted with that choice. Right now I want you to understand that I am not at all certain I'll let you take thirty-five Germans for two Americans. I may very well open up, Lieutenant, with everything we've got. Though of course it wouldn't take much."

"I do not believe you would ever train your own guns on Americans. You wouldn't like it on your conscience."

"Your concern for my conscience deeply touches me, Lieutenant. But let us say I was able to overcome my conscience. Are you willing to pay thirty-six German soldiers for two Americans? That's pretty flattering to us, Lieutenant."

The German smiled. "Not thirty-six German soldiers, Captain. Thirty-six German prisoners. There's a considerable difference."

"Very well, Lieutenant. I have done my duty in informing you of the risk you take. I may not open up on you. But then, I repeat, I may. That is all I have to say, Lieutenant."

"Thank you, Captain. I trust to your compassion."

The German now gave the last of his instructions and had just finished with it when the phone buzzed. The captain took it, talked a moment, then turned to the German.

"Your compatriots are in the boat, Lieutenant."

"Very well. Kindly give the officer the remainder of the instructions, Captain."

The captain took one last look at the .45 pointed at Horner, then spoke into the phone.

"Fairchild? Now listen to me. I don't want the slightest deviation from what I'm about to tell you. I want you to get someone who can operate the boat, and get a volunteer. Explain to him that the Germans are going to attempt to make it to German-held territory on the mainland, north of Cassino, and that he is to go with them. When you have done this, stop the ship. Don't do anything else. Under no circumstances, I repeat, make any attempt to rush the wardroom. Don't attempt anything. Is that absolutely clear, Fairchild? The German says you have five minutes to get someone and to stop the ship. One final thing. Send someone to clear the decks of all personnel except for the man who is going with the Germans, and the man who is lowering the boat. Have these two men stand by the boat. That's it, Fairchild."

The captain waited a moment to make sure Fairchild had it, then put the phone back.

"Now, Captain, there remains only the selection of the officer to accompany us on our voyage," the German said. He nodded toward Horner then Barclay. "Which is it to be, Captain?"

"I'll go, Captain," Barclay said.

"Captain," Horner said with some fervor, "I'm the one who ought to go. I got us into this."

"Nobody got us into anything," the captain said. "Okay, Barclay."

Then they could feel the ship slowing. Presently she had stopped.

"All right, Captain. You first, then you," the German indicated Barclay. "You"—he motioned to Horner—"will stay here."

The captain and Barclay rose. "Incidentally, Lieutenant," the captain said, "before we part, would you satisfy my curiosity as to how you got the gun?"

The German smiled. "Gladly. Immediately after supper. The only route out of the wardroom leads directly by the staterooms. Your officers leave these rooms open and every imaginable thing lying around. Very little discipline. Now let us go."

The captain and Barclay started out the door and now Barclay could feel the German behind him, the .45 pressing lightly into his back. They emerged into a star-filled night over a quiet sea. The decks stood deserted. The captain led the way to the starboard boat. They could see the heads of the Germans who now filled it and Barclay could see two of the crew, standing alongside. They were Carlyle and Nelson. Barclay wondered which was to go along to operate the boat and which to lower it away. Each man was qualified in both skills. The German lieutenant spoke.

"Captain, as one final precaution, will you please face inboard—you and whichever man is to lower the boat."

Nelson turned with the captain. Then, keeping them carefully covered with the .45, the German ordered Barclay and Carlyle into the boat. He spoke some words to one of the Germans in the boat, quickly handed him the gun, and while this one kept it on the two Americans who were to be their fellow passengers, the German officer climbed in himself. He then took the gun back, ordered Barclay and Carlyle to face forward, and spoke to the captain.

"All right, Captain. We're ready. Thank you for your hospitality."

The boat was lowered away. It touched the sea softly.

The strangest thing of all to Barclay was to see the big shape of the LST standing perfectly motionless in the open sea. Momentarily the desires of Barclay and the German officer coincided, which was to get underway as quickly as possible. The German, so that they would be on their way to German-held territory; Barclay, so that the ship would not be sitting there as a target for some wandering submarine. The German glanced up quickly at the stars, then back at the North Star, which was aft and slightly to the port side of the boat, the ship also being on the port side. The German had made his plan clear. He had instructed the captain to let the boat proceed until it was some one hundred yards dead ahead of the ship, at which point it would cut across the ship's course and turn in to the mainland. After that the LST could get underway. The German gave instructions quickly to Carlyle now, and the seaman got the boat underway.

The Luftwaffe officer had said something in German to his thirty-five countrymen aboard. It must have been to tell them to stay low in the boat for they all now crouched down into the welldeck, so that no one showed above the gunwales except Carlyle standing at the wheel, Barclay standing by the engine cover directly forward of him, and the German standing in such a way as to form the other point of a triangle the three men made so that the American .45 he possessed could make sure the other two points of the triangle did his bidding. Barclay could almost admire the extreme care with which he must have thought all of this out and the equally careful and able execution of it. Beyond that he did not think, there certainly appearing nothing to do. The boat rode on through the still water.

They were approaching their turning point some one hundred yards ahead of the LST and Barclay was anxious that they should now cut across it so that the ship could get underway. It was for this reason that he looked up now at Carlyle. And in the starlit darkness he thought that for the barest fraction of a second the sailor's eyes held his and then went into a fixed position. It could have been his imagination but Barclay turned his gaze away and followed that of Carlyle. Later he would remember what eyes Carlyle had. Now he saw, beyond the ramp of the LCVP, just slightly to port, and in the exact course the LST would take once it got underway, a vague shape in the water. It seemed to appear, then disappear, then appear again, bobbing. The boat was moving slowly and now the shape, coming into view again, took on a slightly clearer outline. The stars flashed down and Barclay saw that shape. It was unmistakably round.

They scarcely needed a signal. In any event it was impossible to make one, with the German standing there. Barclay could sense, without looking, that Carlyle was keeping his eyes straight ahead, as was Barclay. But he knew also that the seaman was thinking the exact same thought as himself, which was that they must do something now, with the LST about to resume course over this very pathway of sea. He had to believe, too, that Carlyle had resolved, independently, on the identical course of action that Barclay himself, in that flash that came in the only time they had, had resolved on. And he knew one thing more: that Carlyle would wait for him to make the first move, that, occupied as he was at the wheel, with the German forward of him and to his left, there would be no opportunity for him to take his hands off that wheel and make the first move himself. Barclay, free and unoccupied there, had the only chance to do it. And now it must be made quickly. The boat was now no more than ninety or eighty yards from the object. Barclay waited, unmoving but tense and he felt rather than saw the German officer look up at the stars and heard him say to Carlyle:

"Now, we will turn presently. There, on the North Star . . ."

Carlyle turned the boat just fractionally to port. Barclay was about to take what thin chance there was and go for the German when he heard him ask: "Will the boat go any faster?"

Barclay spoke immediately. "Yes, if we cut off the underwater exhaust. The exhaust then comes out above water, Lieutenant. More noise, Lieutenant—but much more speed."

"Then cut it off, Lieutenant. We have no fear of noise."

Barclay stooped down behind the engine cover, found the exhaust valve lever and switched the damper to horizontal position. Immediately the engine became considerably noisier and the boat jumped forward. Then, raising up with an almost convulsive movement and using the engine cover to give him purchase, his feet shot out violently at the groin of the German officer. He felt his heavy field shoes grind into the German, heard a cry in German, and heard the sound of metal striking metal, as the .45 flew out of his hand. He leapt for the German, could hear Carlyle locking the wheel in place, feel him joining him savagely on the German officer, then both of them pushed him up bodily and flung him across the engine cover, where he lay draped and apparently unconscious. The whole thing had taken only seconds.

"Jump!" Barclay said.

Springing onto the gunwale, Carlyle gave a mighty dive aft, Barclay doing the same thing immediately behind him. Surfacing, he could see Carlyle just glance sideways a moment to see that he was up and safe. Then the two of them began swimming away from the boat with great overhead crawl strokes. They stroked hard through the smooth water, putting space between themselves and the boat. They could hear vaguely the raucous sound of the VP's engine as the boat proceeded swiftly on the course fixed by Carlyle. Then they heard the explosion. They felt their bodies shaken, themselves stunned, a fear consciousness would go, then the knowledge it would not go, that they were all right. They turned, treading water, and one could see in the distance a pattern of debris on the water. Nothing else. The mine, made to take an LST apart, had chewed up the small LCVP and its contents as if it were a toy boat and its passengers little wooden figures.

Already from the LST the other boat was being lowered away. They swam toward it and were pulled in by a covey of hands, reaching over the side, among them being those of Ensign Horner. The moment the LCVP was in its davits the ship got underway.

Ship's company was always grateful to the German Luftwaffe officer for saving them from that mine. But no one was ever to know the answer to the question Horner raised the following day when they were having some coffee in the wardroom.

"I wonder," Ensign Horner said, "if he could have been the one that actually dropped the mine."

"Let us hope so," the captain said somberly. He sipped at his coffee and looked thoughtfully at Barclay.

"By the way, I forgot something."

"What's that, Captain?"

"I meant to congratulate you and Carlyle on a particular talent you both displayed."

"What talent was that, Captain? Discipline?"

"No. It's a talent which on the whole I deem to be of a higher order even than discipline. Adaptability."

14

THE WEEK

No one could have foreseen that the destruction of the LCVP would lead to such a stroke of good fortune. The crew all knew that the boat would have to be replaced, of course, but that unfortunately was only a matter of finding another one and hoisting it into the same davits. But the cerebrations of those in the upper levels of naval command should never be under-estimated. Someone on that level had decided that while the LST 1826 was getting a new small boat, it might as well get that additional 40-millimeter gun that some of the ships were now being outfitted with as added capability in the renewed battle; by the latter phrase being meant the augmented effort the Germans were now making in the sea lanes between Naples and Anzio, with aircraft, with submarines, and even with an in-genious new one-man sub which operated by attaching its for-ward end, which was an explosive, directly to the hull of a ship then sailing off in the after end. The crew was delighted to get an additional 40-millimeter gun. It would take a week to install. Captain Adler being a highly permissive sort of ship's captain in his way, only a very minimum of crew had to stay aboard at any one time. After all no one wanted to get in the way of the welders. Ship's company was unexpectedly presented with the most liberty it had had since leaving the States.

Seaman Second Class Carlyle got away late that afternoon and went swinging with long strides up the Pozzuoli street, and whistling happily; the Italians often turned to stare at Carlyle's height and his hair and now they turned and stared at his hap-

piness, and some smiled, for whatever it was. Carlyle was eager
to surprise Coco with the good news. But when he knocked
on the door and she opened it, it was he who received the
surprise.

Her habitual attire was a clean but worn black dress and a
pair of wooden shoes. Now she stood there wearing a blue silk
dress which looked just out of a box. She was wearing very
thin black stockings. She was wearing a pair of new, shiny black
shoes with high heels—it seemed to him almost the most astonishing thing of all to see her in high heels. He stared at her in
amazement. Then he laughed and a sentence of joy burst from
his lips.

"How beautiful you are!"

It did not occur to him to ask where she could have got all
these things. If it had, he would have supposed that they repre-
sented translations of the cigarettes, C-rations, and the like which
he brought her, but he would never have dreamed of calling
attention to his own benevolences. And in fact he felt such delight in how stunning she looked that there was no room for his
mind even to touch on the source of what made her so. He was
filled with her beauty, so much so that he did not notice that
she was a little surprised at his being there just then. This hit
him only when she spoke.

"Red, I have to be going out now. I'm just waiting for Rebi
to come to stay with the baby."

"Going out?" he said, not understanding. "Fine, I'll go with
you. Let's go! Where are we going?"

"Red," she said. "I didn't know you were coming in. You
can't expect me to just sit and wait for you."

"No, I suppose not," he said. It was his first suspicion. "No,
I guess you didn't know. Anyhow you know now!" he said,
brightening. "Wherever you're going, I'll take you."

"Red, you can't go where I'm going."

"I don't understand," he said. "Where can't I go?" He laughed.
"Americans can go anywhere over here. We're the conquerors,
remember?"

"Red, I'm going to the Navy officers club. They won't let you in there, will they?" She said this, not with the slightest content of cruelty, but merely as a fact.

He looked at her for a long moment before speaking. Abruptly a fury flashed through him that she, a civilian, could go where he could not. "No, I don't suppose they would," he said. "Not in the front door anyhow."

"Oh, Red, I've got to go out sometimes. I've got to have some gaiety in my life."

"All right. I'll take you somewhere."

"Where?" she said immediately.

Then it occurred to him that in all of Naples there was literally no place an enlisted man could take a girl—to dance, to drink, to do anything in the way of fun; no place, that is, except places where prostitutes met the men, places everyone knew existed just for that. He would certainly never take her to one of those.

"Where will you take me, Red?" she pressed him. "I've got to have some gaiety in my life!" Her voice rose a little for the first time.

"Do you have to go to the officers club to get it?"

"It is a very beautiful club. They have dancing there. It is very gay there, very beautiful. And also I get a very remarkable meal when I go there."

"You sound as if you knew it very well."

"I do! I cannot sit in this hole forever."

"How many times have you been there?" His voice was low and even now.

"I don't count them." She had never meant to be harsh, but because his voice had been angry hers became so and besides she didn't like to be cross-examined, by anyone. So she said it.

"You're only a sailor," she said. "You can't expect me to save myself all the time for a common sailor when all these officers are here. They can take me to places you can't go, you understand? And they like me. They like me very much, do you understand that?"

The sailor's face was very white. "What do they give you?" he said. "What do the officers give you? Did they give you that dress and those shoes and those stockings? Do you have underwear now? Do they give you that underwear you always wanted? Is it silk and lacy?"

He was on the verge of asking her how she had paid for the clothes she was wearing. But he was terrified to hear what the answer would be. And, furthermore, some instinct made him draw back; told him that if he asked that question, it would be the last of them.

She looked at him coldly. "You don't own me. I am not to be bought for a few bars of soap and some packs of cigarettes, and a C-ration. Now suppose you get out of here until you learn some manners."

The word stung him. He left the room in a blindness of rage. That night Seaman Second Class Peter Carlyle had the first drink of his life. And then he had several more. He went to one bar after another drinking. Some of the vino being sold in those bars, some of the "cognac" were enough to test the most accustomed stomach. With Carlyle, who in addition didn't know one drink from another and mixed everything, the effect was deadly. The first thing anyone knew about it was when a shore patrol jeep pulled up in front of the bow ramp, where Barclay had the watch. One of those mistral-like winds that come suddenly upon Naples had begun to rise, bringing cold and an intimation of rain with it, and Barclay had sent the messenger to get jungle-cloth jackets for the watch and they were just putting them on.

"Is this one of yours?" the shore patrol boatswain's mate asked.

Barclay, Lord Nelson, who was the boatswain on watch, and Mason, who was the messenger, walked over to the jeep and peered in. Spread out in the back seat between two other shore patrol men was what certainly looked like Carlyle, though a Carlyle they had never seen. Nelson even took off his hat to make sure.

"Carlyle drunk!" Nelson said. "I wouldn't ever have believed that. But that's his hair all right, Mr. Barclay. No doubt about it! There isn't another head of hair like that in the Mediterranean."

"Yes, I guess it is," Barclay said to the shore patrol boatswain's mate. "It's one of ours all right."

"He sure tied one on," the boatswain's mate said.

"It looks like it," Barclay said thoughtfully.

"Do you suppose someone could have held him and forced it down him, Mr. Barclay?" Lord Nelson said. "I never even seen Carlyle *near* a bar."

The shore patrol boatswain's mate regarded Nelson cynically. "Yes, they forced it down him all right," he said. "He's so small and delicate. When we got to him he was sitting by himself at a table and yelling at the waitress something that sounded like 'Drink! Bring me anything you got.' Oh, yes, they sure forced it down him all right."

"I'd never have believed it," Lord Nelson said, shaking his head. "There must be something here we don't know about."

"Well, the whole thing is probably very academic anyhow right now," Barclay said judiciously. "Where did you find him, Boats?"

"In one of those off-limits poison bars off Via Roma, sir," the boatswain's mate said. "It took all three of us to tie him down."

"Yes, he's a big boy all right," Barclay said.

"I'd hate to take him on when he was sober," the boatswain's mate said.

"Oh, he's all right when he's sober," Barclay said.

It took Nelson, Mason, and Latimer, the pharmacist's mate, to get Carlyle, who, all hands and arms, was sprawled all over the back seat, like an intoxicated giraffe, out of the jeep and start him on his way to the bow ramp. Lifted up, he came slightly to life and began singing "Shenandoah" quite drunkenly, bearing down on the words . . .

> They said I was a dirty sailor
> Away, away, I'm bound away
> 'Cross the wide Miss-ur-uh . . .

Then he almost collapsed. Propped back on his feet he faced Barclay and attempted a salute which was not very successful.

"Permission to come aboard, sir!" he said drunkenly. "Mr. Barclay! How are you, Mr. Barclay?"

Barclay smiled. "Better than you right now, Red. Come on, let's get aboard."

Carlyle held up a waving finger. "Just a moment, Mr. Barclay. Just one moment please! Have you thanked these gentlemen?" and he bowed so deeply to the shore patrol that he would have fallen on his face if Nelson and Latimer had not caught him by the arms, which they were grasping firmly. "Have you thanked these good gentlemen for bringing me in?"

"Yes, they're all properly thanked, Red," Barclay said. "Now let's go."

"Mr. Barclay, I just want to say one thing. Just one thing! Lately, just lately, I have started hating officers. But I still like you, Mr. Barclay. And that's a fact."

With that he passed out completely and was carried aboard, the three men carrying him by two arms and a leg and Barclay on the other leg.

"Would you men like some hot coffee?" Barclay asked pleasantly—and calculatingly—of the shore patrol men when he came back. He was thinking any report on Carlyle might be softened a little.

"That would taste very good, sir," the boatswain's mate said. He lifted his head to the sea as if to scent the cold wind that was coming on. He was an old sailor, Barclay knew. "I think we're in for a big one tonight."

"I think we are," Barclay agreed. The wind was rising steadily, slapping the sea against the vessel. Barclay knew—they had been through this before—that it would bring storm and heavy rain before this night was over. When Lord Nelson returned from bedding down Carlyle he sent him to make sure all was lashed down aboard that needed to be. They were going to get a pretty big one all right and he was glad Carlyle had got in before it hit.

In Coco's apartment Rebi awakened suddenly. He lay there for a moment wondering what had done it and then he heard the baby cry. At about the same moment he felt something that told him why. A chill wind was blowing through the window, which he had left open in the warm night. He walked over and shut it.

He went over and looked at the baby and held his finger out to it. This pleased the baby, he had learned, and now he played with the finger a moment then tumbled back to sleep. Rebi went back to the bed and sat on the edge of it a moment. Despite the window being down, the room was getting colder. He walked over and looked out. He could see a gust of wind hit a large, wayward can and rifle it up the street. At that sight he knew what it was. It was known to every boy who grew up down by the sea in Naples. It was the mistral, which could come so suddenly, and drop the temperature so fast. Pozzuoli, sitting down on the sea, always felt it first. And Rebi knew it would get colder that night. Much colder. He heard the baby cry.

He went back to the crib and stood looking down at it thoughtfully. There was a thin blanket over the baby and he pulled it up. It would not do for long. He could hear rain begin to drill against the window. Finally he went over, picked the baby up in its blanket and brought it to his own bed. He put it with himself under his blanket and toward the wall side so it would not roll off. He lay there for a bit listening to the wind. He could hear it rise more, that sudden anger of the wind that he was so familiar with, as familiar as with the bone-numbing, wet cold it always brought. The baby coughed and cried again. He drew it up against himself, shielding it under his own body and trying to pass over to the baby what warmth was in himself. It was getting less. He was beginning to shiver himself and now he heard the rain come on in full violence, flung by a deafening wind. He pressed as much of himself as he could over the baby, and shivering uncontrollably from time to time himself, did not move from that position.

In the cherub room, the wind and the rain could have been heard, too, if anyone had been awake to hear them, though, being farther from the sea, not so strongly. It was only toward morning when the wind had reached gale force and the rain was slamming against the tiles of the house that a girl awoke beneath her comforter. She was too sleepy to think even where she was. She knew only that it felt cozy and warm there and contentedly she started to pull the luxurious comforter up around her and go back to sleep. Then she heard a burst of rain like shot against the French doors and a flash of lightning which illumined the whole room. She was looking up at the ceiling at that moment and, in that second of terror that can come like a nightmare from being awakened unnaturally, she saw the cherubs and felt they were staring down at her. For a moment then she could hear only the singing fury of the wind and she knew instantly it was the mistral. Then the thunder burst seemingly right over the roof. She sat up violently in the bed. Another flash of lightning came, filling the room, and in only a second another appalling burst of thunder which set the French doors vibrating. She could feel the great cold out there. She reached over and with both hands started shaking the big form sprawled so blissfully beside her, his sleep impervious, apparently, to anything short of a typhoon.

"Shanley!" she cried. "Shanley, wake up! I've got to go home. You've got to take me home quickly. Shanley!"

Once he was awake, he was instantly so. In less than ten minutes Shanley was outside buckling the rain windows onto the jeep—at times the wind almost tore them out of his hands. Then he pulled the jeep under the portico so she could get in dry and they started over the long drive to Pozzuoli. The wind intensity kept rising the nearer they got to the village on the sea, and at times seemed as if it would suck the rain curtains right off. Shanley could see nothing in front of him. He was driving into a wall of water all the way. By the time they reached the town it was almost dawn and would have been if it were not that the rain was keeping the dawn back. She mumbled some kind of thanks to Shanley for the evening, for the dinner, and ran up the stairs. She came into the room to hear the baby coughing stridently and rushed over to him. Rebi was still lying there, wide awake, trying to shield the child. The room was icy and damp. She looked, said nothing, and then impulsively rushed downstairs. Shanley was gone. She ran back up the stairs. She took the baby up and held it to her, almost enveloping it unto herself, and spoke to the boy.

"Rebi," she said. "Go get the doctor."

There was no need to say which one. There was only one in Pozzuoli, and everyone knew where he lived.

"Hurry!" Coco said. "Hurry, please hurry!"

Rebi ran out of the room, took the steps going down two at a time, and emerged into a gust which slammed him against the wall of the house. The rain came down to where he could see only a few steps ahead. Clinging to the walls of the houses, he started fighting his way up the street and then up a small hill where the doctor had his house.

Seaman Second Class Carlyle awakened next day in a specific kind of physical misery that was entirely novel to him. The storm had raged unheard against his total sleep. A shower and breakfast pretty well removed his physical tribulation but even then the mental misery over her which so far exceeded it hung on and chewed at him. Finally, after going to Barclay and apologizing for last night, he went ashore.

The wind blew coldly as he walked up the street but the rain had slackened some. He had not even needed to think over what he was going to do. There was nothing to think over, since he knew he could not possibly do anything else. The simple fact was that nothing could ever touch his feeling for her, nothing that anybody else or even she herself did. He had to keep her—he knew nothing else but that. And whatever she was doing—and he didn't want to know—it was his fault. He should have brought her more, a great deal more. Well, he would now. If *they* were bringing her things, he would bring her more. And if she was doing anything she would stop doing it. But he didn't even want to ask her to do that. He didn't want to know anything or for her to commit herself to anything. He only wanted to be with her. To give her up, not to have her, never to see her again—it was not even conceivable to him. So there was really no decision for him to make. Then he was walking into a scene so harshly different from last night's that his own emotions about himself and his needs and desires were instantly swept away, to leave him focused entirely on what he found.

She was wearing the plain dress and her wooden shoes. There was an Italian civilian there and Coco said he was a doctor. She looked distraught and overcome, and helpless as a child. The man was bending over the crib. Presently he stood up. He paid no attention to Carlyle. Hardly any to the mother herself but spoke as if to the room in general.

"The child has pneumonia," he said. His shoulders shrugged. "It is no wonder. A place like this. No heat." He shrugged again. "It's very cold in here," he said, as if conveying news. "I feel cold myself right now."

Coco looked too stunned even to speak and the doctor spoke up to the room in general.

"Who is the father?" he said.

"I am," Carlyle said.

That made the doctor look at Carlyle. He looked for a long moment.

"I see," he said finally. He made the two words seem like a pronunciamento.

"Is the baby bad, Doctor?" Carlyle said. There was a crispness in his voice which would have sounded very unusual to anyone who knew him.

"Pneumonia is always bad," the doctor spoke to the room again. He was a very sententious man. He shrugged again.

"Doctor, I'm going to say this just once and don't make me have to say it again." Coco, brought out of her daze by this unaccustomed manner of Carlyle, looked at the sailor. His voice came low pitched but with an unmistakable tone of authority and even, slightly, of menace. "Do you understand, Doctor? And look at me when you speak, not about the room."

The doctor, it must be said for him, was a judge of men. He regarded the sailor standing there, his feet a little apart, his height looming almost to the ceiling, a young man of obvious physical capabilities. He reached a quick decision that it might be a wise, not to mention healthy, thing to be slightly civil.

"Very well, what is it?"

"Can you save him, Doctor?"

"I believe he can be saved. If we can get medicines. And more food. And you need heat here—and blankets. You need a great deal here."

The doctor was looking at Carlyle now. "It should be easy for you. The Americans have everything. Since you are the father," he said.

"I will get it all," Carlyle said.

"Good!" the doctor said. "And by the way. While you are getting things will you get me a carton of American cigarettes? I prefer Camels—but Lucky Strikes if there are no Camels."

"I'll get you a carton of Camels, Doctor," Carlyle said. "Will you come back this afternoon if I get you a carton of Camels?"

The doctor smiled a little. He was even happy to see that he was not dealing with a fool, as he always assumed at the outset with an American.

"Certainly," he said. "I was planning to come anyhow."

"The Camels won't keep you from coming though, will they, Doctor?"

The doctor smiled in wan appreciativeness. "I shall see you parents at two."

"Doctor, one more thing. If you save this child, if you stay here a good deal, and make many visits, and if you save him, there will be a great many cartons of cigarettes for you—Camels, Doctor. And a lot more."

The doctor looked at Carlyle a moment. "I understand," he said. "I find I can be back in an hour instead of this afternoon."

When the doctor had gone Coco held to Carlyle and started crying. "How cruel I was last night," she said.

"Let's forget last night. Last night never happened."

"Yes, it did. This is a punishment of God. Both for my cruelty to you and for leaving the baby. The baby will die for my punishment."

"Don't speak nonsense," Carlyle said, rather brusquely. "I've never believed that about God punishing parents by killing off their little children. I couldn't believe in that kind of God."

"But I was cruel to you," she said, sobbing against him, "and I should never have gone out."

"Now you must stop this," he said sharply. "Do you hear me? We've got a lot to do and we have no time to cry. Listen to me now."

At these tones of command, she looked up at him. "Yes, you're right," she said. "This is not the time to cry. Tell me what to do."

She was astonished at his quick intelligence, at the authority, at the ability to cope which he at once threw into the fight. Suddenly she was taking orders from him, and doing exactly as he told her. She looked upon him now in awe and with a fresh variety of respect, as together they, with Carlyle in charge, set out to try to save the child.

It was Carlyle who saved that baby. He saved it by taking charge. And he saved it by what he brought. First of all, he got medicine from the ship. Then quickly he took a step which he had resolved on before entering the room and finding the baby ill. Then it seemed necessary. Now it seemed urgent.

Given a certain amount of intelligence and resourcefulness, it was not really so difficult. And the opportunities were heightened for anyone on a ship, such as an LST, which carried troops. The fact that rations for the troops were drawn from the Army gave someone from the ship access to Army dumps. Reserving a little for other uses did not mean that the troops were going to be on short rations on their overnight trip to the beachhead, since an amount over and above any conceivable need was always drawn. If a can or two of 10-in-one rations, for example, departed the Army dump but somehow did not reach its destination of the ship no one even noticed. There were so many other cans and no one bothered to keep any close inventory on such materials. On steaks, when they were available, yes—these were inventoried as carefully as a shipment of diamonds; even on cans of peaches. But the ordinary ration things were so plentiful. The

American genius for supply was really one for oversupply, to always assure there would be far more of most items around than could ever possibly be used. Army dumps became one source of Carlyle's appropriations. In the natural course of things it sometimes fell to him to take a truck to some Army dump to pick up supplies. More of this duty was always available for anyone who volunteered for it. Carlyle began volunteering a lot. In addition Navy storekeepers and Army supply sergeants would generally give the person picking up the stores any item within reason he wanted, and this was just handed over outright. The two-piece suit of Army woolen long underwear, for example. Carlyle could easily ask for and get one for himself when he made the trip. A man with a little personality to throw around at the storekeeper or supply sergeant found no trouble in gathering up items like these.

A 10-in-one ration, a tin of corned beef, a set of wool underwear: these items brought astonishing sums from a hungry and cold populace, and completely changed the life in the apartment. It blossomed with a stove, with clothes and blankets and food. The sailor's enterprise also fed the doctor the cigarettes and other items which kept him in almost constant attendance on the baby. Want, the oppressive, almost literally killing want, disappeared. And the Army and the Navy, it was not difficult for Carlyle to detect, still had plenty to spare. He could reason accurately enough that he was taking only what amounted to surplus goods; harming no one; depriving no one; and helping a household besieged by material need to the point of threatening not only its morals but its very life as well. Carlyle knew what to take and what not to take. Cigarettes, for example, were a dangerous item, due to the fact that men would complain more loudly if they were short-rationed on cigarettes than on anything else, hence a closer check was kept on their distribution. This presented Carlyle with a problem since cigarettes were the one thing the doctor wanted most of all. The sailor solved the problem with interesting ingenuity. He bought the American cigarettes on the black market, with proceeds derived from sale of other Navy and Army items.

As the week of the ship's stay in port drew to an end, Carlyle looked around for a good-sized haul that would carry Coco and her baby along during his absence, and for a while afterward if anything should happen to the ship. On a trip to the Army dump he had discovered something interesting while chatting with one of the supply sergeants. The sergeant badly wanted one of the Navy jungle-cloth jackets. This was a superb garment, lined with heavy wool. It would turn aside wind, water, and intense cold and the Army man felt, with a certain service disloyalty, that the Army had nothing quite like it. He spoke almost soulfully of the Navy's jungle-cloth jacket; and by allusion suggested that he would trade off almost anything the Army had to get one. Talking with Coco, Carlyle had learned that the storeowner to whom she traded U.S. items for food had his soul equally set on another, very different item, which was American flour. He would give more for it than for anything. The Italians virtually lived off bread and pasta yet flour of any kind was in very short supply. Even when they got it it was a gritty gray stuff that made the teeth grind. White flour, which they really longed for, was almost nonexistent. If the storeowner could get one of those 100-pound sacks of flour which the Americans had, he would keep Coco and her child and Rebi, who now was practically a member of the household, supplied with food for an entire month. Just this one item would set Carlyle's mind at ease when the ship left. He decided to pair off the Army sergeant's and the Italian storeowner's deepest longings. He had got the jungle-cloth jacket and set up the flour. But now he needed a jeep to go pick up the flour. He asked Barclay if he knew where he could get one for a couple of hours and Barclay arranged for him to use Shanley's. Carlyle hitched a ride into town on a weapons carrier to pick it up. Shanley was very pleasant to him and Carlyle was overcome by the sight of the cherub room. He wished Coco could see it. Shanley showed him the room's features, including the armoire, with its dresses above and its cans of 10-in-one rations, cartons of cigarettes, stacks of soap below. The sight reaffirmed Carlyle in what he was doing. If an officer took these things, it was certainly all right for him to do so. He also

believed that he had a somewhat better reason than the officer's, Shanley being quite bland about the uses to which he
put these items.

"Well, I've found a few," the officer said as they stood at
the armoire. "Though lately I've been concentrating on one in
particular. She's a doll. A real doll. I can actually put my two
hands around her waist and they'll close."

"She sounds really small," Carlyle made polite conversation.
"Of course you've got large hands I see."

"The best of them over here," Shanley said in nostalgic tones,
"the best of them . . . well, I don't know that there's any
better beauty anywhere."

"I'm inclined to agree with that, sir," Carlyle said.

"And this one is the very best of them. Incidentally, did that
storm the other night do any damage in Pozzuoli?"

"No damage, sir. Just shook things up a little."

Up above Carlyle looked in admiration at the rack of dresses
and wished he had some for Coco. He could not help thinking
of the room as a contrast to hers. But this stirred no resentment
in him. It was the way things were. But he found himself idly
wondering how Coco would look in some of those dresses.

"Well, I guess I'll be going. Thanks very much for the jeep,
sir," he said. "I'll have it back in two hours."

"Take your time," Shanley said. "I won't need it today. In fact
I won't be here, so just leave the jeep in the parking lot on the
other side of the villa, will you? And stick the key on the mantel-
piece here. This room is usually kept open anyhow."

He seemed a very generous man, Carlyle was thinking as he
drove off. He drove along idly reflecting about this and about
Iowa a little and, less idly, about Coco and the baby. He was
also reflecting on what he felt was a valuable conversation he
had had with the Army sergeant at the dump. He had discovered
that the sergeant had a mania for collecting German war
souvenirs. It was a mania that existed more in the back lines
than in the forward ones. The sergeant had mentioned that he
would value indeed a German Luger if Carlyle could get hold of
one on one of his trips to the beachhead. Carlyle had felt glad to

discover the sergeant's hobby as a source for future trading for items Coco could use and had filed the Luger request for action. Occupied with all these thoughts he was not aware that another jeep was following him. The people in it had become increasingly interested in a jeep labeled BOMB DISPOSAL.

When the ship at last sailed from that week, when the new LCVP was in its davits and the new 40-millimeter on its mount, a great many things had taken place. The baby was well. And Coco and Carlyle felt as welded to each other as that gun was to that deck. They felt as if their feelings for each other had been but a kind of toy before, a method of speaking, a ritual one went through. Now the feeling was imbedded deep in them so that surely nothing could tear it out. They felt indeed that the child was theirs. And in a sense now, it was. Their feeling had graduated, without their even saying it, into what was probably love.

Whatever it was that Barclay and the nurse had, whatever its name, also deepened that week. And it brought him one clear fact.

He had called her the moment he could get off the ship and told her the news of the week the ship had in port. She was as excited as himself.

"Look," she said. "I think I can trade off duty. Trade off a lot of duty I mean. I'll have to work practically all the time next week, and the next, most likely. But it'll be worth it. Let's see Naples this week. Let's see Naples together, and things around Naples, everything there is to see. It will be something for us to have, to have seen it together."

Barclay had four of those seven days off and she managed to get the same ones. One day they went out to Pompeii. Another they took the boat that now carried troops on liberty over to Capri and spent the day climbing around the island. Another they got Shanley's jeep and drove north through the countryside where now and then a burned tank or a damaged artillery piece stuck up from the waving green grass, and through towns where it was a problem to find one complete house standing. Out of one heap of stones stuck a surprising sign, JESUS SAVES, and

Barclay wondered if an Italian or an American had put it there. It didn't sound very Roman. It was cold that day but along the way they could see Italian refugees headed south, most of them barefooted, all carrying their remaining belongings in the eternal little bag on a stick over their shoulders, wandering down the railroad tracks, or on the sides of the road. There were signs saying No CIVILIAN HITCHHIKERS—there was no question who put these up—but Barclay and the nurse picked up a family of five which piled into the back seat and took them into the next town where they disappeared among the stones, scraggling around for some piece or others of theirs that might be left, or perhaps just to verify what they already knew, that nothing was. Coming back they stopped into a large cathedral they both wanted to see, and the guide, anticipating cigarettes, took them on an eager tour ending with a climb up a long flight of spiral stone steps to the great organ, a trip which he assured them he by no means tendered everybody. "Play!" he invited them—as though all Americans played the pipe organ. "One of you play something!" He said it like a gift, figuring a couple more cigarettes maybe. He didn't seem at all surprised when the nurse sat down and played some passages of something Barclay liked but had to ask the name of. It was Bach's *Toccata and Fugue in G minor* and the great sounds swept out through the empty cathedral and its old, cold stone which Barclay always liked to touch.

The fourth of their days they spent in Naples itself. Churches were the main things to see in Naples, in fact about the *only* things now, but this was all right with Barclay, who had always been interested in church architecture since his father "built" several churches, and they hit three of them, the fourth-century Basilica di Santa Restituta with its five naves; the Church of San Domenico Maggiore to see also the adjoining monastery where Thomas Aquinas was a professor of philosophy, "I'd liked to have been a student in *his* class," Barclay said; the Santa Anna dei Lombardi with its Renaissance sculpture; and finally standing before the tomb of Virgil on the heights of Posillipo and reading there the inscription "*Arma virumque cano . . . ,*"

"I sing of Arms and of Men and deeds of Valour"; then descending to the city and doing what they both most liked to do, which was to walk up and down Via Roma. Barclay never tired of seeing that street, with its troops of so many different nationalities, and it turned out she got the same excitement from it as did he. But there was something different about the street now. Neither had seen it for a couple of weeks or more and they both saw the difference at once, with a certain startlement for the meaning it carried to both and neither mentioned.

Via Roma was filling up, that was the difference. It was always crowded but now great throngs of troops and sailors in many uniforms filled the sidewalks solid and bulged over into the street. And they were not, now, just those back for a rest from Anzio and Cassino, not even just that normal number one would see headed up as replacements for the wounded and dead from those two places. Now there was a vast horde of unblooded troops, so many, many of them that it could mean only one thing, that the effort for the big breakthrough at Cassino and the breakout at Anzio, so long talked about, could not be long away now. The troops had to be there for that, there could be no other reason. There could be one other reason actually, which was that they were headed for another invasion somewhere else. But Barclay didn't believe it. No one did. Those troops were the harbinger of something new at Cassino and Anzio. Never had the pulse of the street beat so loudly, so eagerly, almost so avariciously for whatever was to be had. One could sense the bars and the brothels fattening and see the vendors and pimps run about with a frenzy which seemed to suggest that they, too, knew they would never have such a chance again, such a flood-tide of eager customers, there being no customer so prodigal as he who does not know if he will be around tomorrow to be one, and the sellers sensed strongly this identity of these men. It would have been like a carnival had one not known of the admission price to be paid up the line and in the sealanes to Anzio. Barclay looked at that huge crowd, and thought of all the others waiting to replace *them* if necessary, and thought: There was not a sane man alive, or at least one in whom remained the ability to assess

facts, who did not know how this war would end. But the war had
to go on.

And as it did so, and even as he walked down the street slowly
with her through that crowd, he was aware that the days of their
being able to see each other were drawing to an end. For a while
Barclay had found himself torn. If the time came soon for
Cassino and for the breakout at Anzio, and surely they would
happen at the same time, it would mean she wouldn't have to go
to the beachhead. It also meant the ship would be taken away
somewhere. But, now, he found himself hoping for it to come
soon. Though it meant leaving her, he wanted very much that
she wouldn't have to go to Anzio. For he was remembering
suddenly an infantryman they had taken back recently on the
ship, what the infantryman had said: "I don't know exactly that
the German artillery is *aiming* for those field hospitals. Size of
that beachhead what it is, I think they can just throw anything
down from up there and be sure of hitting something, it has to
hit something. Anyhow they've been taking a terrible beating,
those field hospitals. I don't think there's any place I'd hate to be
on Anzio worse than a field hospital. Elsewhere you can at least
dig in but at those hospitals you're in a *tent*. . . ." He had taken
to questioning Army people they took back and forth to the
beachhead as to when the breakout might come, even questioning
prisoners-of-war. There were as many different guesses as men
he talked with. But now he did not need ask anybody. He knew
now, walking on Via Roma, that it would be soon. He tried not
to think about the fact that soon now they would not be together again during the war. For the one clear fact that week
brought him and which he was to keep and hold with him was:
at the end of it he could wonder if he had found any pleasure in
life greater than just to be with her. And he wished he had a
name for that.

He had had a sense, that last day, of their being followed, a
curious imagining, he felt. The sense was still with him when
toward the end of it he took her into a little shop off Via Roma.

"I want to buy you something," he said.

The store didn't have much to offer but he did find a silver half-bracelet with an oval malachite stone set on it and he bought that and put it on her wrist. He paid for it in the coin of the realm, in lire. Then, coming out, he turned and looked up quickly and saw two men get in a jeep and drive off. There was only one distinctive thing about them. He had got just enough of a glimpse of them to see it. It was this: They wore American military uniforms, but with no insignia of rank, no marking whatever. He kept thinking but could not remember and decided he would have to ask Shanley. Now as they came up to the jeep he did remember. He remembered he had heard that the CID did that. At that moment he looked up and his eyes rested upon the two large words on the front of the jeep, BOMB DISPOSAL.

15

DUSK OFF ANZIO

It was dusk off Anzio. They had brought up a load of fresh American troops and watched them leave the ship under full field packs to go up into the line. Instead of taking something else on immediately for the run back, the ship had been ordered to drop anchor and wait overnight to take on tomorrow something which was apparently not quite ready to go today. Whatever it was. No one had bothered to tell them that, or perhaps no one knew yet.

Now the PCs and the destroyers were running around the harbor producing the smoke screen which was always laid on at dusk and dawn, the two periods, being the times of lowest visibility for ship's lookouts, favored by the Germans—or any enemy of surface ships—for striking. They had a lot of targets to choose from in that anchorage, which was jammed with a variety of vessels. The white screen added to the problems of the German planes looking for something to drop a bomb on and German submarines looking for something to put a torpedo into. But it also increased the possibility of the ships ramming each other, and the LST 1826, like all the ships, had a full quorum of lookouts stationed, not only on the fo'c'sle and fantail but also along both sides. The captain kept on the flying bridge atop the conning tower with a bull-roarer in his hand. And all over the ship all was quiet, both to detect the approach of other ships and prevent ramming, and because the smoke itself seemed somehow to encourage the blotting out of sound as well as sight. The smoke brought a strange feeling to the ship. Men talked, when they did, in whispers. No one could see more than a few yards away. The men on the fantail could not see their own ship's bridge or the men on the bridge the ship's bow. Once a destroyer appeared abruptly out of the mists in that small yardage directly upon them—they could see the destroyer's bridge before they could see the ship itself, so that the men on it appeared to be standing on a cloud—and the captain sang out through his megaphone: "Destroyer! You are on collision course with LST!" The destroyer heeled over hard and the men could make out a few smoke-wreathed, helmeted figures in kapok jackets and then three numbers on the bow before she sheared off no more than ten feet from them and was swallowed up in the white mists from which she had emerged so ghostlike.

"Jesus H.," Ensign Horner said softly. He was standing near the captain. "Sometimes I don't know if these smokescreens don't hurt more than they help. There's not much to choose between being hit by a JU-88 and being rammed by one of our own destroyers, is there, Captain?"

The question was highly rhetorical but the captain gave it an answer. "Well, we have to use those smoke pots," he said. "We can't waste valuable materiel like smoke pots, can we, Horner?"

"That's a point, sir," Horner said, and grinned. "I wonder if a destroyer could ram us hard enough to get us sent back?"

"Yes, back to Naples," the captain said. "They have a very good ship's repair department in Naples, I'm told."

"I hear the one in the Brooklyn Navy Yard's not so bad either, sir," Horner said.

"Naples is a little closer. Unfortunately."

Horner waited a moment then said in a voice of absent forlornness: "I'd like to be in Brooklyn. It's so close to Manhattan."

The ship stood at general quarters and Red Anzio, meaning there were German planes in the vicinity, had been declared an hour ago. The conning tower watch listened with a kind of idle attentiveness to the reports coming over the TBS radio from the control ship.

> 2016—2 hostiles about 5 miles east of Rome coming southwest, 2 other hostiles coming south from the Rome sector. Several hostiles at the mouth of the Tiber coming south

They looked reflexively toward the sky, forgetting momentarily that they could see nothing through the smoke. The voice from the radio kept up its chant.

> 2020—We have about 15 hostiles approaching Anzio from the northeast and northwest. One hostile along the coast of Anzio about 10 miles

> 2025—About 6 hostiles 5 miles north of Anzio coming south

> 2027—We have 25 hostiles coming into the area

It sounded a little, it occurred to Porterfield, the helmsman on watch, like an auctioneer hawking doubtful wares.

> 2029—Still hostiles north of Rome coming south

> 2030—PC this is Tinian stand by to smoke on order

> 2033—All hostiles now diving on the harbor

They could hear the sound of guns from both sides, to shore and to sea, but they sounded far off. Perhaps the shroud of smoke made them seem farther off than they actually were.

> 2036—We have 30 hostiles in the area

> 2037—PC this is Tinian start smoke

> 2038—We have more hostiles approaching Anzio from north of the Tiber

Now the screen was breaking some and they could see blobs of black smoke mattressing up from the shore; then, as the screen broke still more skyward, smaller patches of ack-ack above the darkening blue sea.

> 2050—We have white flares in the area

They could see these about the same time the lookouts on the control ship did, for the sky was suddenly lighted up to sea, showing glossy, glistening water and on it the naked shapes of the ships riding. The flares would have been dropped from the German planes hopefully to light up some targets. In their moment of sight they saw a plane, German or friendly, corkscrewing down the sky then hit the water in a red rash of fire. Then, apparently from the PC, great bundles of smoke began to roll across the harbor and the scene was again blotted out in opaque white.

2102—Hostile about 3 miles northeast of Anzio the aircraft is strafing out

2106—Still have hostile aircraft in the harbor

Their eyes kept turning automatically in the directions the radio gave, but on all sides and above they were now wrapped in smoke, though they could hear planes cackling somewhere above them. They waited, saying nothing, but listening more carefully now to the squawking radio.

2109—Still have hostiles north of Rome coming south

2112—1 hostile north of Lake Albano

2120—We have hostiles at Cisterna coming south

It was seven minutes when the voice came again.

2127—Stop smoke

They waited, knowing what that meant. Then in ten minutes they heard the two words they waited for.

2137—White Anzio

By that time the smoke had begun to clear, first to sea, then toward the shore. It was night now and they could see three red flames on the beach. The flames were very large.

"Must be gas and ammo dumps," someone said.

The captain waited a few moments then ordered the ship to secure from general quarters, adding, over the p.a. system:

"All hands are cautioned to keep their clothes on throughout the night." The men started taking off their helmets and kapok jackets. They were all glad to be out of the smoke. It gave you claustrophobia. Porterfield went below to get the nightly game going.

An LST was not deemed of sufficient size to warrant a chaplain being carried aboard. Only at cruiser-level did the Navy take into account the spiritual needs of a ship's company. The LST 1826 was, therefore, perhaps fortunate to have a man who filled this need in addition to his other duties.

Edgar Allan Poe Porterfield had not chosen to exercise the option of staying out of the war which his ministerial studies gave him (he was just on the point of being ordained). He decided instead that it might be useful experience for a man who was going to devote his life to try to save men's lives and souls to be among them for a while, so he joined the Navy. When the ship was in port he let the full-time chaplains take over but if Sunday caught the ship at sea he held a service on the large Number 2 hatch, and the captain would have the church pennant—white with a cross and the only banner ever to fly above the colors on a United States Navy vessel—run up the mainmast. It was a rather curious service. The service even had music, guitar music supplied by Carlyle, who played hymns he knew. The LST 1826 numbered in its company men of at least three radically different ways, so they supposed, of worshiping the Creator and men of no way at all and even though Carlyle happened to be a Methodist and therefore played Methodist hymns, men who ordinarily worshiped in a different fashion when they did so at all decided it wouldn't hurt to sing them and anyhow the rhythm of them was nice, and in some uncertain way the hymns, floating from Number 2 hatch out over the sea, seemed to suggest hope for an end to the lives they had and a return to the ones they had left. A number who had never heard of them learned such hymns as "Faith of Our Fathers," "Beulah Land," and "How Firm a Foundation, Ye Saints of the Lord." In an ecumenical spirit Porterfield got hold of copies of the

Missal and the Torah and for the short service would read from
these as well as from the Book of Common Prayer, which is
Episcopalian. Porterfield himself was a Presbyterian. Porterfield
read very well aloud and the men liked to listen to him. The
services on Number 2 hatch were well-attended. Sometimes in
addition to the spiritual passages he read profane poetry. Some
of the men understood what he was reading and some didn't,
and some of the latter came to understand over the months, but
all, from the first, liked to hear Porterfield read. He had a rich,
soft, somewhat drawling voice that was pleasant on the ear.

"That's the goddamndest sort of religious service I ever seen,"
Mason, the second-class cook, said once. "Excuse me." But he
never missed one.

Porterfield was a gangly man, mostly bones, and so tall he had
almost to hunch over the helm when he had it. In his non-
sermon speech he was equally soft-spoken and had a slow deliberate way about him, except at one place. At the helm his reactions
were lightning quick. His hands seemed to have a peculiar sensi-
tiveness to the ship's helm, as if there was a special understanding
between the hands and the helm. The hands seemed almost
loving on it, as if they were playing a beautiful instrument.
Whatever it was, no one on the ship even pretended to be in
Porterfield's class as a helmsman.

He was a rather singular chaplain. For one thing he loved
poker. He was one of the finer players aboard and a regular
participant in the running poker game which convened in the
steering gear room. His reading of Scripture had not yet revealed
to him a single verse forbidding gambling. He hoped it never
would. He sometimes softly hummed a hymn when dealing the
cards or studying his hand. And even some of the other men got
in the habit after a while, humming and even singing a little so
that a man might be quietly and unawarely giving out with "In
the Sweet Bye and Bye" while studying an ace in the hole or
trying to decide whether to draw to an inside straight.

Other than Porterfield the game's most consistent regular was
Mason, who was a pretty steady loser but could stay in the
game because he had the advantage of a steady side income.

LSTs were not supplied with any appliances for washing clothes but the crew had chipped in and bought an old Maytag in New Orleans and installed it in one of the after troop berthing compartments adjoining the shower so that water could be piped from there. Chiefly as a means of acquiring money for the poker game Mason did all the ship's washing and at any given hour of the day or night was absolutely certain to be found in one of four places: the conning tower, the steering gear room, his bunk, or feeding the washing machine, the last-named being the place where he spent most of his time in order to keep up with the demands a crew of this size would make on one wringer model. There was a more or less steady stream of complaints about the cleanliness of Mason's finished products but on his behalf it must be said that he and the Maytag had a considerable load to carry and as Mason himself always observed whenever such complaints were made to him, anyone was free to take his business elsewhere.

The other regulars in the poker game were Latimer, Nelson, Wiley, and Abbot. However, since not all of these were always off watch at the same time, others sat in from time to time. It was not, ordinarily, an excessively high-stakes poker game, its main purpose being to talk, over and between hands, in a congenial framework and pass the time. It passed a great deal of that, for it had been running almost from the commissioning of the ship. It had started in New Orleans, continued across the middle Atlantic, into the Mediterranean, and had survived the invasions of Sicily, Salerno, and Anzio. That night, the men sat on the deck with their helmets and kapok jackets beside them, occasionally getting up and putting both on as they went to their various battle stations when a Red Anzio was proclaimed and the general alarm sounded.

For some reason Barclay had never felt so lonely as he did that night while watching the battle of Anzio. He had the 2000–2400 watch and when he came off it he did not feel sleepy as he almost always did the moment he got off watch. He had some coffee in the wardroom, where he listened to the German propaganda radio in Rome, which had all the best tunes, play in succession "I Get a Kick Out of You," "Just One of Those Things," and "You Do Something to Me," which all happened to be by Cole Porter, who happened to be Barclay's favorite composer of songs, got up and prowled restlessly around the ship, stopping to talk with men he ran into. He went topside again.

He still knew sleep wouldn't come and he walked up to the forward part of the ship where he could get a better view of the shore and stood with his foot on a bitt looking out over the dark sea into the black mass of Anzio. There was no breeze and an acrid smell of smoke hung in the air. The water lay almost noiseless, he could hear the soft murmur of it against the sides of the ship and see it surflessly touch the beach. On the fo'c'sle he could make out the silhouetted shapes of the two lookouts standing alongside, one mainly a sky lookout, for planes, and the other a surface lookout, for, especially, the new one-man submarines they had been warned so much about and none of which they had seen. He could see their heads angled differently, one up, one down, one pair of eyes scanning the sky, the other the water, for the enemy. Every once in a while the two men traded scanning targets to balance the keen strain on their neck muscles. The flashing of shelling from both sides kept streaming across the sky and the long, aching whines of it, interspersed with the chains of red tracers racing upward from the ack-ack guns and blanking out the stars. He thought of the death and mutilation being inflicted on both sides tonight and of how it was the most extreme form of lunacy, the most consummate of follies, and yet had to be. All around him, black and silent, stood the shapes of other ships. A tremendous red explosion erupted ashore, quite nearby, fading away after a while into a steady, glimmering red patch, almost like a campfire, and he wondered idly what had caught fire. In the starlight he thought he saw a plane maneuvering high up. He looked forward and saw that the bow lookout had also seen it. If it were friendly, presumably the control ship knew, and if it were not, presumably they would have a Red Anzio. They had had five already that night.

There was nothing much to do. The ship, along with most of

those in the harbor, had tried firing once at something high up, all of them together in such close space making a fearful clatter, until an angry voice broke over the radio from the senior naval officer present on the control ship. "This scandalous firing will stop at once." The SOPA apparently felt the ships, being so numerous and anchored so close to one another, were in more danger from their own fire than from any planes, and he may have been right. It was probable, with that message, that a certain showering of American shrapnel had fallen on the control ship —indeed the 1826 had received a few pieces herself. In any event the ships were ordered not to open up unless something came in on a direct run on them. They would have felt a good deal better if they could fire. Since they couldn't there really wasn't much to do except for the lookouts to keep a sharp eye.

He tried to think what it was that made him feel so particularly lonely tonight, and could think of no one specific reason. He was lonely to be on the ship right now, lonely for Sarah, lonely most of all because of the war, and because what the war did more than anything else was to make you lonely, incredibly lonely. He thought about back home, and of the years going by, and that made him more lonely. He thought about the nurse, and that made him more lonely still, because he knew it was coming to an end. It had to come to an end, anything like that did. The men over on that black mass were doing the things that would bring it to an end, and the men down the coast at Cassino were doing the same thing, which was to kill Germans, kill lots of Germans, giving up in fair exchange some indeterminable number of their own, American and other lives, and bring their two cymbals of hard fighting clanging together, and everyone to march on Rome. And that would bring all of it—Anzio, Cassino, himself and the nurse—to an end, which was a desirable thing, since it would get on with the war. He wondered what the people in Rome, so near where he stood, were doing tonight. Readying themselves, accustomed Romans since the Caesars, to receive one more in that long roll-call of invaders, or liberators, bannered and blood-bought, over the centuries? Yes, liberators. The word, he believed, had validity. At Anzio and Cassino they must get on with the

war, and whatever he and Sarah had would come to an end, a
microcosm invisible and unvalued, properly so. Whatever it was.
He didn't know, only that he was lonely without her. Then the
simple thought occurred to him that it would have been very
strange if he hadn't been since any man would have preferred to
be with almost any girl as opposed to standing up here on the
forward part of a ship looking at Anzio. The rational thought
didn't make him any less lonely. Rational thoughts seldom do.
And also she wasn't any girl. But he did not, he told himself
again, want to be in love in the war. That was the last thing he
wanted. It was simply impossible, he felt, ever to know in war if
it was a valid thing in itself, or if it was the war, making you
reach out for anybody, which had brought it on. Just as he didn't
believe in any of the after-the-war talk. It was just something to
talk about, something to live ahead for since no one liked living
in the present. He was aware someone was approaching and
turned his head a little. He could not make out the man until he
spoke.

"It looks pretty active over there, doesn't it, Mr. Barclay?"
Carlyle said.

"Hello, Red. Yes, pretty active," Barclay said. Their conversation came soft and quiet, the aimless, easy talk of two men who
were comfortable with each other. Barclay suddenly felt a little
less lonely with someone there to talk with.

"Where do you think we'll go when it's done over there, Mr.
Barclay?"

If there was any one favorite subject on the ship, it was this:
where they would go next.

"I wish I knew," the officer said. "I guess our side will be going
into Southern France or the Balkans, one or the other. And I
guess they'll be going into France across the channel too. And
I would guess that we would be in one of them. I'm guessing a
lot. I don't know."

"We could be sent home, too?" The surprising thing about the
question was the lack of eagerness in its tone.

"That's always possible. I think last year a ship was sent home."

He could hear Carlyle's soft laughter. But when he spoke he

sounded more serious, as if he were trying actually to sound out for information and was not just talking the eternal talk of the possibility of the ship going home.

"Well, I don't think they'll send us back," Carlyle said convincingly. "I think we'll stay over here."

"Well, there is always one more invasion to make."

It was the favorite phrase—"one more invasion" and everybody would go home. Only there was always one more invasion after the present one. Indeed a prevailing belief, voiced sometimes with resignation and at others with bitterness, was that when they ran out of places to invade on the continent of Europe the LSTs would then be sent through the Suez Canal to the Pacific and thus successfully avoid touching the United States at all. A star shell burst over the beachhead, sending a brilliant gleam of light across the water and spilling over the LST. By its light they could see a shell kick up water, a distance off. They watched the star shell until it was extinguished. Then the shelling began to pick up sharply and both men put their helmets on.

"Of course they'll have to keep bringing troops and supplies to Italy for a long time yet, won't they, Mr. Barclay? I mean, from places like Africa and Sicily. What I mean is, isn't it possible we could be put on a run to do that, so that we'd be making runs from Sicily and Africa to Naples to bring in troops and supplies for the Army? I mean they're going to keep going up Italy, aren't they, and they'll need more men and supplies."

The long ranging whistling whine they knew to be the German 170-millimeter sang across the sky and they listened to it until it faded away, hitting or not hitting something.

"That's true," Barclay said thoughtfully and wondered what the sailor was getting at. "I suppose they'll put some of the ships doing that. I guess it's what numbers they draw out of a hat. I'd like to watch them make that drawing sometime."

Carlyle apparently couldn't put it off any longer. But when he said it he said it very quietly, as if the Germans or someone else over on the beach would hear him and do something about it if they overheard.

"Mr. Barclay, would it surprise you if I told you I'd fallen in love with a girl over here."

The officer waited only a moment. "No," he said quietly, "I don't think it would too much. There are some mighty pretty girls over here."

"This one is that mother," Carlyle said. "That mother who had a baby on the ship. Do you remember her?"

Barclay turned a moment from looking at Anzio and looked at the sailor. Under the helmet he could see only the shadow of his face. Carlyle seemed to find it necessary to say a little more, now that he'd said that.

"She's not like so many of the girls over here," he said. He said just that, with no elaboration, but both knew what he meant.

"I'm sure she isn't," Barclay heard himself say. He felt immediately that he had lied. Suddenly all his senses were awake and he had forgotten his own loneliness. He wondered if he should tell Carlyle what he knew about the girl and Shanley, even if he had a responsibility to do so. Then he thought: Well, what do I know? Really know. He had never been very good at giving unsolicited advice. And even if Carlyle had asked him for it—which he was not doing, at least not explicitly—he didn't know what he would say. It might be a good thing—who could ever tell about a thing like that?—and he hoped Carlyle wouldn't ask him.

"She's a very pretty girl," he said. "She looked pretty even that night and I can imagine how she would look under better circumstances."

Even this was deceitful, he thought, since he *knew* how she looked under better circumstances. But he had not made up his mind how to do this with Carlyle, or what to do, if anything.

"Well, I'm glad you like her," the sailor said. "I'm glad you think she's so nice, Mr. Barclay." Barclay couldn't recall that he had said quite that. "Because I believe I'm going to ask her to marry me." He laughed a moment. "Of course, I don't know if she will. But she's a very unusual girl, Mr. Barclay. She has courage, she has—well, I'm in love with her, and want to marry her, let's put it that way. I hope she says yes."

Barclay visualized the young sailor and the young girl and the very young baby together. Everyone involved in it seemed very young for this kind of operation and he wondered if Carlyle had thought out the enormity of things involved here, a very long list starting with where would they live and what would they live off of. It didn't seem possible, and yet he was an exceptionally intelligent man.

"She certainly showed she had courage," Barclay said. He started to say something else. But at that moment they heard something which seemed to be rushing with great force directly down upon them, saw a huge geyser of water and then very quickly heard an explosion directly on the beach nearby. Once, later, he wondered if he would have said it, and if so how it might have been that an explosion on the beach at Anzio, by keeping him from doing so, might have changed Carlyle's future. They felt the ship vibrate distinctly, the deck under their feet making a noise from it and sending an odd, tingling sensation up through their bodies. Simultaneously three star shells burst like huge white flowers out to sea. They made enormous light and they could see dozens of ships revealed as naked as lovers in the dark caught by some great brutal lamp turned suddenly on them.

The general alarm started to gong. The sailor and the officer had already started for their battle stations.

There were a number of identifiable German guns shelling at them or somebody else at Anzio and the crew liked to guess from the sounds what they were. There was the 170-millimeter, which had a long, quite shrill, fading whistle and whine and was of course called the Whistling Willie. There was the 280-millimeter, which sounded like a runaway train coming at immense speed straight down the tracks toward you and was soon called the Anzio Express. Then there was the 88-millimeter, which may have been the finest gun on either side during the war. There was the 150-millimeter, known as the Screaming Meemies, which appeared to have been designed for demoralization as well as destruction, with holes in the sides of the shells so that they screamed out through the night a terrifying noise as they came over and in. There were the 210s and the 240s. When the ships heard a shell they didn't know whether it was coming at them, the Army, or what, and the tension came from the knowledge that they could always be next. The sound was entirely useless as far as getting out of its way. They knew a shell's destination only when one landed in the harbor fifty or fifteen hundred yards off and performed its splash. A man might then contemplate where the next one would fall. If so, he did it only as a ritual, not as an exercise to avoid it. The worst thing about the shelling was that there wasn't the slightest thing to do about it. Except try to guess what it was, which may have been done because there was nothing else to do. Porterfield was generally held to be the best man aboard in this game of identifying a shell from its sound.

In the steering gear room, where the poker game was rapidly turning into the supreme tribute to a good session, an all-night game, the shelling was heard less clearly than topside. But the vibration from whatever it was had been felt much more strongly, the room being at the ship's waterline in the after part of the ship. The game had been interrupted already by five Red Anzios and each time it picked up with renewed strength, as if the Red Anzios gave a curious sort of vigor and impetus to the game. In the few minutes before the vibration, several hands had been played off with considerably larger pots than had been accumulated earlier in the evening, possibly because the game, from starting with dealer's choice, had matured into seven-card, one-wild-card stud almost exclusively. It is a deadly game, with the first two hole cards down, the next four up, and the last down, at which point the player bets on his best five cards. With the frequent cards there are many calls to bet, and with three of the five betting cards down, the game can be like an explosion. There are few deadlier games known to man than seven-card stud. It was shortly before the vibration that Porterfield made his suggestion.

"You know, I've been thinking," he said as he raked in a pot and Mason started shuffling the cards to deal the next hand. Porterfield's drawl took him longer than most people to get through a sentence. "I think we're going to be getting out of this thing soon. I surely do. As soon as Anzio's over they'll be taking us somewhere else, that's a fact."

"Anzio over?" Abbot, the signalman, said. "Who said anything about Anzio being over? I expect they'll keep it going the rest of the war. Maybe even *after* the war."

"It's going to be over," Porterfield said. "All you've got to do is walk down Via Roma and see all those troops."

"Hell, they're going to the Balkans or somewhere," Abbot said. "We can't let anything happen to Anzio, you know that. It's become an institution."

Porterfield smiled softly. "That's possible. But I don't think so. That thing just can't keep going on much longer over there."

"I didn't see any signs of them krauts pulling out tonight," Mason said. "They've got a lot of stuff left, them sons-a-bitches."

As if to verify Mason's estimate, a long sound cruised over them and they waited, listening closely, heads cocked a little, for it to hit.

"The 210, I believe," Porterfield said by way of identification. "Well, let's just say it *might* be over. What I thought was, before we left Pozzuoli for wherever we're going it might be appropriate to have a party aboard the ship. A big party."

The men all brightened at this. "Hell, maybe Anzio will be over sometime," Abbot admitted. "I'd never want it said that any doubts of mine stood in the way of a party."

The shelling had been picking up considerably and they listened for a moment to its flat sound, its long flat whining.

"We could have the signorine from the cave," Lord Nelson said. "They're pretty scattered now but I imagine they could be rounded up with a little effort. I'll be happy to make that effort personally. I've kept in touch socially with one or two of them."

"In touch?" Mason said ribaldly.

"I vote for that," Wiley, the carpenter's mate, said. "I vote for the signorine."

A screaming noise came from afar, rose in shrillness as it came nearer, then disappeared.

"The 150, no doubt about that. Well, I don't see why not,"

Porterfield said judiciously. "The signorine would surely help a party."

"I ain't sure the captain's gonna let a flock of hoors come aboard this ship for any party," Mason said.

Porterfield raised his eyes slowly from his cards and looked balefully at Mason. "We won't be having them in the capacity of whatever their means of employment happens to be," he said gravely. "For the purposes of the party, they will be signorine. They will be present aboard as our guests. I'm sure the captain will be glad to let us invite them provided they are treated with the respect due guests."

Mason didn't understand all of this but he had great confidence in Porterfield's ability with words.

"Don't get me wrong," he said earnestly. "I'm for any way we can get them hoors aboard."

"We could even round up a band of some kind in Naples and have a little dancing maybe."

"Well, that means we *need* the signorine then," Mason said brightly. "If they's gonna be dancing they's got to be signorine."

"It might also be a nice thing to have the bambini," Porterfield said. "The signorine and the bambini might—well, let us say, balance each other. Also they'd like it and I think we'd like having them."

No one seemed to find any objection to this. They talked about it for a little as they played the next hand. It grew into a big pot and it was Wiley who raked it in.

"Yes, sir," Porterfield said, as Wiley began to shuffle the cards. "I think it could be quite a party. Maybe it ought to be a kind of benefit," he added mellifluously.

"A benefit? What the hell's that?" Mason said.

"That's what I'm coming to," Porterfield said. The next round of cards was laid out. Mason's ace was paired, he checked, and Porterfield decided to look at his hole cards. "First, though, I think I'll make a little bet."

Nothing but a seven of hearts had been added to his up cards of a diamond jack and a trey and four of hearts but the acting chaplain bet heavily on it.

"You're really bluffing tonight, Poe," Mason said. "Damned if you ain't. I'll just call—and raise."

Porterfield lifted the edge of his second hole card again then looked expressionlessly at Mason's cards. "Call—and raise you back," he said.

Mason looked surprised but he and everyone decided it was necessary to protect his investment and stayed through the two raises. The pot grew. Wiley started to deal then paused a moment with a card held out and down. They all listened to the deep, accelerating whine. It was a specific sound, and only one gun made it. It grew, seemed to be rushing toward them like an express train, then to pass over them and find water, earth, or target somewhere.

"The 280," Porterfield said, "I would surely say."

Mason had his two aces showing. He looked at his new hole card, then at the other two.

"Well, I don't have much," he said. "But it's going to cost anybody plenty to find out I don't."

And putting out both hands, heels down, he put all that was allowable, the game being pot limit, in, giving the pot a very creative lift. Now everyone settled back, looking at his three hole cards and his own and his shipmates' four up cards and estimating the situation for the final bet. Still everyone was resting a little before making it. Porterfield looked briefly at his last hole card, then sat back a little and talked some more.

"I'd say what we need to do is to raise about 250,000 lire for the benefit."

The other five men in the game looked across at him.

"What are we going to do with a quarter million lire?" Wiley said.

Porterfield's fingers drifted over the cards and his gangly body leaned forward a little. "I don't really know," he said. "I'd like for us to think about it between now and then. Maybe something to leave behind for the bambini."

"That's sure a lot of lire," Mason said at this time.

Porterfield tapped his cards gently. "Well, I had this idea. I thought we could start the fund with our poker game. Let's say the winners each night give half of their winnings to the fund until we reached the two fifty. The losers wouldn't have to give anything naturally. We could start with this pot right here." He looked at the pot. "It'd make a pretty good start."

Mason looked at his hole cards quickly and then at the pot. He had two aces showing and there must have been over a hundred dollars in that pot.

"Half the poker winnings?" Mason said indignantly. "Beginning with this pot? This is a helluva time to mention something like that!"

Porterfield smiled softly. "Don't you think the Lord might watch over us a little better if we gave one-half of the action for the benefit?" he said resonantly.

"Jesus god," Mason said. "*Half* the action."

Wiley grinned. "What a pious bastard you are, Poe."

Porterfield smiled broadly. "The winner still keeps half. There's not too much to lose."

"The hell there ain't!" Mason said. He took another darting look at his hole cards. "Give up half the winnings!" he said in disbelief. "Jesus Christ, I don't need *that* much watching over . . ."

At that moment the men heard a loud noise different entirely from any previously and felt the whole steering gear room start to vibrate. The vibration rocked them back and tumbled Mason over. Mason looked startled for a moment, as if he had been struck by an act of God. Then they heard the general alarm sounding. They got hurriedly to their feet and started for their stations, putting on their battle helmets and kapok jackets as they went. Mason looked back long enough to see that, although the cards had slid a little they had not been disarranged and no hole cards had been turned up.

"Nobody touch them cards!" he said as he left.

The sixth Red Anzio was the oddest of any that night. Boland, the surface lookout in the gun tub on the fantail, had reported seeing two things at almost the same instant: Something coming fast toward the ship through the water; and almost on top of this object and just abaft the port beam, a tremendous spouting of water. Many had also heard the shell at about the same time, and from its sound and the splash it made, it was almost certainly the 280. The other, running object had disappeared under the after part of the ship just before the explosion ashore, where it had apparently detonated against the mole. It was not difficult to calculate that had the ship been loaded and thus lower in the water, the torpedo might have passed into instead of under her. The word passed rapidly through the ship and it was a long hour before the ship once again secured from general quarters. The six men returned to the game. The cards lay undisturbed.

"That was close," Mason said soberly. "It must have passed right under here about," and he pointed to the deck.

"Bets?" Wiley said.

"Before we do," Porterfield said, "how about the benefit?"

Mason looked lovingly at the large pot. He seemed anguished, almost tortured in spirit about something, as if pulled equally both ways by a major decision he must make. Then he gave a deep sigh.

"Well, speaking for myself, I think it'd be a good idea—I guess," he said with considerable reluctance. "I'm for the benefit long as it benefits me too. Count me for it. I guess."

"All right, we're all for it," Wiley said, a little impatiently. "Now let's bet."

"Well, I've got too much in now," Lord Nelson said, and he covered Mason's bet. So did everyone else, and Porterfield even raised, and the bet was back to Mason, who looked again at his hole cards. "Call," he said; so did the others.

Mason turned his three hole cards up. One of them was an ace and one a wild deuce. He grinned happily.

"Only four aces," he said.

Porterfield sighed and turned up his cards. He seemed almost as if he hated to do it. There were five hearts spread out.

"Only a flush?" Mason said, starting to rake in the pot. "I swear, I thought you had more than a little old flush."

"Gerald," Porterfield said gently to Mason.

"Yeh, Poe?"

"I'm afraid those hearts are all straight."

Mason looked in disbelief. True enough, the hearts started at the trey and went through the seven, with a wild deuce for the six of hearts.

"Well, I'll be damned," he said. "Imagine being beaten by a piss-ant little straight flush like that. I'll be goddamned." Then his face brightened suddenly with a happy thought. "Anyhow I lose only half."

Edgar Allan Poe Porterfield counted out the pot. It came to a hundred and eighty-four dollars. Then he counted out ninety-two of the pile and gave the money to Mason.

"Why don't you be treasurer, Mason," he said. "For the benefit. We'll try to think of what to do with it. Anyhow it ought to be a pretty good party, with the signorine and the bambini. Lord Nelson, why don't you start rounding up the signorine to be on the alert."

"That I will," Lord Nelson said. "That'll be a very pleasant thing to do."

No bombs or shells fell near the ship the rest of the night. It was Porterfield's turn to deal, and humming "Lead On, O King Eternal," he started peeling off the cards.

There were three more Red Anzios that night, the ninth and last just before dawn. Having been in and out of their bunks nine times, and with daylight at hand, even the men not on watch stayed up when the ship secured from general quarters. It wasn't worth going back to bed. The dawn broke upon a scene of complete quietness on the beachhead and out over the water, where the ships still rode at anchor, largely safe through the long night. Out over the sea not a ruffle broke the blue and only a wisp of fog sheeted it, a sea of that peculiar smoothness that is like satin, smooth enough to pick up cloud shadow. They waited around awhile and when no orders came the captain signaled the shore. Back came the instructions: LST 1826 PROCEED TO NAPLES EMPTY.

"Well I'll be a son-of-a-bitch," the captain, who had not been to bed the night through and had scarcely left the conning tower, said. "They could have sent us back last night."

16

A LONG DAY

At Caserta, in a forested setting sixteen miles from Naples, stands the Queen's palace. From the palace a long and straight mall of great beauty and bordered the entire distance on either side by rows of boxwood drawn up like a guard of honor ends at a waterfall over which stand, with their attendants, the sculptured figures of Diana and Actaeon. The palace, most ideally, served now as Allied Headquarters and the mall, from time to time, as a parade ground for honors to be done to men of war for deeds performed, above and beyond the call of duty, in the mountains not so far to the north and upon the waters not so far to the west. In the case of Seaman Second Class Peter Carlyle it was a Bronze Star for his part in the sinking of the LCVP-load of Germans. That morning, before a pride of flag and general rank, Carlyle lined up there with thirty-eight other Navy men, in addition to a considerably larger number of soldiers of various nationalities, and medals were pinned on their chest, the pinning in the case of the Navy men being executed by Rear Admiral Haynes Doddridge, Commander Amphibious Forces Mediterranean, who had come over from Algiers for the purpose. A ceremonial band played, trumpets sounded, and the colors flashed by. Carlyle remembered the sun glinting from the trumpets, the intense green of the boxwood and of the eucalyptus behind it, the enormity of the palace, the riotous profusion of the statuary, and a setting overpowering in its splendor.

Carlyle had never seen Coco and the baby looking better. Really, he thought, he had brought them very little, but this little had made all the difference. But then food does, he thought simply. There was a glow in the customary paleness of both of them and it showed also in the happiness with which Coco greeted him when he came over late that morning from the ship after returning from the ceremonies at Caserta. He had got away just long enough to tell her he was back and that he did not have liberty today but would tomorrow, a long big one. He told her he had come across a way of getting a jeep sometimes and if he could get it tomorrow—he didn't know yet if he could—maybe they could even take a ride somewhere. As far as he knew, she had never been in a jeep. The idea, anyhow, of having one for a full day and riding in it out into the countryside excited her a good deal.

"Maybe we'll go to Pompeii," she said. "Have you been to Pompeii?"

"No," he said.

She smiled. "You must be the only American over here who hasn't. I'm glad. I'd like for you to see it first with me. What fun to drive out to Pompeii with you!"

He had to get back to the ship but, knowing he would see her for such a long time tomorrow, he was not unhappy when he left. Then going back he remembered he would have to get some things for her. Her keeping that health and that sense of well-being, for both herself and her baby, depended now on his continuing to provide what had brought it about in the first place.

Carlyle had not the slightest sense of wrong in taking these things to her. It was so very little, actually—who would ever miss a sack of American flour in the thousands of such sacks that were stored in American warehouses? No process of reasoning could now have brought him to the feeling that there was anything wrong in taking so little when it meant so much to this girl and her child. If he had had to reason himself up to this point, he could easily have told himself that others were taking much more, and using what they took for a personal gain. But in fact no such reasoning was necessary, since the thought of what he was doing having any stigma of "wrong" attached to it no longer occurred to him. No one suffered for it, and two people gained much. They gained, the fact was, life itself.

Back on the ship, he asked Mr. Barclay if there was any chance of getting his friend's jeep tomorrow. Barclay said he would ask about it and unless the jeep was being used on some sort of bomb-disposal business he imagined he could get it for him—in a way, then, it depended on there being no air raids tonight, and there had been few lately. Carlyle explained that he wanted it to take Coco out into the country.

"She wants to show me Pompeii," he said.

"I think I can get it," Barclay said. "I suppose you ought to see Pompeii."

"Why don't you come along and see it with us?"

Barclay felt the invitation was polite and also that he would not increase Carlyle's happiness by accepting.

"I've seen it," he said. "You see it with Coco."

Carlyle was, in fact, glad of the refusal. So much so that he blurted out something he had no intention of saying.

"I'm going to ask her tomorrow to marry me, I believe, Mr. Barclay."

Barclay looked at the sailor solemnly. He looked so young, it seemed impossible that he was about to take on a wife and a young child all at the same time. He wondered, very practically, whether they would live in Naples or in Iowa.

"Then you certainly don't want me along," he said.

Carlyle grinned. "No, I suppose not."

They talked a little more and Barclay mentioned that he was going to use Shanley's jeep tonight himself, and he would find out at that time if it was available tomorrow. Then he too said something impulsively, prompted perhaps by the feeling that any-one who was going to get married, any friend, should have things done for him.

"I have a date myself," he said. "That is, half a date. She has to be in by nine. Would you like to use the jeep tonight too? You could drop me and my date and pick us up later."

Carlyle started to explain that he didn't have liberty. Then it occurred to him he could trade off one, and that while he had the jeep he could use it for something else. They were hard to get, and with his need for one to get things for Coco, he had better take it while it was available.

"Why, yes, I'd like that," he said. "I'd like very much to have the jeep this evening if you won't miss it too much."

"I won't," Barclay said. "Shanley is picking me up about five. Why don't you come along, we'll pick up my date, you can drop us off at the officers club and pick us up about eight-thirty."

"That'll be fine, Mr. Barclay. Thanks very much."

Barclay smiled. "It's not my jeep but you're welcome."

Back in her room Coco had decided on something. Shanley had been nice to her and she felt she must tell him she could not see him any more. She asked Rebi to go into the city, go to the BOQ villa, and ask Shanley if he could see her tonight for a while. It was late afternoon by then and Rebi went over and caught the interurban into Naples. By the time he reached the villa, Shanley had left. Rebi was very good at waiting and he simply went around to the garden in back, skinned over the wall, found himself an obscure place from where he could see the lights in the officer's room when they came on, and sat down on a marble bench to wait. Above him was a trio of marble statues which he didn't know the names of. After a while he felt a little sleepy and lay down on the bench and dozed off looking up into their faces. They were very pretty. Their names were Salacia, Neverita, and Venilia, the sea goddesses.

Shanley picked Barclay up, Carlyle came along with them, and they dropped Shanley at his BOQ villa. Then they drove out to pick up Sarah. She and Carlyle seemed to like each other at once and the three of them drove back to the officers club, where Carlyle dropped Barclay and the nurse and took the jeep away. He drove away thinking this, "Mr. Barclay and that nurse are very fond of each other. I'm glad. She's a very beautiful girl. Got style." Being so very happy himself he wanted everyone else to be the same. He drove on slowly, headed for the Army dump to see his sergeant friend there. He had a German Luger for him.

Rebi awakened and saw someone moving around in the room. He walked across the garden and knocked quietly at the French doors. The naval officer seemed a little surprised to see him and his face looked thoughtful and pleased when the boy told him he had a message from Coco. She would like very much to see him for a while tonight.

Shanley called the base O.O.D., explained that he had loaned his own jeep, that a serious matter involving bomb disposal had come up, and he needed a jeep right away. One was promptly dispatched. He and Rebi got in and drove to Pozzuoli. Rebi stayed in the jeep and Shanley walked up to her room. She was already dressed ready to go out.

"Can we take a drive?" she said.

"Certainly," Shanley said. "Now?"

"Now, please," she said.

They went downstairs. She noticed idly that it was not his usual jeep, the words BOMB DISPOSAL being missing.

"I loaned it to a friend," he explained as they were getting in. "Where shall we go?"

"Anywhere," she said. "Let's just drive."

Rebi went up to stay with the baby.

As Carlyle pulled up in front of the office of the Army warehouse, another jeep parked a half-block away. Two men sat in it and talked a little. They were dressed in civilian clothes but they spoke unmistakably the American language.

"It certainly does make it easy to follow," one said. "Using a jeep with those big words BOMB DISPOSAL on it."

"That's the only thing that worries me," the other said. "That anyone would do it in such an obvious jeep."

"Maybe that's what he figures, too," the first man said. "That it's so obvious no one would suspect."

"Maybe," the other said. "Well, we'll see."

"Yes," the first man said. "We'll certainly see, very soon."

At the officers club Barclay and the nurse were dancing and talking. It was as gay as ever there. They had never danced together before and he could not remember when he had been this happy. He was very happy until later in the evening when she told him.

"I don't like to have to tell you this tonight," she said. "But I promised to tell you whenever I knew. Our detachment is going up to the beachhead in two weeks."

"It's firm?"

"It's very firm," she said.

"I'm glad you told me."

"Matthew, I don't know what to say."

"Don't say anything. We've got two weeks. Maybe Anzio will be over. Maybe the war will be over and we'll all go home."

She smiled a little. "Maybe," she said. "I guess anything can happen in two weeks."

"Anything can," he said.

They went back to their table and he ordered some more Scotch.

Carlyle took a walk through the warehouse with his friend the Army sergeant. The warehouse teemed with goods of all sorts. Enormous stacks of Army clothing. Equally enormous stacks of every kind of Army food, save for fresh food—every kind of ration, C-rations, K-rations, 10-in-one rations. Stacks of sacks of flour. Carlyle wanted such a little bit of it. Even so you could hardly ask for it. The ritual was that you had to trade off something. He pulled from his peacoat the item the sergeant had expressed a desire for, if Carlyle could ever pick one up on the beachhead, and he had, the last time up. It was a beautiful gun. A German Army officer's Luger. The sergeant fingered it lovingly.

Presently the sergeant went out and opened a gate. Carlyle drove his jeep in, and the Army sergeant put a 100-pound sack of flour in the back seat. Carlyle started to drive off.

"Wait a minute," the sergeant said.

The sergeant returned with a poncho and spread it over the flour.

"It won't hurt," he said. "You can bring the poncho back next time."

"Thanks," Carlyle said, and grinned, since one thing plentiful was ponchos. "I'll take good care of that poncho."

The sergeant grinned back. "You do that," he said. "And, oh, by the way. One other thing I'd like is a German bayonet. Do you think you can get one from the beachhead for me?"

"I'll try," Carlyle said. He was very grateful for the sergeant's passion for German war souvenirs. "Next time we go up I'll try."

He drove out and the Army sergeant shut and locked the gate behind him. In the street Carlyle switched on the jeep's headlights and started driving to Pozzuoli. Some distance back of him another jeep started up. It drove with its main lights off, using only the two thin pinpricks of lights used in blackouts to show a vehicle was there if one were driving toward it.

"Well, I think we're in," one of the men in the jeep said.

"It looks like it. Provided he has something in that jeep. We've got to catch him doing it."

"Of course he's doing no more than a lot are doing," the first man said.

"That's just the point, chum. A lot are doing it and I know they want to get someone—*anyone*—and make a real example of him. I mean really throw the book at him—and maybe stop what so many others are doing, or slow it down anyhow. It's just too bad it has to be *somebody*."

"He looks like a nice kid to be made an example of."

The second man shrugged. "We're not judging on nice looks," he said.

Shanley took Coco to his room. She had said she wanted to talk and that is all they did. She didn't drink but he had a couple of Scotches while she told him. There was nothing at all dramatic about it and the thing lasted no more than half an hour. She said simply that she liked him, and she wanted to explain why she would not be seeing him again.

"I've fallen in love with someone." She laughed abruptly. "I may be overestimating but I think he's going to ask me to marry him. And if he does I'm going to say yes. Anyhow I love him."

Shanley grinned. He thought what a girl she was, beyond any-

thing he'd seen over here. "Well, personally I'm opposed to marriage. Very obsolescent institution. But congratulations anyhow."

She smiled. "Thank you. He's a very good man."

"American, British, or Italian?"

She smiled again. "American."

"Well, I'm glad our side got you anyhow. Do you want to go
back now?"

"Yes, please," she said.

That was all there was to it and he drove her back to Pozzuoli.
It was a pretty evening and they drove very slowly. Just before
they left he had opened the doors of the great armoire and told
her he would like it if she picked out one of the dresses for a
wedding present. She picked a very pretty, very red one.

Carlyle was surprised to see another jeep parked in front of
Coco's place when he drove up. Then he dismissed it as being
another of the Navy or Army calling on another signorina in that
row of houses. He got out and walked up the stairs. He had just
arrived on the landing when he saw Shanley coming toward him.
He was too startled to say anything. The officer looked equally
startled at seeing him. Then he was gone and Carlyle walked on
and knocked at Coco's door. She let him in, he closed the door
behind him.

"What was Lieutenant Shanley doing here?"

She turned, startled.

"Do you know him?" she said.

"Does that answer my question? Do *you* know him?"

"Yes, a little," she said. "He's taken me to the officers club a
few times. I decided I wouldn't go any more and I wanted to tell
him so."

"It must have been very important if you needed to tell him
personally."

"Red, don't you understand—I was breaking it off between us."

The statement seemed to inflame him more than anything.
"What was there *to* break off in the first place?"

"Nothing. I was just being polite."

"I don't believe you."

At that moment his eyes caught a red dress he had never seen before spread out on the bed. He looked at the dress, then at the girl. Then he hurried out.

He went downstairs to the jeep, pushed the poncho back and hoisted the 100-pound sack of flour easily to his shoulder. He walked up the stairs with it, thinking idly that it would support her for a month and not caring any more, put it down on the floor.

"I've brought you what you want from me," he said. "Good-bye."

He had just turned to leave when he saw two men standing in the doorway. They were pleasant looking men, dressed in civilian clothes, better clothes than most Italians were wearing these days. For a moment he thought they were Italians following him to steal. Then one spoke. He spoke very quietly.

"I'm sorry, sailor, but you're under arrest." The voice could have belonged to someone from Iowa.

The man showed him a card. It had a name on it and the words *U. S. Army—Criminal Investigation Division.*

"I'm sorry," the man said simply again.

From the moment Sarah had told him she was leaving in two weeks, the officers club had seemed like a prison to Barclay and he wished he had not loaned Carlyle the jeep and would never have, had he known. He would have liked to take her somewhere, anywhere they could be alone and talk. Then when Carlyle did not show up and it was time for her to get back to the hospital, Barclay assumed he must have had an accident with the jeep and called the base transportation pool, explained the situation, and asked for something to take her back to the hospital. It was awhile getting there and when it did it was a weapons carrier. The driver took them up to the hospital, the nurse sitting between the two of them. At the hospital door Barclay told her he would see her tomorrow.

"We'll talk about the two weeks tomorrow," he said. "Don't think about it at all until then and we'll go into the whole thing tomorrow."

"I won't think about it," she said, "until tomorrow."

He had the driver take him back to Pozzuoli and the LST. He arrived there to find a surprising sight. In the darkness troops and weapons carriers were being loaded. The captain was very busy and could only tell him that they had been given sudden orders to take these men to Anzio tonight, why, he didn't know, but that they were shoving off the moment they were aboard. And he told him one other thing, that a shore patrol man had dropped by the ship to tell them that Carlyle had been arrested and was being detained on a charge too serious to let him go even to rejoin his sailing ship.

Barclay hurriedly wrote two notes. One to the nurse, explaining that he could not see her tomorrow. The other to Shanley, asking him to look into whatever the thing was with Carlyle, that apparently there had been some mistake. In both notes he said he expected to be back the day after tomorrow and would immediately be in touch with them. He put the notes in envelopes, sealed and addressed them, wrote *Urgent* on both and went over and left them at the little base office on the mole, with a request they be delivered tomorrow on the regular courier trips to military points in Naples.

He went back to the ship and dug in to help with getting the trucks and troops aboard. The weapons carriers were packed in, main and tank decks, and then the troops came on in long files in the night. The loading took place very fast and immediately they were on, the ship raised its bow ramp, closed its bow doors, backed off by pulling against its stern anchor, swung slowly around and stood out for Anzio.

17

REINFORCEMENTS

Now as the ship pushed north through the night, he knew there was hardly any secret to it any more. The ships had been taking up more, many more, fresh troops to the beachhead than they were bringing back casualties. Anybody could have added it up. It would be soon now, and the only question was, which week, which day. The nurse had told him that the time for her detachment to leave for the beachhead had been set for two weeks from now. But these were definitely replacements, since she knew that other nurses would be coming back when they arrived. But the troops they had aboard tonight were no replacements. They were strengthening forces for a breakout. He was sure of it.

He walked along the narrow passageway in troops quarters to see if there was anything the Army needed of the Navy. From the four-tiered canvas bunks rigged almost deck to overhead on each side a foot stuck out here and there or a hand drooped down and there was the sound of soldiers sleeping and the smell of many men in close quarters. Some of the soldiers had inflated their CO_2 lifebelts for pillows, which was never to be done, in case the lifebelts were needed for their designed purpose. Barclay smiled a little and walked on. Near a watertight door he stepped around a poker game still on at 0200 under the dim light there. In a bunk nearby one soldier was still awake reading a comic book, head and book leaning out of the bunk to catch the light as he read with concentrated frown. Just beyond Barclay met their company commander walking toward him and stopped to talk a moment.

"Good evening, Captain. Everything okay?"

The captain was young, lean, and hard. He was small, Barclay towering over him, but he looked as if he could take care of himself even without the .45 which looked very big on him, hanging by the web belt from his hip. Barclay would have guessed he was a West Pointer.

"Pretty okay, Lieutenant. Okay as things can be on a ship."

Barclay grinned. The men were of a veteran division and had fought in Africa, and at Sicily and Salerno. Barclay waited a moment. He had to know, whatever knowledge this man had.

"Captain, you aren't replacements, are you?"

The Army captain grinned broadly. "Lieutenant," he said, "I don't know nothing." Then he said quietly, "No, we're not replacements. Nobody's told me but I don't think so. I surely don't."

"You're going to Rome?"

"We hope we're going to Rome, Lieutenant. I'd prefer to go to Rome than sit on that beachhead. I've never liked sitting in a shooting barrel."

The Army and Navy officers stood there a moment. "Anything you want, Captain," Barclay said then, "just let me know. We don't have any Scotch and soda but anything we got."

"Thanks, Lieutenant. I think you've done everything you can." He waited a moment then said, "I'll say hello to the Pope for you."

Barclay grinned. "Do that, Captain."

He went on topside. It was a good night and some of the men had chosen to sleep up here. He could see a scattering of humped bodies under blankets on the main cargo hatch, and the pulled-up shapes of other men sleeping in the trucks tethered topside. Far off, near Cassino, the light of artillery fire could be seen, as ever. It seemed as if it had been there always, as part of the sky, a man-made aurora borealis. No one was staying awake to watch it. These men had seen it, or one like it, many times, and there was no point in staying awake to see it again. They would see it plenty more anyhow. A few were sitting in a circle on their helmets passing a canteen of coffee around. But they were just talking quietly, not watching the shelling. Barclay looked up at the sky. It was perfectly clear and the stars flowered down. No moon, he was glad. Between the washings of the dark sea against the ship he heard one soldier talking with quiet longing of the trout season in Michigan, which he said would be on right now. Another say, "I'd like to make leave in Rome." Then, another man in the circle begin a story . . .

"The night before I left my girl got a crying jag . . ."

He went on back to his room. It was 0300. They would beach early and that was his job getting the trucks that were jammed on the tank deck off. He got into his bunk and was asleep instantly.

It seemed he had been asleep no more than a few minutes but he could sense, even in the blacked-out room, that light was outside. He got dressed and went to the wardroom and got a cup of coffee. No one was there and he sat and drank his coffee and thought about two people in Naples. He thought how Sarah would be making this same run in a couple weeks. He visualized her in field clothes walking off the bow ramp and into a truck and disappearing up that road, walking off the bow ramp and right out of his life. He tried to think whether he hoped she would go in this ship or not. He couldn't decide. Then he decided not. He didn't want to see her get into a truck and it drive away into the beachhead. He wouldn't choose that for his last sight of her. Anyhow he had nothing to do with it. He shut that off and turned to thinking about Carlyle. Carlyle arrested! It didn't sound possible. It must be some big foulup of a mistake. He would find out all about it when they got back tomorrow night and he and the captain would do something about it. He had already talked with the captain. They both knew it was a mistake.

"Hell, that boy couldn't do anything wrong if he tried," the captain said. "We'll get him out as soon as we get back. They got the wrong man or something."

The Army captain came into the wardroom. He looked clean and shaved.

"Good morning, Captain," he said. "Get any sleep?"

He got up to get him some coffee.

"Thanks," the captain said when he brought it back. "I can't sleep on a ship. No reflection on your ship, Lieutenant. I can't sleep on any ship. I can sleep in a foxhole, but I can't sleep on a ship."

"I'm sure I couldn't sleep in a foxhole," Barclay said, grinning.

"Then it looks like we're both in the right place. Good coffee," the captain said. "They always have good coffee in the Navy."

They talked aimlessly a little while and the captain told Barclay a story of something that happened at the beginning of the war when a train berth from Chicago to New York had been sold to three people including himself.

"We stood there arguing about it," he said, smiling a little at the far-away reminiscence. "Finally an old lady showed up who didn't have a ticket for anything and we gave it to her. I sat up all night talking with a Wave."

Barclay laughed quietly and they talked a little more over the coffee. "Where do you go after the beachhead is over?" the captain asked.

"I don't know, Captain," Barclay said. "Some other invasion, I guess. Wherever that is."

"Well I don't think we'll be in it," the captain said. "They've more or less said we're rotating, probably soon after Rome. Another reason to get to Rome. Though I'd personally prefer to get to New York."

"Wouldn't we all," Barclay said. "But you're due it if you've been here since Africa."

"Yes, these men are due it," the captain said. Barclay noticed he didn't say himself. "I didn't use to believe it. It got to be like the wolf story. But this time I think they're really sending us back. In a month or so, I'd guess. Right after Rome—I'd guess. Thanks for the coffee, Lieutenant."

The captain left to see about his troops being ready to go off. Barclay went out on deck. He could see the shape of Anzio, still quite far off. There seemed no activity whatever, only a great quiet. Anchored farthest from shore, and deliberately so, he knew, a good, identifiable distance from any other ship, he saw a hospital ship big and gleaming white where all other ships were gray, and with the big red cross on her. Pretty soon he could begin to make out the shape of ships in the harbor. The soldiers were stirring, and beginning to have their breakfast, and getting ready to leave the ship and begin whatever they were being sent to Anzio for. If it was to beef up for the breakout, and they were not replacements, at least they should have a few days before moving into the line. Though this didn't mean much. That beachhead was plenty small for what was there, German artillery could cover it all, and one part of it was about as bad to be on as another. No, not quite. The line was the worst.

Now the ship neared the harbor and their noncoms were beginning to get a vague muster of the men, some topside and some still in troops quarters, he knew. The men, bent under their full field packs, looked incuriously at the land. Still Barclay felt a desire in them to get off the ship and into their own element.

The ship moved on toward the harbor. A blinker light was going from the beach and Barclay could read it telling the ship where to beach and hear, just above him, the mosquito buzz of their own blinker saying received and that it would comply. The ship headed very slowly in. It was remarkably quiet. The air was clean and crisp. No clouds hung down.

The LST made its way carefully between a couple of freighters anchored out and aimed for its spot on the beach, probably five hundred yards away now. Barclay turned and started to the tank deck to be there when the bow ramp came down to start moving the trucks on the tank deck off first before they started bringing the main-deck cargo down on the big elevator. He could see Anzio and their spot of beach just over the bow which for a change rose and fell ever so gently. Then it hit.

At first he thought it must be a lone shell thrown down by the railroad gun far up the coast and coming in on a lucky hit. It had landed not far aft of the fo'c'sle into some trucks and men there. Then another shell shot up a geyser of water off the starboard beam and he knew it was no aimless railroad-gun lobbing. It was a 170, or something like it, and it had the ship in range. He heard the general alarm begin to gong and he started moving rapidly forward. He looked down at the water and could see that

the ship was proceeding, despite the hit and the miss. Then a
third shell spilled in not far from the cargo hatch just forward of
the superstructure. He looked over the bow and saw that the
beach was being shelled too. But the ship came on. Then he saw
two soldiers on fire just beyond him and standing facing each
other, squared off like boxers and each trying to beat out the
flames on the other. He had started toward them when suddenly
they both rushed over to the life line and leaped over the side.
Barclay looked down. The men were in the water but they continued to burn as brightly as ever. Then he knew: The shells
had been phosphorous shells, which create a fire inextinguishable
by water. Now he could see the white tracers which phosphorous
shells leave racing toward the ship. He turned back and started
running toward the forward ladder leading to the tank deck and
flung himself down it. He reached his station by the bow ramp
just as the ship came up against the mole.

The bow ramp came down and unfolded the mole immediately before him. Now Barclay saw a bulldozer grunting across
the mole with two men in it. He was looking at it when a shell
landed close in front of the bulldozer and he saw the driver
flung upward, seem to fly apart and disintegrate, and disappear.
The bulldozer started careening wildly toward the water. The
other man in it leaned over to where the driver had been and
grabbed the wheel and swung the bulldozer inshore. Another
shell arrived and this man too was gone. The bulldozer zig-
zagged crazily down the mole and then headed straight for the
water and went riderless into the sea.

Over the noise he heard Coxswain Jerry Boland, who was filling in for Carlyle as bow ramp talker on the offloading detail
and wearing that oversized helmet made for phone talkers to
wear over earphones, say, "Sir, the captain says to put your ear
to the speaker."

By pressing a button on it while talking a speaker could be
used as a two-way voice channel, which was quicker when seconds were important, allowing the captain to talk directly to you
rather than the talker repeating the words. Barclay leaned down

until his ear was against the speaker on Boland's chest and heard the captain say:

"Matthew. Get everything off as quickly as possible so they can disperse ashore. Unless the Army captain wants to keep his men aboard. They've probably got a better chance ashore. But tell him to do as he wishes. Ask him."

The Army captain was standing by him and Barclay gave him the captain's message. The Army captain smiled softly.

"Tell him we want off the ship," he said. "Tell him we'll go off, with pleasure, and thanks for the ride."

"They're going off, Captain," Barclay said into the speaker. "They're on their way."

He stood up and began directing the traffic off. The trucks roared up over the bow ramp and headed toward some shells of buildings beyond the road. There the drivers stopped the trucks, jumped out, and raced for the cover of a little rubble, clawing into the dirt. The Army captain was directing off in an orderly fashion such of his men as were not driving trucks. As soon as they were over the bow ramp they started running and spread out widely and burrowed their way into the artillery-shattered buildings.

A shell landed directly on the waterline and Barclay felt himself slammed down on the bow ramp. He got up and out the mouth of the bow ramp saw, about twenty feet across the mole, two figures lying still, faces up. He ran across the twenty feet and up to them. The shell had divided them forever. One, the Army captain, was dead, his helmet with the two painted silver bars on it flung out beyond him and his .45 ripped away and somehow stuck upright in the rubble, the muzzle pointed helplessly skyward, and the other, a corporal, alive, one leg held to his body only by thin strands of flesh. Barclay leaned over and not for a moment was he aware that the blood dripping heavily down on the corporal was his own. He moved his hand carefully over his head and felt a mass of blood and torn flesh. He lifted the corporal, cradling him carefully in his arms so that his leg would not be jolted off, and started back into the ship with him, tossing his head now and then to keep the blood out of his eyes. He laid him down in an empty space by the bo's'n's locker, picked up a dirty cloth lying there and mopped the blood out of his eyes. He told Boland to ask for stretcher bearers. He had just turned back when another shell hit closer and caught and ignited a soldier just beyond the bow ramp. The soldier started running toward the water. Barclay ran up to him and pushing his hands into his flaming body shoved him back hard.

"The water won't put it out," he heard himself say. "They're phosphorous shells and the water won't do anything. Roll yourself in the sand!"

The man either didn't hear or was crazed by the flame for he tried to fight around Barclay toward the water. Barclay tripped him and sent him sprawling. He leaned down and began rolling him over until the fire on him was gone. He picked him up, smelling the seared flesh, and started back with him to the ship through what seemed to him a haze of shrapnel hurtling around him from fragmenting shells, he would have guessed, set to explode a few feet above the ground. He got the burned soldier up the bow ramp and laid him on the deck. He stepped back to the ramp to get the traffic on off. The trucks were roaring off now, almost leaping over a huge jagged tear in the bow ramp plates which Barclay was only now aware of. Litter bearers, both Army and Navy, were moving back and forth between mole and ship, gathering up the wounded and bringing them back to the ship they had just left. He saw a shell hit comfortably a way off and spout up a geyser of water and sand. The trucks kept coming off, the tank deck emptying. Soon it was emptied entirely and Barclay had Boland tell the conning tower to have the elevator start the vehicles on the main deck down. This was slow going by comparison. But now the shells came more infrequently. Two bracketing the ship, harming nothing. The goddamn thing about it was that the ship's guns had nothing to fire on. The 170, if it was a 170 and the shells sounded and fell like it, was dug in somewhere on the high ground above the beachhead and had a fix on them. The only thing they could do was get the ship emptied as quickly as possible, giving the soldiers a better chance spread out ashore,

and then get out of there themselves. He heard another shell hit
with violent nearness.

Turning, now out the bow ramp he could see perhaps thirty
feet across the mole two soldiers lying there, both hit, and one
trying to crawl away, trying also to pull with him the other soldier,
who apparently was too badly hit even to crawl, back toward the
LST. Barclay ran down the ramp toward them, felt a shell explode
nearby and fragment into flying shrapnel, felt himself knocked
down. He got up and with a kind of staggering plunge threw
himself forward toward the two soldiers. He looked quickly at the
soldier who could not even crawl and though seeing not a mark
on him saw his eyes which only the dead have looking up at the
sky. The other soldier who had been trying to pull him back with
him and still had a hand clutched tightly to his field jacket at the
shoulder had been hit in face and chest so closely that they ran
together and you could not determine where his face ended and
his body began. But he was the one who was alive and Barclay
pried his hand from the shoulder of the dead man, having to pry
the fingers off one by one to get the hand loosened, and picked
him up and got him back inside the ship. The stretcher bearers
were putting the wounded directly on the tank deck now, not
taking the time to carry them up to the wardroom which was
used for casualties. Both Army medics and ship's crew were working on the men laid out there, trying to keep them alive. Mainly
they were either pumping blood plasma into them, one man
holding the big bottle high while another placed the needle in
the arm of the wounded man and let the plasma flow in; or getting morphine into them.

He stepped back to the bow ramp. Two soldiers were just starting a man up the ramp on a stretcher when the next shell came
in. Barclay saw one of the soldiers hit and fall and his end of the
stretcher drop to the deck. He stepped forward and took his
place and he and the other soldier got the man inside the tank
deck and they laid him out in the row of them there. He could
hear the p.a. system from the bridge directing a repair party to go
to the starboard bow where this shell or another had opened up
a hole in the ship's side. The elevator was still functioning. Go-

ing up and down, resolutely bringing from the main deck its cargo of trucks, which then shot off over the bow ramp even as the elevator started up again. He could see on the stretcher the bones of the soldier's thighs bared, stripped of their flesh by shrapnel from the same shell that had got the other soldier and got him again even while he was on the stretcher, and could see Latimer bending over him applying a tourniquet. The wounded were beginning now to form a considerable row on the tank deck where rivulets of red ran down. Some of them, he could see now, were missing arms and legs and some you could not make out their faces at all, shattered out of all identification as faces by either shell fragments or burns. Very little moaning or crying came from the wounded, and he felt a moment of wonder at this, that they could lie there soundlessly, and they had been soundless even before the medics got the morphine in them. He felt dazed from his own wound but he was able to keep directing the ups and downs of the elevator and the exiting of the trucks, the latter needing little directing. He kept mopping the blood off his face to keep his eyes free to see.

He had no notion of time any more. Suddenly a shell came in what he thought was some distance away but he saw Boland fall across the bow ramp and lie there motionless on his back. He and a soldier got him back inside. He was unconscious but how badly hit Barclay didn't know. He could only see blood oozing out around the speaker which was still on his chest. Instinctively he looked up and saw that the tank deck was empty. He got down on his hands and knees and was just able with his own blood-slippery hands to press the button on the speaker on Boland's chest that would make it a voice channel if it were still working. He spoke something, released the button, and immediately put his ear on the speaker, knowing that he would be unable with his hands to get the earphones off Boland's head. It was the captain telling him the main deck was clear of cargo and asking him to verify that the tank deck was ready for the bow ramp to be raised.

"There's a hospital ship anchored out," he heard the captain say. "We're going there to offload casualties."

Barclay had reported the break in the bow ramp plates earlier and he said now: "It may not come up fully, Captain. I'll see."

Presently the bow ramp came up and closed but from where he stood before them he could see the bow doors, apparently buckled by the shelling, close only partially, leaving a hole of daylight. Barclay had to get down on his hands and knees again and found himself barely able to do so without passing out, to put his mouth against the speaker on Boland's chest. He felt for the button with both hands and with all his will held it down long enough to get his report off.

"The ramp's closed, Captain. The doors won't close all the way —I think they're sprung. You can see some daylight. But it's good enough to get us out."

He could feel the ship starting to back off. He looked again at Boland's face. He could not tell if he were alive or dead. He leaned down and put his head against Boland's chest and thought he heard something. He stood up, almost blacking out again as he did so, to find someone to see about Boland and to see to the carrying up of the stretchers to the wardroom. He realized Latimer, the pharmacist's mate, was standing there.

"My God, Mr. Barclay, your scalp. Your scalp's laid clean back. Let's have a look."

"All right, Latimer, in a moment," he said. "Right now take a look at Boland, will you—then let's get these stretchers up."

The teams of men started carrying them up to the wardroom. When the last of the wounded were out of the tank deck Barclay went on topside. He could feel blood flowing thickly over his hair and down his face and despite his almost continuous mopping with the now-soaked rag everything was murky before him but he could sense that on the beach the shelling seemed to have stopped. All seemed enveloped again in strange silence, almost serenity. The ship was swinging around and standing out and he was aware of a blur of blue beyond which would be the welcome sea. The ship was just leaving the harbor and he had started aft, moving with great difficulty, and hoping he could keep off unconsciousness long enough to get to the wardroom to get something done about his scalp and had reached about midships when he felt a great explosion seemingly immediately beneath him. He felt himself flung down onto the deck and he felt his head hit something hard and ungiving. He could see nothing any more and he felt it must be because of the wetness flowing very heavily now down over his forehead and into his eyes. Entirely blinded, he felt himself trying to claw forward along the deck and then he decided he had better stop where he was lest he crawl right over the side. Then he knew no more.

18

THE LOST SIGNORINA

"The ship broke in two," Barclay heard someone say, not to him. He heard the voice above a falling rain. "We'd been ordered to rendezvous with a hospital ship anchored out and alone and to offload our wounded from the beach. We were approaching the hospital ship, maybe it was about 1500 yards off right then, when we knew it. There was a plane, a Junker 88, went right above the water, no more than fifty feet above it, I'd say, and way off our starboard beam when it let one go. The torpedo scooted through the water—several men topside saw it a fair ways off, but LSTs just don't turn very fast. There's really no such thing as maneuvering an LST, nurse, to get out of the way of a torpedo. Unless you get the plane dropping it first, or unless the thing just plain misses, there you are. We knew it was going to happen, and it did. You never saw a more exact hit. It came in not far forward of the superstructure but that could have been a blessing—if it had hit either farther forward or farther aft the ship would undoubtedly have gone down, bow first, or stern first, as the case may have been. But hitting where it did it broke the ship into two parts. And there we were, sliced clean through and where there had been one ship there were two ships. It was the damndest thing. There was about thirty yards of water between, the men on one part standing and looking at the men on the other part, and not able to believe it, but both floating prettily enough, swaying quite a bit of course, but neither part giving any sign in the world that it intended to go down. And neither did. We got off a blinker message to the shore at Anzio and they sent out two tugs and an LCT. The LCT took off our wounded and dead, from the beach and the JU-88 hit, and took them on over to the hospital ship. Then the tugs each took a part of us under tow and got both parts clear back to Naples here and put them in drydock. And can you imagine what they're doing there? That damn ship-repair officer says they can put it back together again. I thought someone was nuts at first but I believe the damn fool's going to succeed in doing it. Look, the man's awake."

Barclay had opened his eyes at just that point, waiting until the captain, whose voice he soon recognized, had run through it, not wanting to cause interruption for fear he would never hear the story just this way again. He listened with great attentiveness, wondering only idly who the other listener might be. When he opened his eyes two things happened at once. His head began to hurt violently, and he saw who the listener was. She was in nurse's uniform and she was Sarah Clark. He could still hear rain falling.

"Hello, Lieutenant," he said. "My head hurts. Would you get me some aspirin?"

The nurse broke into spontaneous laughter. "He wakes up and immediately gives an order to a nurse as to what medicine he is to have," she said to the captain. "What kind of discipline do you have on that ship, Captain?"

The captain now laughed abruptly also. "I would estimate him as the kind to be a very trying and difficult patient."

She got the aspirin and after talking a bit left them.

"That's quite a girl," the captain said. "Very handsome young lady, very bright too. She has the class. You have good taste, Barclay. Very good taste. Remarkable. Did you hear everything I said about the ship?"

"I heard it."

"You must have been coming back from the bow ramp when that JU got us."

Barclay's memory had not yet reminded him in any detail of the action on the bow ramp getting the troops off. Now he remembered it. He remembered first the dead infantry captain

on the beach and for some reason he remembered the captain's
.45 in the rubble pointing to the sky.

"Which part of the ship did I end up on?" he asked.

The captain laughed. "The after part. Just barely. You were
just over what was then the bow of the after part when we got to
you. Five seconds earlier and you'd have been just about in the
direct path of that torpedo. Not a very pleasant thought, is it?
I think it was about time for the dice to roll your way. You got
quite a working over on the bow ramp."

This statement made Barclay for the first time bring his hand
up and softly feel his head. It felt a thick bandage.

"What's with my head, Captain?"

"Just a hell of a lot of stitches. I think they had to use a sewing machine. Latimer said your scalp was laid clean back down
there on the ramp. We got a little information about what you
did down there. You're being put in for the Navy Cross, my boy."

"Hell, it doesn't rate a Navy Cross," Barclay said.

"I think it does. Anyhow I think they're a little short in their
quota of giving out Navy Crosses."

"They must be," Barclay said.

"It'll be that or a Silver Star." The captain grinned. "I agree
you don't deserve any of this but I thought it would make me
look good as the captain."

"Well, in that case, I'll hope fervently it'll come through."

"It will."

Then Barclay's memory served up Carlyle. He remembered
that Carlyle was always with him on the bow ramp offloading
detail and he remembered the man with him lying dead, he felt
or sensed, on the tank deck at Anzio.

"Carlyle's dead, Captain?" he said.

"Carlyle? No. Oh, I see what you're thinking. No, that was
Boland, Matthew. He was filling in for Carlyle. And the torpedo
—it got four in the engine room," and he named them off.

He felt glad for Carlyle, sorry about Boland and the others.
"But Carlyle?" he said.

Then Barclay's memory served it all up to him. "I'd forgotten.
Carlyle was behind in Naples, wasn't he?"

"That's right. Under arrest by the military people. Probably the luckiest thing that ever happened to him. He's alive, anyhow —thanks to that arrest."

"What about Carlyle, Captain? What gives with him?"

"Well, I went down to see. It seems they're holding him for dealings on the black market."

"The black market?" Barclay repeated incredulously. "Carlyle?"

"I know. I couldn't believe it. I still can't believe it. It must be some kind of foulup that could happen only in the Navy. They claim Carlyle's been feeding supplies from the ship and from some Army dump onto the black market, via . . . You remember that young lady who had the baby aboard?"

"Yes, indeed," Barclay said. "What's she got to do with it?"

"This is the damndest thing. They claim Carlyle's been trading on the black market, using her as his go-between. I thought the shore patrol people, the CID people, and the rest of them must be on heroin or something to make a charge like that. I doubt seriously if Carlyle knows there *is* a black market."

"What does he say about it?" Barclay said. "About all these charges I mean."

"Well, I've been in a couple of times to talk with him. At first he wouldn't, or couldn't, even discuss it. He'd heard about the ship being broken up, and there he was, caged up without being able to get any poop on it, and I think he was a little wild to get down there and see what had happened, to the ship and his shipmates. So I went over it all with him for a long time. Then, and only then, would he talk a little about the thing he was in. The damndest thing of all about it is that he admits it. Oh, not to dealing on the black market. But to taking things like rations, soap, that sort of thing, and I think a couple of sacks of flour he got hold of at the Army dump—how he's not saying— he admits taking these things to the girl. It couldn't have been very much and I imagine he did. No reason for him to say he did if he didn't. But, hell, he couldn't have taken enough for it to amount to anything."

"But the black market. How does that come in?"

"Well, they're saying the girl sold some of these things Carlyle brought. Personally I can't see that any great harm would have been done by it. But right now they're bound and determined to put a stop to even a bar of soap falling into what we generally call unauthorized hands. I paid a call on the legal officer at the base and you definitely get a sense of the tumbrils clattering across the Place de la Concorde. That character in the legal office almost shot his bolt when I said, hell, it's only a few bars of soap, Commander, a few cartons of cigarettes, and some cans of C-rations and fruit here and there. I said it was too silly for words to go after a man for a routine thing like that. Well, I thought for a moment, the way he reacted, I was dealing with Inspector Javert. He said what I called 'little' amounted to a hell of a lot when a million men did it—I never knew that was the figure for the number of men we had in Italy, did you? but the legal chap seemed to like to talk in round figures, preferably large ones. He said what if a million men stole one can of C-rations a day? That's the way his mind works, if you can believe it. He promised me winningly they would do everything they could to 'get' Carlyle. Those were his very words. Anyhow, that's it and Carlyle's getting a general court."

"A general court?" Barclay said, feeling fear. "My God."

"The legal officer was pretty frank about it. He's the frank sort. He said they had to get at the black market which he said was chewing up supplies to where it had become a *very* serious matter. He said they'd thought about a summary court but a summary can only give a bad conduct discharge. Not enough to get the point over to the rest of us liberators, quoting him. To do that, he said quite calmly that they've got to get a dishonorable discharge."

"My God," Barclay said. "They're going for a dishonorable discharge?"

"Yes, that's it. It seems if there's one thing the Navy hates it's theft of naval supplies by one of its own. They hate it so much —I found this out by looking it up in *Naval Courts and Boards* —that a man can get a DD for any kind of theft from one cent on up. I tell you for a fact, that legal officer acts like the prosecutor at the Old Bailey with his hands on the man who filched the Crown jewels."

"Well, we've got to get somebody plenty good to defend Carlyle."

"I know. Between times of being down at the drydock while they strap up the ship—I don't know why the hell I go down, it's all in ship repair's hands now, and I think they even resent my being around, but it fascinates me what they're doing and after all it is *my* ship . . . Between times I've been scouting the lawyer situation at the base. As a matter of fact, I've cased it pretty thoroughly. They've got two or three in various departments with pretty hot lawyer records back home. Naturally we can have any of them. Besides, any of them would be only too glad to be a lawyer again for a change. No problem about a good lawyer, fortunately. Except Carlyle."

"How do you mean?"

"Well, for some reason he's holding back he doesn't seem eager to *have* a lawyer just yet. And the court's, let's see, ten days from today."

The captain waited a moment. "Actually Carlyle told me he'd like to talk to you first. I told him you'd got conked at Anzio and I didn't know what shape you were in."

"I feel all right. My head feels a little odd. I'd like to go see him. What does the doctor say about me getting out of here?"

"Well, you know how it is. They always like to keep people around. I talked with *him*, too. He said two weeks would see you out of here. He said he couldn't see it before two weeks. I imagine we might work that down a little."

"We've got to. I don't know what Carlyle wants to see me about. Obviously he has to be shown he's got to get the best lawyer, and get him fast. Which of those hot-shots did you find out was the best?"

"Fellow named Lyman I believe is our man. Works in the H.E.C.P. He was eight years out of law school when the Navy got him and he had those eight years with a firm I know very well indeed in New York. It's one of the best."

"All right, I'll go talk with Carlyle and we'll get Lyman started on it."

"That's a fine program. How the hell do you propose to get out of here?"

"I'll figure some way. We'll see how much pull that nurse really has."

"I don't know about her pull but . . . Well, we'll see. Now I must go down and see them strapping the ship up. I wish you could see it. Personally, if they'd have asked me I'd have said she was ready for the nearest junk heap. As it is, they're working around the clock on it, Navy and Italian civilian workers both, and it's the damndest thing to watch them—putting in new plates and welding on doublers—in fact giving her a big new steel belly . . ." The captain sighed. "Then out of the drydock—to float as in olden times or go straight to the bottom. It'll be interesting to see which, won't it?"

"Yes, I'd like to be on hand for that one. How long if it works?"

"The ship-repair officer says he'll have the thing floating right as ever—his words, not mine—in two weeks. Provided, of course, she floats at all."

"That means whatever happens to Carlyle we'll be here to see him back on the ship—or back home."

"Yes," the captain said evenly. "That's what it does mean."

The captain stood up. "I'll check in tomorrow, Barclay. Give the nurse what we call the big picture."

"By the way, where is Carlyle?"

"Oh. They've made a brig out of a room at the enlisted men's barracks. Not a bad brig, if you have to be in a brig. It has a view of the harbor."

And the captain, picking up his rain slicker, was gone. Barclay could still hear the rain coming down.

Soon after the captain had left Sarah stopped by again and they talked for a few minutes. She said at one point, very somberly:

"I'm glad you got through, Matthew. Our luck's running, isn't it?"

"It seems it is. What's wrong with my head?"

"Not very much. You looked very bad when you were brought in and when I saw it was you . . . Well, let's just say I was very scared. But you're going to be all right. You'll have a scar but I think the kind that makes men handsome, the dueling scar kind."

"I could use some of that."

"And you'll even be up in two weeks. Dr. Jarvis says."

"Dr. Jarvis? Is he the man who decides about these things?"

The nurse smiled. "Yes, Dr. Jarvis is the man who decides about everything around here."

"Tell me about this Dr. Jarvis. Is he a reasonable man? Can he be talked to?"

"Well, he's got his own mind. How do you mean?"

"You remember one night when I picked you up I had a man named Carlyle with me?"

"The one with all that red hair? Yes, I remember very well. He seemed nice and intelligent."

"Yes. He's so nice and intelligent that right now he's sitting down at the base in a brig."

And Barclay related all he knew about the matter, beginning with the birth of the baby on the ship, Carlyle's involvement with the mother, his apparent taking of Navy and Army goods to her, and his arrest. She listened intently.

"Good heavens," she said when she had heard the story. "Was a baby really born on your ship?"

"Yes indeed. Anyhow Carlyle's in my division aboard ship, and he seems to be stalling about getting a lawyer. He's going to need one very much indeed and the captain's found a good one. But Carlyle wants to see me first—for some mysterious reason. The trial's in ten days. It's very important the lawyer get to Carlyle to start preparing his case. I've got to get out of here today."

"Today! No, I'll tell you this much about Dr. Jarvis. He'd never stand for your leaving here today. Not if your mother was about to go on trial."

"Well, tomorrow at the latest. I'll settle for that. Now I want your help in this," Barclay said briskly. "I want you to help me work on Jarvis. You see the importance of this to Carlyle?"

"Yes. I see that. But I wouldn't be too sure myself if you got up before a week at the least."

"That won't help. It's got to be today or tomorrow. I'm asking you to help me get Jarvis to okay it. Are you going to help me?"

"Matthew," she said quietly, "I'll do anything you want."

"Fine. That's what I want. How do we go about it?"

"Let me think for a little bit and see what I think's the best plan. Probably it's for me to go to Jarvis first myself."

"All right, but let's move fast on it. Let's get going on it, shall we?"

She smiled a little at him and shook her head slightly. "Yes, sir, Lieutenant. Right away, sir. Incidentally, do you know what Jarvis' rank is?"

"No, what does that have to do with it?"

"It has this. I'm a second lieutenant, you're a lieutenant junior grade. And Jarvis, he's a colonel. A full colonel."

"Good," Barclay said. "Then he'll have the rank to get me out."

She couldn't help bursting out laughing.

"What in the world are you laughing at?"

"You," she said, and laughed, walking away lightly.

Colonel Jarvis of the Army Medical Corps was the roundest-looking man Barclay had ever seen, at least in uniform. Barclay believed a tape measure thrown around his chest just under the shoulders and applied every few inches down to his hips would have shown a variation of no more than an inch over the entire route, and the tape would have had to be stretched plenty far out at that. He appeared very little over five feet tall, had a mass of thick black hair parted in the middle, and his eyebrows were minor forests above very light brown eyes which seemed to look out upon the world as dedicated to killing itself by failing to follow his directions. His hands were as fat and stubby as padded boxing gloves and Barclay could not visualize their even holding a surgical knife. The nurse told Barclay he was one of the five or six greatest surgeons in America. He appeared to function exactly as if the military did not exist as such, and that if it did, it knew less than nothing about his business.

"Young man," he said when he dropped by Barclay's bed that

afternoon, "Clark tells me you want up and out of here. Ordinarily I wouldn't bother even to discuss such a ridiculous request, but Clark is a bright girl for a nurse and I sometimes at least listen to what she has to say. Of course you can't possibly move for two weeks. First of all if you stood up right now you would immediately collapse into unconsciousness—making more work for us, and we've got far too much as it is. Secondly, even if you didn't collapse here, you would pretty soon somewhere, and also that wound would undoubtedly get infected and we'd have to amputate. Since the wound is on the head that would be pretty serious."

Colonel Jarvis appeared to have a fairly ghoulish sense of humor, though he was certainly not smiling at all.

"You've lost a lot of blood in case you don't know, and in case you don't know that some rather odd things happen to the body when it loses a few quarts of blood." The colonel spoke to Barclay as if he ranked just below the village idiot on the IQ scale. "I shouldn't be taking the time to explain this to you. I'm much too busy to explain things to the several thousands of patients we get in this hospital. However, Clark is a rather remarkable girl, for a woman."

"Yes, she is, Colonel." Barclay felt somewhat bristling himself. "Did she tell you why I needed out?"

"Yes, she told me all that," the colonel said, as if he were really too busy to be bothered. Barclay was bristling, but still there was something about the colonel he liked. "Something about one of your men being in a jam and needing to talk with you. Naturally the reason doesn't make the slightest difference. Well, I've got work to do. I can't stay here all day talking with the Navy. But for Clark's sake I wanted to be courteous."

"Colonel, this is terribly important. The 'jam' is a general court and the man's up for a dishonorable discharge. How would it be if I tried it. If I collapse, you can always put me back in bed."

"A very foolish statement," the colonel said. "I wouldn't possibly risk it today or tomorrow. What if I let you try to kill yourself day after tomorrow on one condition?"

"I'd be very grateful, Colonel. What's the condition?"

"Clark has been working like a son-of-a-bitch. She has three days' leave coming up. I suggested the rest camp over on Capri. But the ignorant woman says she'd be willing to spend them looking after you. This is much too big a war for one man to be assigned to the care of one nurse. However, it's Clark's own time and if she wants to spend it so ignorantly, I never stop my subordinates from doing ignorant things on their own time. That means you can check out of here day after tomorrow under Clark's care, provided you check back in by six each evening. She's promised to pop you back anyhow if you show any critical signs, such as your heart stopping, and Clark never lies. Will that do?"

"That will do very well, Colonel," Barclay said. "I'm very grateful, sir."

"I hope you live through it," Colonel Jarvis said. "I can't give you any more time. My time is more valuable than Mark Clark's. I told the general that once when he was up here on an inspection and he agreed."

"I'm sure he did, Colonel," Barclay said, meaning it. He couldn't visualize three stars even disagreeing with Colonel Jarvis, at least on his home territory.

"Try to stay alive," the colonel said. "It'll help our statistics."

He was gone, waddling away down the aisle. Barclay decided he probably was, after all, one hell of a surgeon.

Barclay left two days later. Shanley came up to pick him up and the nurse rode in the back seat. Getting into the jeep with the markings BOMB DISPOSAL made him feel, with all that had happened since he first saw that jeep, as if he were getting into some old family-flivver of his childhood. Shanley was in a mood which was a mixture of good spirits at taking Barclay out like this, and of reflectiveness about Carlyle. He talked about the sailor as they drove down the hill toward Naples.

"I went over to talk with him, Matthew, after getting your note," he said. "He just didn't have much to say. Very polite—so polite it bothered me, just froze me out—and that was it. Matthew, I want to ask you one thing. When I started going around with her a little bit I didn't have the foggiest idea that the girl Coco even knew Carlyle—I want to know if you believe me?"

"Why should you lie to me, Shan? I believe anything you say."

"That's good because as a matter of fact I *wouldn't* lie to you. Now let me relate a little story to you."

Shanley told how he had met Coco, taken her to the officers club a few times, of how she told him one night she couldn't see him any longer because she was in love with an American whose identity she didn't disclose and thought he was going to ask her to marry him, of how he then dropped her by her room, and of how, coming back down the stairs, he ran into Carlyle.

"That's the first time I knew that Carlyle and Coco even knew each other."

"Well," Barclay said. "Well. That explains a lot. At least I *think* it explains a lot."

It occurred now to Barclay that if he had told Carlyle, long back, about Coco and Shanley seeing each other, when he had seen them together at the officers club, possibly it might have saved Carlyle this court-martial, by making him stop seeing the girl. He didn't know if he would have stopped. And there was no way to ask him, and no point in doing so now even if there had been. But it remained a small knot of self-reproach in him. He heard Shanley saying:

"Well, it's some background for you anyhow."

Barclay looked carefully at Shanley. "Any more background?"

Shanley watched the traffic. They were going up another hill. They passed some weapons carriers full of soldiers in combat dress, with slung rifles and wearing helmet liners. "Not at this moment," he said. Then they were pulling up at the enlisted men's barracks. "Here we are, Leftenant."

Shanley and the nurse sat outside while Barclay was taken to Carlyle. The "brig" was just another room in the enlisted men's barracks, the only difference outside being that a shore patrol guard sat at the door, and, inside, that some crude bars had been cemented into the window. It wasn't a bad room actually, as the captain had said. The building had been a resort hotel in peace-time and was set into a cliff high above the sea. Barclay walked over to where Carlyle was standing at the window watching, through the bars, the sea pound in on some rocks far below. It was a straight drop of a hundred feet and Barclay wondered why the bars were necessary. They turned back into the room.

He seemed to Barclay more bewildered than anything else. He was without any nervousness at all, only looking around him oc-casionally as if wondering what in the world he was doing here. And sitting down and getting up and walking around from time to time as if a boy who had known only the wide acres of the farm and the great expanses of the sea could not accustom himself to the confinement. But his talk was entirely calm. First he asked Barclay about his wound, and Barclay told him the fact he was here was proof the doctors knew he was doing well. Then he wanted to know about the ship, from the time of the shells coming in on their approach to the beachhead, to the shelling on the beach itself and of the wounded and the dead. He must have heard this in some detail from the captain, who was the only member of ship's company who had been allowed to visit him, but still he wanted to hear it from Barclay, possibly because his station on the ship during offloading had always been alongside the officer on the bow ramp, so that what Barclay told him was exactly what he would have seen himself had he been there. Barclay related it in detail from the time of the first shell dropping in, and Carlyle listened very carefully. When Barclay had finished he said:

"The captain says they're actually going to put the two parts together again. How about that?" he said in wonder. "How long will it take?"

"Only a couple of weeks, or so they claim. If it works."

"Two weeks!"

And Barclay knew what Carlyle was thinking, which was to wonder whether he would be on the ship, if and when she sailed. Neither mentioned the thought. Instead, Carlyle, with the greatest abruptness, brought up the subject which Barclay wanted to get to, for he felt somewhat weak and wanted his energies expended on that subject. He brought it up as if reading Barclay's thoughts.

"Mr. Barclay, I think I'd better get to what I want to say. I mean with that head of yours. The main thing I want to say is, I want you to defend me. Will you?"

Caught entirely off guard, Barclay looked at the sailor in the most utter startlement. "Me defend you? Listen, Red, they've got some real legal brains on this base—the captain found that out. Me, I've got one year of law school . . ."

Barclay must have spent fifteen minutes then trying with every weapon of argument he could think of to persuade Carlyle. He told him of how the captain had found an officer to defend him he considered ideal; how the captain had checked his record; how he knew the firm he worked for in New York and how it was one of the best; how this lawyer had had eight years of civilian legal and trial experience. One would have thought, the way Barclay built up this man he didn't even know, that he was the reincarnation of Clarence Darrow. Barclay said in the strongest terms that Carlyle would be far better off with such a lawyer, and he urged him repeatedly to let this officer come at once and that he tell him everything so that he could begin his preparation of the case. Carlyle listened patiently and when Barclay had finished said:

"Mr. Barclay, I appreciate every one of those arguments. And ever since the captain talked about it and about this officer he'd found, I've tried as hard as I could to convince myself it's the thing to do, to have him. It doesn't work. Something in me, *something*, keeps telling me I'd be better off with you."

"Listen carefully, Red. Repeat: I've had one year of law school. That's practically nothing. The other man has a law degree and eight years of practice."

"I know all that. I've gone over it again and again. But I wouldn't care if you'd not even been *near* the law or courts or anything. I feel I'd still be better off, have a better chance, with you defending me. But here's the important thing I want to say, Mr. Barclay: I don't believe this is just emotional, I mean the fact I know you and trust you. I think it's also the most *practical* thing in the world. I've thought this thing through very carefully and

I figure it's far better even from a *practical*, a *logical* angle, to
have someone who knows so much of the story from the beginning, who was present on the ship when I first saw Coco, who saw
her have her baby like I did . . ."

For the first time Barclay began to feel that perhaps Carlyle had
a point, that his basic intelligence, expending so many hours
thinking in this room above the sea, may have penetrated to what
might be the one real fact that lay at the center of the matter:
that, in the case of a Navy court and above all given the circumstances of this case, he should be defended if possible by
someone who by being there knew firsthand all, or most, of the
story. Carlyle talked on and finally he put the question directly.

"I'm asking you to defend me, Mr. Barclay. Unless either one
of two reasons is there: That you don't feel up to it"—and he
looked at the officer's bandaged head—"or that you feel for any
reason at all—and you don't have to tell me what the reason is—
that you'd rather not. That's all I've got to say."

The sailor was silent, and Barclay, too, for a few moments. The
room seemed all of silence except for the sounds of the sea. Barclay walked over to the window and for a few moments looked
down at the sea pounding the rocks and then away in the distance
at the gray ships riding at anchor in the harbor. Somewhere down
there was the drydock with the two parts of the LST in it. He
turned back. They seemed to have been silent a long time, then
Barclay said quietly:

"No, neither reason holds. And I've changed my mind—I think
you would be better off with me defending you." Barclay laughed
slightly. "I seem to be getting lawyer-cocky already. I'll do it. All
right, let's get to work. I want you to start with the time you saw
Coco aboard ship, and tell me everything, up to right now, that
I don't know."

Just before Barclay left Carlyle said:

"Could you do one thing for me, Mr. Barclay? Could you go see
after Coco?"

Barclay looked straight into the eyes of the sailor, but he could
not tell his thoughts.

"Yes," he said. "I'll do that."

After leaving Carlyle, Barclay, with the nurse and Shanley, drove on out to Pozzuoli and Via Giuseppe Mazzini 36. Shanley went in to check and got no answer to the knock on Coco's door. Downstairs an old woman was sitting in a chair set against the front of the building. Barclay got out and talked to her.

"Signora, we wish to see the Signora Coco Comparo," he said in Italian. "Do you know when she'll be back?"

"Sigarette?"

Shanley gave her a half pack he had. The woman lighted one up and stuffed the others in the pocket of a worn old apron she was wearing.

"I doubt very seriously if the signora will be back," the woman then opened up.

"How do you mean, signora, that she won't be back?" Barclay said.

"I mean what I say. She's moved out. Gone."

Barclay took a deep breath. His head was hurting. "Do you know where she's gone?"

"Leef Savers?" the old woman said.

"My God, she wants Life Savers," Shanley said. "Wait a minute." He went over and looked in the dash compartment of the jeep and sure enough there was a package there. It looked a little beaten in. He gave it to the old woman, who opened it, put one between her toothless gums, still smoking, and what with the puffing of the cigarette and the sucking of the Life Saver an expression almost of bliss came over her face.

"I'm very fond of Leef Savers," she said. "They are the greatest thing the Americans have brought us." It was not an anti-American statement. To her it was really a great gift from the liberators.

"Signora," Barclay said. "Forgive me but we are in a hurry. We need to find Signora Comparo on a matter of great importance. Do you have any idea where she went?"

"No. She just left. Her and her baby."

"Those Life Savers were a lot of help," Shanley said in English.

"Thank you, signora," Barclay said. "Thank you very much." And they drove off.

"Well, I've about had it for today," Barclay said. "Can you take us back to the sausage factory, Shanley?"

"What a way to refer to the 300th General," the nurse said.

They drove on back up the hill to the hospital. On the way Barclay told them of Carlyle's urgent desire that he defend him, that he had tried to persuade him to obtain a professional lawyer, that Carlyle was persistent, and why, and that he had at last agreed to do so. By that time they were at the hospital. Barclay arranged for Shanley to take him to see Carlyle next morning. Inside he went straight to bed, feeling considerably dizzy as Colonel Jarvis had predicted, and was almost immediately asleep. He slept fourteen hours, woke up, ate breakfast, and when Shanley arrived went with him and the nurse down to see Carlyle again. Carlyle supplied him with some more random details he remembered. Again Shanley took Barclay and the nurse back to the hospital. Barclay did another fourteen hours in bed, on the button. When he woke up, he felt better than anytime since he had got in there. The nurse took his bandage off, one of the doctors looked at his head and made the observation that it was healing "beautifully" and the nurse put another, smaller bandage on. He went down to see Carlyle briefly, came back, and that day and the next stayed in bed working from a clipboard the nurse had brought him and all but memorizing the copy of *Naval Courts and Boards* the captain had got for him.

His entire energy now was on the question of what the defense should, or could, be, and he knew before long that he would settle for the second verb as he thought about it long hours, reading that book or just sitting up in bed penciling not very artistic designs on the clipboard and around him aware of the many wounded from the land and the sea. He read up intently on dishonorable discharges; the language coming cold off the page chilling him even more for its very matter-of-factness: "The Articles for the Government of the Navy do not make any sentence mandatory. The statutes of the United States, however, provide that any person convicted of certain offenses shall be forever incapable of holding any office of trust or profit under the United States. The sentence of the court in such a case must provide for the dismissal or discharge of the accused . . ." And: "Where the court deems an offense found proved serious enough to warrant a sentence of imprisonment it should, except under most unusual circumstances, or where not allowed by the limitation of punishment, include in its sentence dismissal or dishonorable or bad conduct discharge; a man who has committed such an offense is not a proper person to remain in the service. Furthermore, such a sentence puts the accused in prison in a status altogether different from that of other prisoners. A court must be careful in sentencing to confinement to include accessories in its sentence, as otherwise the man will continue to draw full pay." They hadn't overlooked a thing. He read: "A general court-martial may sentence an enlisted man to a dishonorable discharge alone, without adjudging a period of confinement and 'other accessories.' But this sentence is not ordinarily deemed advisable." He read on with mounting depression, in the prescribed section 622, to find out what these "accessories" might be and read: "The words 'other accessories of said sentence' when hereafter used in the sentence of a general court-martial in the case of an enlisted man should be understood to include the following: (a) The person so sentenced shall perform hard labor while confined pursuant to such sentence and (b) shall forfeit all pay that may become due him during a period equivalent to the term of such confinement (or if sentenced to dishonorable or bad conduct discharge, during his current enlistment)." And he read last and worst, "The stigma of a dishonorable discharge is in itself a severe punishment." He visualized all this happening to Carlyle and knew that he, as himself, or for that matter he would imagine virtually anyone would far rather be killed. Unfortunately the book didn't give you that choice.

He closed his eyes to rest them awhile and by pure will shut the picture out, determined to, knowing he must, keep emotion out and concentrate dispassionately, coldly himself, on the job, and do it, and do it as well as possible, and read grimly on under a section entitled "Schedule of offenses and limitations" setting forth the possible sentences for theft, broken down with such precise dividing lines: "Above $100—Confinement for 4 years and dishonorable discharge. Between $50 and $100—Confinement for 18 months and dishonorable discharge. Under $50—Confinement for 1 year and dishonorable discharge." It was all too plain that the Navy viewed *any* theft with the most extreme gravity. He didn't have to consult the book to know that a year's sentence would take away virtually all a man's citizenship rights, all that gave him any sense of self-respect: Right to vote, right to hold office, right to do or be much of anything except to exist, and pretty hard sometimes to do even that for a man with a dishonorable discharge. They might as well, he thought lying there, tattoo the letters on his forehead. He could detach himself enough to see that the Navy had its point. Theft of naval supplies—the Navy felt, and had so from times ancient, that excepting only cowardice in battle or desertion, there was nothing more heinous, more despicable, of which a man who bore the uniform was capable. They had their point, as a moral position they had it, and even more as a practical one, considering circumstances in which a ship might be long at sea and men's well-being, even lives, dependent on trust, on non-theft, and the way things had to be left lying around on any ship, none could function for long where theft existed. And he had himself heard enough of the increasing black marketeering to know that they had their point there too. But *Carlyle*, he thought. Carlyle and the circumstances under which he did it. The book seemed to offer nothing in the way of a defense and he felt a surge of hopelessness. At that moment something happened.

He had just looked up to rest his eyes from the heavy headache he was getting from all his reading and to get his mind away from it for a moment, too, and had looked down the aisle of the ward and seen two stretcher bearers carrying someone whose neck was in a surgical brace making movement impossible except to look straight up and following them he could see they were headed out of this ward and taking this wounded to another and his bed being near the door he saw, just as the wounded passed him, a short mass of curls around the head and he became aware with a start that it was a girl, a woman, a wounded nurse it would be from Anzio or Cassino. In that swift glimpse he had of her, her face seemed pretty and he looked only for the briefest second then his eyes came back to his work and there it was.

Among the shuffle of papers and pages his eyes fell on one of them and upon one sequence of words which caused him to look up, look back, focusing intently, and look up again and to feel caught up and held in some profound stillness of insight. There were only nine words and he held them to him as something impossibly precious, saying them over and over to himself . . . over and over . . . "applies to his own use or benefit, or wrongfully . . ."

He shut the book. He sat very still. He looked for a few moments around the ward of wounded. And he felt his first lifting of spirits in days, and some shimmering of light where before all had been but a dark woods. And he knew: Whatever defense they had, he now had it. They had something. They had nine words, to be precise, but they had *something*. He went to work on his clipboard, filling pages, making notes from the book; then at last put book and clipboard aside and lay back.

He got another long sleep and when he awoke on this, the seventh day, he felt no dizziness at all and felt that he had it made insofar as the head wound was concerned. The doctor said pretty much the same thing, and Colonel Jarvis came around and even admitted himself the recovery was quite remarkable, warned him something could still happen, however, such as sudden, unexpected attacks of dizziness, and even said he could sleep somewhere else that night if he preferred. He also said he was sure he could navigate now without the help of the nurse, and that he would use her that day on surgical duty if Barclay didn't mind. Barclay gave him permission.

Shanley picked Barclay up and drove him down first to see Carlyle again. Barclay spent the entire session meticulously going over with him his strategy for the trial and in precision what their line of defense would be and how it would be set up, having himself gone over in the most exact detail, using *Courts and Boards*, every foreseeable step of the trial, but knowing how many could never be foreseen. Then Shanley came for him and drove him down to an empty room in his own BOQ he had got for him. He left him there to go down to the base where he had a couple hours of letter-censoring duty coming up that day. Barclay lay down on the bed for a while and tried to think. God in heaven, he thought, he *had* to find Coco. The words came to him again, words that really never left him now . . . "applies to his own use or benefit, or wrongfully . . ." Whatever chance or case Carlyle had depended on her, that he knew. He had told Carlyle he felt the best thing he could do was to plead guilty to the specifications of unauthorized taking of Navy and Army materiel, and to rest his case on the motivation involved, the fact that he had taken these goods to a young mother in great need of them to save herself and her baby born on Carlyle's ship. With all the taking of Navy and Army goods by sailors and soldiers to pass off to the Italians out of motivations, generally, not so high as Carlyle's, Barclay felt Carlyle had a chance with this defense. In any event it was the only defense he had and Barclay intended to push it for all it was worth. Fat chance it was, he thought, if he couldn't even find the girl who had got all this help. If the young woman who was the object of all Carlyle's aid was not there to testify . . . Well, Barclay felt, though he had not told Carlyle as much, that then they had no chance whatsoever. None. They had to have her to testify that but for Carlyle she and her baby would have gone under. Two days to go before the trial, he thought, urgency coming upon him. Where in the hell could she be? It seemed obvious that at the first sign of trouble she had simply taken off. Whatever it was, Barclay had felt he had to lie to Carlyle about it, that the sailor was simply not in a position to take the fact that she had vanished. When Carlyle had asked him about Coco on the visits following the first one he pleaded his own injuries.

"I just haven't felt up to getting out there," he said. "I will any day now. I'm sure she's all right. Don't worry about her."

Barclay looked at his watch: 1:30. He decided he had to get

out and walk some if he were ever to think his way through this
and also staying in bed seemed to bring on dizziness.

His bandage had been reduced a little each day until now
it fitted, if snugly, under his cap. He adjusted the cap carefully
over the bandage and left the BOQ and started walking in the
direction of the city. It was not far. When he turned into Via
Roma he could hardly believe what he saw. The last time he had
been down this street, which was on a walk with Sarah, they
had found it thronged with troops, more than they had ever
seen there, and the number of those troops told them that the
great drive for the breakthrough at the Gustav Line and the
breakout at Anzio was surely near. Now the present traffic on
the street made that last time look rather small. Now there
was literally not an inch of sidewalk or pavement to be seen anywhere, only a solid mass of troops and sailors coursing slowly
back and forth, paying little if any attention to the shouting
horns of jeeps and weapons carriers trying to get through. Seeing
it, Barclay would not have been surprised to wake up any day to
find that they had all gone north, to Cassino and Anzio, and
had broken through, joined up, and were marching on Rome.
He remembered the nurse would be leaving any day now, something they had deliberately not talked about. It seemed nearly
certain that his ship would never be repaired in time for the
breakout—but then a thought hit him. If this were so, why all
the haste which the captain said was going on down at the
drydock? It hardly made sense if someone knew the ship would
not make it in time to carry troops up for the breakout anyhow.
And suddenly Barclay felt he had a special, and secret, piece of
knowledge: that someone had determined that the LST could
make it in time for whatever the date was, and that therefore
the work going on on the ship was an excellent gauge to the day
set for the breakout, that it would not come until the ship was
ready. Not that they were waiting for her but knew that with
this kind of work she could make the already-set date. All of this
was reinforced by a fact he knew all too well, which was that
there were never really enough LSTs, they were ever in desperate
need.

He stepped into the crowd on Via Roma and let it carry him along—his only choice actually—swaying along with it, occasionally getting a glimpse of a store front and occasionally finding an Italian civilian in front of him, somehow squeezed into the crowd of fighting men, or about-to-be-fighting men, with something urgent to sell, such as a rosary or a woman. He soon decided he would take the first opportunity to stop somewhere he could sit and drink something for a while. If he could ever find such a place. A chair would be a precious possession on a day like this, not likely to be relinquished. His head was beginning to give him a considerable little amount of pain, a decided dizziness, and he began to get a fixation on finding a chair, one empty chair, in all those innumerable bars he was passing. Finally, from down a side street, he could hear music coming from a place. It was American popular music and it came to him with remembrance. He walked on, drawn to it, keeping a bearing on its ascending volume, until he stood in front of the place it was coming from. Then he was inside it. The place had scores of extremely small tables, all occupied by Army and Navy of a dozen different nationalities, but then moving on in he found one over against the wall that for some reason was empty. It must have been that someone in the last half-minute had had all the vino he could hold for the time being and had stepped or been carried out. Barclay's eyes focused blessedly on the empty chair and in a moment he was in it. With all the racket and the dank darkness of the room it still seemed an unconscionable relief to be sitting down.

After a while he began to feel that a cognac, even the cognac of wartime Naples, would taste good. He felt in general disconsolate at the thought of Carlyle, and he wished Sarah were here, he didn't like to sit there thinking that they were about to part in this war and not see each other for a very long time, if ever, if ever. They had had a total of perhaps two and a half minutes alone, which were walking from the jeep when Shanley dropped them at the hospital. He felt the urgency of time and apartness closing in on them. Then he was thinking about the court-martial again, never absent long from his thinking, and

again of the fact that even a chance for Carlyle depended on
his finding Coco, and how he had but two days now, and that
crowded in on him. He felt everything crowding in at once and
he decided he wanted, and needed, a cognac. He was able to
intersect one of the flying signorine, mainly on the strength of
a burst of fluent Italian which caused her to stop while literally
running for the bar to fill a host of urgent orders. Hearing
her language caused her to smile through the frosting of sweat
on her face and very quickly he had a cognac sitting in front
of him. Tasting it, he even had the idea that maybe the language
had brought something that was kept beneath the counter instead
of the usual mouth-searing bar stuff. It tasted quite good.

He sat back sipping and now enjoying the scene a little more.
Commerce other than the mere selling of wine was being conducted in that place, he could soon see. Some of it was of
the direct-sale variety, with the signorina talking with a soldier
or a sailor, and some of it had a middleman, in the eternal
form of small boys who crept through the room like swift-footed
kittens soliciting the drinkers to further pleasures available if only
they would accompany them out the door. And some went along
with the little boys, who obviously deposited their customers
nearby, for they would soon come trotting back through the
doorway and pad around looking for a fresh customer to be
ready the moment the merchandise was again available. He had
one more cognac and was preparing to leave when one of the
boys approached him.

"Something very special, Tenente," he said. "Only for officers."

Barclay felt a small, tickled burst of laughter coming on. Now
again he gave out with a fluent chatter of Italian which caught
the boy by surprise.

"You mean there are some for the soldiers and sailors and
others only for the officers?" he said.

"Yes, Tenente. That is how it is. Some for the simple *soldati*,
but others, the very best, for the officers. Some will have only
officers. And one, best of all, for very few officers, but for you
who speak Italian so well, I am sure she would for you. Very

expensive but worth it. You have never seen anything like this, Tenente. Very special."

"Not today," Barclay said. "Some other day. I have to be somewhere else now. But thank you."

He stood up to go, leaving some wads of lire on the table for the waitress and handing some additional notes to the boy. He started out through the darkness, but the boy still followed and tugged at him.

"Tenente, you will regret it until the day you die if you don't try this one. She is . . ."

Then, right then, something about the boy's voice came through to Barclay's memory. And he said:

"All right. Come along."

"Good! You'll never regret it, Tenente."

Out in the sunlight Rebi went ahead. Barclay, following, wondered if the boy would recognize him when he turned. They had seen each other only twice, on the ship, and again when he and Shanley gave him a lift from Pozzuoli into Naples, and the last time had been quite some time ago. He might have instructions not to offer the wares to anyone he knew to be from the ship, and recognition, if it came, might lose forever what Barclay so much wanted. And he felt that a great deal rode on the next minute and a half or so. So far the boy hadn't looked back. He moved rapidly along close to the walls of the buildings, turned a corner and started up a hill into a section of not bad-looking apartment houses, on the corner one a faded and chipped bit of blue tile that said "Via Apollo." Then he had turned into one and they were in the shaded darkness of a lobby without Barclay's being identified. But even then the boy did not turn around. He seemed intent only on leading his persuaded customer to the apartment and he hopped swiftly up two flights of stairs, Barclay after him, turned down a corridor, stopped at a door, knocked three times, Barclay heard a voice inside asking who it was, heard Rebi say it was himself with an *ufficiale*, then the door was unlocked, Rebi waited a moment, obviously by arrangement, before opening it, then opened it, stepped inside, Barclay followed and stood in still another pool of darkness, a small hallway. Then Rebi, just before leaving the apartment quickly, opened another door, disclosing a large, quite good-looking room in half-light and standing there, in a posture of natural grace, perfectly adorned in black and silk—black silk stockings, a black, unornamented silk dress, black pumps, long very black hair done back, and all of it setting off the astonishing light-olive smoothness of her skin and somehow, also, her almost extreme-seeming youngness, there standing quietly amid the barest scent of perfume was what Barclay felt was surely the most beautiful, and the most desirable girl he had ever seen.

"Hello, Coco," he said.

19

VIA APOLLO 24

"Who are you?" she said.

The half-light came into the room through partially closed shutters. Barclay stepped closer to her where she stood near the windows, bringing himself more into the light.

"Don't you remember?" he said.

"Lieutenant Barclay?" His name came from her as a gasp. But then she had recovered herself into that presence he had always known in her. She gave a small laugh.

"What are you doing here, Lieutenant? What the others are?"

"How long have you been here?"

"Not very long, Lieutenant. About a week."

"A week?"

"You're wondering how much business I could conduct in a week? Well, quite an amount, Lieutenant. It pays very well."

"So I see," he said, looking around at the room.

"It is better than the Via Mazzini, certainly. But sit down, Lieutenant."

Only then did he take off his cap. "The bandage, Lieutenant!" she exclaimed. "What has happened to you?"

Her solicitousness, he felt, was very sincere but it meant nothing to him now. He explained as briefly as possible. Then he sat on the sofa, and she in a chair across from him. Watching her cross her legs, with a whispering of silk, he thought how even now her beauty was not a whore's beauty. Even in her dress calculated to entice. She enticed all right, she was an object of great desire, but even so she had complete taste. He felt no man could help desiring her a great deal.

"That's a pretty dress. And so are the shoes and the stockings."

"They should be, they cost enough. But, as I say, this business pays very well. Very well indeed. It has taken only a week to find that out."

He said bluntly: "Why did you run away?"

"Run away? I wasn't aware I had run away. I was afraid they might arrest me. Remember that I have a child, Lieutenant. You should remember, it was born on your ship. And one of its names is yours. Do you remember—you were almost a midwife with me. I don't know what I would have done if you had not been there to speak my language. It seems a long time ago."

"Haven't you wondered what has happened to Red?"

"Yes, very much, Lieutenant. I wonder all the time about him. Is he back on the ship now?"

"Not exactly. He's being held for trial."

"Held for trial!" the phrase burst in shock from her. "For what, Lieutenant?"

"For taking things to you."

"You mean they're going to try him for *that*? For taking a few cans of rations and some soap and flour?"

He realized that her surprise and incredulity were genuine. But he felt nothing for her. "Yes, they try them for that. You see, they feel that the goods belonged to them."

"They, *they*. Who are *they*?"

"They are the Navy and the Army from whom he took the goods."

"But it seems so little, with all they've got."

"They don't consider that exactly the point."

She sat a moment in dumbfoundment.

"After all you saw him arrested," he said. "What in the world did you think they were arresting him for?"

"I knew it was for that, of course. But I couldn't imagine they would do much to him. Maybe just lecture him and tell him not to do it any more and let him go. Could they do more than that to him?"

He did feel that this was no act, that she was either very innocent or very unschooled in the methods of naval and military justice. It still didn't help.

"They could do considerably more," Barclay said and his voice came quite hard now. "They could give him a dishonorable discharge, which is as great a disgrace as can come to an American in uniform. What is more it marks him for life when he returns to civilian life. When he tries to get a job, when he tries to vote. It's a very terrible thing to happen to a man, do you understand that? It makes a kind of moral eunuch out of him in everybody's eyes, do you understand? Most men would rather be killed than to get one of them, do you understand that?"

Now he saw the great worry and fear in her but it exacted not pity in him but the prospect of usefulness. And for a while she sat as in a pool of it, not speaking.

"I really had no idea, Lieutenant," she said finally. "No idea at all that such a thing, such a horrible thing, could happen from what he did. Do you believe me, Lieutenant?"

"Yes, I do believe you. Not that it makes much difference now."

"What can I do, Lieutenant? For Red, I mean. Is there anything? I will do anything, anything."

Barclay sighed deeply. "As a matter-of-fact there is. Something. That's why I've been trying to find you for almost a week now."

"What is it, Lieutenant? Tell me and I will do whatever it is."

"We need you as a witness. As our main witness really."

"A witness? How would that help Red?"

"It might not help him at all. But it could help a great deal." He paused. "It might save him. In any case it's the only chance in the world he has. I don't believe there's much chance for him—but this way there is a little chance."

"Just tell me exactly what to do, Lieutenant."

He sat back and talked for a while then, going over with her his strategy for the trial. She agreed again to do anything he wanted.

"Very well. The first thing you can do is to stop this work you're doing." He spoke bluntly, an edge in his voice. "It won't help things in that court-martial if they discover your present occupation."

"I would rather stop it than anything in the world, Lieutenant. But my child has to eat. I have to eat."

"If I get you the money to take care of you both, will you stop it?"

"Of course, Lieutenant. Though I don't like to take money—for nothing."

He said brusquely: "The time for worrying about the way you take money is past, a long time ago in fact. I'm doing this for Carlyle—not you."

"I see, Lieutenant."

"Then listen well. I'm going from here to the Navy disbursing office and cash a couple of paychecks I have. They'll keep you quite awhile. You must wait here, and I'll bring them back to you. And meantime you're to do nothing. Do you understand that?"

"Yes, Lieutenant," she said meekly. "I'll do exactly as you tell me . . ."

Three knocks sounded on the door.

"If that's Rebi with another customer," Barclay said at once, and sharply, "send the customer away. Then tell Rebi to come in here."

She walked to the door, said a few words through it to Rebi, then Barclay could hear the boy speaking in broken English to someone. The someone began to protest in a very American voice, to protest rather strongly. Barclay got up and walked to the door and opened it and stood in the doorway. He saw a man wearing the crossed rifles of an infantryman on one collar tab, the gold oak leaf on the other. He looked stocky and very fit.

"Can I do anything for you, Major?"

"I was given to understand the signorina wasn't busy."

"You've been given to understand wrong, Major. She's very busy."

"When will she be through, Lieutenant? Or should I say, when will you be through?"

"I'm not exactly sure, Major. I've been quite awhile at sea."

The major hesitated then grinned slyly. "Pretty good, eh, Lieutenant?"

"The best, Major," Barclay said. "The best in Naples."

"That's what the boy said. Of course that's what they all say. I didn't know whether to believe him or not."

"He spoke the truth, Major."

"I'd like to find out for myself. I think I'd like to have a look at her."

The major started around Barclay, who put his hand on the door jamb, blocking his way.

"I'm not sure you understood me, Major. I've got her tied up. She's blocked out for as long as my ship's here."

The Army officer looked with a sudden flaring anger at Barclay. The major appeared clearly unaccustomed to having his way blocked without at least removing the block.

"How long will that be, Lieutenant?"

"About a week, Major. You might try back in a week."

Suddenly the major relaxed. "Well, I don't suppose the Army and Navy should stand here arguing over a whore, should we, Lieutenant? Not with so many of them around."

"I couldn't agree more, Major. Why don't you try somewhere else then come back in a week if you're still interested. One week ought to do it."

The major gave a short laugh. "Lieutenant, in a week I don't think I'll be in a place where one is confronted with choices of this sort. Well, have fun, Lieutenant."

The major started away and Rebi started away with him. Barclay reached out and yanked the boy in after him. Barclay closed the door and they left the darkness of the hallway and went into the living room. For the first time the boy looked up at Barclay with some vague sense of recognition.

"It's been a long time, Rebi," Barclay said, and grinned down at the boy. "You remember the ship that took you to Anzio?"

"The lieutenant!" Rebi exclaimed. He seemed only happy to see him, and totally undisturbed at the trade Barclay had found him practicing.

"Rebi, you're to stay here now," Barclay said. "You can take a vacation—at least for a couple of weeks. I'm going to get something so you and the signora can take a vacation."

The boy seemed as pleased with giving up his trade for the time being as he had seemed undisturbed by practicing it. Barclay thought, maybe the young ones take it more in stride than anyone else. He even felt a certain envy of the attitude. Or maybe the fact they did was the worst part of what it did to them. He turned to Coco.

"I'll be back after a while," he said. "I've got to get over there before the thing closes."

"Lieutenant?" He had turned to go but stopped, looking down at her.

"Yes?"

"Lieutenant, do you have to tell Carlyle?"

At that moment Barclay felt no sympathy for her. He saw her only as someone who had brought all this on Carlyle, and who now had the audacity to ask him to shield her whoring from the man who had so risked himself to help her. Then looking at her, with all her beauty, and with all that valid sorrow that was in her face, he realized how wrong he was to feel hard on her. The hell that had been fashioned for her by this war was surely worse, far worse, than any that Carlyle or any of them had endured. He saw like a blow across his face the young mother, little more than a child herself, lying on the wardroom table, where she had seemed to him the very triumph over all the folly and evil that war was; and now a whore, available to any man—or maybe only to officers, he thought bitterly. And he felt an almost unbearable sadness.

"No, I won't tell Carlyle, Coco." He would not have told him anyhow, for Carlyle's own sake in trying to get him emotionally prepared for his trial. But now it was for her sake as well that he wouldn't tell him. "You really do love him, don't you?"

"Why of course I love him, Lieutenant," she said, in surprise that there could be any doubt about it. "I love him very much, Lieutenant."

"I won't tell him anything. Except that I've found you and that you are well."

"Yes, tell him that, Lieutenant."

20

THE COURT-MARTIAL OF
PETER CARLYLE

The Morning

It was a setting of considerable beauty, a small ballroom in a palazzo where in another age ladies in flowing gowns and gentlemen in doublets and hose had danced the minuet and the contre. The platform where the string orchestra had once played was still there, at one end of the room. The floor was of a marvelous teak inlay and from it, on one side, windows rose almost all the way to the high ceiling. These faced to the east so that of a morning sunlight flooded the room. Standing at these windows one had a view of one of the world's fairest harbors. The view was breathtaking, for the palazzo sat on a hill and one could see not only the harbor and the men of war riding at anchor, but beyond them the cone of Vesuvius, often smoking red in those days. Immediately outside the windows was a green lawn, still well kept, then the land fell away abruptly into trees so that the tops of the trees made a green stairway which led to the white roofs of the city, traversed these, and ended in the blue sea stretching away. There was surely no better view in the city and the selection of the palazzo for the Navy's Administration building was a tribute to the unfailing esthetic taste of Navy requisitioning officers. The ballroom was not used very often, and then it was generally for large staff planning conferences, and highly secret naval operations, great and small, had been laid out around long tables in that room. And occasionally the room was used for its present purpose. This purpose was identifiable at a glance.

Near the wall containing the windows and near the opposite wall, which had no windows but for recompense did have an enormous mural of Garibaldi and The Thousand routing thirty times their number on the field at Reggio Calabria, were a small table and two chairs, so that the tables faced each other across perhaps thirty feet of floor. Precisely in the middle of this open space was a very small raised platform, just large enough to accommodate one chair, and set back enough not to obscure the view between the two tables. The chair also faced forward to the large platform at the end of the room which had once been the orchestra's. On this platform was a table capable, with comfort and armroom to spare, of taking nine chairs ranged along one side of it. Only five of these chairs were at present occupied, the center one, which was of a higher back than the others, by a full commander of the line, the chair on his immediate right by a lieutenant commander wearing the insignia of the Medical Corps, and three other chairs by lieutenants of the line. The chairs at the window table were occupied by two additional naval officers, one a lieutenant commander and one a lieutenant. The chairs at the mural table across from it were occupied by Lieutenant (jg) Matthew Barclay and by Seaman Second Class Peter Carlyle, wearing dress blues. Halfway between the large platform and the small raised one and slightly to the side two Navy yeomen sat at a small table, one with stenographic pads and a row of sharpened pencils arranged before him. Still another table immediately in front of the platform provided the most incongruous sight in this beautiful room. On it were a sack of flour, some cans of C- and packages of K-rations, a couple cans of mixed fruit, a few other cans of food, two bars of soap, a few packs of cigarettes, a tube of toothpaste, a can of talcum powder, and finally a red dress, neatly folded. The commander in the high-backed chair on the large platform spoke.

"I declare the court-martial of Peter Carlyle, seaman second class, USNR, member of ship's company of the USS *LST 1826*, opened." A time was spent in oath taking by the members of the court, Barclay hearing the words almost as an echo over the great room. ". . . do each and severally swear that you will truly try without prejudice or partiality, the case now depending, according to the evidence which shall come before the court, the rules for the government of the Navy, and your own conscience . . ." The president spoke: "Judge Advocate, will you please read the charge and specifications."

At the window table the lieutenant commander rose and Barclay pressed his hand on Carlyle's back to indicate to him to do the same. The judge advocate, facing the court, began reading from a sheet of paper. He read in a relaxed and easy, almost monotonic voice, giving no emphasis to any of the words.

"The charge falls under Article 14, paragraph 8, of the Articles for the Government of the Navy, reading: 'Fine and imprisonment or such other punishment as a court-martial may adjudge, shall be inflicted upon any person in the naval service of the United States who steals, embezzles, knowingly and willfully misappropriates, applies to his own use or benefit, or wrongfully and knowingly sells or disposes of any ordnance, arms, equipments, ammunition, clothing, subsistence stores, money or other property of the United States, furnished or intended for the military or naval service thereof.'"

The judge advocate paused a moment then continued in the same unemphasizing voice. "The specifications are as follows:

"Specification One: 'In that Peter Carlyle, seaman second class, USNR, while serving on board the USS LST 1826, did on April 28, 1944, and May 4, 1944, each, feloniously take, steal, and carry away from the possession of the United States, to wit from the 162 1st Army Supply Depot in the city of Naples, Italy, one 100-pound sack of flour, the property of the United States intended for the military service thereof, and, without proper authority, did knowingly hand said articles over to civilian sources for sale or other unauthorized disposition; the United States then being in a state of war.'

"Specification Two: 'In that this same Carlyle did, on at least eleven separate occasions between April 16, 1944, and May 4, 1944, feloniously take, steal, and carry away from the possession of the

United States, to wit, from the USS *LST 1826*, various articles of Navy property and, without proper authority, did knowingly hand said articles over to civilian sources for consumption, sale, or other unauthorized disposition; the United States then being in a state of war. Said articles included, but were not necessarily limited to . . .' "

If one had been watching the table in front of the platform one could have tallied off all the items on it with the exception of the red dress. The judge advocate finished his reading and across the room addressed Carlyle.

"Peter Carlyle, seaman second class, USNR, you have heard the charge and specifications preferred against you. How say you to the first specification, guilty or not guilty?"

Barclay had gone over in great care with Carlyle what he should say here, and gone over with him also what the result of the pleas they had decided upon would be. Barclay was threading, or would try to, a very narrow corridor. None other lay open to him, none which would allow Carlyle to present his case.

"Guilty," Carlyle said.

The judge advocate spoke: "To the second specification, guilty or not guilty?"

Carlyle: "Guilty."

The judge advocate: "How say you to the charge, guilty or not guilty?"

"Guilty," Carlyle said, and paused a moment. "Except as to the words 'applies to his own use or benefit' and the words 'or wrongfully.' "

Barclay made certain to be watching the judge advocate carefully at this point. He observed that his expression varied only quite momentarily. He turned and waited upon the court. There were moments of silence, then the president:

"The court wishes to address the accused."

The president leaned forward from his high-backed chair toward the sailor standing at the defense table and spoke slowly and with meticulous care.

"Seaman Carlyle, it is my duty as president of this court to warn you that by your plea of guilty except as to the words 'applies to his own use or benefit' and the words 'or wrongfully' to the charge, and guilty as to both specifications of the charge, you deprive yourself of the benefits of a regular defense as to those specifications and those parts of the charge thus admitted. That is to say, you cannot after such a plea of guilty go ahead and prove that you are not guilty on these specifications and charge, so that the court would be left with no alternative but to return a finding of guilty. You may, however, by changing your plea, introduce evidence of mitigating circumstances, in extenuation. Do you understand what I have just explained?"

"I do, sir."

"Understanding this, do you persist in your plea?"

"No, sir," Carlyle said promptly. He was doing perfectly, Barclay thought, and in these earliest moments of the trial felt a moment of encouragement as to how Carlyle would perform as a witness. All so far was going as to plan. "Sir, I wish now to change my plea."

The court: "Can defense counsel on his own responsibility verify and will he stipulate that accused understands what he is doing?"

Barclay stood. "He understands thoroughly, sir. On his own responsibility defense counsel so verifies and stipulates, sir."

"Judge Advocate," the president said, "will you please restate the questions as to plea to the accused."

The judge advocate once more looked across at Carlyle, studying him for a moment, then glanced narrowly for the barest moment at Barclay as if studying him, too, then spoke: "How say you to the first specification of the charge, guilty or not guilty?"

Carlyle's voice came in clear tones: "Not guilty."

"To the second specification of the charge, guilty or not guilty?"

"Not guilty."

"How say you to the charge, guilty or not guilty?"

"Not guilty."

The judge advocate, as Carlyle sat down, addressed the court. "I ask the court's permission to call the first witness."

"Permission granted."

The judge advocate spoke to a sailor standing at a large double door and wearing dress blues, white hat, white leggings, on his right arm the insignia of a boatswain's mate first class, and around his left arm a blue brassard bearing the letters in yellow "SP."

"Will the orderly please call First Lieutenant Thomas Gibbs."

The shore patrol man opened one of the doors, spoke a name, then held the door back. The doors seemed very thick. An Army lieutenant walked into the room, crossed it to the small platform in the center, stepped up into the chair there and was sworn. The judge advocate, standing easily in front of the prosecution table, began to question him in a quiet voice.

"State your name, rank, and present station."

"Thomas Gibbs, first lieutenant, Criminal Investigation Department, United States Army, Naples, Italy."

"If you recognize the accused state as whom."

"Peter Carlyle, seaman second class, United States Naval Reserve."

"Lieutenant, I direct your attention to the afternoon of April 28, 1944. On that afternoon did you follow the accused to and observe him enter the 162 1st Army Supply Depot located at the corner of Triontale and Valfonda avenues?"

The judge advocate then led Gibbs through the evidence of the sacks of flour and the musette bag and the delivery by the sailor in each instance to the address of Via Giuseppe Mazzini 36. He then asked:

"Will you tell the court how you know the man you followed to be the same man you later knew as Seaman Carlyle."

"Well, sir, first of all he had the same physical description. He was of about the same height, build, and age—and he had his red hair. It is rather identifiable hair. He was also, both times, driving a jeep with the markings 'Bomb Disposal.' And finally, we followed this man out of the jeep and arrested him."

"Witness, what led you first to suspect the accused?"

"We had followed a young Italian boy—his name was Rebi, we later learned—and had observed him disposing of Navy and Army goods. It was this boy who led us, not knowing he was doing so, to the accused."

"What do you mean by 'disposing' of Army and Navy goods, Lieutenant?"

"Well, the boy would carry a bag containing American C-rations, K-rations, bars of soap, that sort of thing, and sell them to Italian intermediaries on the black market."

"And why did you not arrest the boy while so witnessing?"

"We were after the source of the materiel, which we considered a good deal more important."

"And the boy led you where?"

"We followed him one day to the naval BOQ on Via Fonte Bella. We saw him ride away in a jeep marked 'Bomb Disposal.' Thereafter we took to following the jeep itself. It was in this way that we turned up the accused, who apparently had use of the jeep, access to it I mean."

"Lieutenant, aside from the two visits to the Army depot, did you at any other times observe accused in possession of what you believed was Navy materiel which later was to leave his possession?"

"At least eleven times, sir."

"Would you identify those occasions in general for us, Lieutenant."

"Yes, sir. It was in the trailings of the accused from his ship. He would often carry a musette bag when he left the ship. The bag was obviously full."

"Lieutenant, what approximate distance is it from where the LST 1826 customarily put in to the address of Via Giuseppe Mazzini 36?"

"It is no more than three blocks away."

"So that the accused needed to conceal the musette bag only for a distance of three blocks?"

"Objection," Barclay said. "No evidence of either needing to conceal or concealing."

"Sustained," the president said.

"Lieutenant. Tell us what you saw while trailing the accused from his ship to Via Mazzini 36."

"We saw him enter this address with the musette bag, obviously carrying something. Then when he came out the bag would be flat."

"How long would the accused be in the building?"

"It varied. Oftentimes four hours."

"Four hours. I see." The judge advocate paused, then repeated: "Four hours. Lieutenant, I direct your attention to these items of American goods."

The judge advocate stepped over to the table in front of the main platform. One by one, he held up the various items there, all but two, naming them off then setting them back quietly. "Three cans of C-ration . . . Two boxes of K-ration . . . Two cans of mixed fruit . . . Two bars of American soap . . ." He merely placed his hand on the sack of flour and said "A one-hundred-pound sack of American flour." And he disregarded the red dress.

"Lieutenant, were these all confiscated and brought in by you?"

"Yes, sir. By me and my colleague, Lieutenant James Craig."

"Where did you bring them from?"

"From an apartment on the second floor of the building at Via Mazzini 36."

"Was the accused present when you took them?"

"He was. Lieutenant Craig and I had just observed the accused carrying the sack of flour up the stairway."

"Tell the court what you did then."

"We followed the accused up presently and placed him under arrest. The other goods were found in the apartment at the time."

"Do you know who occupied the apartment at that time, Lieutenant?"

"Yes, sir. A Signora Coco Comparo. She was present at the time of the arrest."

"The arrest was made immediately after the sailor had delivered the flour?"

"Yes, sir. He still had the white dust from the flour sack on his shoulder."

"So that you arrested accused," the judge advocate said, "in act of delivering United States property intended for the military or naval service thereof to an unauthorized civilian person and at the same time took from the apartment where the arrest was made the objects you have just identified as being in the courtroom."

"Yes, sir. The arrest of the sailor and the confiscation of the objects were made at the same time."

The judge advocate addressed the court: "I have no further questions, sir."

"Defense counsel?" the president said.

Barclay addressed the witness. "Lieutenant, did the accused offer any resistance to the arrest?"

"None," the witness said.

"Did either the accused or the woman offer any objection to the searching of the apartment?"

"None."

"And when he was transporting these items from the ship to the apartment in a musette bag where did the accused carry the bag?"

"By the strap over his shoulder."

"So that at no time did he attempt to hide the objects he was carrying?"

"Only in the musette bag. It appeared to be very full."

"Exactly, Lieutenant. This obviously very full bag was carried in full view at all times, in the open, with no attempt at concealment?"

"Not of the bag itself. It would be difficult to conceal a full musette bag."

"Lieutenant, whether or not there are ways to conceal a musette bag—and I would suggest it to be a not insurmountable feat—my question is only whether there was an attempt to conceal it. Was there or was there not?"

"There was not."

"Thank you, Lieutenant. And when he came out of the building and the musette bag was empty, where did the accused carry the bag?"

"The same way. By the strap over the shoulder."

"So that anyone in the world watching him both when he went in and when he came out could have told readily that he went in with a full musette bag and emerged with an empty one?"

"Yes, sir."

"Lieutenant, did Seaman Carlyle, during the course of your following him, appear at any time to have a furtive, secretive air to what he was doing?"

"Objection," the judge advocate said. "Counsel is asking witness to interpret the 'air' of a man, whatever that is. Question is objected to as being too vague and subjective."

"Sir," Barclay addressed the court. "I submit that the 'air' of accused is of vital importance to our case. We wish to establish that the accused made no attempt to hide what he was doing. Witness is a highly trained observer."

"The witness may answer the question."

The CID man said: "No, sir. Insofar as I could tell there was nothing furtive or secretive about the accused's actions."

"Thank you, Lieutenant," Barclay said. He walked around to the front of the defense table. "Now I call your attention, Lieutenant, to the jeep used by the accused to transport the flour. You have said that it had markings in the form of the words 'Bomb Disposal' on it. Where were these words situated, Lieutenant?"

"On the front, just under the windshield."

"Is the lettering large or small?"

"It is large. At least six inches high, I would say. I have not measured it."

"And just under the windshield, so that it is highly visible?"

"Highly visible. That is its purpose, I imagine."

"Would you say then, Lieutenant, that it was what you might call a conspicuous jeep?"

"Yes, sir, it was."

"Lieutenant, I ask you this: Did it not strike you as odd that a man would use such a jeep to transport goods if he felt the activity to be an improper one?"

"As a matter of fact it did. I remember mentioning it to Lieutenant Craig."

"Mentioning what, Lieutenant?"

"I said to Lieutenant Craig something like, 'It seems strange that a man would do this in a jeep so easily followed.'"

Barclay paused. He looked out the windows over the bay, as though pondering his next question. By the time he turned back several seconds had elapsed during which silence and the last line of testimony had held the court. He then addressed the court stenographer as though to pick up the thread of testimony.

"Yeoman, will you please read the last line."

The yeoman read: "I said to Lieutenant Craig something like, 'It seems strange that a man would do this in a jeep so easily followed.'"

Barclay waited a handful of seconds longer; then turned to the witness. "Thank you, Lieutenant." And to the court, "I have no further questions, sir."

In a voice carrying the faintest touch of irritation the judge advocate said: "Lieutenant, the sack of flour which the accused transported in the jeep to Via Mazzini 36, just before his arrest, was it concealed?"

"It was."

"In what manner?"

"It was covered by a poncho."

"Could the poncho have been for protection against the weather?"

"I don't think so," the witness said. "It was clear weather."

"Thank you, Lieutenant."

Barclay said: "Lieutenant, we are dealing here with two separate occasions—and two only—in which the accused transported sacks of flour from the Army depot. Was the poncho used both times to cover the sack in the jeep?"

"No, sir, only one time."

"The other time the sack of flour was carried in the open—that is to say, uncovered."

"Yes, sir."

"And it was easily visible, let us say, from your jeep?"

"Yes, sir."

"No further questions."

"Witness is excused," the president said. "Your next witness?" he said to the judge advocate.

"Will the orderly please call Signor Tomaso Gabini."

The shore patrol man saw the CID officer through the door and presently brought in a small Italian man of past middle age who looked considerably frightened. He stepped into the chair on the little platform and gripped its arms with shaking hands. The other yeoman, who was an interpreter, came forward and translated the oath to him. The yeoman remained at his side.

"Your name, sir?" the judge advocate said.

This was translated and he replied, "Tomaso Gabini."

"Signor Gabini, you are in business in the town of Pozzuoli?"

"When there is business to be made I am in business."

"And what is your business, sir?"

"The selling of groceries and green things, when there are groceries to be had. Mostly there are just green things to be had these days, and few of them."

"Thank you, sir. Have you ever had American flour to sell?"

"Very seldom," the signore-groceryman said. "Almost never. We get very little American flour for a people who eat almost completely things made of flour."

"Sir, I did not ask you how many times you have had American flour to sell. I asked you if you had *ever* had it. I will ask it again. Have you ever sold or traded American flour in your store?"

"I have—rarely."

"Can you recall one specific time having sold or traded it?"

"Yes, I can just recall one time."

"Fine. In what size sack did the American flour come to you?"

"In fifty kilos, by approximation."

"And who brought it to you?"

"Signora Coco Comparo. She is a nice young lady."

"And did you pay this nice young lady for the fifty-kilo sack of flour?"

"Never in cash!" the signore exclaimed proudly. "Only in other things. Italian things."

"And this nice young lady, did she bring you other American things?"

"Sometimes."

"What things?"

"Sometimes a bar of soap."

"American soap?"

"Yes, American soap. Not very often."

"And what else?"

"One time cigarettes. Various items. One time a man's underwear. I wore that myself and it was the color of an olive. But mostly American soap. Nothing very often."

"And did you pay for these items?"

"Never in cash! Only in Italian things."

"No further questions."

Barclay said: "In return for these American packages the signora brought, did you ever give her anything except things to eat?"

"Never!" the Italian exclaimed. "Never cash! Only in things to eat."

"Milk sometimes?"

"I get very little milk."

"But when you did get it, did you sometimes trade milk to the signora in exchange for the American items?"

"Yes, milk more than anthing else. She seemed to want milk more than any other single thing."

"Did she say why she wanted milk more than anything else?"

"She has a small baby. These drink milk in Italy."

"Yes. Did the signora ever talk about the baby?"

Now a rather lovely smile broke suddenly over the Italian grocer's face. "Yes. Obviously she was very fond of the baby. And very worried. That was why she wanted the milk."

"Did the signora ever tell you where this baby of hers was born?"

The Italian frowned thoughtfully. "She told me he was born on an American ship. That always sounded very remarkable to me."

The members of the court-martial looked at the grocer and then at Barclay in surprise.

"The signora said her baby was born on an American ship,"

Barclay repeated in English, though looking at the Italian. He did not wait for a translation.

"Sir," he said to the court. "I have no further questions."

The Italian was led off the witness stand. His nervousness was now all gone and he bowed and smiled his way out of the room, to everybody, including the members of the court and the judge advocate. As Barclay had expected an Army sergeant was brought in. Barclay wondered idly what would happen to him. The judge advocate established in a few questions that the sergeant was stationed at the 162 1st Army Supply Depot and that he had twice given 100-pound sacks of flour to Carlyle. The sergeant seemed reluctant to hurt Carlyle and Barclay knew he was in a bind, that he had to give his testimony. The judge advocate established that on the second trip the flour had left the depot in a jeep with a poncho over the sack. Barclay then had the witness.

"Sergeant, how did the first sack of flour leave the depot, covered or uncovered?"

"Uncovered."

"Seaman Carlyle did not suggest covering it?"

"No, sir, he didn't."

"Sergeant, did Seaman Carlyle in any way attempt to hide the first sack of flour in the jeep?"

"No, sir. He just put it on the back seat."

"Not even on the floor?"

"He put it on the back seat."

"Then it would have been easy to see in the jeep?"

"If anyone had looked that way."

"Now the second sack of flour, Sergeant. Let us go to that. It was also placed on the seat of the jeep?"

"Yes, sir."

Barclay disliked to ask the next question, realizing the sergeant was there unwillingly. But he had to ask it.

"Sergeant," he said. "Was it Seaman Carlyle who suggested putting the poncho over that sack of flour?"

"No, sir." The sergeant did not flinch and he spoke very clearly. "Sir, I was the one who made that suggestion, sir."

"Thank you, Sergeant. That is all."

"Judge advocate?"

"Sergeant," the judge advocate. "Did Seaman Carlyle in any way object to your putting the poncho over the sack of flour or in any way attempt to hinder you from doing so?"

"No, sir. He just laughed."

"No further questions. Call the Italian boy," the judge advocate said to the shore patrol sailor at the door.

Rebi came in looking very curiously about the room, at the officers at the various tables, out the window at the view, up at the ceiling and the mural. Finally, with the assistance of the shore patrol man, he got up into the witness stand. The judge advocate was gentle with the boy. He led him through his identification, his acquaintanceship with Signora Comparo, the fact he came to live in her apartment.

"Did you notice that someone was bringing some packages of American goods to the apartment?"

"Yes, sir."

"Who brought these packages, Rebi?"

"Red brought them." The boy said it as a tribute.

"Is Red in this room?"

"Oh, yes. He is the sailor sitting at that table." The boy smiled at Carlyle.

"Let the record show," the president said, "that the witness has identified the accused as Seaman Carlyle."

The judge advocate: "Were some of these packages given to you to do something with?"

"Yes, sir."

"What did you do with them?"

"I sold them. Here in Naples."

"And what did you do with the money?"

"I gave it to Signora Coco. Except for the fare on the interurban."

"Thank you, Rebi. That's all."

Barclay said: "Rebi, what did the signora use the money for?"

"Why to buy food. For myself, for her baby, for herself."

"No further questions."

The judge advocate next called the base supply officer, a full commander. He then walked over to the table containing the confiscated articles and picked up a bar of Palmolive soap.

"Sir, how much would this bar of soap sell for on the black market?"

"About one dollar."

The judge advocate picked up a package of cigarettes. "And this item?"

"Between fifty cents and one dollar."

The judge advocate picked up a tin of corned beef. "This item?"

"Varying considerably. Anywhere between three and five dollars."

"Thank you, Commander. No further questions."

Barclay: "Commander, what is the approximate price for each of the three mentioned items to the Navy or to a Navy man in a ship's store?"

"The bar of soap, four cents. The pack of cigarettes, five cents. The tin of beef, oh, about sixteen cents."

"Thank you, Commander. No further questions."

The judge advocate stood and faced the court. "The prosecution rests."

The president looked at his watch. "This court will stand in recess until fourteen hundred hours. Will the defense be prepared with its first witness at that time?"

Barclay stood. "We will, sir."

"Very well. The court is in recess until fourteen hundred hours."

The Afternoon

"Will the orderly please call Signora Coco Comparo."

The lightest of shadows lay upon the great room as Coco walked in. As he had seen before with the same stimulus, Barclay caught the startlement of the members of the court-martial confronted with the beauty and youth of the girl. She looked once over at the sailor seated at the defense table. Carlyle, at the same time, looked at her, then away. It was their first sight of each other since the night of the arrest. Barclay walked up and stood lightly at her side.

"I ask the court's permission," he said casually, "to conduct my questioning of the witness in Italian and for the interpreter to translate the Italian for the court."

"I object, sir," the judge advocate said. "It seems to me an American court-martial should be conducted in the English language. The interpreter can translate counsel's questions to the witness, as he has done with all other Italian witnesses."

"Defense counsel?" the president said.

"Sir, I believe addressing the witness in Italian will prevent any possible misunderstanding. She is a very vital witness, sir. The interpreter can then translate. He is a good interpreter. I am surprised that the judge advocate objects. Interpreter will provide full protection against any slipping of instructions to the witness, if that is the judge advocate's concern."

"It is a good deal too early for counsel to develop a persecution complex," the judge advocate said. "I was thinking only of procedure."

"The court sees no reason against the proposed procedure," the president said. "There will have to be translation one way in any event since all of us do not speak both languages. Which way the translation is made seems immaterial to me. Defense counsel may proceed."

"Signora Comparo." Barclay turned to Coco and addressed her in Italian. "I would like for you to tell this court under what circumstances you first met the American sailor, Peter Carlyle."

The girl testified to her experience of being taken off the beachhead with other Italians onto the LST 1826, to becoming aware enroute to Naples that she was going to have her baby, to how the baby was born after many hours, to Carlyle's coming to see her about two weeks after her return from the American hospital and arranging to take Italian lessons for two hundred lire whenever the ship came in from Anzio and Carlyle had liberty and to the fact this was her sole means of support. Barclay said:

"So at the most you had four hundred lire a week from him for the lessons?"

"About that."

"Signora, how much does a litre of milk cost?"

"Forty lire is the fixed price. It is nearly impossible to get for that. If you will pay three or four hundred lire a bottle, it can be had more readily."

"How much for a loaf of bread?"

"Twenty-five lire, the fixed price. But it is almost never come by for that. But it can be come by for one hundred lire."

"So the four hundred lire would not begin to support you and your child?"

There is no living thing it would support."

"Did there come a time when Seaman Carlyle began to bring you American articles?"

"Yes. But that was at my suggestion. All of it was at my suggestion."

The judge advocate: "Does the court understand that the matter of whose suggestion it was that the accused take Navy materiel has no bearing on the question of the guilt or innocence of the accused?"

"The court needs no instruction in the nature of the charge, Judge Advocate," the president said with some acerbity. "Please continue with your questioning, defense counsel."

"So at your suggestion the sailor Carlyle began to bring you American articles. What was the nature of these articles, signora?"

"Some of them were things we could eat. C-rations and K-rations they were called. Once there was a can of peaches. We ate that. Some other things were things I would sell or trade. These would be things like a bar of soap, a razor, a set of men's underwear."

"How much would a bar of American soap sell for, signora?"

"At least one hundred lire."

"Or about one-third the cost of a litre of milk?"

"About."

"At any time did the sailor Carlyle bring you these articles in wholesale amounts? That is to say, a case or twenty-four cans of C-rations or peaches?"

"No, it was always one or two items of each thing."

"Then after a while did he begin to bring you larger things?"

"Yes. He brought a hundred-pound sack of American flour. That paid for a great deal. He did this two times—though the second time it was taken away. He would bring me this larger thing when his ship was leaving. I believe it was because if something happened to his ship, he knew it would take care of us for a while. That one sack of flour would support us for an entire month."

"Did Carlyle ever bring anything else to you?"

"Yes, once when my baby became ill. Red—Carlyle brought medicine from his ship. And he brought things to pay the doctor. And he put something in to heat my place. A stove."

"What was the child's illness, signora?"

"Pneumonia."

"Signora, did you ever use the money obtained from your disposal of the items the sailor Carlyle brought for any purpose other than the most basic things, such as food and rent for yourself and your child, and most of it by far for food?"

"What else would I use it for, Lieutenant?"

Barclay decided to dispose of a point which he believed would be less damaging if brought in by the defense rather than if the judge advocate somehow discovered it and brought it out.

"Signora, one last point. Did there come a time when you moved out of the room into an apartment?"

"Yes. In the same building."

"What was your reason for moving, signora? Was the apartment more elegant than the room?"

Coco smiled faintly. "There is nothing elegant in the building at Via Giuseppe Mazzini 36, Lieutenant. The apartment differed only in that it had two rooms instead of one."

"Why did you need two rooms, signora?"

"Red brought a young boy named Rebi to live with myself and the baby. He said it would make him feel safer about us when he was away on his ship. And Rebi had no home—he was living in the sulphur caves at Pozzuoli."

"Thank you, signora." Barclay turned to the court. "I have no further questions, sir."

"Judge Advocate?"

The judge advocate stood up and walked around facing the witness. "Signora," he said, "are you a qualified teacher of the Italian language?"

"I have no degree to teach it, if that is what you mean."

The interpretation went the other way now. "And yet you consented readily to teach the language to the sailor?"

"A number of Italians are teaching the language to Americans now who never did it before. Or doing any other work they can find, even if they never did it before."

"Is Carlyle the only pupil you have ever had or have there been a good many others?"

"He is the only one."

"I see." The judge advocate paused. "Signora, how long were the lessons in the Italian language which you have testified you gave Carlyle?"

"Usually four hours or more."

"Isn't a session of four hours at a time very long for the study of a language, even for a very devoted scholar?"

"I would think it would depend on a person's intelligence. And how badly he wanted to learn. If both of these were present, I would think four hours could be usefully taken up."

"And the sailor Carlyle is intelligent?"

"Highly so, I consider him."

"And he wanted to learn?"

"He was very anxious to and he did learn, very rapidly. But with lots of study."

"And the sailor Carlyle did nothing during those four-hour sessions but study the language?"

"Sometimes he would stop and pick up the baby and hold it for a few minutes. And sometimes we stopped and ate a C-ration. Then went back to studying."

"I see. Signora, you have testified that the things which the sailor Carlyle brought you were used only for the barest necessities. Is that correct?"

"Yes, sir."

The judge advocate walked across to the table in front of the court containing the objects. He stood looking down at them a moment. Then, using both hands as if they were a tray, he picked up the red dress and brought it over and stood close to the witness.

"Signora, can you tell me what I am holding?"

"Yes. It is a dress. A red dress."

"Would you say it would be an expensive dress?"

"Yes, I would say so. It would be expensive even in Italy before the war. Today it would be very expensive, and very hard to come by even so."

"Would you say that if a man gave this dress to a woman it would be a rather personal gift and would suggest that he was a very good friend of hers?"

"Yes. Any girl would like a dress like that."

"Signora, whose dress is this?"

"I don't know whose it is now. At one time it was mine."

"Do you have any idea how it got where it is now?"

"I can guess. The dress was taken from my place on the night the men came to arrest Red—to arrest Carlyle."

"You called him Red, signorina?"

"I imagine anyone would, with his hair."

"Signora, if you used the money brought in by the Navy and Army objects you admit the sailor Carlyle brought you only for the barest necessities of life, as you have testified, how do you explain your possession of this dress? Would an expensive dress like this come under the head of 'necessity'?"

"No, not today."

"How did you or Carlyle, as the case may have been, happen to buy the dress if you had barely enough for necessities, signora?"

"I did not buy it, Commander."

"Then Carlyle traded some of these objects he took from the Navy and Army for dresses and other luxuries for you? At least this dress. We do not know if there were others. Do you know what the sailor Carlyle traded to get this dress to give you?"

"He didn't give it to me, Commander."

The judge advocate's eyebrows lifted. "Oh? And how did you get it, signora?"

"Some one else gave it to me."

"His—or her—name, please."

The witness waited a moment. "His name is Lieutenant Shanley."

The judge advocate looked very surprised, something seemed to leap in him, and Barclay knew what it was: Though failing in his line of questioning, in the very failure he had stumbled onto something of possibly far greater importance.

"Would you know this lieutenant's first name, Signora?"

"It is Allen."

"Is he an Army or a Navy lieutenant?"

"Navy."

The judge advocate waited a moment, then turned to the court and spoke softly.

"I have no further questions at this time, sir. I would like to reserve the right to recall witness if necessary."

"Very well."

Coco was led away and out the door, which the orderly then shut. The president looked at his watch and addressed Barclay. "How many more witnesses does defense counsel have?"

"Only one, sir."

"Who is the witness?"

"The accused, sir."

The president explained to Carlyle that as the accused he was not compelled to testify and exacted the reply that he did so of his own free will. Carlyle walked around the table and to the small raised platform. He remained standing for the oath, then sat down. His rangy body seemed confined by this tiny throne and for a while, during the preliminary questions, he shifted around, either to get comfortable, or from nerves. But as the questioning proceeded he seemed to come to an amnesty between himself and the platform and chair and sat relaxed. His voice at all times was clear. Quickly Barclay brought him to the point where Coco had been carried on a stretcher from troops quarters to the ladder leading topside.

"What did you do then?"

"I picked her up and carried her up to the wardroom and put her on the table. You, sir, decided—it was decided it would be too risky to try to get a stretcher up the ladder. She was very light."

"How long after you placed her on the wardroom table was it before she gave birth?"

Carlyle figured for a moment. "It was over ten hours, sir. It was a very long time. She had a bad time of it."

The judge advocate stood and addressed the court. "Sir, I have refrained until now but I must protest what appears to be an obvious intention on part of defense counsel to build up a sympathy for the Italian woman in the minds of members of the court-martial."

Barclay said: "Sir, the judge advocate errs in assessing my intentions. I believe it unnecessary to 'build up,' as the judge advocate puts it, sympathy for any Italian civilian caught in the situation of this woman. I believe, sir, that such a sympathy would naturally exist for such a person on the part of any of us, including the judge advocate. But I do have an intention in my questioning, sir, which is to establish the identification of the accused with the woman and the set of circumstances which provoked him to come to her assistance."

The judge advocate: "It is the same thing."

Barclay: "It is a very different thing."

"The object is the same. To reduce these proceedings to a matter of sympathy for starving Italians, whether young ladies with babies or otherwise. Counsel is correct that such conditions evoke the sympathy of us all. But this is a different matter from justification of criminal acts by naval personnel. It happens that the latter is the issue at hand."

"Defense counsel?" the president addressed Barclay.

"If it please the court." Barclay spoke quietly and carefully. "The question at issue here is of the greatest importance to the defense case. It is the defense intention to disprove the words in the charge 'applies to his own use or benefit, or wrongfully.' To disprove the first part 'applies to his own use or benefit' the defense must be allowed to establish that a need other than the accused's own, someone else's need, led him to take naval and military goods and that the accused received no compensation of any nature whatever for handing these goods over. To prove that he did not take the goods 'wrongfully' it is essential that the defense be allowed to establish the series of events and the circumstances which moved the accused to his acts. It will be the defense contention that these events and circumstances were of such an extraordinary nature that the accused was justified in committing what would ordinarily be a grave offense against the naval code and law. Judge advocate will have every opportunity on cross-examination to prove, if such be the case, that these needs and these circumstances are all a tissue of lies invented by the accused after the fact to save himself. The court can then judge which of the two contentions is the true one. But if the sailor Carlyle is not to be allowed the opportunity to prove his contention that he did not indeed apply the naval and military goods 'to his own use or benefit' and if he is not to be allowed to present the urgent and highly unusual circumstances which the defense contention shall be both led to the acts and rendered them not done 'wrongfully,' then the court, I submit respectfully, sirs, will in effect be depriving the accused the right to defend himself against the very words of the charge." Barclay paused a moment in the quiet attentiveness that had come over the court. "Sir, I rest on the judgment of the court."

The president of the court waited a few moments, looked to his right and then to his left along the line of the other members of the court.

"The court rules that counsel has the right to establish his client's motives and any pertinent circumstances that caused him to act as he did. Counsel may proceed."

"Yeoman," Barclay said, as the great importance of the ruling to Carlyle's case flashed through him, "will you please read the last question and answer."

The yeoman: "How long after you placed her on the wardroom table was it before she gave birth?"

"It was over ten hours, sir. It was a very long time. She had a bad time of it."

Barclay said: "The sea was rough toward the last?"

"Objection. Counsel is telegraphing answers to his own questions to witness."

"Sustained."

"What was the condition of the sea in the couple of hours immediately before the birth?"

"It was very rough. Especially the roll of the ship. Two men had to stand on either side of the wardroom table and one man at each end to keep her from rolling off."

Barclay asked: "Where were you during this entire period?"

"In the wardroom. Except when I went to help get hot water from the galley for the pharmacist's mate, who was with the girl—with the signora."

The president spoke up in tones of both surprise and admiration: "That woman's baby was delivered by a Navy pharmacist's mate?"

"Yes, sir. That late after the invasion, sir, we no longer had a ship's doctor aboard."

"Proceed."

"So during the ten hours in which the signora was in labor pain you were in the wardroom. Except for your trips to get the hot water?"

"I went out once to get my guitar. It was thought playing guitar music might soothe her a little."

"What were your feelings during this time in respect to the girl?"

"I was very afraid for her. I think we all were. She was very young."

"But the baby was born soundly?"

"Yes, sir. About five in the morning."

"Then the ship put into Pozzuoli, the woman was taken up to the hospital. You have heard her testify that you visited her later and continued the visits, taking lessons in Italian. Why did you want to take those lessons, Carlyle?"

"At first it was an excuse to see her," Carlyle said candidly. "Then I was very glad I did because I could talk to her."

"Did you pay her in money for the lessons?"

"I did, sir."

"You have heard her testify that you also began to bring her things from the ship—C-rations, K-rations, soap, the sort of things you see spread out on that table there. Is this true?"

"Yes, sir. I brought her all of those things."

"Is it your belief that she used these things only to buy food for herself and to pay her rent, aside from the stove and to pay the doctor to which she testified?"

"There wasn't enough to use for anything else. She needed all of it just to stay alive."

"So that having seen the baby born, indeed born on a Navy vessel, you felt that the Navy had some undefined moral obligation to see that the child and its mother did not starve . . ."

"Objection, objection!" The judge advocate was on his feet, shouting and red with anger. "Sir, I must protest the defense's continuing, blatant attempt to sentimentalize this proceeding. Defense has done everything but present the accessories to the charge as the Madonna and Child and now is endeavoring to present the accused himself as, I presume, Joseph or St. George— I hardly know which. I submit that none of this has anything whatsoever to do with the matter we are considering here, which is the theft of Navy materiel. In addition defense counsel in the most outrageous manner is framing the accused's answers for him in his questions!"

"Very well, Judge Advocate. The latter part of your point is well taken. As to the first part, the court has ruled that the defense may establish motive. But be so good, defense counsel, as not to articulate it yourself. If accused felt moral obligation let him state it in his own way."

"Thank you, sir. I apologize for so stating what I feel to have been the accused's motive. I will rephrase the question."

Barclay turned back to Carlyle. "Why did you bring Navy things to the woman?"

"To keep her and her child from starving to death."

"Many have gone very hungry in this city and surely not a few have starved. Why did you feel this particular obligation toward this woman?"

"Well, sir, I saw what she had gone through on the ship. I admired her. She had great courage. I felt in some way I can't explain that the Navy just couldn't take that mother off Anzio, bring that baby into the world—good as that was of the Navy— and then drop it there. I felt the Navy had to follow through. I don't express it well, sir."

Barclay's face lit up. "You express it very well." He turned slightly to the prosecution table. The judge advocate was livid. "I wish to thank the judge advocate for so properly stopping me from phrasing accused's answer and letting accused phrase it himself."

Barclay looked out the windows a moment at the green path of the treetops sloping down to the blue bay, then turned back to the sailor. He spoke quietly.

"Carlyle, did you have reason to fear that if you did not bring these objects—the rations, soap, and the like—to the young mother, had you reason to fear that she might have to turn to certain work to support herself and her child?"

Carlyle was tense for a moment. But he spoke quietly also. "I did, sir."

"What work did you fear she would have to do if you didn't bring her these things?"

Again Carlyle hesitated. But then again his speech marched forward quietly, his voice firm and bell-like over the room.

"I was afraid she would become a prostitute, sir."

"Why did you feel that?"

"Because it is the main way—about the only way—for girls in Naples to feed themselves and their families these days. I guess we all know that. And she is a very pretty girl."

"Was the belief you had that she would become a prostitute

if you did not bring her things—was this just an assumption—
something you thought up yourself?"

"No, sir. She told me. Or started to tell me before I stopped
her."

Barclay paused a few moments. "Carlyle," he said then, "I ask
you: Did you ever receive money or any other compensation of
any nature whatsoever for bringing these goods to the girl?"

"I did not, sir."

"Did you in any way apply any of these goods to your own use
or benefit?"

"I did not, sir."

"Were they not considered payment for the language lessons?"

"No, sir. I continued to pay her for those."

"I ask you: Did you at that time consider that you were taking
the goods wrongfully?"

"I did not, sir."

"Do you today consider that you took them wrongfully?"

"I do not, sir."

"No further questions."

The judge advocate walked around his table and stood directly
by the witness.

"Now we are given all too clearly to understand that your
motive in appropriating Navy—and later Army as well—materiel
was to keep the mother from one of two fates—starvation or
prostitution. Is my understanding of this correct?"

Carlyle hesitated. "I would say it is, sir, if you put it like that."

"How would you put it?"

"I am satisfied with the way you put it, sir."

"So that your motive was wholly altruistic?"

"What is altruistic, Mr. Barclay?" Carlyle, turning his head,
said over to the defense table.

"Never mind asking your counsel for definitions! I will rephrase
it. You had no selfish motive for bringing her these things?"

"Selfish, sir?"

"Don't you understand English, young man? Must you keep
repeating words after me?"

Barclay said to the court: "Sir, would it be possible for the judge advocate not to badger the witness both by talking so loudly and by questioning his understanding of the English language. Accused knows it quite well, I believe, especially if counsel would address him in somewhat civil tones."

"Judge Advocate, I believe we can assume that any member of the naval forces is literate," the president said mildly.

The judge advocate said a little more quietly to Carlyle, "Was there nothing you expected to get out of bringing the signorina these Navy—and Army—things?"

"Only her friendship."

"So that your relations with her were entirely platonic?"

"What's platonic, Mr. Barclay?"

"Sir!" The judge advocate's temper flew up. "I really must ask the court to instruct witness that if he does not understand any terms I use, he simply ask me. I will be more than happy to define anything for him."

"The accused will not address his counsel when he is witness. You may define the term platonic, Judge Advocate."

"I will rephrase the question, sir. You contend that you had no relations with this young lady in whose apartment you spent up to four hours a day that were anything more than one friend to another?"

"No, sir. I was a student, too, I guess. Those hours were spent studying the Italian language."

"I see. Carlyle, you have heard the signorina testify about a move she made out of a room into an apartment. Would you consider an apartment as compared to a room a luxury rather than a necessity?"

"Not for three people, sir, and not if the apartment only had two rooms. You wouldn't if you saw the place, sir. It isn't a place anyone like yourself would want to live in."

"I see." The judge advocate paused then turned sharply to Carlyle, catching him by surprise. "Who was the father of her child? Did she ever tell you?"

"No, sir, she never mentioned it."

"And you never asked?"

"No, sir. I felt it was none of my business."

"You seem to have made plenty of other things concerning her your business. You hadn't the remotest notion who the father was?"

"Not really, sir. I used to think it was an Italian officer. It may have been from something she said. Or I may have just felt that. She never actually said."

"An Italian officer?" the judge advocate said.

"Well, it couldn't have been an American officer," Carlyle said innocently. "We weren't here yet."

A loud startling laugh broke abruptly from the furthest-seated lieutenant on the court. The president looked at him sternly and he quieted at once. The judge advocate turned back to Carlyle and his voice this time was self-controlled, surprisingly quiet, almost friendly.

"Carlyle," he said, "do you find the signorina attractive, I mean to say, physically attractive, appealing to the eye?"

"I find her attractive in every way."

"How do you mean, 'every way'?"

"Well, she is unselfish and she is courageous. She doesn't let life get her down—and this life around here could get some pretty strong people down. She tries to deal with life, cope with it. And I like being with her. I like the way she walks across a room. She is very graceful, she has a dignity about her. She is beautiful."

"You appear to find her exceedingly appealing." The judge advocate now spoke in entirely friendly tones. "I must say that in respect to those of her attributes as have come within my observation . . . I must say that I find myself in full agreement with you. She appears to be an unusually appealing creature. And anyone with eyes could see that she is beautiful. She is, in fact, extremely—" the judge advocate paused and moved a step closer to the sailor—"desirable."

Now quickly he came down until he was very near the witness. And then in crisp and even tones he said:

"Carlyle, you contend that you had a motive in bringing unauthorized Navy materiel to this young lady. You state that your motive was to keep her from starvation and that this was further justified by the signorina having given birth to a baby on your ship. Let us agree that this motive existed. But I submit to you that there was an additional motive of a quite different character than the one stated."

The judge advocate paused, glanced out the window, toward Vesuvius, then turned back quickly to the sailor.

"Carlyle, I submit to you that those long, four-hour sessions which you spent with the girl in her apartment when your ship returned to port were devoted not, as claimed, to the scholarly pursuit of studying the Italian language. I submit that you desired this beautiful signorina as you have never desired anything else in the world; that your motive was to make this highly desirable woman your mistress and that she did in fact become such; that in fact, it was for this reason that you moved her out of a room into an apartment, and that the K-rations, the C-rations, the cans of food, the flour, all of it, were payment for her sexual favors, because she was your mistress, and to assure that she would remain so." The judge advocate stepped swiftly to the table and lifted some of the items and set them down with a clatter that rang through the chamber. "That was your motivation. These times were what this Navy and Army materiel paid for. Is not this the real truth of it, Carlyle?"

Carlyle's hands clenched the arms of the chair as though to restrain himself from some act of violence upon the officer setting forth this picture. The judge advocate did not waver. In fact, he had crossed back to the witness from the table and had brought himself even closer to Carlyle, so that his face was inches away. He spoke insinuatingly.

"I ask you: Do you deny that this is the true picture of the facts?"

Carlyle waited as if to gain control of himself. Then said: "I deny it completely, sir."

The judge advocate stepped back a couple of paces. He shrugged.

"You deny absolutely that you engaged in sexual intercourse with the signorina?"

"I deny it."

"Not even once?"

"Not even once."

"Very well. Then since defense has seen fit to bring in motivation, indeed to base its whole case upon it, let us, this final time, make your position perfectly clear. Defense has been so anxious to sum it up, I shall sum it up myself." He looked at the sailor and spoke slowly. "It is that you brought the young lady Navy materiel solely in order to keep her from starvation or from turning to prostitution to save herself from starvation and that you had no motives and received no favors of the sort I have described beyond that. You are willing to stand on that testimony and that your case rest upon it?"

"I did, sir. I do, sir."

"You are sure?"

"I am completely sure."

"And your bringing her these things accomplished this purpose?"

"Yes, sir."

"Thank you. Thank you very much."

By that time Barclay knew but there was nothing in the world he could do about it, except to realize what an able adversary he had in the judge advocate. The judge advocate turned quietly to the court.

"We have no further questions, sir."

"Defense counsel?"

"Very briefly, sir." Barclay stood up, walked over and picked up a book lying on the court stenographer's table, and walked over to Carlyle and handed him it.

"Carlyle, will you tell the court-martial what book you are holding."

"It's a Bible."

"In what language is this Bible?"

"It's an Italian Bible."

"Will you open it and start reading wherever you open."

Carlyle opened the book and began to read. "*Salvo che il Signore edifica la casa, in vano vi si affaticano gli edificatori:*

salvo che il Signore guarda la città, in vano vegghiano le guardie. . . ."

When he had read a half dozen verses, Barclay said: "Will you translate into English what you have just read?"

Carlyle began to read: "Except the Lord build the house, they labour in vain that build it: except the Lord keep the city, the watchman waketh but in vain. . . ."

Barclay took the Bible back. "I ask the court's permission for the court's interpreter to testify briefly."

"Very well."

The interpreter took the stand and was sworn as witness. Barclay said, "I believe we have no need to establish the witness' competency in the Italian language, since he is the court's official interpreter. I ask the witness: What would you say as to the competence in the Italian language of the witness who has just testified, that is to say, the accused."

"I would say it was excellent, sir."

"Both the pronunciation and the translation?"

"Both, sir," the yeoman said. "He is proficient and I think with not much more study could become entirely fluent in the language."

"No further questions, sir."

"Witness may step down."

Carlyle walked back to the table and took his place.

"Defense counsel?"

Barclay stood. "The defense rests."

"Judge advocate?"

"We would like to call one more witness, sir."

The president looked surprised and a little irritated. "Another witness, Judge Advocate? We were given to understand you had presented all your witnesses."

"Sir, I apologize, and I thought I had. Need for the witness has only just been created by accused's testimony."

"Very well," the president said. He looked at his watch. "It is 1630 hours. I am afraid we will have to put this over until tomorrow morning. Can the judge advocate definitely finish then?"

"Easily, sir."

"Please give the name of the witness."

"The witness' name," the judge advocate said, looking down at a piece of paper in his hand, then across at Barclay, "is Lieutenant (jg) Allen Shanley."

The Second Morning

"State your name, rank, and present station."

"Allen Shanley, lieutenant (jg), USNR, bomb-disposal officer, NOB Naples."

At the identification the president of the court-martial leaned slightly forward. The judge advocate established quickly that the jeep Carlyle used was Shanley's but that the officer had no knowledge of the use to which it was being put. He then said:

"Lieutenant, I have brought you here to answer but one single question. It is of considerable importance to this proceeding and I trust you will give it your careful attention."

The judge advocate waited a moment, looking through the tall windows where the morning sun flooded in.

"Before I ask the question, Lieutenant, and before you answer it, I believe it my function to state that the prosecution is prepared to produce witnesses who saw a young Italian woman whom they can identify enter the BOQ where you reside at 11 P.M. and not leave it until 4 A.M. on the night in question, both arriving and leaving in your company. I might further point out that the reason these witnesses remember that particular night so well is not because of the woman's visit to the BOQ but because there was a very considerable storm that night. This weather circumstance might also, incidentally, help to refresh your own memory concerning the events of that night. I mention this, Lieutenant, not because I feel that you would in any event tell this court anything but the truth but to save the time of the court and speed up this proceeding."

The judge advocate again looked out the window—he seemed to be making a study of the cone of Vesuvius in the distance—then rather slowly turned back to Shanley.

"Lieutenant, my question is this: Did you on the night of April 22, 1944, or on any other night, commit fornication with an Italian woman by the name of Coco Comparo?"

Shanley waited. Then he said: "I did."

Barclay did not look at Carlyle but he could sense that the sailor was looking, not at the witness testifying this thing, but straight ahead through the great windows.

"Thank you, Lieutenant," the judge advocate was saying. "I have but two short questions more."

He looked at Shanley. "By the time of the night of April 22, 1944, do you have knowledge that Signora Comparo was well acquainted by that time with the sailor Carlyle?"

"I did not know it then. I have learned it since."

"And finally: Did you at any time give presents of any description to this woman?"

"I did."

"What were they, Lieutenant?"

"Clothes. A couple of dresses. Some stockings. A pair of shoes. One of the dresses is on that table there."

"Thank you, Lieutenant. No further questions."

Barclay said: "How many times did you and Signora Comparo engage in fornication?"

"One time," Shanley said evenly.

"No further questions."

Shanley stepped down and walked out the door. The judge advocate said: "Sir, I would like to recall one witness briefly."

"Very well."

"Will the orderly call Signora Comparo."

Coco came in once more, stepped up onto the little platform, and sat down. The judge advocate spoke from in front of the prosecution table.

"Besides the red dress on the table there, did Lieutenant Allen Shanley give you anything else?"

"Yes. He gave me some stockings. Some shoes. Another dress. I am wearing it."

"And you look very attractive in it, might I say. Signorina, what were your relations with Lieutenant Shanley?"

"He took me a few times to the officers club and to the officers mess for meals."

The judge advocate waited briefly then walked over to a point directly by the witness. He spoke quietly.

"Signorina, this court has just received testimony from Lieutenant Shanley that the list you have just given as to your relations with him is not entirely a complete one. Is it your testimony that the list is complete or would you like the opportunity to supplement it? If so, please take as much time as you need to refresh your recollection."

Coco listened to the translation. Hesitated. Then said: "I went to bed with him. One time."

The girl did not look over at Carlyle, but even if she had, their eyes would never have met. Carlyle, since the moment in Shanley's testimony, had not moved his gaze from that same position, dead ahead, out the tall windows.

"Did this act occur during the time in which the sailor Carlyle was bringing you Navy and Army goods?"

Coco: "Yes. It was during that time."

"Now you say you engaged in prostitution with Lieutenant Shanley . . ."

Barclay came to his feet and spoke to the president. "I object, sir. I object strongly."

The judge advocate affected surprise. "Two persons—and they the participants—have just so testified she did."

"Sir," Barclay said to the president. "They testified no such thing, and judge advocate knows it. Witnesses said they were in bed together one time. Even to us in America that hardly constitutes prostitution."

"I withdraw the word since it seems to offend counsel so," the judge advocate said in sardonic tones. "They did not engage in prostitution. They went to bed—one time. Signora," he said. "Did you go to bed with Lieutenant Shanley for the same reason you did with Carlyle? That he was to give you things."

Barclay was on his feet to object but before he could Coco answered. The trap was wide open. She did not fall into it.

"Commander," she said quietly. "I never went to bed with Red—with Carlyle."

"I beg your pardon, signora," the judge advocate said elaborately, "for impugning your virtue—in relation to the man Carlyle. I will rephrase the question. Why did you go out with the lieutenant, signora?"

"I wanted some gaiety in my life. I felt I had to have a little gaiety. And Lieutenant Shanley took me to the officers club and to the officers mess where he lived. The officers club is a very gay place—and the officers mess has food such as one can get nowhere else in this city."

"So you went out with Lieutenant Shanley for purposes of 'gaiety.' Is that also why you slept with him, signora?"

The girl was calm. "No, that wasn't the reason, Commander. I did that, perhaps in gratitude."

"I see. Lieutenant Shanley gave you gaiety and clothes and meals and you gave him your expression of gratitude—which you did not, interestingly, give the sailor Carlyle."

"No. But I was never in love with Lieutenant Shanley." She hesitated. "I was with Red."

"I am glad to hear, signora," the judge advocate said drily, "that at least you were not in love with two members of the Navy simultaneously. That you were only in love with one and slept with the other. In regards to that, signora. Why was it only one time that you slept with Lieutenant Shanley?"

"Red—Carlyle—started to bring me other things. But also it was because I came to know I was in love with Red."

"Oh, I see. You gave up sleeping with the officer when the sailor brought you *more* things."

The judge advocate stepped dramatically over to the table containing the various American products.

"Signora," he said from this distance and his voice rose through the room, "this court has heard testimony that the reason Carlyle brought you these naval and military stores . . . the C-rations . . . the K-rations . . . the soap . . . the cans of fruit . . . and how much more only God knows . . . This court-martial, I say, has heard testimony, signora, and offered as absolution for the accused, that the reason the sailor Carlyle brought you all of these was to keep you from the very prostitution in which you nevertheless engaged. If that were his intention, signora, would you say that he failed?"

The question was translated and Coco hesitated in answering. The judge advocate pressed in: "I ask you, signorina, would you say that the sailor Carlyle failed in his goal?"

"Let the judge advocate lower his voice please," Barclay said, chiefly to give Coco time to measure her answer.

"Let the witness answer!" the judge advocate shouted, enraged at the obvious device.

Burgan spoke mildly to the court. "Sir, we would also appreciate the judge advocate's making up his mind as to which form of address he prefers with witness. We would be satisfied with either signorina or signora. We would appreciate consistency."

"*Signorina*," the judge advocate said tensely, "would you answer the question?"

"It is not for me to say who failed and who was successful, Commander. Is one such act considered prostitution in your country?"

"Signorina," the judge advocate said with great sarcasm, "I'm afraid neither I nor this court has the time, especially in the middle of a very difficult war one purpose of which is to liberate your country, to furnish you with an education in what are considered proper moral standards in the United States. The fact remains that you engaged in sexual intercourse with one man while telling another that if only he would bring you goods which belonged to the American Navy you would not do so. Is that a fact or is it not, signora?"

Coco said quietly: "It is putting it very simply and it was never put that way. But I suppose it added up to it. What you say is a fact, even if a partial fact."

"All we are after is facts, even simple ones," the judge advocate said drily. "Now I ask you again: Would not your testimony as to your sexual activity effectively destroy the validity of any contention that the man Carlyle brought you Navy goods to save you from prostitution, since in all fact you were sleeping with a naval officer at the very time you were telling a Navy enlisted man you needed things to keep you from prostitution? Would it not, signorina?"

"Carlyle never knew that I was even seeing Lieutenant Shanley," Coco said. "Nor that I was in love with him, Red. I was going to tell Red so after I had gone to see Lieutenant Shanley to tell him I couldn't see him again. But that was the night Red was arrested, so that I never had a chance to tell him I loved him."

"How inconvenient of the arrest," the judge advocate said. "No further questions. Oh, one moment."

The judge advocate had turned away and Coco had started to rise to leave. Then the judge advocate, picking up a sheet of paper from the prosecution table, turned back.

"I do have just one further question."

He walked slowly toward her, looking at the paper, and stopped a couple paces away.

"Signorina," the judge advocate said. "I have before me a list of eight members of the American armed forces, including Second Lieutenant James Craig of the Army's Criminal Investigation Division. These men are all in Naples and they are available to testify here if it becomes necessary. Among other things, they are available to testify that they have, one and all, and in the last ten days, spent time in an apartment at the address Via Apollo 24. Lieutenant Craig, I might add, was sent there as a bomber pilot, and in the course of duty, and the other seven men went there of their own accord and desire and were questioned only on leaving; there being one further difference in the visit of Lieutenant Craig, namely, that while he, like the others, made payment, he alone of the eight did not accept the proffered services. As I say all eight are quickly available to testify to these facts and to various occurrences in the said apartment. But perhaps we can save the court's time, and the necessity of calling these eight witnesses, by a few questions. Let us in any event try.

Signorina, are you acquainted with the address of Via Apollo 24?"

Barclay thought of how it now seemed obvious that of course they would have continued to trail her, that they knew everything. A blinding fury held him for a moment, particularly over the planting of Craig. It seemed to go too far, to exceed the bounds of fairness, that the prosecution should go after the girl to the extent of keeping in reserve eight men to testify to relations with her, and worst of all to have sent one of these men there for that purpose. He had a notion to call Craig and do everything he could to destroy him. Then he knew that was useless, and would only harm her more. He made his fury subside a little. But he could not help rising to his feet and he spoke angrily to the court.

"Sir, is the girl on trial here?"

The judge advocate turned blandly to the court. "Surely we have the right to probe the character of so important a witness—an importance greatly insisted upon by defense counsel himself."

"You do, Judge Advocate. Proceed."

"Will the court stenographer please read the last question."

"Signorina, are you acquainted with the address of Via Apollo 24?"

"I am," Coco said. "I am now living there."

"You have moved out of Via Mazzini 36?"

"I have."

"And Via Apollo 24 is a better place, would you say?"

"It is much better."

"And much more expensive, I imagine?"

"Much more."

"Signorina. What is your present occupation?"

Coco said nothing and Barclay helplessly heard the judge advocate's voice leaning in.

"Signorina, I don't know if you heard the question. I will repeat it. Signorina, what is your present occupation?"

"I am a prostitute."

The judge advocate gave a slight bow. "I am sure the court

appreciates your saving it the time-consuming necessity of listening to eight additional witnesses. No further questions, sir."

Barclay sat there as in a nightmare, stunned. He forgot for the moment even where he was. His brain seemed numbed and yet somehow working with a terrible swiftness. And then suddenly, like something flowering, he saw that perhaps the judge advocate, instead of introducing the most damning of evidences, may instead have unwittingly introduced the best possible substantiation of the defense's case. But if so, why had he done it? Perhaps the plain inability not to use such character-destroying evidence, perhaps in his triumph at having it even being blinded to another meaning it carried. It was not for a while that he heard the voice of the president of the court addressing him. He must have been doing so for some little time.

"Defense counsel. I ask if you have cross-examination or are you finished with the witness?"

"I am not finished, sir."

Barclay came to his feet, walked around the table and up to the small platform where Coco sat.

"Signora, was it before or after Carlyle's arrest that you moved out of Via Mazzini 36 in Pozzuoli and into Via Apollo 24 in Naples?"

"After. I could never have afforded the Via Apollo with what Carlyle was bringing me."

"Now, signora, I ask you this. Other than the one time with Lieutenant Shanley did you at any time commit fornication with anyone from the time you first knew the sailor Carlyle until the night of his arrest?"

"No. Never. Only that one time."

"So that it was only after Carlyle's arrest that you began to engage in prostitution. Is that true?"

"It is."

"And why did you engage in it then?"

"Because Red was no longer there to bring things to support myself and my child."

"So that with Carlyle bringing things to support you, you did not engage in prostitution, and you had to begin doing so only because he was no longer there to bring these things to support you?"

"That is true."

"And you have in fact not even seen the sailor Carlyle from the moment you moved into the apartment at Via Apollo 24 and commenced the practice of prostitution until you saw him in this very room?"

"That is true. I have not seen him since I saw him the night of the arrest at Via Mazzini 36."

"No further questions, sir."

"No questions," the judge advocate said.

Coco was taken out. She went away without looking at Carlyle. Barclay, though feeling his case may actually have improved by the last part of her testimony, and remembering that he must stress it heavily in his argument, felt at what a terrible price the improvement had been had, and could not, himself, bear to turn and look at Carlyle just then. He heard the president of the court speaking.

"Judge Advocate?"

"We have no further evidence to offer."

"Defense counsel?"

"Defense is finished," Barclay said.

"Gentlemen," the president said. "I had hoped we could conclude this matter this morning. I was mistaken. We will have to go over until this afternoon. Gentlemen, the facts, as best they can be brought out—and I must here commend both counsels for bringing them out so well—are before us. I would certainly see no need for extended arguments. Would a quarter hour each suffice for you gentlemen. Defense counsel?"

"We will need no more time than that, sir," Barclay said. "Probably less."

"Judge Advocate?"

"I desire to make no opening argument, so fifteen minutes will be sufficient to answer counsel, sir."

"Then I will depend on it that we can conclude this case this afternoon. Until fourteen hundred hours this court-martial will stand in recess."

The Second Afternoon

"Gentlemen," Barclay addressed the court, "the accused, the sailor Carlyle, has at no time denied, or attempted in any way to deny or evade, the charges that he took Navy and Army goods and diverted these goods to civilian Italian use. By no standard, however, is it suggested that these amounts were large. They may have been continuous, over a period of weeks, but by no measurement large. A musette bag containing C-rations, K-rations, a can of peaches, a bar of soap. Accused's ship was in port no more than twice a week, or at the most three times. The implication, and indeed the evidence, here is that on each of those occasions accused took one musette bag containing such items to the Italian girl who has testified here, and to her child. Other than the articles contained in the musette bag, it has been established that the accused on two occasions only carried larger items to the girl. Two one-hundred-pound sacks of flour, worth, in the United States, about six dollars each. In the case neither of the musette bag, openly carried, nor the sacks of flour, transported in a highly identifiable jeep, did accused make any effort to conceal his activities. Furthermore, no one has established that the accused in any way used any of these items for personal profit. His motivation has been established beyond any doubt. Accused took the items in order to prevent the young woman and her child from becoming the victims of starvation and the mother from having to turn to prostitution. On the latter point, the judge advocate himself has brought out evidence, based on unceasing trailings by the Army's CID, that the girl did not in fact turn to prostitution until *after* the sailor Carlyle's support was withdrawn as a result of his arrest and did so as a direct consequence of this withdrawal. There could be no better proof of the validity of the accused's motivation. The evidence concerning the girl Comparo's engaging in prostitution after being parted from the accused has served to destroy the girl but it has also served, as nothing else could, to assert the strength of the accused's case that he supported her precisely so she would not engage in prostitution, since she did not in fact do so until after the support was withdrawn. As to the girl's activities *before* the arrest, which *are* pertinent, I trust only that this court will not synonymize one night of fornication with the practice of prostitution, as the judge advocate urges. That would indeed be a far-reaching judgment. In sum, then: It has been established clearly, first, that the accused took Army and Navy items to save the woman and her child from starvation and the mother from prostitution and, secondly, that in this he succeeded. Whatever decision may be recorded as to accused's judgment in taking these items, no one has successfully challenged his motivation.

"What was behind this motivation, sirs? The young girl whom the sailor Carlyle undertook to aid found herself, at the height of the battle of Anzio, caught, with other Italians, on that beach, with no family, no home, no possessions. Her only difference from her fellow-Italians was that she was about to give birth to a baby. And indeed this baby was born on the American naval vessel which took her, and the others, off the beachhead at Anzio. The birth itself may be said to have been a kind of victory, whether by act of Providence or resolution of ship's company, in that the baby was born safely, and in rough seas at that, despite the absence of any physician on the ship. The accused in a sense assisted in the birth of the child. It happened that his sympathy went out to this mother. It would have been strange had it not.

"But Seaman Carlyle's identification with the mother and child, gentlemen, did not cease when the mother left the ship. In a short time he had gone to seek her out, to visit her and the child, in her room at Pozzuoli. Finding her without resources, he undertook to help her, out of his own sympathy and also out of a moral conviction that the Navy, having been involved in the child's birth and the saving of its mother, could not then stand aside and leave them helpless before the conditions of war. He misappropriated Navy, and later Army, goods. The fact is not denied. Gentlemen, misappropriation encouraged, certainly the naval and military would suffer grievously. But another, and possibly even larger, question is implied and you cannot turn away from giving it your answer, gentlemen. That question is this: Is misappropriation never justifiable? Whatever the want? However great the distress? Certainly, sirs, no wrong, no evil, was intended here. On the contrary only good was intended, to give sustenance to a child born on the accused's ship, and to its mother. Sirs, was Seaman Carlyle to let the mother and child starve? And yes, was the Navy to let them starve? I cannot accept this. I could hope that you, naval officers, equally could not.

"There is another fact that torments against any contrary decision, gentlemen. It is this: It is the most common of practices for officers and men, both those on shore and those on ships, to take various items of naval materiel to Italian civilians, and out of motivations, in many instances, certainly far less altruistic than those which prompted Seaman Carlyle to do so. Is there an officer or a man in this room who can say that he has not either given or traded—in a word, misappropriated—a single item of Navy materiel to the Italians? Is there one here, or anywhere on this base or on the peninsula of Italy, or on any ship which comes to this harbor? Is there one such officer or enlisted man, gentlemen? I venture to say there are very few. If the sailor Carlyle is guilty, gentlemen, we are all guilty. I suggest, sirs, that there is no guilt unless the guilt be that of the conditions of war itself.

"The war brings many things, and among others it brings hunger. Among them it brings loneliness. And the lonely individual can buy his way out of his loneliness, if only for an hour, from the hungry one. It is a fact of war. And yes the war also brings compassion, and it brought it to the accused Carlyle. And the price, whether of loneliness or compassion, is a certain amount of taking of Navy and Army goods and the diversion of these goods to the civilians in need around us. If you are to condemn the accused, gentlemen, you are to condemn a condition of war which no man can change. The war came and produced the conditions that called out to Seaman Carlyle. And I venture to say that they called out to the best in him, or in any man. They called out the desire to succor a human being in great distress. He did so, and the war goes on. The few cans of C-ration, the few bars of soap, the two sacks of flour, have not delayed the progress of Allied arms one minute or one inch of enemy ground, gentlemen. All they have done is to save two human beings from starvation. Condemn this man, and you condemn all that is best in man, and truly best if even war cannot crush it. I cannot believe you will do it, gentlemen.

"Sirs, I have but one point more. I could not let this court-martial close without confessing to a certain unease at the lengths to which the prosecution has gone to 'get' the accused and, so it would seem, the girl herself. I refer specifically to and for the record I would protest the trailings of the girl after the accused's apprehension. These seem to me to have served no useful purpose, to border on persecution, and to exceed every bound of fair play and decency known to our people and to the naval and military services of the United States. Was it really necessary for the prosecution, in building its case, to send a CID agent to the girl's apartment and there, in the guise of a bomber pilot, buy her favors? Was it necessary to follow and pursue her at all after her relationship with the accused, whatever that relationship might have been, had ceased as a result of accused's arrest? Sirs, it was not in the slightest necessary, and it is somehow out of bounds. One wonders—or stands appalled—at the great number of military man-hours thus expended amid this war which would seem to need all the man-hours available to combat what is surely a more formidable enemy than one Italian girl and a man abducting a few cans of C-ration. It may be, sirs, that it is possible to have an excess of zeal and I could not let this court-martial close without saying I believe the prosecution to have been guilty of it. It may be, sirs, that one can go too far, that one can be too anxious to damn, to blacken, and, yes, to convict. I do not know and we leave that to the mercies of Providence and the judgment of this court-martial."

Barclay sat down. There was a slight rustle on the platform where the members of the court-martial sat. The judge advocate came slowly to his feet.

"Members of the court. I applaud my fellow officer's eloquence —and skill. I will go further and predict for opposing counsel, on the record of his having defended so well on such absence of real defense material, a brilliant future in the law. He has defended his client well indeed. He appeals to the best in us. He has repeatedly dwelt on the accused's motivation in helping an individual or individuals in distress. Indeed this has been his entire case. Gentleman, I can only point out that motivation is not relevant here. Purpose is not relevant. It may sound hard to say, but the Navy's presence here is not to prevent people, even babies, from starving, or to prevent signorine, even young and beautiful ones, from engaging in prostitution. The Navy, and other instruments of the United States, have done much to aid the civilian population. But that is not the Navy's purpose here. And above all it is not the function of any single Navy man to decide how naval materiel is to be used. If we were to hold the contrary, if we were to leave such judgment to the millions of individuals in uniform encountering need in this war where need is everywhere, if we were to turn every man, every officer in the Navy loose to act on his own motivations, whatever they might be, in distributing Navy materiel, we would have consequences that would be so patently disastrous that I need not belabor the point. Counsel argues the special circumstances for his client, as if we could have one rule for one Navy man and another rule for all others. The idea is false on its face. Naval or other appropriate authorities, not *any* individual Navy person, are to judge how such help as the accused Carlyle chose to undertake on his own is to be dispensed. Equally irrelevant is the matter—although really unestablished one way or the other in testimony here—of whether or not accused sought to conceal his activities in taking naval and military stores he was not authorized to take. It is the duty, and the only duty, of this court-martial to act on the question of whether naval or military regulations have been breached. The motivations, however we applaud them, the methods, whatever they were, are not our concern here, gentlemen.

"Moreover, the validity of this motivation itself, thin as it is, has been struck down by the testimony of the young lady involved herself. Even defense's efforts to present the woman Comparo as some kind of Virgin Madonna have run aground on the fact that she was engaged in sexual activity at the very time she was telling the accused that if he brought her Navy goods she would not be obliged to do so. Whether it was one or twenty times, it was, gentlemen, an act or acts of prostitution, which in event defense counsel does not know is defined legally as fornication in return for reward of any nature, whether it be 'gaiety,' meals, clothing, or whatever—which exchange the woman Comparo herself has testified did take place in her relations with the officer Shanley. But even had she not so engaged, even if the accused's alleged purpose in saving her from such enterprise had succeeded, he would remain without justification. The sailor Carlyle has not been appointed by the Navy to preserve the virtue of the women of Naples. And I might add that if every girl in Naples were given Navy materiel to abstain from prostitution —admitting that to be a good thing—there would soon be nothing left for the Navy to fight the war with. Accused says that he aided the woman out of sympathy, that it was for this reason he brought and continued to bring her Navy and Army materiel, and that he received no favors of any kind in return. I do not question that the accused felt sympathy for her, nor that this sympathy was in part evoked by the circumstance of her child having been born on the accused's ship. But the plane is so high that our credulity is strained. You have as much right, gentlemen, if we are to get into the matter of *why* the accused misappropriated Navy materiel, to believe that the girl became accused's mistress and that the price she extracted for her sexual favors was a continuing—and increasing—flow of Navy and Army materiel, as to believe the other stated motive. The point is that whatever the motive was, it is entirely without relevance or importance. What is of importance is that the accused violated well established naval codes, and indeed has admitted doing so.

"For added justification, counsel mentions that others have done things similar to what the accused has done. It is a curious defense. I daresay not many have taken hundred-pound sacks of flour. But be that as it may, this court is not convened to decide whether others of the naval or military forces have misappropriated supply items for the civilian population and to what degree. Our only concern here is with the actions of the accused. The naval and military code are not selective, gentlemen. They do not choose among all possible offenders and judge and sentence only the worst. Agents of the naval and military law must catch those they can catch. And courts-martial must sentence those who are caught and adjudged guilty. It is useless to talk of those who are not caught, those whose acts may be worse, less well motivated, than those of the accused. They are not here for us to deal with, gentlemen. We must deal with the one who is caught. If we were to accept the premise that the guilty man who is caught shall go unpunished because other guilty men roam free, it would be the end of all law and order.

"But let us freely admit, as counsel contends, that the practice of illegal diversion of Navy and Army materiel in this area onto the black market is widespread. Counsel for defense uses this fact to excuse accused's actions. We use it, sirs, as the most imperative reason of all for this court-martial to act. And act firmly! What are the facts? They are simplicity itself, gentlemen. Accused Carlyle took Navy materiel he was not authorized to take and directed this materiel to unauthorized use and ends. He did so increasingly and over an extended period of time. Specifications and charge have been proved beyond all question—indeed, have not even been challenged. Gentlemen, you have but two choices before you: You must state and state firmly, by appropriate disciplinary action, so that all shall know, that such conduct is not to be tolerated. Or you must, by absolving the accused, approve such conduct and put the entire naval and military in this area on notice that it is wholly appropriate to take and disperse to whomever naval and military materiel—provided only one approve of one's own motivation. Is the latter alternative even conceivable to this court-martial?

"And finally, gentlemen, I would pass over entirely defense counsel's objections to the methods used to obtain evidence in this case. I would, of course, disagree entirely, the methods having been entirely within the proper and established framework of evidence-gathering, but again the point is wholly irrelevant, as is so very, very much of which the defense counsel speaks. And there is a reason for so much irrelevancy, gentlemen, which is that counsel has almost nothing which *is* relevant to the case, and so must strike out blindly where he may. I will say no more on that.

"Gentlemen, you really have but one choice in conscience. It may be a painful choice. Courts-martial often are. But the effects of a contrary decision would be far more painful, and not merely to one man, but, by encouraging the depletion of our supply lines maintained over great distances at much cost of labor and lives, to the cause of our side in this war. The decision may be difficult for you, gentlemen. But naval officers are not selected for their ability to avoid difficult decisions. Gentlemen," the judge advocate said softly, "I know—you know—defense counsel really knows—that you have but one choice, a choice that may avoid further pain and prevent just such courts-martial as this one. Gentlemen, I ask—and I truly regret to ask it—that you find the charge and specifications proved and that the accused be given the maximum sentence under this charge."

The judge advocate sat down. The president spoke.

"The court will be cleared to deliberate and arrive at its findings."

Verdict

The day had begun to fade from the room when the parties to the court-martial took their places. The president spoke:

"Will the accused please step forward."

Carlyle stood up, walked around the table and diagonally across the room to a point but a few feet in front of the raised platform. He stood there erectly. The president spoke quietly.

"This court-martial has found as follows: the first specification of the charge, proved. The second specification of the charge, proved. And that the accused, Peter Carlyle, seaman second class, USNR, is of the charge guilty."

He looked down at the sailor. "Seaman Carlyle, is there anything you wish to say before you hear the sentence of this court?"

"No, sir," Carlyle said. His voice came clear and steady.

"Very well." The president of the court-martial put on a pair of glasses and looked down at a piece of paper in his hands.

"The court therefore sentences Peter Carlyle, seaman second class, USNR, to be confined for a period of eighteen months, to be dishonorably discharged from the United States naval service and to suffer all the other accessories of said sentence as prescribed by section 622, *Naval Courts and Boards*. Will the master-at-arms please take the prisoner into custody. All business before this court having been completed the court stands adjourned."

The master-at-arms stepped forward toward Carlyle. Barclay stood up and also moved across the room toward the sailor, who stood unmoving, still facing forward. In the distance out the great windows Barclay could see the cone of Vesuvius erupting brilliant red showers of lava into the sky of the fast-oncoming night.

21

LAST PICNIC

Now the spring had lit up the countryside and they had a good day for it, a better day in every respect than the last time they had come along this road. It was a mid-May day, warm and windless, and not a cloud anywhere in all that blue sky which merged into the sea far below them with hardly any change of color. To the other side of the mountain road the fields stretching away in a rolling topography gave only signs of peace. No burned-out tanks, no gray files of refugees with packs on sticks over their shoulders marred the esthetics of the countryside, no shelling disturbed the air. It was a quiet day, of a quietness one could feel its hand reach out and soothe. They had folded back the canvas top of the jeep and every curve of the road brought a new and peace-giving view of the brown land or of the blue sea meeting the shore on one small beach after another, each embraced by a pair of rocky arms pointing out to sea.

"I haven't felt so far from the war, from everything, since I can remember," she said. "I wish we had a week instead of an afternoon." Then added: "But I'm glad to get an afternoon."

They could see the shape of the deserted fishing shack which identified their beach even from high on the mountain road above it and they started descending. He drove the jeep up to the edge of the sand and stopped. There was no sign of life here or from here and but for the shack no sign that life had ever been here. Enclosed by the promontories on either side, and with the mountains quickly behind them and only the sea ahead they were almost walled off, they could have been the only life this

spot of earth had ever known, and probably were the only it
had known in a long time.

"I don't think *anyone* ever comes here," she said. "And it's
such a very nice, a lovely beach. It's hard to believe no one
except us ever uses the beach, even now."

"Maybe we've just lucked onto one that isn't used. Beyond
that promontory there is another beach. Then there'll be another
promontory beyond that, and another beach, and so on down
the coast. Hundreds of these small beaches. We just got one
closed for the duration, I imagine."

They got up and walked down the beach toward one of the
rock promontories. It was good sand and clean and the water
very clear. He would have liked to be in it.

"Are you a good swimmer?" she said, as if thinking with him.

"As a matter-of-fact I am a good swimmer."

"If your head was all right, we could swim. But you can't
swim with that head."

"I know. I'd like to."

"Do you feel it much any more?"

"No, not really. I get a little dizzy sometimes. The eminent
Dr. Jarvis said that was perfectly normal for a couple of weeks
more or so. He used a new word for me. He said it was expectable."

"Well, that's better than expendable anyhow."

"Yes, I prefer it. If you want to swim I'll wait."

"Thank you but I don't believe so. Not alone. I'm a little
afraid of water, I think. Not on a ship. But in it I'm scared of
it, a little." She gave a short laugh. "Probably because I can't
swim. I love the sea, being by the sea, or on the sea, more
than almost anything. But to be in it, it still frightens me a little.
I must be scared of drowning."

"Not that I'm anxious to either, but if it had to be, well, it's
probably the easiest kind of death."

"I suppose so. Look, there's a bird on the end of the promontory," she said, as if to change the subject.

It took flight in a sweep of winged black and disappeared on
the other side before they could identify it, or try to. They walked
a long time on the beach and came back tired and hungry and

he got the poncho and spread it out on the sand. Even the materials of the picnic were much better today. Instead of K-rations, there were some deviled eggs and tuna fish sandwiches which he guessed she had made in some nurses' kitchen, and he noticed, as an item to notice, that the crusts were cut from the bread. She sat on the poncho with her legs tucked under her and her back very straight and her arms moving out, arranging things on the poncho as if it were a tablecloth of damask. He felt he had never seen anyone with more grace. The sun slanted down across the promontory, touched her light walnut hair and her bare legs where tiny shoots of blonde hair glistened.

Not having had either deviled eggs or tuna fish sandwiches, with or without crusts, for so long, they tasted very good indeed, and even the wine was better too. Barclay had got Chatham to get him a bottle from wherever he got the wine for the five-gallon can aboard ship that he kept supplied. It was much better wine than they had had before, much the best wine Barclay had had in Italy. It left a very dry and clean feeling in the mouth. They finished the food well before the wine and sat drinking the rest of it very slowly.

"Do you know when the ship's leaving the drydock?" she said.

"Five days, they claim." He laughed quietly. "Then everybody stands and watches and sees if she floats or not. They won't completely know if it works until she's out of that drydock."

"What will happen if it doesn't?"

"Well, there are two theories about that. One theory is that we'll all go into some replacement pool—I think they've got one over here somewhere, Bizerte I believe—for reassignment to other ships over here. The other is that we'll be shipped back to the States for reassignment. The second theory is highly improbable but the more popular of the two."

She laughed. "You mean they aren't happy about the ship being repaired?"

"Well, they are and they aren't. They feel completely both ways, if you can understand it—or several ways. They think it's a neat trick that the ship is being repaired and in a way they approve of it, of the ship being that tough. Also everybody would be overjoyed, naturally, to get sent back to the States. However, this depends on the no-ship theory accomplishing that. They feel if you get in a replacement pool you more or less disappear forever. In that case they'd far rather have the ship—it has to take them home sometime and they'd be on it and they'd be together—and some, especially those on from the beginning, actually have a sense of ownership about her, weird as that might seem with a thing like that. They feel several ways, if you can understand it."

"I think I can," she said.

They watched the sea for a few moments then she said, "Matthew, I promised . . ."

From the sea he turned and looked at her.

"They've put us on alert. Not telling us the date of course. But we're to be ready to go on twelve hours notice—and not more than four hours at one time out of the hospital. The favorite guess is four days from now."

"You'd go up in four days?" He had long expected the fact. Still, with it here, it was hard to deal with.

"Maybe we'll go up on your ship," she said in a moment. "If the repair works."

"There's always the chance you will. After all we've had experience in transporting nurses."

"I remember. I remember the first time I saw you. We talked about mules."

"Yes, you seemed very interested in mules."

"And we watched the night shelling at Cassino. And I remember hearing Red playing 'Shenandoah' on the guitar and my singing it a little for you. He played very well, didn't he?"

"Yes, he's been good on the guitar ever since I've known him."

"Matthew, is Red . . ."

"He's back under guard at the barracks. I saw him this morning. They're waiting for the findings to be reviewed in Algiers before shipping him home. But that's usually just routine."

She saw he did not want to talk about it.

"Have you seen Shanley lately?" she said.

"No, I haven't," he said.

She looked at the sea a moment. "I wonder how far ahead of time they make the assignments. I mean who or what is to go on which ship?"

"I don't know how far ahead they make them but we usually get told the same day—or the day before at the most. It was the same day when we took you up before. I remember the captain calling a meeting in the wardroom."

"About what?"

"He wanted to remind us to quit ourselves like gentlemen with this particular cargo."

She laughed quietly again. "You did. Everybody did. You don't sound very enthusiastic about having the same cargo again."

"I don't like to think of having to watch you walk away into that beachhead," he said suddenly, and unexpectedly. He hadn't meant to say it. "I think that would be a very hard thing for me to do."

"I'm not very good at goodbyes either," she said. "Do you have any more idea where the ship, if it works, will go when Anzio is over?"

"No, nobody does. At least nobody on the ship. I suppose they know somewhere."

"Could it still be in the Mediterranean?"

"If there's another invasion. And I suppose there will be. France or the Balkans, I guess it would have to be. There aren't any other places left. I remember that infantry captain telling me the same thing."

"What infantry captain?"

"I'm sorry, I thought I might have mentioned him. We carried his company up that last time. I talked with him a little going up. He didn't get farther than about ten yards into Anzio."

She had heard about the shelling from Captain Adler but not about the infantry captain. He thought of her leaving the ship as the infantry captain had left it. He thought of the conversation he had had that time with another infantryman about the beating the field hospitals at Anzio had been taking from the German artillery. He didn't mention it to her. Undoubtedly she knew it anyhow, from the other nurses. In any event it was nothing to talk about, as was anything you could do nothing about. If there was anything the war taught you, it was not to talk about, and to try very hard not to think about, things you couldn't do anything about. Learning not to talk about it was not difficult, and it was surprisingly easy, too, with practice, to learn not to think about it. But it wasn't too easy right now. She must go to Anzio and he to wherever his ship would take him, if there was a ship, and wherever else somebody else would decide, if there wasn't, and no force on earth, no will, could stop these two things from happening. If there was anything neither he nor she could do anything about, it was the fact that they would part soon, whatever happened with the ship. But he found it very hard not to think about it.

"Matthew," she said, "if I could know always where you were, it would help."

"Yes, I'll let you know."

"You won't just drop out of sight? Do you promise me that?"

"Yes. I promise you. I won't drop out of sight. I'll always let you know where I am."

"And I'll let you know where I am. Wherever we are, we'll know where the other is. I don't know why that should make things so much easier but it does."

It didn't with him.

"The worst thing with me would be if you just disappeared. If you promise not to, promise to let me know always where you are, I'll be all right. If you do that, I'll be fine . . ."

Then she was crying, very quietly. He put his hand on her shoulder, holding it there a little tightly, as if somehow to give her some reassurance, to let something pass out of his body into her and maybe strengthen her a little.

"No, it doesn't make it all right," she said. "It doesn't make it fine. I can't pretend it, and I can't say that's the way it has to be and then be all right. I hate it, Matthew. I hate the idea of our going apart and not being able to do anything in the world about it and never knowing when or if we'll see each

other again. I hate the thought of disappearing up there and
you disappearing somewhere and it won't be fine at all, it won't
be all right. I'm not good at this at all and I can't pretend to
be."

He let her talk and he kept his hand on her shoulder until
her crying had stopped. He said gently: "Try not to think about
it."

"I'll try," she said. "It won't help but I'll try. Can we walk
some more? Let's go down and look at the dory again, can we
do that?"

He stood up and reached down a hand to pull her to her feet.
They went down the beach toward the old fishing shack at the
end of it, looking ahead at the arm of the rock promontory
and occasionally out to seaward over the still water, the sea
flowing west to Gibraltar, west to home. He did not, he told
himself for the hundredth time recently, believe in the feelings
of war, for all within that iron framework was distorted and
larger than life, whether it be hate or love or desire or selfishness
or greed or compassion or cowardice or courage. War blew them
all up much larger than any of them ever was freed of the
echoing, distorting walls of war. He did not believe in the emotions brought on within the framework of war. But even up
against this, he dared put a sure knowledge that here was a
highly unusual girl, one of goodness, one of warmth, one of
grace, one of a desire to live, not outside, but in the middle of
life, that life should be lived to the full, one who was very much
a woman. And believing this he knew that if he let himself, if
he should let himself go for even one moment, he would be
lost, lost in her and in the fullest of commitments to her. And
on another day, another war-less day, he would have wanted
nothing better than that commitment, nothing better than to so
lose himself in her. But he knew also, with time closing in on
them and about to erect that wall of apartness between them,
that if he did lose himself, did make the commitment now,
that every day from the moment of that apartness would be a
day of longing and misery, every day until this war ended, and
the war showed every promise of continuing for a very long time

to come. And he could not face the abyss that was that misery. One suspended, thoughtless moment, and he would be in it for so long as this war should go on.

They had come to the fishing shack and they peered inside. The dory with several holes in the side was still sitting there, ghostlike within the walls. There was no way to turn now but back. They lingered, then turned away facing toward the sea.

"I'm afraid of being in the sea," she said again as they went along slowly, "but I would be happiest to live my life on the sea, right down on the sea."

"Yes, I would myself. I'd like to live right on the sea."

They stopped, as if by the same emotion, and stood in the sand, looking at each other.

"With nothing between oneself and the sea," she said.

"Nothing," he said.

She waited one moment, then said, "I must get back. My four hours will be gone."

He waited, looking down at her and knowing that now, this moment, was very probably the last time they would be alone until the war, the long war, was over. Then he reached over and with one finger touched away from under her eyes a damp spot, half a tear, which remained from her crying.

"Come on, I'll take you back," he said.

22

SENTENCES AND CITATIONS

It was what Rear Admiral Haynes Doddridge, USN, called his "Sentences and Citations" hour; one hour a week out of the passionately busy schedule of a desk officer who would far rather have been at sea, where indeed he had spent most of his life. Admiral Doddridge had said a hundred times and had had said a hundred times to him (nearly always by officers of rank superior to his own who were trying to keep him there, for he was a brilliant organizer) that someone had to be at the desks, and this included some very fine fighting officers of high rank. Admiral Doddridge's time for it had happened to fall in the last half of 1943 and the first half of 1944, which was a very busy season for fighting men. His only consolation was that the year was drawing to an end which he had been promised by a *very* high ranking officer—in fact, the Chief of Naval Operations—would be a maximum and that at its conclusion he would again be given sea command.

Meantime he did a superb job at the desk. He had organized the desk work, since it had to be, with the efficiency he applied to everything else. And also with whatever small arrangements would make it more bearable, such as in the present task, deliberately doing the two matters together: the dislike of reviewing and approving—generally—the sentences of courts-martial would be somewhat offset, he reasoned, if at the same time he would review the recommendations of commanding officers of citations for bravery or work well done of one kind or another. It made for a balance. In this labor he worked from two baskets set on opposite sides of his desk, as if representing the polarities of naval behavior. One was labeled COURTS-MARTIAL and the other CITATIONS. He had refined his method to the degree he alternately took a paper out of one basket, dealt with it, then took a paper out of the other basket and dealt with that, until one basket was empty. Then he worked straight through the remaining basket. Sometimes the COURTS-MARTIAL basket would be finished first and sometimes the CITATIONS. He preferred it when the COURTS-MARTIAL basket was emptied first.

That day he was not far from the bottom of both baskets when he picked up a small file from the COURTS-MARTIAL basket and settled forward with one elbow on the desk, arm up, and head leaning forward a little into the hand. He read:

"Sentence of Dishonorable Discharge in the case of Peter Carlyle, seaman second class, USNR, of the LST 1826."

The first page, a summary prepared by his legal officer, contained the essential facts of the case. It related in brief, formal, and dispassionate language how the sailor had been charged with and adjudged guilty by a general court of taking various Navy and Army materiel, mostly food, over a period of time and passing it on to a young Italian woman who then either used these items directly for herself and child, traded them for items of Italian food, or sold them on the Naples black market and used the money thus obtained to pay for other of her expenses, such as rent. The sailor himself had not, the summary said, dealt directly on the black market but had been aware the woman was doing so with the articles he brought her.

Admiral Doddridge looked up a moment and sighed wearily. He had read enough. The admiral had little sympathy for any member of the Navy caught dealing on the black market. It was a plainly offensive act to him and he had not hesitated to approve all sentences for such activity that had come his way, including that of a lieutenant commander who had operated in a really big way and for his enterprise was now doing five years in Portsmouth Naval Prison.

At the bottom of the first sheet, Admiral Doddridge saw, was the usual typed form with a blank space in which he was to write the word *Approved* or the word *Disapproved* and below it the first word lightly penciled and the initials "SRA" indicating his legal officer's recommendation. He was about to write the word *Approved* in this space and his name and pass on to the top paper in the CITATIONS basket when he became aware that his flag secretary was standing in front of the desk.

"Yes, Baker?"

"Sorry to interrupt, sir, but there's a message from Naples I thought you might like to see."

Admiral Doddridge took the despatch the flag secretary was holding out. It had been broken from code and it read:

> Strapping job on LST 1826 completed and ship sailed successfully this date out of Naples drydock to home port Pozzuoli all flags flying. Ship in all respects stands ready for sea. Please forward fagairtrans case of Scotch. Simpson.

Bowie Simpson (his nickname derived from an unallowed absence one day at the race track not far from Annapolis which very nearly got him expelled) had been in Admiral Doddridge's class at the Academy and the war had landed them both on the shore in the Mediterranean, Simpson as commanding officer of the NOB at Naples in the recently revived rank of commodore. Admiral Doddridge knew the case of the *LST* 1826 very well. Its torpedoing off Anzio could not have come at a worse time. The Anzio breakout was about to happen and he desperately needed every landing craft he could get his hands on. He was in Naples the following day taking a look at what was left of the ship—a wreck, split in two, she was obviously done for—then conferring with Simpson and a rather brash young ship-repair officer of Simpson's, a reservist commander named Jellicoe. He was flabbergasted when Jellicoe proposed to put the two parts of the ship back together, and in a couple of weeks at that. Admiral Doddridge remembered looking at the ship-repair officer, about whom all he knew was that on the outside he had been first a naval architect and then had taught the subject at MIT, as if he had gone, or was about to go, around the bend. He was surprised when Simpson had backed Jellicoe up fully—he had had the ship-repair officer with him from the first days of the activation of the Naples NOB, and he seemed to look upon the man as a freak, or a genius, as one chose; in any case to believe, from experience, that Jellicoe could do anything he said he could do in the realm of marine flotation, including possibly walking or making someone walk on water.

"Flat bottom, that's what makes the job possible, Admiral," the man had said "—that is to say, certain."

Admiral Doddridge cast a baleful, almost bellicose look on the commander.

"I must say, Commander, no one could ever accuse you of lacking in confidence," he said drily. "Very well, Simpson. If you fools over here have time to waste trying such a thing, proceed. I need LSTs any way I can get them. It won't work, of course, but you have my permission to try."

"A bottle of Scotch on it?" Simpson had said.

"A case of Scotch if you want. I can get a case of Scotch much easier than I can an LST. And I hope you can too when you lose this bet."

Admiral Doddridge read the despatch again.

"Son-of-a-bitch!" he said. "The sons-a-bitches did it." He looked up at his flag secretary and spoke crisply. "Can you get a case of Scotch on its way today to Commodore Simpson?"

"I'll have it on the 1400 courier plane," the flag secretary said, and smiled.

"And oh, Baker."

"Yes, sir?"

"As a matter-of-fact, send two cases of Scotch and mark one 'Jellicoe.' "

"Descended from the admiral of the same name?" the flag secretary said wittily.

"He should be, with what he's done."

"Aye aye, sir. Two cases of Scotch."

The flag secretary left and Admiral Doddridge, remembering

precisely where he had been, reached for his desk pen. He was about to write the word *Approved* when he remembered something and his eyes moved to the top of the summary sheet. They rested on the figure 1826.

Reflexively and with a very slow motion movement, the admiral put the pen back, finding the holder by feel and still reading the papers. Then he sat back and read some more. He finished reading the summary. "No charge of personal profit for the accused was either made or sustained . . ." The accused's defense was stated in brief: "Seaman Second Class Carlyle admitted to taking the items. His defense was that they were for the support of the young mother, age seventeen, and her child born at sea on the accused's ship."

Christ, the admiral thought, the LST 1826, fresh out of drydock, was the same ship that had had that baby born aboard a few weeks back while carrying refugees from Anzio. He had heard of the incident, how a pharmacist's mate had actually delivered the baby, and he had never forgotten it. As a matter-of-fact he had always maintained great pride in the incident as yet another proof of the Navy's ability to cope with any situation. All he had forgotten was the actual number of the ship. He pressed a buzzer on his desk.

"Yes, Admiral?"

"Baker, please don't let me be disturbed for, say, twenty minutes except for an emergency."

"Yes, sir."

Picking up the entire folder, the admiral sat back. A record of proceedings of the court-martial was appended and he began reading it. As the name Carlyle kept reappearing on the pages he began to believe he had even heard *that* name before, but decided he must be imagining connections. He read on. He came to a passage in the testimony, a part where a CID man was testifying, and he read the phrase, "And he had his red hair. It is rather identifiable hair . . ."

The admiral looked up as if he had had a visitation of some kind. Caserta! If it was the same man, he himself had seen that hair and it was surely the reddest hair in creation. He had seen

it on the parade ground at Caserta. He was sure of it. He pressed
his buzzer.

"Yes, Admiral?"

"Baker, will you check our Citations file and see if there's a
man named . . . it's Peter Carlyle, seaman second class, USNR,"
he read from the paper in front of him ". . . see if we gave a
man by that name some kind of medal."

The flag secretary, carrying another sheet of paper, was back
in the office in less than two minutes.

"I believe this is it, sir. A Bronze Star to Seaman Second Class
Peter Carlyle, USNR . . ."

"The *LST 1826?*" the admiral cut in.

"Why, so it is," the flag secretary said, looking at the paper.
"So he is, sir," he repeated slowly.

"That'll be all for the present, Baker. I'll take that paper."

The flag secretary passed it over and left the room. The admiral
refreshed his memory by reading Carlyle's citation. Then he read
some more of the court-martial proceedings. He turned the last
page and there was a letter addressed to him. He read slowly
through it . . .

> ". . . It is my opinion that Seaman Carlyle felt the
> Navy had some obligation to support the mother and
> the child she gave birth to on a Navy ship. Doubtless
> Navy Regulations do not cover this contingency, but I
> believe the moral obligation was there in Seaman
> Carlyle's mind. Certainly no crime was intended. It may
> be, sir, that little was done. Seaman Carlyle is a Navy
> man of the first order, and, incidentally, the best lookout
> on this vessel. He has performed with a high degree of
> skill and imagination his duties aboard this vessel through
> three invasions and throughout the long support of the
> Anzio beachhead. I urgently and respectfully recommend
> that his sentence be set aside and that Seaman Carlyle
> be returned to his ship."
>
>   (Signed) Jacob Adler, Lieutenant, USNR,
>   COMMANDING, LST 1826

Abruptly the admiral's movements became swift and decisive. He reached for his pen and across his legal officer's summary page wrote: "Sentence is disapproved, for extenuating circumstances." He hesitated a moment and then wrote: "Namely, baby born aboard Navy vessel." It was cryptic in a way, but in another way, he felt, perfectly clear. Everything had started with and derived from the birth of that baby on a Navy ship; the legal officer could work out the formal language. He signed his name with a firm stroke. He put all of it back in the folder and put the folder in his OUTGOING box. The admiral then forgot the matter and reached for the top paper in the CITATIONS basket, dealt with it, then alternately worked through the papers in the two baskets. He was down to the third paper from the bottom of the CITATIONS basket when he plucked out and read:

> Recommendation for the Navy Cross. Subject: Lieutenant (jg) Matthew Barclay, USNR. For conspicuous gallantry and intrepidity in action. Subject officer, when his ship was taken under severe attack on the Anzio beachhead, unhesitatingly and in an entirely exposed position coolly continued his duties as bow ramp offloading officer, getting a company of U. S. Army infantry with equipment off the ship. During the heaviest part of the attack, Lieutenant (jg) Barclay, with complete disregard for his own safety, repeatedly entered the beach and while exposed to intense flying shrapnel, brought several wounded from the beach onto the ship, continuing such activity even when he had himself sustained severe scalp wounds. Lieutenant (jg) Barclay's prompt action and high courage were in the highest traditions of the Naval Service and in all probability saved the lives of several wounded Army and Navy personnel until his ship, the LST 1826 . . .

Five minutes later the admiral buzzed for his flag secretary. "Baker," he said. "That LST 1826. That seems to be a rather unusual vessel, in, I would say, a number of respects."

The flag secretary smiled softly. "It is that, sir. We seem to be constantly getting some kind of correspondence about the LST 1826."

"Not just correspondence," the admiral said. "Well, the main thing is that she's ready for Operation Buffalo. That does make me happy and gratified. Yes, indeed. However in addition."

"Yes, sir," the flag secretary said dutifully.

"In addition I had a thought, Baker."

"Yes, sir. What was the thought, Admiral?" the flag secretary, a most trained and attuned man to his job, said.

"The thought, Baker, was that that ship deserves something."

"Deserves something, sir?" Baker said. As a good flag secretary he had learned even to echo the admiral's very phrases.

"By way of reward I suppose one might call it." The admiral looked keenly at his flag secretary. "Baker, what would you say would be any ship's preferred cargo to carry over all others?"

The flag secretary felt he could afford the smile of one who can say what is already in his admiral's mind. He could say it in one word.

"Nurses," he said, "sir."

23

DESPATCHES

At 1830 on Monday 22 May, Barclay walked off the ship, down the mole, and into the small shack at the end of it. He took the field phone out of its leather case, turned the crank on the side of the phone, and finally got put through to the 300th General Hospital. As always, it took a while to get her on the phone, and as always when he did the connection was not very good and they both had to do an amount of yelling to make themselves heard. He had an extremely uncertain date with her for that evening, and they had arranged together for him to call first to see if she could get away. Now he knew at once from the guarded tone of her voice what had happened. The only thing she said on the phone about it was that she could not see him this evening. She gave no reason but then he didn't need one. When he hung up he knew one thing: that she was going; and didn't know another: on which ship it would be. And he knew one thing more. "I have an appointment at your place tomorrow with Colonel Jarvis. Will I see you?" he had asked. "When's the appointment?" "Eleven-thirty." "Yes."

He went back to the ship and startled Ensign Horner, who had the bow ramp watch, by telling him that if he cared to go into Naples this evening he would take his watch for him. Horner, overjoyed at this deliverance, was off the ship in fifteen minutes and on his way, on the interurban, into the city.

The bad thing about a port watch was that there was not much to do except think, and he sometimes felt that war was chiefly an exercise in learning not to think. He would try to stop it but the thoughts would come on, rushing. He thought about Carlyle. This made him think about Coco. She had moved back into Via Mazzini 36 and he was still turning his paycheck over to her. He wished he had done it long ago. If he had, Carlyle would be here now. And he thought also of the futility of thinking how things might have been, if and if and if. Then, helplessly, he thought about the nurse, of her and her detachment being restricted to quarters and of the fact this meant she would be going, any day, any hour, any hour after noon tomorrow. He wondered on which ship. Then he thought about his own ship and wondered when their first run to Anzio would be since being put back together. She was all ready, apparently, to go, and that also could be any day, any hour. He thought about when he would be given orders to rejoin the ship on a "permanent" basis. Right now his status was that he was staying aboard but was not to sail with the ship if she sailed. But he was seeing Colonel Jarvis again tomorrow and he had promised to let him know then.

He felt all right. An occasional attack of dizziness would still hit him, without warning, to where he would have to go, wherever he happened to be, and find a place to sit down or lie down. But he wanted to sail with the ship when she sailed. He was not doing much, that, he felt, was one cause of the attacks. And they would not let him do much while the ship was in port. He felt that once the ship had sailed, they would have to let him do everything he had done before—there would be nobody but himself to do it then—and that once he was fully back and the ship going up again to Anzio and him doing his regular job, he would be thoroughly all right. He remembered that he would have to try to explain all this tomorrow to Colonel Jarvis. He remembered that he would have to be very alert when Jarvis examined him tomorrow, and above all to concentrate on not having any of these attacks of dizziness then, to will Jarvis somehow into approving his return to the ship. Cassino had fallen. There were reports that the Germans were falling back on another line but six miles north and its christened name of the Adolf Hitler Line at least suggested that they intended to make a stand there, which if successful would hold up any breakout at Anzio. Nevertheless, he felt in him that Anzio was about over, any trip could be their last one. He had not come this far to stay behind, now, and he was not going to. He was not. A couple of times during the watch he felt a minor wave of dizziness come over him, strong enough, the second time, that he told Lord Nelson, the boatswain on watch, that he was going to his stateroom and would be back in ten minutes. In the room he pulled the door curtain and lay down on his bunk and lay very still. He would have to make sure this didn't happen tomorrow, he kept telling himself. After a few minutes of lying down he got up and went back to the bow ramp and resumed his place there.

"It's a nice night, isn't it, Mr. Barclay?" Lord Nelson said.

"Yes, very pretty night," Barclay said, looking up at the stars and at the large moon.

"It'll be full tomorrow night," Nelson said.

At 2100 Monday Carlyle was standing looking out the barred window at the great gathering of ships spread out in silhouette far below and beyond him in the moonlight when he heard a key turn. He turned reflexively and saw standing there a shore patrol man. Leaving the door open, he walked over and stood by Carlyle and looked out at the view with him. The shore patrol man was unarmed.

"It is quite a view at that, isn't it?" he said. Then added: "Be better without the bars though."

He waited a moment, looking, then said: "Well, come along. You're wanted below."

"What for?" Carlyle said.

"They didn't confide in me. They hardly ever do. They just said to fetch you."

Carlyle had hardly needed to ask. He knew it must mean his sentence had been reviewed and approved in Algiers and that he would be leaving on the early flight tomorrow on the long trip which would take him home from Naples. During the days in this room he had outwardly maintained composure; inwardly he felt chiefly numbness. The numbness was fortunate, for it kept him from thinking, though sometimes a thought, of a court-martial,

DESPATCHES

of a girl, or of a ship and his shipmates on her, would break
through the shield and hold him in its grip for a moment; then
often, too, came a plan he had.

With the shore patrol man he walked down the wide corridor
of the building which had once been a resort hotel. If there were
elevators—Carlyle saw none—they apparently were not operating
for presently they came to a staircase and he and the shore patrol
man started down it. There were five flights and when they
reached the ground floor the shore patrol man guided him into a
room opening off what had been the lobby of the hotel. He
found himself standing in a small office at which sat a chief
petty officer in khakis with the insignia of a boatswain's mate on
his upper right sleeve and four hashmarks on his lower left representing sixteen years of naval service.

"Seaman Second Class Carlyle?" the chief said.

"I'm Carlyle, sir."

"I'm not an officer," the chief said mildly. "However, if you'll
read this . . ."

He handed a Navy despatch form across. Carlyle read it, and
did not comprehend. Then read it again. This time he did comprehend.

ORIGINATOR: COMPHIBMED

ACTION: CO NOB NAPLES

ORIGINATOR HAS THIS DATE REVIEWED AND DISAPPROVED
REPEAT DISAPPROVED COURT-MARTIAL SENTENCE OF
SEAMAN SECOND CLASS PETER CARLYLE USNR ATTACHED
YOUR COMMAND ON INTERNMENT STATUS. ON RECEIPT OF
THIS DESPATCH YOU ARE HEREBY DIRECTED TO RELEASE
SUBJECT ENLISTED MAN IMMEDIATELY FROM CUSTODY AND
TO DELIVER TO HIM THE FOLLOWING ORDERS COMPHIBMED
HAS THIS DATE DISAPPROVED SENTENCE OF COURT-
MARTIAL OF SEAMAN SECOND CLASS PETER CARLYLE USNR.
ALL PRIVILEGES OBTAINING BEFORE SAID SENTENCE ARE
HEREBY RESTORED. ON RECEIPT OF THESE ORDERS YOU
WILL REPORT TO THE COMMANDING OFFICER LST 1826
REPEAT LOVE SUGAR TARE ONE EIGHT TWO SIX BY 2400
HOURS 23 MAY FOR DUTY ABOARD

The chief with the sixteen years service—they were red instead of gold hashmarks so that his career had not been wholly free of infractions—stood up, smiled softly, and held out his hand.

"Welcome back aboard, Carlyle," he said.

Carlyle stood there a few moments unable to think even to the extent of planning such a simple thing as where he would sleep that night. The chief helped him out.

"Schedule of carryall trips into the city ended about an hour ago," he said. "I guess you'd better spend the night here. However, that choice is up to you."

"Yes, I guess that would be best," Carlyle said.

"Okay," the chief said. He smiled abruptly, spoke to the shore patrol man. "No need to lock the door any more."

Carlyle walked—alone—back up the five flights of stairs. He went into his room and closed the door. Then he opened it again just to enjoy the sensation of being able to do so. He closed it and walked over to the window and stood there briefly looking down over the moonlit harbor and the ships. He came back, stripped to his skivvies and T-shirt and lay down on the bunk on his back, looking up at the ceiling partially moonlighted. His mind could not in any fullness yet absorb the big thing. Instead it went off on relatively small matters, such as how he would spend tomorrow. He had the entire day and evening before he had to report to the ship. He couldn't remember when a thing like that had happened even before the court-martial, in all his time on the ship. He dozed off into a deep sleep.

At 2305 Colonel Jarvis settled behind his desk in his office at the 300th General Hospital and faced the paperwork, which he hated but knew he could never be free of. There was a lot of it in his civilian life and an unbelievable amount of it in the military. He wondered sometimes how any actual medical or surgical work got done at all. He dived in. During the course of an hour and a half of this labor, of checking the reports of men who had lost legs, arms, faces, sphincter muscles, genital organs, of men who had contracted hepatitis, gangrene, dysentery, of men who had lost part or all of their minds, he came across a report on a

Lieutenant (jg) Matthew Barclay and then remembered this was Clark's friend, the one with the head wound. He noted that he was to see the naval officer tomorrow forenoon. There was a report from the Army doctor who had attended Barclay and another from the nurse Clark herself. The latter was unusual—nurses didn't as a rule participate in these reports, certainly not to the point of making recommendations—but Clark, he noted, had intelligently used the advantage of having observed the patient on the outside to add these observations. The nurse said patient appeared to be progressing well, but that she would recommend that he not be returned to full duty for at least a week, that she was disturbed by continuing, if infrequent, attacks of dizziness. Colonel Jarvis had a remarkable memory. He wrote a few words on the paper and put it aside and went on to the next one.

At 0800 hours on Tuesday 23 May Captain Adler was sitting in his cabin with the door open having a cup of coffee with Commander Jellicoe, officer-in-charge of the NOB ship-repair department. Commander Jellicoe had been on the ship since 0700 taking another careful look at her with the captain. During the days of Jellicoe's putting the ship together the two men had struck up a liking for each other and now the ship-repair officer had just finished his coffee and was preparing to go.

"I'll say once more, Commander," Captain Adler said. "That is quite a job you did. Frankly, I didn't believe it could be done."

"Between you and me, Captain, I wasn't sure myself. But I *thought* it was possible, with an LST. I thought there wasn't any harm in trying. Frankly, too, I've always wanted to try it." Commander Jellicoe grinned. "I'm grateful to you for giving me the opportunity."

"Highly involuntarily, I assure you," Captain Adler said. He waited a moment, and asked, not chiefly for reassurance, but more as form: "It'll hold, you're certain? These ships take a pretty heavy beating in not much of a sea."

Commander Jellicoe smiled again. "It'll hold, Captain. If anything, with that new belly I think the ship is stronger against stress than when she was new."

Captain Adler returned the smile. "I'm glad to know it. We can use all the strength against stress we can get."

When Jellicoe had left, Captain Adler sat down at his desk again. He looked a moment at the photograph on it in a silver frame from Jensen's of his wife and children. It occurred to him that the man responsible for the fact he was not with them, this very day, in New York, was the one who had just left. He stood up and looked out the open port. It was on the sea side and it was a pretty, sunny day out to sea. He wondered for a moment what kind of day 23 May would be in New York. May could bring some lovely days to the city. Still, under the circumstances, he was glad to be here. He would have liked to be with his family, but certainly not at the price of a lost ship. In any event it would not be long. Things were coming to an end over here and it couldn't be long . . .

"Captain?"

He turned. Ensign Horner, the communications officer, was standing in the doorway holding a despatch.

"This just came in—I just broke it," Horner said. He came forward and handed the despatch over and Captain Adler read:

ORIGINATOR: COMPHIBMED

ACTION: COMMANDING OFFICER, LST 1826

URGENT   TOP SECRET

YOU ARE HEREBY DIRECTED TO STAND IN ALL
RESPECTS READY FOR SEA AND PREPARED TO TAKE
ON DETACHMENT OF FIFTY FOUR UNITED STATES
ARMY NURSES FROM 300TH GENERAL HOSPITAL AT
1600 HOURS 23 MAY

The captain read it again then looked at the ensign.

"Would you please assemble all officers in the wardroom at once, Horner. On second thought, make that fifteen minutes from now. And send Porterfield in now, will you."

It was just past ten o'clock Tuesday when Carlyle, wearing his dress blues, walked down the steps of the enlisted men's barracks. The wide walk split and circled on either side a fountain in which sculpture stood but no water now flowed and as the walks converged again before another long bank of steps the sailor turned and looked up at the hotel. He was surprised how large it was, and how pretty, but he looked only a moment then descended the steps and came out onto a road which led down a long hill toward the harbor and the city. He could have got a ride into the city but he wanted to walk. The soreness in his legs from the walking actually felt good and it was an uncanny pleasure merely to be able to walk continuously without having to turn around after a few steps and cover the same ground back and at first his attention was directed entirely to that pleasure. Then he began to notice the villas set on the sides of the hill. They were attractive, white buildings, some scarred now, imbedded in deep green growth. At the point where the road flattened somewhat he found himself in a cluster of much meaner looking houses and he saw a few Italians wandering around. He realized he didn't know the best way down into the city and presently he would ask one of them. Then he saw sitting in a doorway a family—at least he assumed it was one family—of mother and father and something like eight children. He went up to them with the idea of seeking directions into the city. Then he decided he would like to do something else first for a while. He decided he would like to stop and talk. Just talk.

It was some time back that the captain had given permission for "The Benefit Party." Now, in the course of events, it had developed that the party was to be a kind of commemoration of the return of the ship as well as of the fact that the ship would, any day now, be making its last voyage from Pozzuoli and the crew had expressed a wish for the party before the ship left for good. The arrangements for it, rather elaborate, had all been laid on and the party had been set for tonight, Tuesday. Now, of course, since the ship would be making its first run since its reconstitution then, they would have to postpone it. The captain told Porterfield.

"Let's make it Thursday and pass the word, will you?"

"Yes, sir." Porterfield's face broke into a thoughtful smile. "That's going to be some party, sir."

"I can well imagine. Believe me, I'm looking forward to it," the captain said.

Porterfield left and alerted the men in the crew who had been making the preparations. Presently: Lord Nelson left the ship to go into Naples to pay a quick call on his chief contact, herself a member, who had previously been alerted to keep the Ladies of the Cave free for tonight to make that Thursday night instead and to ask her to pass the same word to a Signor Alfini, a bassoonist by profession, and his small band; Chatham left the LST to pay a call on the owner, now a long-time friend as well as a part-time ship's chandler, of perhaps the best vineyard in the Naples area, to tell him to hold off that exceptionally large delivery for two days; Mason, back on his rating for this occasion, belayed the preliminary cooking preparations which he had been about to start and Wiley the laying of planking over Number 2 hatch for dancing; Plimpton merely stepped off the ship, walked a few paces, and informed the children of the change. Porterfield started to get the strongbox from Mason to go into town. Then hesitated. . . .

Ever since the all-night poker session at Anzio, when the idea for The Benefit had been broached by Porterfield and finally agreed to in principle, the fund for it had been rapidly accumulating. The nightly poker sessions had been interrupted only briefly by the torpedoing of the ship, and the sessions were promptly resumed at the Naples receiving station, where the crew were billeted until such time as the work in the drydock should determine whether they would have a ship to return to. The men having a great deal more time now, the poker sessions became even longer, and the fund proportionately stepped up. It had now well passed the set goal of 250,000 lire and was still growing. In the meantime the men had continued to discuss, from

time to time, what to do with the fund and at last Porterfield
had had an idea.

"You know," he said one day while dealing out a hand at the
receiving station, "the main thing those kids are starved for is
play—fun. Wiley, you remember when you made them those
stilts? How they went nuts over them?"

"Yeh," the carpenter's mate said, grinning, "they liked those
stilts all right."

"King's betting. And how they're always after us on the dock
to play catch with them, or any game we can think of? They
don't seem to have any place to play. If we could find a piece of
land in Pozzuoli," Porterfield said thoughtfully, "and buy it. If
we could do that and then deed it in perpetuity to the children
of the town as a playground . . ."

"Deed it in what?" Mason said.

"It would belong to them as long as there was an Italy,"
Porterfield translated. "We could buy the land and put up a few
things ourselves. The people of the town whenever the war gets
over and they get back on their feet again could put up other
things for them to play on. Matter-of-fact something just occurred
to me."

He studied his hole cards for a moment then talked while
dealing the next round. "It might even work out for *us* to keep
it up ourselves, after the war, from wherever we are, to furnish
and maintain it I mean. Wouldn't cost much. And that way it
would keep us in touch when we're back in civilian life. Anyhow
at least they'd have a place. Pair of Jacks bets."

The general idea had been accepted. Porterfield, in anticipation, had already diligently cased the town, done a good deal of
inquiring around, and finally come upon a piece of land not far
from the port that he considered ideal, a roomy plateau overlooking the sea and the actual place where the LST came in. He
then had gone into the NOB, got an appointment with the
base's assistant legal officer and asked for his help in checking
the thing through to make certain it was legal. The legal officer
became an immediate admirer of the plan. He looked, himself,
into the land Porterfield had spotted, found out it could be

transferred legally, and that the owner would be happy to part with it for 275,000 lire. After that it was just a matter of having enough poker sessions to raise the amount, which they had now reached. There remained only the final meeting with the owner and the legal officer, who had drawn up papers deeding the property to the children of the town of Pozzuoli, for the signing of these documents and the delivery of the 275,000 lire. Mason, as treasurer, had been keeping the money in a strongbox in the safe in the communications shack. Now, returning from his talk with the captain, Porterfield started to get the money and take it in. Then he decided to wait until Thursday. There would be plenty of time for it then and the fund would be even richer and so enable him, on his trip into Naples, to purchase certain added attractions for The Benefit.

Barclay, with the other officers assembled in the wardroom, had received word of the ship's departure that afternoon and of the identity of its passengers shortly before leaving the ship to go up to the 300th General to keep his appointment with Colonel Jarvis. That did it. His resolution was now absolute. If she was going, so was he. Whatever it took, he would do it. He walked into the hospital at 1120, found Colonel Jarvis' office, sat in the waiting room for five minutes and promptly at 1130 was shown in. Colonel Jarvis was a man who ran on schedule. Barclay was down for exactly five minutes and the colonel got briskly to it.

"The report's not bad," he said, looking at a paper he held before him. "I promised you something definite this time, didn't I?"

"Yes, you did, Colonel. And I feel fine now, perfectly all right."

"Not so fast, please. You'll be back on your ship in a week. I've written the orders. Here." And he handed a sheet of paper across.

"A week?" Barclay said, taking the paper. "But the ship's sailing tonight, sir."

"Is that so?" Colonel Jarvis received this highly incidental information emotionlessly. "Well, I envy you, an extra week in

Naples. Just take it easy and I don't think you'll have to bother with us except one more look, end of that week. Good luck," he said, dismissing the naval officer politely but briskly.

"Colonel."

"Yes?" The colonel looked up from his desk as if surprised to see Barclay still there.

"I'd like to get back on the ship now, sir. There's nothing in the world wrong with me . . ."

"Are you out of your mind, boy? Dizzy spells less but continuing, the report says. And are you trying to tell me my business? Let's don't be so reluctant about an extra week in Naples, shall we not? Now get the hell out of here," he said, the edge off his words. "I've got lots of work, lots of work. You're throwing my schedule off. Get out, get out," he said, waving his hand.

Barclay waited a moment then, knowing it would be no use, left. Outside he looked at the piece of paper. Then he went downstairs to the reception desk and asked the corporal on duty there if he would see if he could turn up Lieutenant Sarah Clark. The clock behind the desk showed ten minutes past noon. Time was hurrying on, he kept thinking. Only four hours now. Then she was walking across the lobby. They stood in the middle of it, talking very quietly. She wore field clothes.

"Listen, Sarah," he said. "I've got very little time. I want you to do something for me. I want three sheets of the hospital stationery."

"What for?"

"I don't want to be asked. Will you get it for me or not?" he said brusquely.

She looked up at him a moment. "Wait here," she said then.

In five minutes she was back with an envelope which she handed him. Suddenly he grinned.

"It won't be necessary to say goodbye now," he said. And he was gone.

Back on the ship Barclay went to the communications shack, unlocked it, went inside and locked the door. He rolled a sheet of the stationery in the typewriter and beside the typewriter placed the orders Colonel Jarvis had given him. They were on identical stationery and he read them now:

SUBJECT: RETURN TO DUTY
TO: MATTHEW BARCLAY, LT (JG) USNR
YOU ARE HEREBY NOTIFIED THAT SURVEY OF YOUR
HEAD WOUND INDICATES APPROXIMATELY ONE FURTHER
WEEK OF RECOVERY, BARRING COMPLICATIONS, BEGINNING
THIS DATE AFTER WHICH YOU WILL BE RETURNED TO FULL
DUTY. YOU WILL NOT SAIL WITH SHIP UNTIL APPROVED
BY THIS COMMAND. YOU WILL DELIVER THIS MEMORANDUM
IMMEDIATELY TO YOUR COMMANDING OFFICER.

(Signed) W. J. Jarvis, Colonel, MC, AUS
COMMANDING OFFICER,
300TH GENERAL HOSPITAL

Barclay typed the "Subject" and the "To" carefully and then typed out:

YOU ARE HEREBY NOTIFIED THAT DUE TO SATISFACTORY
PROGRESS OF TREATMENT OF WOUND, YOU MAY, EFFECTIVE
THIS DATE AND ON RECEIPT OF THESE ORDERS, REJOIN
YOUR SHIP AND RESUME YOUR FULL DUTIES. YOU WILL
DELIVER THIS MEMORANDUM IMMEDIATELY TO YOUR
COMMANDING OFFICER.

He made one typing error and was thankful he had remembered to ask for three sheets of the stationery. He got it errorless on the second try. Then he found a pen and sat several moments studying Colonel Jarvis' signature. He tried it a few times on a blank piece of paper until he was satisfied. Then with great care he wrote at the bottom of the new order

W. J. Jarvis

He gathered up all the materials, put them in the same envelope the nurse had given him, and walked down to his room and shut the door. He removed his new copy, put the envelope under his

pillow, and walked down to the captain's cabin. The captain
wasn't there. He went up on the bridge and he wasn't there.
Finally he found him in troops quarters checking the bunk rigging
with Polk and Wiley. He walked up and held out the paper.
The captain read it and grinned.

"Well, well," he said. "We are unusually glad to have you
aboard, especially now. You feel like doing some work for a
change?"

"I feel great, Captain."

"I'm glad to hear it. If you'll take over here, I've got things to
do topside. Same arrangements we had with the nurses that last
time. Been a long time, hasn't it?"

"A long time, Captain."

"Do you remember how you did it before?"

"I think so, Captain."

"Well, just do it the same way."

The captain turned to go then stopped.

"And oh yes, Barclay."

"Yes, sir?"

"Even though we have the value of experience I think we'd
better be on the safe side and put up signs as before. Somebody
might just forget."

For a moment Barclay didn't know what signs he was talking
about. Then he remembered.

"It'll be good to see those signs up again," the captain said.

"Yes, sir. I think we still have the same ones."

The captain left. Barclay sent Wiley to find the NURSES
COUNTRY—DO NOT ENTER signs. It occurred to him that he was
glad he had saved them. He couldn't for the life of him remember
why.

It was quite a talk Carlyle had with the Italian family. He
could not have remembered in any substance what they talked
about, only that it was highly pleasant to do so, but he was
surprised, looking at his watch, to realize he had been there so
long. He said goodbye to them, and with the directions they
had given followed down ancient streets, hilly and winding. After

considerably more walking he came out at a landmark he recognized—the San Carlo Opera House.

Suddenly he felt tired. He walked on a few blocks more until
he came to the liberty landing where whaleboats from ships
anchored in Naples harbor put in and he sat down on a bollard
and looked out over the water. His freedom, by its suddenness,
remained too large a thing to comprehend fully. What continued
more immediate and surprising, and something he could comprehend, was that he actually had a whole day in which to do
whatever he pleased. Though so many ships out there, there was
little activity on the landing, liberty parties having already been
deposited. He looked out at the long promontory which obscured
Pozzuoli where the 1826 would be and which would be about
ten miles from where he sat and anywhere from a half hour to
a full hour's trip on the uncertain interurban. His mind working
really actively for the first time in days, he gave himself up to
the leisure of choice. He considered the various things at which
he might spend the rest of that day and evening. He ran over in
his mind places to sightsee in Naples. He thought of two or
three he had seen but would like to see again. Then it occurred
to him that the greatest pleasure of all might be simply to wander
about the city, letting his steps take him where they would. He
decided firmly on this and was about to get up to do so. At
that moment his eyes swinging around from the sea, he found
himself looking up at the heights above the city. He tried to find
the place where he had spent what had seemed the longest time
of his life in that room with the bars on it. Presently he thought
that he could make out the building but was not sure. Then
suddenly a strange thing happened with him.

He realized that he didn't want to sightsee at all right now
or wander around—or do anything else except one thing. He
found himself caught up in an overpowering compulsion to get
back to the ship, to see and to talk with the men of that ship
who had been his world and his friends for so long. And his
mind was made up in an instant. As a whaleboat slid in along
the landing, he got up and started back in the direction of the
interurban station. For two blocks the route ran along the Via

Apollo but he never noticed that. He did look at his watch and notice that it was a few minutes before five. He hoped he made the five o'clock interurban. Now that his mind was made up, he would as soon not have to wait around for the next one, an hour hence. He started walking a little faster.

They started coming aboard from the weapons carriers lined up on the mole at a little past 1600 on a sunny Tuesday, their barracks bags carried as on the other time by the sailors stepping out from the ship to help them. There was nothing different from the last time. They wore field clothes and they looked as good as ever in them and they brought to the ship, as they had then, a special air. Barclay was standing at the top of the bow ramp when she came up and she paused only a moment, looking at him and both knowing, and then followed the sailor carrying her barracks bag. By 1700 they and their effects were all aboard and it was the same as last time, a gladness to have them aboard, and if there was any difference at all it was only in the heightened feeling that large events were imminent in the place where they were going. By 1745 the ship was secured for sea and from the conning tower the order was passed down, "Heave in stern anchor. . . ."

At that moment Lord Nelson, standing at the bow ramp to supervise its raising, heard a yell, looked up, and saw a sailor in dress blues hurrying toward the ship. He saw him pushing his way through the large crowd of children gathered on the mole, as always, to see the ship off.

He just made the five o'clock interurban, though not in time to get a seat. It was hot and incredibly crowded and it seemed to be stopping everywhere but he felt in no hurry now that he was on his way. He got off at Pozzuoli and started down the main street toward the mole. At one point he passed within one block of Coco's old apartment and he wondered where she was now. Surely not there. For a moment he debated detouring a little and stopping by the house just to see. Then he decided he would rather go to the ship first. He could find out about her there from Mr. Barclay.

He was not in sight of the ship until he turned a corner of a building, then there he saw her about two hundred yards away. He was astonished at what he saw. A crowd of children was on the mole yelling things up to the crew. Not for a moment did he recognize this as the familiar scene of the ship's casting off. Then he started running. As he got nearer he began to yell. He could see the bow ramp beginning to be raised. He pushed his way through the crowd yelling. He thought he heard someone call his name from the crowd but he ran on. The bow ramp was a considerable way up by the time he reached it but he made a leap, was just able to obtain a purchase with his hands and pulled himself up and over and half-slid, half-stepped down the incline into the tank deck.

"Mary Mother of God," Lord Nelson said. "Look who's here."

Now water began to appear between ship and mole, the distance slowly increasing. Carlyle stood by the life line looking at the crowd of children waving goodbye. Suddenly he saw a figure running toward the ship, come up to the very edge of the mole so that she was alone before the crowd, and stand there where she could go no farther. He could make out that she was holding a baby. Then he heard his name being called and he saw the girl raise her free arm and begin to wave, still calling his name. He began to wave and to call her name back. The interval of water steadily increased until he could hear his name no more. He borrowed Lord Nelson's binoculars and through them kept her in sight. She was still waving when she could no longer be seen even through 7×50 binoculars.

The ship stood out to sea, then, swinging slowly, stood north to Anzio. The sea was smooth. A full moon was just rising over the hills to starboard.

24

THE NURSES GOING TO ANZIO

The May sea stretched away motionless under the full moon, with not a whitecap nor even a break or bump in the skin of the sea anywhere. It was a remarkable sea and Barclay was certain he had never seen a better one. From the conning tower he could see the silhouetted figures of nurses at the life lines looking out upon it as if in wonder that there could be a sea like that. When it came well in the war, he thought, it came very well. Twice now they had taken up nurses, which would surely be any ship's favorite cargo, and twice been blessed with that kind of sea and moon. The ship even had an odd new, and better, sound to it. Barclay had always thought the sound of an LST underway was nearest of anything to that of a creaking porch swing. Now it still sounded like a porch swing but as if its chains had been oiled, so that the movement was smoother, the creaking almost gone. Almost. Besides putting the ship back together, the Naples ship-repair department seemed actually to have improved her with that huge new steel belly. Carlyle was back, he was here now on the 2000–2400 watch which Barclay had and for this reason also it was an unusually satisfying watch.

Everything seemed better, everything except one thing, which was Barclay's knowledge that in about nine hours one of those nurses would be walking ashore at Anzio with the others, walking into the beachhead and out of his life. He tried with some success not to think about it, to think only, where she was concerned, that as soon as he was off watch at midnight he would be seeing her, one more time; they had arranged to meet then in the space forward of the starboard boat. It was only a little over an hour away. He thought of the good sea tonight and of the men with him on watch, Nelson boatswain, Porterfield helmsman, Abbot signalman, Mason recorder, Carlyle phone man, and of all the watches they had stood together and of how he was closer to them than he had ever been to anybody. He thought how he had lived so long on the ship, and with these men, that he had almost an affection for this ship, for this hybrid, rolling thing that wasn't even built very much like a ship, and that was something he would never, never have predicted. He thought what a good thing it was to have Carlyle back. Outwardly he seemed no different at all. But even inwardly, Barclay felt, he was pretty much all right. There had been only a very little talk about the fact that he had been away and for what reason, and this had taken place in Barclay's stateroom soon after the ship was underway. Barclay waited for Carlyle to bring it up, if he should want to, and he did so, in a very natural manner.

"Have you seen Coco, Mr. Barclay?" he asked.

"Yes, I have that, Red. She's back in her old place on Via Mazzini."

"How is she?"

"She's fine actually. She's very well, I think, and the baby too. I've seen them several times."

"Do they need anything? I mean food and everything?"

"No," Barclay said, and he knew Carlyle would feel better to know. "I've been giving them money. They don't need a thing."

"That's nice of you, Mr. Barclay."

"I don't have much to spend it on over here anyhow."

Carlyle waited a moment. "The first thing we get back day after tomorrow . . . The first thing, I'm going right over there."

"I'm glad to hear it, Red. She's had a rough time."

"Yes, that's it. Nobody has any right to blame her, no matter what in the world she'd done."

"No, they don't. And I think I'd better tell you, too, that I didn't think so at first. I was pretty angry with her, at first. To myself, I mean. I thought how she had messed things up so much. Then I realized what a stupid anger that was. She didn't mess things up."

"No, I'm the one who messed things up," the sailor said.

"No, I didn't mean that," Barclay said quietly. "You didn't mess things up, Red, and she didn't. The war messed things up."

Carlyle said: "It's strange but I feel about her exactly as I did before any of this happened. Except more so. I mean that, well, I suppose I love her if anything more than ever. Is that strange?"

"No, I don't think so. I think it's the way it would be if you really loved someone. I mean, you would love them more if you went through something like that."

"Yes, that's what I mean," Carlyle said, with a certain quiet excitement. "When I was sitting there in that room—after it was all over—it suddenly hit me that that court-martial was probably a lot harder for her than for me. Do you see what I mean?"

"It was hard enough for both of you. But yes . . . it couldn't have been harder on anyone than on her."

"Testifying to those things she had to testify to," the sailor said it. There was no embarrassment for him in saying it now. He seemed to say it as the successful analysis of a problem which had long bothered him. "I can't think of anything harder any woman would have to do. And I think she did it for me. Because . . ."

Carlyle faltered a few moments. Barclay said, "Let me tell you something I haven't told you, Red."

And the officer related briefly of looking for and finding Coco, and how she had been prepared to come forward as a witness, no matter what happened to her.

"She could easily have just run away," Barclay said. "Vanished, disappeared, faded out. She didn't. When she knew the jam you were in, she stayed, and wanted to stay, and testified. If a girl had done that for me I would imagine myself thinking that she must love me very much, very much indeed."

"I think she was about all I thought about up there. And then I knew something. I knew I was going to try every way I could find to get back over here as soon as I could, and that whenever I did I'd find her wherever she was and if she wasn't already, I'd marry her. That's the only thing I was really sure of."

"I remember the first time you told me that—I mean about marrying her. I couldn't see it, not a bit. One reason only—I didn't think you knew what the hell you were doing, didn't know what a load you were taking on, that it was the war . . . How little I knew."

"What do you have to do to get married over here—does somebody, some command I mean, have to approve it?"

"I imagine so. They do everything else. But I imagine it shouldn't be too much trouble. Would you like for me to look into it when we get back?"

"Yes, sir. I'd like it very much if you would."

"All right, I will—and I'll come to your wedding. Well, it's another watch."

"Mr. Barclay, do you believe in fate?"

Barclay, who had just stood up and was reaching for his kapok on a bulkhead hook, half-turned, waited a moment, "No, I don't think so. Yes and no, I guess. More no."

"I mean that I was meant to come back in order to marry her?"

"No, I don't believe in fate." Suddenly Barclay grinned a little. "But I believe in love."

Now in the conning tower he checked the time down through the voice tube into the wheelhouse, then ordered a course change.

"Right rudder to course two eight three."

"Right rudder to course two eight three," he heard Porterfield's long-familiar voice back up through the tube; felt the ship move slightly to starboard; heard Porterfield's voice again: "Course is two eight three, sir."

"Very well."

"I've never seen a prettier night, Mr. Barclay," Mason said alongside him. "Look at that moonlight out there! It gets fatter and lighter every time there's a full moon, doesn't it?"

"May, I guess," Barclay said.

"May moons were always big ones back home too," Abbot said.

"Home. That reminds me," Mason said. "I've got a bet down we'll get orders for home by the Fourth of July."

There was general laughter at this. And so the watch passed.

Barclay went below and found her standing in the shadows of Number 1 boat. Just beyond them the deck was pure white in the moonlight. No wind stirred across the flat, bright sea. They stood by the life line looking over toward the mainland.

"This is where I came in," she said. "Was it a long time ago, Matthew?"

"Yes. Two months. That's a long time in a war—they tell me."

"Well, they're wrong about that. It really seems much more short than long to me, now . . ."

She didn't finish it, but he did in his mind . . . Now that we're leaving, now that we're parting. It seems such a short time, now that you're leaving in seven hours.

"Matthew," she said in a moment. "You shouldn't be here. Colonel Jarvis is going to pop when he hears what you did to those orders of his. And maybe a great deal more than pop."

He smiled at the mildly lecturing tone in her voice. "Well, he won't hear. I'm not going to tell him and you're not going to tell him. Nobody else knows."

"No. But he might hear some way."

"Well, let's say he does. What can they do to me?"

"Quite a bit, I imagine, if they make up their mind to. And I don't even need the imagination to know what they've worked out for people who forge orders."

"They?"

"The military. The naval. All of this that runs our lives."

"Oh, that they."

"Besides that you shouldn't be here anyhow. That wound of yours. It really needed another week."

"Well, I'm here. And I feel better because I'm here."

She waited, then said it as a statement, not a question. "You did it because of me."

"Well, it gives us a few hours more."

"Yes. A few hours more." She repeated that. "A few hours more . . . Will you write?"

"Yes, I'll write."

"Do you have that APO number of mine somewhere you won't lose it?"

"Yes, it's in my billfold," and he patted his hip pocket.

"Be sure you don't lose it."

"I've got it memorized anyhow."

"I'll write if you write. I'll write even if you don't write. But I hope you'll write."

"I will."

"Please write, Matthew. I'll write and tell you where I am. If I'm in Rome will you try to get there to see me?"

"Yes, I'll try. Maybe I'll get to Rome," he said, knowing that however many times he might get within thirty-seven miles of Rome, the distance from Anzio, it would take a major miracle to get any leave to do those last thirty-seven miles, and he had seen no miracles, major or minor, floating around lately.

"We were going to see Rome together. You were going to take me to Rome."

"It might still happen," he said, and he knew it wouldn't.

"Wouldn't it be lovely if you got a liaison job to talk to the Italians there. We could go around Rome together. The way you speak Italian, you ought to be just right for a liaison job—is that what they call it?"

It sounded funny, the simple, dreamlike, hopelike, hopeless-like way she put this impossible thing.

"Yes, that would be lovely. I doubt if there's a great demand for Italian-speaking Navy jg's for liaison jobs in Rome. I imagine the line forms at the right for any job like that. The line probably ends with lieutenant commanders."

"Would they ever take some one off a ship for a job like that?"

He thought what a fancy this was, so much so as not even to be torturing.

"They'd be a pretty long time taking anyone off a ship for a job like that."

"Would you like it?" she went on with the fancy. It seemed even to make it easier if they could talk of an impossible thing like this. "Would you like it rather than the ship?"

He thought a moment about the beaten-up LST. "Well, I'll cross that bridge when . . . I doubt seriously if it'll be offered me."

"No, I suppose not."

Presently they could see the familiar artillery shelling on the mainland, but still only a little farther north than usual, even though Cassino had fallen.

"How far have they got over there?" she said.

"Not too far. About six miles, I saw earlier today. They're still hitting up against some very rough opposition."

When they had talked some more, she said suddenly: "Look! Up ahead!"

Off the starboard bow and far up ahead of them at Anzio they could now begin to see the light of shelling, of red flak and flares, of great intensity. As the ship moved farther north it, along with the activity on the Fifth Army front opposite them, seemed to fill the sky.

"My God, I've never seen so much, up there . . ."

The p.a. system from the conning tower cut him off.

"Now hear this," it said. "Now everybody hear this. This is the captain speaking. We have just intercepted a message in clear from Allied Headquarters. I think everybody would like to hear it. Here it is: 'Allied Forces have broken out of the Anzio beachhead and are driving the German enemy before them. Simultaneously, Fifth and Eighth Army forces are assaulting in force the Adolf Hitler Line north of Cassino. These two major offensives are aimed at a linkup for the march on Rome. The long-sought liberation of the Eternal City is at hand.'

"That's it," the captain said.

There was one moment of unbelieving silence. Then a ragged shout began to rise from the main deck, and more shouts, rising until they seemed to become as one mighty shout. And suddenly

there was running over the ship. Those who were awake began
running along passageways near the wardroom, in the crew's
quarters and in troops quarters awakening those who were asleep,
until soon nobody slept on the ship, and all but those on watch
crowded topside to share in the momentous news.

It was over an hour later before Barclay and she were alone
again. In him was an unmarred happiness that seemed the first
he had known in years and it was explicit: For the victory,
for the fact that she would now be put ashore on a beach, not
being shelled by the Germans but being broken out of. Even
any feeling over parting was wiped out by the news. It might
return later when she walked ashore but for now it was gone.
And he knew now he would be glad forever that he had taken
it upon himself to change those orders and had come along. Something seemed finished that ought to be finished. And then a
curious thing happened. He thought suddenly, in a way he could
not understand and that was like a mystery, that the finishing of
that somehow gave him breathing space to begin something
else . . .

For there, standing there by the life line forward of the starboard
boat, it came over him. Up ahead they could see the great shell-
lightning, and between it and the moonlight the night seemed as
day. All about them was a festive air. Around the corner of the
superstructure they could just see the edge of the crowd gathered
on Number 2 hatch, could hear the talking and laughter, and from
the fantail in the other direction could hear also the playing of
Carlyle's guitar and the singing to it, could hear that song "Shenandoah" he had come to love, could hear, as though faint and
faraway, those lines of loneliness

> Farewell, my love, I'm bound to leave you,
> Away, you rolling river . . .

but could hear and feel above them, too, and even in them, the
jubilation in which the ship was caught up. And everything,
everything seemed changed. Somehow the fact that the beachhead,
where so many had died, was exacting its last toll and that also,
as a consequence, the end of the war was that much nearer to

some day in the future, however indefinite, when it would be over entirely . . . Somehow this seemed to make all things possible; to give belief to the idea one could never really believe before, that things one wanted for a future might actually come to pass. It came over him that he must tell her, that it was the most urgent thing in the world to tell her, despite all his earlier resolves not to do so, that he could not let her go without telling her, and that this was his last chance for it, their last time alone. He looked at the light on the mainland, glanced over at the edge of the crowd on the hatch. He turned and looked down at her. He had reached out to touch her arm, had said "Sarah, I want to tell you something . . ." Then it happened.

Number 2 hatch, situated just forward of the superstructure, was the largest open space on the ship and the natural gathering place for any large number. It was there that Porterfield conducted his rather distinctive religious services when the ship was at sea. It was there that some of the crew rigged cots and slept on fair, warm nights. It was there, on it and immediately around it, that the majority of the passengers and those of the crew off watch had now gathered; there that Carlyle, sitting on the side of the hatch, had begun playing his guitar, with many crew and passengers surrounding him and singing. At the moment they had sung "Rock Island Line," "Bringing in the Sheaves," "The Old Time Religion," and "St. James Infirmary," and the blended voices of the sailors and the nurses fell softly over the ship and the moon-bright sea. Carlyle moved occasionally with his guitar from the crowd on Number 2 hatch to that on the fantail, the second favorite gathering place for any considerable number, and was there now playing before returning once more to Number 2 hatch. The crew and nurses on and around Number 2 hatch and on the fantail were gathered to share a common joy at great tidings, and nobody showed any intention of sleeping any more that night. The torpedo came in directly under Number 2 hatch.

The torpedo was received immediately under the waterline on

the port side and at an angle. Number 2 hatch exploded and disintegrated with great violence. Thus it was that the lives of a very considerable portion of both crew and nurses were extinguished in an instant, without their ever knowing it, many being blown apart and others being rocketed considerable distances off the ship and slammed down into the sea. All of this number certainly had an easy death, within the definition that that which comes and is over quickly is easy. It came, and was over, for them, in a fraction of a moment.

Of the remaining members of the crew and nurses alive in various parts of the ship, most were in three areas: wheelhouse and conning tower, engine room, and fantail. There were two fortunate circumstances here. One was that of the torpedo entering at an angle and high up so that while it gave the ship a list to port she showed no immediate signs of going down. The other was that the larger number of those left were on the fantail, and so a good deal aft of where the torpedo came in and furthermore, between them and Number 2 hatch was the ship's superstructure, which shielded them in some measure from the blast. Nevertheless several were thrown violently to the deck or against various ship attachments, the anchor windlass, stanchions, and the like, or struck by hurtling objects, as barrels flew through the air, ventilators were blown off, and everything seemed to come apart, inflicting injuries of varying degrees, but all there were alive. There was one other fortunate circumstance to the gathering on the fantail. It was near to the ship's two LCVPs, both of which were situated aft of Number 2 hatch and neither of which, in its davits, appeared seriously damaged.

The immediate problem, of course, was whether the ship could be saved or whether people should be put to the boats. Immediately on the detonation of the torpedo the crew members still alive and able started running to their battle stations a moment before the general alarm began sounding its repeated, staccato gongs. At the same time the nurses who were able began to seek out injured to attend to. A little over eleven and one-half minutes elapsed between the first and the second torpedoes.

In the auxiliary engine room, Rutledge, the machinist's mate, who loved machinery of any kind, whether jalopies or ship's diesel engines, and could never stop tinkering with it, was actually beneath the engine room deck level, on the very bottom of the ship, working on the pumps there, when the first torpedo came in. Floor plates shifted over him and the impact left him but half conscious but he managed to crawl through the remaining space. Then, however, his clothing caught on a loose floor plate and he hung there, injured, dazed, and trapped. Across the engine room from him Joel Chatham, the motor machinist's mate, was leaning down to pick up a wrench. The impact threw him violently against the bulkhead. The engine room began at once to flood, fuel lines fractured, and from them oil began to spray out. The lights went and Chatham saw a shower of sparks erupt across the compartment from him as the engine room switchboard short-circuited. Then, also across from him, he saw a tiny flame glow on the water and knew that the sparks had touched fire to the spraying fuel oil. He was not as panicked as he could have been by these observations for he knew that diesel oil burned slowly, particularly with lack of oxygen as here, and that the fire would take a time to cross the water and get him. Then, however, in its dim light, he noticed that the hatch near him was crushed in beyond all hope of getting up it. The water was beginning to rise steadily now in the engine room and its coverlet of flame very slowly to spread, some of the latter lying between him and the escape hatch on the opposite side of the engine room the condition of which he could not know. But it was that hatch or nothing and he knew that there was but one way to find out and knew also that he should do so at once before the flame spread farther. Ducking completely under the water he crawled and felt his way toward that hatch, actually for a space crawling under the flames, until he emerged beyond the fire. Two steps more and his hands were on the escape hatch ladder. Looking up the trunk he could see that it was free. He climbed up but as he reached the tank deck level, from the engine room from which he had just come he could faintly hear a voice. He started back down the hatch and descended again into the engine room.

The water was now thigh-deep and the fire on the water higher, though there were still areas of the engine room it had not reached. From one of these he heard a voice call weakly, he called back "Who's here?" and heard it say from that same space, "I'm over here." He lurched through the slowly rising water and found Rutledge, who had begun to recover consciousness, discovered he was trapped by a floor plate, and waited there watching the competition between the rising water and the slowly spreading fire as to which would get him. Some of the flames had reached him briefly but intensely, combing across his face and holding there, before being washed back by the incoming sea water and pinned there he had tried as best he could to keep splashing water on his face but Chatham, reaching him, could see in the flame's light that still his face was badly seared and he felt, looking into his eyes which seemed to be looking at nothing, that in all probability he had lost his sight. He unfastened him, murmured, "Rutledge it's me, Chatham. Put your arm around my shoulder and I'll help you along," and with him began wading and staggering over the buckled floor plates and around the patches of flame toward the escape hatch. It was extremely slow going and by the time they reached the ladder the water level was nearly to their shoulders. Chatham started his injured shipmate up the trunk, guiding and pushing him from below, then started up himself, virtually carrying the sailor before him. They were not far from the tank deck top of the ladder when the ship took a terrific jar—it was the second torpedo —and Rutledge tumbled back on Chatham.

Middleton, the radioman on watch, was thrown out of his chair to the deck of the radio shack. As he lay there, momentarily stunned, he realized the lights were gone. He got up, switched the transmitter to battery power, sat in front of it and waited, and very soon received a message from the conning tower to transmit, took it down, then bracing himself against the canted deck, broke radio silence and began sending out in clear the following: URGENT URGENT ALL SHIPS ALL SHIPS THIS IS LST 1826 REPEAT LOVE SUGAR TARE ONE EIGHT TWO SIX HAVE TAKEN TORPEDO POSITION 15 MILES EAST OF ZANNONE ISLAND SURVIVAL IN

DOUBT REQUEST DESTROYER FOR AID AND SUBMARINE SEARCH. He felt intensely alone in the small compartment which had not even a port and where he could measure the minute increase in the ship's list through the very soles of his shoes, the occasional barest sliding of the chair and the consequent necessity to brace himself a little more firmly. He was the only man on the ship who was obliged to merely sit and wait, sending out the message at intervals, instead of doing something of a more active character either on behalf of the ship herself, to try to save her, or on behalf of the wounded, and no one aboard could have had his nerves put to a stronger test. The fractional but relentlessly increasing cant of the ship gave him a sense of impending disaster, but he stayed in the chair with his walls around him. When abandon-ship was passed he got up, gathered up the ship's codes and started out on deck. He got through the deck door but no farther. Suddenly the whole ship seemed to collapse beneath him as he clutched the codes hard to his chest.

Porterfield, the helmsman, was on the fantail, where he was slammed to the deck. He got up, found himself apparently without appreciable injury, and beheld a strange sight. It looked as though raindrops of fire were coming down. It took him a moment to realize that they must be drops of diesel oil spurting out and catching fire in the forward part of the ship, and some of it arching over onto the fantail. He saw a nurse whose clothing had caught fire. He rushed up to her and started beating out the flames. He had done so, turned, saw another nurse also burning and did the same thing successfully with her. Turning to see what else there was to do he slipped on something wet on the deck and came up covered with fuel oil and blood. He saw yet a third nurse with only a sleeve of her field clothes burning, ran up to her, beat this out, but in the process the flame jumped off the nurse and ignited the oil on Porterfield's own clothing. He fell on the deck. He started to get up, slipped on the fuel oil and in a flash of understanding was aware that he was very near the edge of the listing deck, reached out to grab something, found his burned hands unable to do so, and slid over the side. He came up very near an overturned life raft which had been flung off the ship by the torpedo blast. He tried to turn the raft over to get into and get to the paddles strapped underneath but again his hands were too burned to make any purchase on the raft. He felt his whole body in that unmeasured pain of burned flesh bathed in salt water. He tried once more to pull the life raft over. His hands would not do it, and they slowly slipped off it, leaving slivers of flesh behind on the bottom of the raft, and the helmsman slid back, unconscious, onto the sea.

Wiley, the carpenter's mate, was on bow lookout. The first torpedo flung him against the gun shielding. He got up, cut slightly around the head. He first tried the phone to the bridge. It was dead. He looked amidships and could see that the ship was completely stove in there. He realized that he was marooned on a steel island-perch, the sea immediately before him in one direction and in the other the huge burning and impassable section of the ship. He stood there unable to do a single thing except watch and unable to receive any commands at all. He waited, and here on the furthest bow point of the ship he could feel the list very heavily. He had to brace himself and hold onto the gun shielding to keep from going over. He decided finally that the best thing for him to do was to go over the side, swim aft and past the destroyed and burning part of the ship, and try to get back aboard on the after end, where he would both be safer and maybe could do something in whatever fight was going on there to save the ship or to attend the wounded. Then another incentive added itself to this list: The fire was now beginning to move toward him. He let himself over the side and started stroking toward the after end. He gave a wide berth midships—the heat from here was very great—and swam around pieces of wreckage. Suddenly he thought he heard a strange, unearthly noise and looking over his shoulder had a part of a moment to guess and never be sure of such a thing, his eyes just looking upon the small flashing white wake in this still sea, that he and his slight human body were in the very path of a second torpedo rushing toward the ship.

Ensign Horner had been following Carlyle as he moved from fantail to Number 2 hatch and back again, in order to hear all of the guitar music, of which he was enormously fond. Carlyle had gone on to the fantail a couple of minutes before and Horner lingered a moment talking with a nurse then started aft himself. He had gone but a few steps and could just hear the strains of the music from aft when a considerable piece of metal tore through his leg, taking it off cleanly, and draping him over the life line. Mason, the cook, was going the exactly opposite direction, from fantail to Number 2 hatch. The two men could have been no more than ten feet apart. Mason was caught by the blast, struggled for a moment to keep from being thrown overboard, righted himself, saw Horner, and rushed forward to pull him back. He got the officer in his arms, light because of the lost leg, and felt the blood spurting over him from where the leg had been. He felt something hit him on the side of the head. He felt stunned momentarily, came back to consciousness to find that the officer had slid out of his arms and was going overboard, saw him fall into the sea a moment before he could reach him. He dived in after him, clutched at the body, felt unconsciousness returning from whatever the blow was. He tried desperately to hold onto the wounded body. He knew, as the last thing he was to know, that he was not doing so.

Latimer, the pharmacist's mate, had been starting forward from the fantail, to get some coffee. The torpedo blast knocked him down and he lost consciousness. It came back in only a few moments but he could see nothing and thought he had been made blind. Kneeling, he put his fingers gently to his eyes and brought them down, held his fingers close up and was able to see a wet smear, to feel the stickiness and its consistency, and knew that he was not blind but only cut about the head. He got up and started running below for his medical supplies. He got his kit, ran back topside, and, moving through the dark smoke, saw around him everywhere, the decks covered with them, the wounded, the dying and the dead. Kneeling on the deck he crawled from one to the other, determining which, and if he or she were dead moving immediately on. To those who had been severely burned he gave mainly morphine injections. He worked as a man possessed, never standing up but crawling on his knees from one to the next to save time, giving the injections, applying a tourniquet to stop the flow of blood, stopping able persons as they walked by to stay and release and reapply and release the tourniquet, as he hurried on on his knees to the next person. He was giving a morphine injection to a nurse whose face seemed almost entirely burned away and was just beginning to worry about his morphine supply when the second torpedo, which was for him too, came in not far from where he knelt leaning over to push the pain-killing needle into her arm.

Plimpton, the gunner's mate, was serving as watch boatswain and he and Lieutenant (jg) Fairchild, the gunnery officer, who was officer of the deck, were in the conning tower, when a single, very large slice of metal, which was actually part of the ship, flew with great velocity across it, the same piece decapitating Plimpton and almost tearing Fairchild's arm off. Holding the arm to him, Fairchild just managed to sound the general alarm before he fell unconscious and heavily bleeding over the gyro repeater. Polk, the watch recorder, was jarred heavily back against the shielding and came to his senses in time to catch Fairchild's body caroming off the gyro. Looking forward he could see the immense hole where Number 2 hatch had been. Looking down he could see a body without a head and guessed this must be Plimpton. Turning he ran down a ladder, and aft to his battle station as loader on the stern 40-millimeter Bofors, arriving there about the same time as Abbot, whose GQ station was pointer on the same gun. Polk stepped up on the mount and picked up a clip of am-munition to load the loader but as he started to put it in, the ammunition would not go down. He removed the clip and felt inside the loader with his hand and found that the pawls were fractured so that the gun would not take ammunition. Polk got Abbot to accompany him with a stretcher back up to the conning tower, where they put Fairchild on it, folding his arm, hanging only by strings of flesh, across his chest, and carried him down to the wardroom, which was being used as a dressing station and where in the glare of battle lamps the deck ran red now with the blood of the surviving nurses and crew. They had to squeeze around to find a space large enough among them for the stretcher, they placed it down, then ran back out. The battle lamps told them that the torpedo must have taken out the auxiliary engine room and with it all power. Along the port life line they bumped into the captain, who was telling off fire-fighting and damage-control parties, told him about the gun, and were told to join the stretcher working party. They started carrying people and parts of people into the reddened wardroom, which looked terribly to Polk now like some sort of slaughterhouse and where he could see nurses working on those who still lived. So crowded was the wardroom that some bodies were propped up against the bulkhead to save deck space and Polk would have hated to have to try to identify some of them. He and Abbot were carrying a nurse in and did not know whether she was dead or living—only that both hands were chopped off as if by some cleaver—and had just stepped with her into the wardroom when the second torpedo arrived, taking the wardroom with it.

Lieutenant (jg) Abernethy, the engineering officer, had just started on deck from his stateroom, was pitched head first against the metal side of his bunk, flung back and crumpled unconscious on the deck. When in a few minutes he regained consciousness he staggered out on deck, saw the ship in flames and listing to port, quite considerably by this time. He immediately turned back in and started below to the auxiliary engine room with the idea of doing the one thing there was to do, which was to trim the ship—put water into the starboard ballast tanks in an attempt to give her an even keel and try to prevent capsizing. On the tank deck he saw that one hatch was twisted beyond any possibility of getting down it and ran over to the other one. He was preparing to lower himself down the trunk when he observed in the light of what appeared to be considerable flames below what as best as he could make out was one man being pushed up it by another. He lowered himself quickly and reached out a hand to help pull up the injured man. The man's own hand not being held out in return he made a guess that something must be wrong with his eyes and got down yet another couple of rungs to where he could help him in any case. He was just reaching out his hand for the shoulder of the injured man when a tremendous convulsion seized the space and sent the three men hurtling down the trunk into a cauldron of fire and sea water.

The first torpedo slammed Barclay back against the superstructure and instinctively he reached out to place himself over the nurse. They both were punched down the side of the superstructure to the deck, both got up. He felt the ship shuddering uncontrollably under him. He held the nurse by the shoulders. "Are you hurt?" "No." He ripped off his kapok jacket, which he was still wearing from his watch, put it on her and quickly tied the strings. "Go back to the fantail," he said, pushing her a little. "You'll be needed there." She started aft to help with the wounded and Barclay had started up to the conning tower when he met the captain along the starboard life line. Together, through the considerable smoke rolling over the ship, the two officers felt their way forward toward Number 2 hatch with the idea of getting some kind of estimate of the damage and a determination of what effort could be made to save the ship. They came up to the edge of the great gaping wound and looked down into the abyss which was now one massive, smoking coffin.

"I'll go below and try for a look at the auxiliary engine room," Barclay said.

Both officers knew from the lack of power that the auxiliary engine room was almost certainly gone and that if so it would be impossible to trim the ship by ballasting. Both knew, too, that it would be best to make absolutely certain of this. The captain agreed and the two men started aft again, moving now along the port side, toward a point where Barclay would go below. It was going back that they noticed something which conveyed to them deadly news. It was that walking they both were leaning at a decidedly greater angle to port than had been true going forward and even having to hold occasionally to any available object to keep from sliding on the deck toward the side. In the short space of their going forward, trying to survey the damage, and coming back, the list had increased dangerously. The captain reached his hand over onto Barclay's shoulder, held him there, and said the thing Barclay had felt simultaneously.

"Matthew, unless we get those boats away soon we may never get them away if this list continues. We can't take that chance and we can always take everybody back aboard. I want you to lower both boats to the rail, start loading the nurses into the port boat and stand by to load the crew. I'm certain about the auxiliary engine room but anyhow I'll find someone else to check it or do it myself."

"Yes, sir . . ." Barclay had just started to turn away. "Look! There's the sub!"

They stood fixed there and saw it, a low gray shape in the distance. They saw a gun-flash from her, heard the whine of a shell and presently saw the shell hit water about a hundred yards over and beyond the ship. The captain and Barclay stood a moment looking toward the gray, menacing shape of the submarine, just sitting there immune and motionless. No more shells came from her. They could each read what was going on in the German captain's mind as much as if he had blinkered it across the water in detail to them. All of this flashed through their minds in a matter of seconds, and without a word said. The captain spoke:

"Yes, I see. Don't you see, Barclay?"

"Yes, I do, Captain."

"I'm not issuing the order yet. Something might just get here. We might just stay up. We . . . But do as I said before. Make all preparations to abandon ship. Get the nurses and wounded crew into the boats."

"Yes, sir."

Barclay made his way aft as quickly as he could through the twisted metal, the continual tendency to slide overboard now, and having to step over two bodies about ten feet apart and both lying face down on the deck and motionless, one a nurse and one a crew member. He did not stop to see who they were but made his way to the fantail. The first man he saw there was Nelson.

"Nelson, the captain wants us to get the nurses and wounded

crew into the port boat. See that both boats are lowered to the rail."

He did not ask a single question but turned immediately and hurried up to the boat deck and let one then the other boat down. Barclay felt his way through smoke and as he came on crew members and nurses told them what they were to do. The sailors began leading the nurses through the swirling, choking smoke to the port boat and starting them into it, then returning to find other nurses to lead and put aboard.

Barclay had no idea how long they had been doing this, and was conscious chiefly of the ship's growing list, but they had got, he felt, most of the nurses aboard when he saw the captain's figure emerge grayly through the smoke. He spoke quietly and quickly, but every sentence told it.

"Matthew, we've got uncontrollable flooding. The auxiliary engine room is gone. We have internal flooding in the main storeroom and in seven voids, big holes everywhere—even where compartments are not flooded bulkheads are ruptured and they're going soon. We've lost any water-tight integrity. We've got about a 21-degree list now. The ship won't make it." He repeated this. "The ship won't make it. I don't know what that son-of-a-bitch out there is going to do—I could make a pretty good guess—but . . . We're abandoning ship. Let's take one more look."

The two officers worked fast, searching their way through the smoke and saying quietly, "Abandon ship," and "We're abandoning ship." One nurse or man after the other was helped or lifted over into the boat until it was full beyond its normal capacity. Barclay had not seen Sarah again. Then through the smoke, he came on her kneeling on the deck and helping somebody. He leaned down and saw who it was.

"Can you walk, Red?"

"I think so," Carlyle said. "It's just my belly. Something's there . . ."

Barclay reached down and felt a sticky wet mass against Carlyle's groin. He and Sarah helped him to his feet, pulled him to the boat, his feet dragging along the deck, and with Nelson's help got him into it. Barclay spoke to the nurse.

"Get in there," he said.

"No."

"Nelson," Barclay said. "Help me here."

They each took the nurse by the elbow and lifted her over the gunwale and into the boat.

"Now," the captain said to Barclay. "I want you to lower the boat and then get in yourself and get it away from the ship before she turns over on it. I want you in that boat, do you understand that clearly? Most—maybe all—we've got left is in it. I'm going to get the wardroom wounded into the other boat if I can get it launched. Get this one away, then get in yourself, Matthew, is that clear?" He waited a moment then said, "Good-bye, Matthew. God bless you."

"Goodbye, Captain."

And he turned and was gone forward into the billows of black smoke. Beyond, Barclay could make out that the fire was increasing, amidships huge flames, wrapped in pillars of smoke, reaching toward the sky and on the oil-covered decks the fire hurrying aft and toward them. Racing up the ladder to the boat deck he braced himself against the canted deck, and bent over the boat winch. He tried to lift the brake and found to his horror that it was jammed. He stepped over to the wheelhouse bulkhead, grabbed the fire ax which hung there, stepped back to the boat winch, put his foot on the two davit cables, holding them flush to the deck, and started hacking at them. They broke and the boat dropped from its davits. Luckily it was already near the water from the list and he quickly heard it hit with a thud against the sea. Rushing back down to the main deck he leaned over and yelled down.

"Nelson! Nelson!"

"Yes, sir?" he heard Nelson's voice yell up in the darkness of the smoke.

"Cast off, Nelson!"

"Aren't you coming, sir?"

"Didn't you hear me, goddamnit?" he yelled back down. "Cast off! Get that boat away from here."

"Yes, sir."

He heard the boat's engine catch. He had just turned to follow the captain forward where he had disappeared in the smoke when he felt a violent convulsion under him. It was as if the ship were being lifted entirely off the surface of the sea and then slammed down on it with great force. Then he felt himself pitching directly forward as the ship herself seemed to come down on the boat.

A little over eleven and one-half minutes elapsed between the first and the second torpedoes . . . Standing there, Barclay and the captain had put themselves into the mind of the German submarine commander and read their same guess, imagined him, wanting if possible to save perhaps a final torpedo for additional tonnage before returning home, waiting around to see if one would do the job, and not even certain, when he finally sent the second on its way, that one wouldn't have, but judging it unwise to wait around any longer for the arrival of enemy destroyers, knowing as well as the LST herself knew that a distress signal had been sent—indeed, having picked it up. They could read and guess that on intercepting this signal, the German submarine had surfaced beyond what it knew to be the range of the ship's 40-millimeter guns. Then her commander had ordered one four-inch shell to be fired over the ship as a test of any powers of retaliation; the shell lofting over and landing in the water; the submarine commander waiting, receiving no responding fire, and then just sitting there, entirely immune, watching the listing, helpless ship carefully through binoculars as she burned steadily against the night sky. The German commander standing there, thinking of the distress message, thinking of the destroyers which had surely now received it and were enroute to this scene, thinking how he did not know whether they were five or fifty miles away, deciding not to try to sink the LST with gunfire which would give any destroyer even a distance off a pinpoint position, giving the ship perhaps four, perhaps five minutes to go down; when these minutes had gone by, observing her again through binoculars; giving the order for the submarine's last torpedo to be fired from surface; at this distance, and the object still and fixed, the firing platform equally motionless in the still water, at the easiest target imaginable, so easy he would be able to put it on the exact square yard on the ship he chose, a submariner's very dream of a shot; presently the long, slender missile leapt gracefully out of the bow of the submarine and streaked forward in the moonlight; observing it make contact with the ship at precisely the mid-point of her superstructure as desired; then, finally—with a shout aboard that was like an echo of the earlier one on the LST—ordering his boat to dive and, under the water, directing her underway toward the mouth of the Mediterranean, toward Gibraltar, toward home.

He felt himself fighting upward through great masses of water and felt intense pressure on his lungs as if he would never get through it. Not until he burst surface and took in a great gasp of air did he realized he was holding tightly to a rather large piece of board, perhaps three by five feet. The scene rushed in upon his senses. He could see the ship about a hundred feet beyond him and could even feel the heat from the huge flames that appeared now to be consuming her. They made a very great light and he could see the ship listing heavily and immediately knew that she had taken a second torpedo. Instinctively, for a moment he looked around as if expecting to see the submarine. Then something communicated itself up to him from his fingers clutching the board to tell him that probably what happened was that the second hit had catapulted him directly overboard on top of the load of nurses and crew, that the boat must have been torn apart by the torpedo's blast, and that this board was part of it. If so, some of its occupants must be nearby. He started at once looking around him in the water. He could see no one but he could begin to hear weak cries. Letting go the board he started to swim. He saw a form in a kapok jacket, grabbed for it, saw that it was a nurse, and in the flamelight from the ship saw that she was dead. Then the cries came again, this time seeming fainter but whether because he was swimming in the wrong direction or because whoever was making the cries was getting weaker he did not know. He changed direction slightly and struck out swimming again. Almost immediately his arm was encircling another body, also in a kapok jacket. It was some member of the crew but his destroyed face told him that he also was dead and kept secret his identity. He swam away. He proceeded on this grim pilgrimage through some six or eight persons, or once-persons. He examined each for any signs of life. He turned over the shapes in their kapoks, some the faces of ship's company and some of American girls, and some no one could have told which. He came at one point on a shape and looked into the face of his captain. He held his dead body in his arms for a moment and then passed on. He proceeded, finding, occasionally, the faces of the men he had spent the last two years of his life with . . . He saw the face of Ensign Horner, of Latimer, and finally of Porterfield. He heard the cries again, a little louder, and this time unmistakably a girl's voice, and he swam very hard. Then he heard them very near, thrust his arms forward, and was holding a shape. Not until she spoke did he know.

"Sarah? Are you all right?"

She rested gasping in his arms. "Yes, I'm all right, Matthew. All right. I was holding onto something but it got away . . ."

"Where's your kapok?"

"I put it on one of the men, one of the wounded men in the boat. He was very badly wounded, Matthew. Carlyle is around here. I was right by him in the boat. He must be around here."

He heard now other cries, quite near, and pulling her with him swam toward them. They came again through the night, very close now, and swimming backward he hit into him. He swirled around, holding the nurse, saw that it was Carlyle and reached out his free arm for him and bore him up.

"Red, it's me, Barclay. Are you okay?"

"I think I'm all right . . . There's something . . . my belly . . . I'm all right I think."

His voice was weak. Barclay hung there in the water holding one in each arm, his feet working steadily to keep them up.

"Red, can you swim at all?"

"I don't think so, Mr. Barclay . . . I tried. But I'm all right. I just can't seem to move. I'm . . ."

"Rest a moment," Barclay said gently.

Now, pedaling there in the water, he tried very realistically to assess their situation and chances. The radio shack would easily have got off a distress signal between the two torpedoes and there would be American or British ships coming there, he knew of a certainty they would be on their way under flank speed for them this very moment, so that it was a question of whether he could preserve their lives until they arrived. He examined then in his mind the situation of the two persons in his arms. She was unhurt but did not know how to swim and if he let her go she would quickly go down. Carlyle was wounded apparently in such a way that he could not swim. He might be able to stay up for a few moments alone, but only a few. Then he assessed himself and his own strength. He was a very strong swimmer but he could feel the pull on his arms. One he figured he could hold for quite a long while, very possibly long enough for a ship to get there. Furthermore, with one he could pull that one along in the water and look for something for them to hang onto, something broken loose from the ship by the blast. But holding them both, he could not move. He kept trying to think around the fact he knew was there, tried not to think what this fact meant but he knew it was there and that he would have to think about it, and now. If he tried to hold them both he would lose them both. He knew that within a very few minutes he would have to let one or the other of them go.

His mind came back from the choice and he thought there in the sea how he did not want it. He did not want to have to decide which of these two should live and which should die. Even knowing already what the answer would be, it seemed too much to ask of anyone and he tried again to think around it somehow. He could not. Then, as if he was reading both his thoughts and the nature of the decision that was upon him, he heard Carlyle's voice.

"Mr. Barclay, I think I can swim to something. Anyhow whatever's happened to me, I think it's very bad . . . I'm going to get it anyhow, Mr. Barclay. Let me go."

The very contradiction in the two ideas told Barclay that

Carlyle was not speaking the truth, that he was only assessing the decision as he knew he, Barclay, must be doing.

"Rest quiet a moment, Red. Let me think and figure out something . . ."

Then he heard the nurse speaking. "Matthew, he's hurt but not very badly. I saw him in the boat and he can make it. Let me try to get to something, Matthew. Let go of me and let me try to get to something."

He thought how she would not get a half dozen strokes away, and even a moment's irritation flashed through him at their unasked-for selflessness, which was of no help at all to him or the situation.

"Let me go!" she said more urgently.

"Be quiet," he said, almost sharply. "Let me think. Be quiet and rest a few moments."

He could feel the muscles in his arms stiffening, feel the strength being sucked very slowly but very steadily away. He knew he could wait very little longer. Wait, and he would lose them both.

At that moment he saw floating just beyond them a large piece of wood. It seemed to be coming straight on them.

"Grab it!" he said quickly to the nurse. "The board there. Grab it, Sarah!"

She turned and saw it even as it almost hit her, her arms reached out for it, his arm half-lifting her up over it. In a moment she was clinging to it. And he saw, with a feeling of great elation, that it was bearing her up. Holding hard to Carlyle, he steadied the piece of wreckage with his now free left arm and it rested gently in the water beside them. He tried to examine it and saw that it was a considerable piece of board, perhaps three feet wide and seven long and fairly thick—it looked like a mess table top. In a strong sea it undoubtedly would have gone under but in this gentle one it bobbed alongside them like a raft.

"Sarah," he said, "see if you can climb on it."

With her pulling herself and him pushing she got up on it. The board seemed to give very little in the water and it bore her up. She lay on it near to him. It did not sink.

"Sarah," he said, "here's what we're going to do. I'm going

to get Carlyle up on there. It may not hold both of you. It may start sinking. If it does when I have him up there, jump off immediately and I'll hold you. Is that clear?"

"Yes, clear," she said. "I'll help you pull him up."

This time, with her pulling Carlyle and Barclay pushing they got him over the edge and onto the little raft. Immediately it started going down.

"Jump!" he said. But she was already off and he was holding her. Now the board came back up and floated gently and Barclay held the nurse with one arm and with his free hand again steadied the raft as Carlyle lay prone and motionless on it. It would hold one, no more. In any event he felt enormously better. He knew he had gained a great amount of time.

"Sarah, listen to me. When I say to, I want you to try holding onto the board. I think it'll hold you up that way. If it will I'm going to leave you here for a few minutes and swim around and see if I can find something to hold us all up. Do you understand?"

"Yes, I understand," she said. It came through him how calm and coping she was and he was very grateful for that, too.

"All right," he said. "Try it now."

While he held her she reached her hands onto the raft, close to Carlyle's body. It gave only a little in the water. He let his hands go from her but stood ready to grab her. The raft did not give. He waited perhaps two minutes while she held. There was no change.

"Good," he said. "It'll hold you up. Stay right there. I'm going to have a look around. I'll be back in about five minutes. Are you all right?"

"Fine. I'm fine."

He started swimming easily away, the movement feeling actually good to his stiffened arm muscles and loosening them. Beyond, perhaps two hundred feet away, he could see the ship burning dully now. He swam in the direction of the ship, figuring that anything thrown clear that might serve to hold them up would be near her. He swam, passing around an occasional floating body, various pieces of wreckage and debris, including once a mattress floating on the water, but seeing nothing that would serve the purpose. He kept swimming on a bearing for the burning vessel, using a breaststroke to keep his head up and his eyes moving in a wide arc. He was coming near the ship. Right now he was grateful for the fire, for it lighted his search area. Then, and he was perhaps no more than a hundred feet from the ship, his vision caught an object to his left and forward, and, something starting up in him, he abandoned the breaststroke and started swimming with a powerful crawl toward it. As he got near he saw that it was what he thought it was. He felt a leap of joy in him, and then his hands were holding to its side.

It was a ship's life raft, apparently undamaged. The raft, of which the ship carried eight, was a balsa-wood oval, eight feet long, five feet across, with a latticework bottom and it would hold the three of them and more. He ran his hands around inside it and found that the paddles were still strapped on it, intact. He pulled himself over the side.

Now he began paddling back toward the nurse and Carlyle in the water. The life raft was not designed to move fast but he stroked hard and it got along. Once it bumped against something and stopped. He paddled around whatever the object was and on. Suddenly he heard a loud explosion behind him, shaking the raft. He looked back and was startled to see that the ship was much closer than he had thought it was when he was in the water, and realized how easy it was to misjudge distance from there, and realized also that he must have been making much less headway in the raft than he thought he was making with the hard strokes he was using. He knew that something considerable had gone off there, ammunition it was most likely. Then another explosion came, this time shaking the raft quite strongly. Not stopping paddling he looked over his shoulder and saw that the ship was burning much more furiously and crackling now against the sky, and he could feel the heat from the ship strongly on him. Then he saw with true fear that she was listing very heavily and in his direction, and she seemed now a very great deal closer than he had thought her, though it may have been the great flame and the fact of the increasing list being toward him. He knew from the degree of the list that she would turn over at any moment now. For a moment he considered jumping off the raft and swimming away, and he knew that would be a far safer course. Then he thought of Sarah and of Carlyle and knew there was no hope without the raft he was riding. He paddled with all his strength to get away both from the downdraft he knew the ship would make when it went over and from any burning wreckage it might fling toward him. Then he heard a deafening explosion which sounded as if it came from almost immediately beneath him and felt himself thrown out of the raft.

He was under water, but came up quickly. Beyond in the ship's light he saw, very near him, the shape of the raft. His right arm made a crawl stroke toward it but as he started to bring his left arm forward a pain so savage that it almost took away consciousness stopped him in the water. He tried very gently to move the left arm and felt again a stabbing pain through it and down through his entire left side. He brought his right hand around and very gingerly felt along his left arm. He felt an area of torn flesh and blood and a pain unbearable to the touch. He felt his left side. It was also soft and blood-wet but not quite so painful. Using only a kick and his right arm he pushed toward the raft. He threw his arm over the side, leaned over, and saw that the bottom had been blown out of the raft and the side torn away and dissolving under his hand even as he held it. He looked and saw the flames on the ship searching high toward the sky and the moon and the great shape of the ship beginning to heel over. Then the whole of the ship was turning toward him, he could see its deck as a wall. He saw the sea grasp out for the flames and the ship and presently, in a noise that was like some death rattle of the sea, saw it claim both. And even as silence came upon the sea he had struck swimming with all his strength away from the dead ship.

Something from the explosion, he thought. Something from the explosion, or he may have rammed against something when he was thrown off the float. It certainly made no difference what or which and he concentrated only on proceeding back to where he had left the two of them. He did not have the flamelight from the ship now but knew it could not be far. Then very quickly he was upon them.

He saw fearfully that the board which had been supporting Carlyle was gone, blown away apparently by the blasts from the ship. But it had served some little purpose at least. A little strength must have returned to Carlyle while he lay on the board, for he was holding the nurse in the water, bearing her up. Strength or will, or both, for Barclay could make out that he was doing so with his last measure. He grabbed for the nurse with his good arm, tried bringing his left arm up against the pain and this time it came up enough for him to anchor it around Carlyle and even give him a little support in staying up, so that the three again bobbed a moment in the water. And now, holding them both and feeling his own pain, he felt strength going terribly from him. He heard Carlyle's voice.

"Have you got her, Mr. Barclay?"

"Yes. I have her, Red."

"I wanted to hold her until you got here . . . I hope you make it . . ."

"Red," Barclay said. "Red." Then the sailor was gone under the surface and down into the sea.

He stayed there in the water holding her, and neither saying anything. The thought must have passed quickly, the thought of any past whatsoever, even that of a minute ago, for he knew he must give what he had to the present, and he knew that now it was desperate. A massive pain was beginning to move through his left arm and all down through his left side and when he tried in the water to elevate the arm he could not. There, bobbing gently in the water, he examined once more their condition, the condition now of two rather than three of them. He knew he was badly wounded and he could feel blood flowing out of his side into the sea. He would estimate that if they were picked up before long he might make it. Or if they found something to get into they might make it. He might not, either, but there would be a chance, and she would. But he felt the time allotted him for this was very short. He felt continually weaker and he tried to guess how long he could survive holding her in the water . . . Five minutes, ten minutes, a quarter hour. That was the amount of time now. Not much longer surely. If he could get her to some kind of safety before then. Beyond that he did not believe that he would have the strength even to help her up on anything.

Having decided that, he then considered more specifically the situation of the nurse. She was still unharmed, apparently. Shaken up but unharmed. Since she could not swim, the problem was very explicit with her. It was to get her into a kapok jacket. It was as simple as that. In a kapok, she could stay up in this kind of smooth sea for hours, and there would be ships here by then. Without a kapok she would go immediately after he did. He rejected this. He would like to save someone out of this, he was determined to do so, and he would like for it to be her. Then it came to him that there were kapoks all around them, floating bodies in them, and if somehow they could get one of them off one of those that would do it. If he had not been badly wounded, he felt confident he could do it. What he would do would be to turn her around, her back to his front, and while he held her have her untie the jacket, get it off, and then get her into it. That would be an operation even if he were unhurt but he believed a determined man could accomplish it. But there was no point in thinking what they could do if he were unhurt. Then what were the chances of accomplishing it now? Well, there was a risk, he figured, of losing her altogether. If while she was facing the dead body and untieing the kapok jacket now useless to it, he should black out even for a moment, she would be away from him, she would go under, and he would never get her back. But that was a risk he would have to take. Furthermore, he had better take it very soon. The longer he waited, the less chance he would have of bearing her up while she accomplished the untieing, with blood and strength going from him. He made up his mind. They would try it now.

"Sarah," he said.

"Yes, Matthew?"

"Listen very carefully to me. Here's what I want us to do . . ."

And he explained it quickly to her. She said nothing for a moment. Then she said: "Yes. Let's try it."

"Good. I'll pull you along and you look out for somebody."

He started back-pedaling slowly and gently with her. Even this was very painful now and he asked once or twice, "See anything? Anybody?"

"No," she said.

It seemed an age but finally she said, "Here's somebody, Matthew."

He stopped pedaling. "Don't look to see who it is."

"No, I won't. I just want to make sure."

"Yes, do that. But do it quickly and don't look at him."

He felt her arms moving and she said then, "He is, Matthew."

"Now untie the strings across his chest," he said.

He could feel her hands moving. Once she almost slipped away from him and his arm tightened quickly around her. But finally, with great relief, he heard her say, "They're untied now, Matthew."

"Start working the kapok jacket off him."

This took even longer and he felt he could hold her this way very, very little longer. Then he heard her, "I've got the jacket, Matthew. It's free."

"Turn around and face me. Very easy now. Hold tight to the jacket."

She turned around in the water facing him, his arm hard around her. The body had sunk; he felt grateful for that and he could see the kapok floating on the water where she held it.

"Put your arms around my neck," he said. "Leave my arm . . . leave my arms free to help you into the jacket."

Her arms went around his neck. "Hold very tight now."

With his right arm he got the jacket around in back of her. He tried again to move his left arm up. It wouldn't move. He kept bringing the jacket around with his right arm.

"Now take your left arm away," he said, "and see if you can put it through the jacket."

It was excruciatingly slow. It was difficult to find the arm hole but finally, and he felt a major triumph, she got one arm through it.

"Rest a minute. Then the other arm."

She held to him again, around his neck, then took her right arm away and tried for the other arm hole. On that side he could not guide the jacket with his hand. She tried and tried again and still again.

"I can't reach it," she said. "I can't find it . . . Matthew, why don't you try bringing your left arm up. That way we might do it."

"Let's try it again."

They did. She could not find the arm hole. She said: "Matthew, you're hurt. Tell me, what is it, where is it? Something's wrong with your left arm, isn't it?"

"Let's try it again."

They tried again. She could not make it. They rested again, both gasping from the great labor of it.

"Matthew, I'll never do it," she said.

"Just once more," he said.

They tried once again. It wouldn't go.

"Rest a while," he said.

They bobbed in the water, not using strength even to talk. And now the pain stilled him for a while. He began to concentrate on remembering back and how he had reached out to touch her arm there on the ship and tell her something it had suddenly become, in his mind, very urgent for him to tell her and for her to know, had been about to tell her when it happened. He kept trying to remember what it was, for he would like to do this while there was time. It was urgent, terribly urgent, and he must remember and tell her, that was the only thing he wanted any longer to do. He would have liked to get her in that jacket and let himself go and give her some chance against the sea but he knew now it would never happen. The only thing remaining was to tell her. If only he could remember what it was that he was going to tell this girl, this unusual girl, who had grace and had beauty. The pain was very great now and he prayed for a little time or for some numbing of the pain, the time so he could tell her and the numbing so he could get through it without blacking away. They were standing there near the moonlight on the decks and going to Anzio . . . And then he knew. He had wanted to tell her this, let us share it together, let us share everything from this time on together. Now he said the word, the phrase to her, and she seemed to know, for she held to him. He heard her murmur two words, "Yes, share."

He said, "I want you to stay alive. It's a waste for you not to stay alive . . ."

"Matthew, I'm where I want to be. I'm staying where I want to stay. Rest quiet. Rest quiet, my dear."

He held her but he knew he could hold her very little longer. Sweet God, if he could only bear the pain. Almost nothing of him was left any more, he thought. Just enough left to hold her for a few minutes more, then nothing would be left at all. Nothing of what had been that boy, or that young man, and already he felt as if he were looking back down long years on his youth which was but a couple years ago, looking at that young man, who had gone to that small college which he loved, loved what he learned there, and been awakened, headed where he did not know, deciding on the law which might lead him somewhere he wanted to go, and so he had had the year at Yale before the war came, and he had lived that year and liked that place and if he had greed it was a greed for knowledge, all that knowledge stretching away before him. He thought of his father and his goodness. He thought of the ship and all his time on her and the men he had known and he thought of Carlyle, and he thought how Carlyle was gone, the ship gone, and how many of ship's company he didn't know and only the two of them left alone in the sea. Then he was remembering saying something, recently he believed though it seemed a very long time ago, to Carlyle, saying, "I believe in love. I don't believe in fate." And the first, anyhow, was true.

"I love you," he could hear his own voice. "I've loved you for quite a while now."

"I love you. I have from the beginning."

He wished one of them would still be here. He wished that she could. He wished one would be around to see it and take part in it. Even if not to share. Or perhaps it was better to share even the shortest of times. They would have shared a few minutes or seconds of their lives together, and he was very grateful he had stayed around long enough to say it to her. Then he felt, suddenly and terribly, even perhaps that she had not, and for the same reason of the few minutes, really tried to get into that kapok but then he rejected this as surely untrue. He knew it would be very little longer now. And he felt, strangely, some kind of peace. He heard himself saying very quietly, and not in great sorrow,

"Sarah, I'm going quickly now. Are you afraid?"

"No. No, I'm not afraid."

He thought: Twenty-four years, and of that, two months together. And yet it was all, all twenty-four years of it, lived for her, for their lives to meet in however brief intersection. Let the sea come over now. Gentle sea. It was such a gentle sea this moon-bathed night. He remembered his father reading, And the sea shall give up the dead which were in it . . . The dead, the dead, he was about to join their number. Lead me, sweet God. Lead me down into these waters. Sweet God, how terrible the pain was.

He thought he saw, in the distance in the moonlight, the shape of either a submarine or an LCI, both had conning towers not very much unalike in any distance. He knew he may only have imagined that he saw it. He felt very capable right now of a mirage where rescue vessels were concerned, of any number of quite beautiful mirages. If it was an LCI, and if he could just hold her up until it got there, then she would be saved. He did not know for a certain fact whether he would be or not, but he felt it was not something one should bet a great deal on. His left side now felt paralyzed all the way down. In a way he was grateful for that, for it eased the pain. But it seemed also to tell him that even if he were picked up he wouldn't have much going for him. But if he could only hold out for a little longer, and if it were an LCI, and if it found them, then she would be saved. Too many ifs, he thought. They had too many ifs going against them. They always had had.

"Sarah," he said. "Can you see a ship? Toward the moon. Out to sea—out there?"

She looked. "No. I don't see anything, Matthew."

"Then hold me," he said.

"I love you, Matthew. How I love you. And we're together."

"Yes, together." He asked again, "Are you afraid?"

"No," he heard her voice quiet and close; it did not tremble and did not cry out. "Hold me . . . hold me."

And so they held each other and held their love. He began to go down into the water, and she was in his arms. He held his arm tight around her and she held to him and they went down into it together. The waters of the sea moved gently over them, as if in caress for all the young and unfulfilled of the war.

Epilogue

The Mass for ship's company of the LST 1826 was said two weeks later in the small church in Pozzuoli whose bells could be heard ringing from where the ship put in on its return from Anzio. A United States Navy chaplain from the base made a little talk, recalling the fondness the men of the ship had for the people of the town and especially for the children. He told, since he believed the people would want to know, what was known of the last hours of the ship, that the ship had been sunk by two torpedoes from a German submarine and that when the LCI and the destroyer arrived there they could find but one survivor. He was a sailor by the name of Andrew Nelson, the chaplain related, and was the source of what information was available. He had been pulled from the sea lying nearly unconscious across some kind of float. On the LCI he had revived sufficiently to give the captain of that vessel a fairly detailed account of the sinking. Shortly before the LCI itself reached Pozzuoli, this sailor died, apparently of internal wounds.

After the service a girl and a young boy walked out of the church with the others and into the sunlight. The girl was carrying a baby, though she appeared quite young to be its mother.

"Do you want me to carry the baby, Signora Coco?" the boy asked.

"Thank you, Rebi. No, I can carry him. I'm all right."

She saw someone emerge from the church and start toward a jeep which she only now noticed, the words BOMB DISPOSAL large under its windshield. Then he had seen her and started toward her. He came up to her.

"Good morning, Coco," he said.

"Good morning, Lieutenant Shanley."

"Can I give you a lift anywhere?"

"No," she said quietly. "Thank you. We're going home. It's only around the corner."

He stood there a moment. "Well, goodbye then."

"'Goodbye,' Lieutenant? Are you going somewhere?"

"Yes, I'm on my way to Rome," he said. "They say the Germans have left a number of unexploded bombs around and the Army needs some help from the Navy."

"Will you be coming back?"

"I don't think so. I think they'll be pushing on up to Livorno for the next naval base and I imagine I'll be stationed there."

He waited a little. Then smiled. "Would you like a lift to Rome?"

"No thank you, Lieutenant. I don't believe so. But say hello to Rome for me."

"I'll do that. Do you know Rome?"

"Oh, yes," she said. "I know Rome."

He turned and walked over to the jeep, waved once to her, then got into the jeep and was driving away. She started walking away from the church and now began to weep quietly. She wept for many things, for all the men going down at sea, she wept for one of them especially, she wept for herself, for the war, for life itself and what it was. She looked at the baby and thought how the ship where it was born was at the bottom of the sea. She thought how the baby was, in a way, the only thing that was left from the ship and how, but for that ship, the baby might not have been at all. Therefore it deserved. It deserved anyway.

"What are we going to do now, signora?" the boy asked.

"I don't know. I've been thinking. I thought maybe we'd move back on the Via Apollo if that apartment is still there. Would you like that?"

The boy shrugged. "It's a pretty apartment. And we'd eat better there, wouldn't we?"

The girl was no longer crying. She shifted the baby in her arms and straightened up a little and held the baby a little more tightly. Her eyes were bright.

"Yes, we'll eat better there," she said.